Dear Reader,

What do an FBI agent hot on the trail of a black widow serial killer and a man who writes romance novels under a female pseudonym have in common?

Both are driven, determined, intelligent and passionate— and falling in love makes them truly unstoppable.

HQN has reissued two of my older stories—and two of my favorite romance novels—in this collection.

Originally published in 1998, *Love with the Proper Stranger* not only features hero John Miller, a legendary yet troubled FBI agent, but also focuses on John's reluctant friendship with Daniel Tonaka, his much younger, fearless new partner who is completely unstoppable himself! (Shades of Max Bhagat and Jules Cassidy!)

And *Letters to Kelly* is my mother's favorite of my books. In it you'll meet one of my all-time favorite romance heroes, T. Jackson Winchester the Second, a young writer who falls in love with Kelly, the sixteen-year-old sister of his college roommate. He does the right thing by keeping his distance until she's older. But fate intervenes and he's thrown into a Central American prison on trumped up charges, and when he finally gets free she's already married to another man. *Letters to Kelly* takes place years later, and is the story of what happens when the made-for-each-other couple gets a second chance to connect.

I'm always thrilled when HQN combines two of my books in a special collection like this one.

Happy reading!

Love,

Suz

D0974357

# SUZANNE BROCKMANN

# UNSTOPPABLE

HQN™

ISBN-13: 978-0-373-77671-9

UNSTOPPABLE

Copyright © 2012 by Harlequin Books S.A.

The publisher acknowledges the copyright holder of the individual works as follows:

LOVE WITH THE PROPER STRANGER
Copyright © 1998 by Suzanne Brockmann

LETTERS TO KELLY
Copyright © 2003 by Suzanne Brockmann

Recycling programs
for this product may
not exist in your area.

This edition published by arrangement with Harlequin Books S.A.

For questions and comments about the quality of this book please contact us at Customer_eCare@Harlequin.ca.

® and TM are trademarks of the publisher. Trademarks indicated with ® are registered in the United States Patent and Trademark Office, the Canadian Trade Marks Office and in other countries.

www.Harlequin.com

Printed in U.S.A.

# CONTENTS

# LOVE WITH THE
# PROPER STRANGER

For Mary Gray, Kirsten McDonough, Sylvia Micalone and all of the other wonderful Workcamp volunteers who have allowed me to help raise a hammer and build houses alongside them, even if only in spirit.

## *PROLOGUE*

SHE LACED HIS COFFEE with opium.

He wasn't supposed to drink coffee this late at night. The doctor had told him not to. But she knew how much it pleased him to cheat the doctor's rules just a little every now and then.

He smiled as she brought it to him, smiled again as he took a sip. He liked it sweet.

The opium wouldn't kill him. It was part of the ritual, part of the game. She'd given him enough to confuse him, enough to slow his wits, to keep him docile and in control as she prepared for her checkmate.

She kissed the top of his balding head and he smiled again, breathing a deep sigh of contentment—the king, relaxing after a hard day at the office, secure in his castle alongside his beautiful queen.

Tonight, this king would die.

TONY WAS BREATHING HARD. John Miller could hear him clearly over the wire, his voice raspy and loud in the radio headset. Tony was breathing hard and Miller knew he was scared.

"Yeah, that's right. I'm FBI," Tony said, giving up his cover. Miller knew without a doubt that his partner and best friend was in serious, serious trouble. "And if you're as smart as your reputation says you are, Domino, then you'll order these goons to lay down their weapons and surrender to me."

Domino laughed. "I've got twenty men surrounding you, and you think I'm going to *surrender...?*"

"I've got more than twenty men on backup," Tony lied, as Miller keyed his radio.

"Where the *hell* is that backup?" Miller's usually unshakable control was nearing a breaking point. He'd been ordered to sit tight and wait here outside the warehouse until the choppers arrived in a show of force, but he couldn't wait any longer. He *wouldn't* wait.

"Jesus, John, didn't you get the word?" came Fred's scratchy voice over the radio. "The choppers have been rerouted—there's been an assassination attempt on the governor. It's code red, priority. You're on your own."

No choppers. No backup. Just Tony inside the warehouse, about to be executed by Alfonse Domino, and John Miller here, outside.

It was the one scenario Miller hadn't considered. It was the one scenario he wasn't ready for.

Miller grabbed the assault rifle from the floor of the van and ran toward the warehouse. He needed a miracle, but he didn't waste time praying. He knew full well that he—and Tony—didn't have a prayer.

"I QUIT."

The board of directors looked at her in stunned silence.

Marie Carver gazed back at the expressions of shock on the familiar faces and knew that those two little words she'd uttered had granted her freedom. It was that easy. That simple. She quit.

"I've made arrangements for my replacement," she

told them, careful not to let her giddy laughter escape. She quit. Tomorrow she would *not* walk through the front doors and take the elevator up to her executive office on the penthouse floor. Tomorrow she would be in another place. Another city, another state. Maybe even another country. She passed around the hiring reports her secretary had typed up and bound neatly with cheery yellow covers. "I've done all the preliminary interviews and narrowed the candidates down to three—any one of which I myself would have utmost faith in as the new president of Carver Software."

All twelve members of the board starting talking at once.

Marie held up her hand. "Should you decide to hire an outside candidate," she said, "you would, of course, require my approval as the major stockholder of this company. But I think you'll be impressed with the choices I've given you here." She rapped the yellow-covered report with her knuckles. "I ask that you hold all of your questions until after you've read this. If any concerns remain unanswered, you can reach me at home until six o'clock this evening. After that, I'll remain in touch with my secretary, whom I've promoted to Executive Assistant." She smiled. "I appreciate your understanding, and will see you all at the next annual shareholders meeting."

She gathered up her briefcase and walked quickly out of the room.

THE OPIUM WAS working.

His pupils had retracted almost to a pinpoint and he was drooling slightly, blinking sleepily as he watched her dance.

This was the part she liked. This was where she showed him what he would never again have the chance to experience, to violate.

True, this one had been gentle. His soft, old hands had never struck her. He'd been careful not to hurt her. He'd given her expensive presents, fancy gifts. But the act itself would always be an act of violence, always despicable, always requiring punishment.

Capital punishment.

Her dress fell in a pool of silk at her feet, and she deftly stepped out of it. His eyes were glazed, but not enough to hide his hunger at the sight of her. He stretched one hand out toward her, but he didn't have the strength to reach her.

And still she danced, to the rhythm of the blood pounding through her veins, to the anticipation of the moment when he would gaze into her eyes and know without a doubt that he was a dead man.

FREEDOM.

It hit Marie like the coolness of the air that swept through the open door at the end of the hall. It felt fresh and clean, like that very spring breeze, bringing hope and life and renewal. Through that open door she could see her car, sitting out in the parking lot, ready for her escape.

"Mariah."

There was only one person on that board of directors who could slow her departure. Susan Kane. Aunt Susan. Marie turned, but kept moving, backward, down the hall.

Susan followed, her long, batik-patterned dress moving in the breeze, disapproval in her slate-blue eyes.

"Mariah," she said again, calling Marie by her childhood nickname. "Obviously you've been planning this for some time."

Marie shook her head. "Only two weeks."

"I wish you had told me."

Marie stopped walking then, meeting the older woman's sternly unwavering gaze. "I couldn't," she said. "I didn't tell most of my own staff until this morning."

"Why?"

"The company doesn't need me anymore," Marie said. "It's been three years since the last layoffs. We've turned it around, Sue. Profits continue to rise—we're thriving. You know the numbers as well as I do."

"So take a vacation. Take a leave of absence. Sit back on your laurels and relax for a while."

Marie smiled ruefully. "That's part of my problem," she said. "I can't relax."

Susan's face softened, concern in her eyes. "Is your stomach still bothering you?"

"Among other things." Like, for instance, the fact that Marie was thirty-two years old and since her divorce four years ago, she had no life outside of the office. Like, the fact that she still worked long overtime hours to increase profits, to expand, to hire more people, even though the failing computer software company that her father's sudden fatal heart attack had thrust into her lap had long ago become a Fortune 500 business. Like, the fact that each morning she found herself walking into the new, fancy office building into which the company had recently moved, and she wondered, what exactly was the point? What purpose did she serve by being here, by stressing herself out enough to develop stomach ulcers over the mundane, day-to-day operation of this business?

One day she was going to wake up, and she was going to be sixty years old and still walking into that building, still going home much too late to that sad excuse for a condo, still living out of boxes that she *still* hadn't managed to unpack.

And she'd look at her life, and all those meaningless, wasted years would stretch back into her meaningless, wasted past.

Because the truth was, even though she'd dutifully gotten her degree in business as her father had wanted, Marie had never wanted to run this company.

Shoot, it had taken years before she'd admitted that to herself. As far as knowing what she really wanted to do, Marie honestly didn't have a clue. But there was something that she did know.

She wanted to do more than keep a multimillion-dollar corporation up and running. She wanted to have a sense of real purpose. She wanted to be able to look back on her life and feel proud—feel as if she'd truly made a difference.

She was considering running for office. She was also thinking about joining the peace corps. She had found a list a mile long of volunteer organizations that desperately needed man power—everything from accountants for the Salvation Army to hands-on, hammer-wielding home builders for Foundations for Families.

But before she could do anything, she had to handle her stress.

Step one was cutting herself off from this company—breaking her addiction to this job and the company's addiction to her. She was going to do it cold turkey.

The company would survive. Marie knew they'd survive. Any one of her three job candidates would bring a freshness and vitality to the job that she'd lacked for nearly two years now. Whether or not Marie would survive was a different story...

"Where are you going?" Susan asked.

"I don't know," Marie admitted. "I'm just going to take my camera and go. I read in a book about stress-reduction that I should take a few months and leave everything behind—including my name. This book recommended that I temporarily take on a new identity. Supposedly that'll help me distance myself from everything that's been causing my ulcers." She smiled. "I'm going to leave Marie Carver locked in my condo—along with all my doubts about my sanity and my worries that Carver Software will go into a nosedive the moment I leave town."

Susan pulled her in for a quick hug—an unusual display of affection. "The job will be yours again when you come back," the older woman whispered. "I'll make sure of that."

Marie pulled away, unable to answer. If she had her way, she'd never be back. If she had her way, Marie Carver and her damned ulcers would be gone forever.

SHE USED THE KNIFE TO CUT off a lock of his hair.

He didn't have too much, just a light fringe of gray at the back of his head, but that didn't matter. It was the only thing of his that she would keep.

Besides the money.

He was handcuffed now. He'd let her do that willingly, thinking she was playing some new sex game, never suspecting he had only moments left to live.

But when she unsheathed the stiletto, there was a hint of consternation in his drug-glazed eyes.

"What are you doing?" he asked.

She shushed him with a kiss. He couldn't speak. He wasn't allowed to speak.

But he didn't know the rules. "Clarise?" he said, fear pushing past the opium, creeping into his voice, making it waver as she set the tip of the stiletto against his chest.

She felt a flash of regret.

Clarise. She liked that name a lot. It was a shame that she would only be Clarise for a few moments longer. She couldn't use that name again. And she wouldn't. She was too smart to make that mistake.

"This has gone far enough," he said, trying to hide his fear behind an air of authority. "Release me now, Clarise."

She smiled and leaned on the whisper-thin blade, sliding it deep into his heart, setting him forever free.


"KILL HIM."

Domino's order came before John Miller had reached the warehouse doors, and the gunshots—four of them in rapid sequence were amplified deafeningly through his headset.

Tony.

Tony was dead.

Miller knew it. He had no chance of saving his friend.

He had this tape, though, this tape of Domino giving the order to off a federal agent. He had enough evidence to put Domino on death row. Blasting his way through that warehouse door at twenty to one odds would only get himself killed, too.

He knew that as well as he knew his own heartbeat.

But the heart that was pounding in his chest wasn't beating with a recognizable rhythm. And the red cloud of rage that covered his eyes didn't obscure his vision, but rather made it sharper, clearer.

Tony was dead, and the son of a bitch who ordered it done was *not* going to make his escape in a power-boat, losing himself in South America, outside of the FBI's jurisdiction. No, Alfonse Domino was going to burn in hell.

Miller hit the warehouse door at full run, bringing his gun up and into position at his hip, shouting in rage at the sight of Tony's crumpled body lying on the cold, blood-soaked concrete, shooting the surprise off the faces of Alfonse Domino and his men.

SHE HAD HER AIRLINE TICKET all ready, under an assumed name, of course. A temporary name.

Jane Riley. Plain Jane. Plane Jane. The thought amused her and she smiled. But only briefly. She knew she had a noticeable smile, and right now she had no desire to be noticed.

Her hair was under a kerchief for the occasion, and she wore a dowdy camel-colored jacket she'd picked up at a secondhand store downtown.

She took nothing of Clarise's with her. Nothing but the money and her collection. Nine locks of hair.

She traveled light, boarding the plane to Atlanta with only a tote bag that held several novels she'd picked up at the airport shop and two hundred thousand dollars in cash. The rest of the money was already in her Swiss bank account.

In Atlanta, she'd catch a train to who knows where. Maybe New York. Maybe Philadelphia.

She'd catch a show or two, take her time deciding exactly who she wanted to be. Then she'd get her hair cut and colored, shop for a new wardrobe to match her new personality, pick a new town in a new state, and start the game all over again.

And then she'd have ten locks of hair.

# CHAPTER ONE

JOHN MILLER'S HEART WAS pounding and his mouth was dry as he awoke with a start. He stood up fast, trying hard to get his bearings, reaching automatically for his gun.

"John, are you all right?"

Christ, he was in his office. He'd fallen asleep with his head on his desk, and now he was standing in his office, with his side arm drawn and his hands shaking.

And Daniel Tonaka was standing in the doorway watching him. Daniel was expressionless, as he often was. But he was gazing rather pointedly at Miller's weapon.

Miller reholstered his gun, then ran both hands across his face. "Yeah," he said. "Yeah, I'm fine. I just fell asleep—or something—for a second."

"Maybe you should go home and go to bed."

Bed. Yeah, right. Maybe in some other lifetime.

"You look like hell, man," Daniel continued.

Miller *felt* like hell. He needed a case to work on. As long as he was working, the dreams weren't so bad. It was this damned in-between time that was unbearable. "I just need some more coffee."

Daniel didn't say anything. He just looked at Miller. He was relatively new to the bureau—just a kid. He was hardly twenty-five years old, with a young handsome face, high cheekbones and deep brown, exotically shaped eyes that announced his part-Asian parentage. Those eyes held a wisdom that extended far beyond his tender years. And true to the wisdom in his eyes, the kid always knew when to hold his tongue.

Daniel Tonaka could say more with his silence and maybe a lift of one of his dark eyebrows than twenty other men could say if they talked all day.

Miller had had half a dozen new partners since Tony, but Daniel was the only one who had lasted for any length of time. Next week it would be, what? Seven months? The kid deserved some kind of award.

Miller knew quite well the reputation he had in the bureau. He was "The Robot." He was a machine, an automaton, letting nothing and no one get in the way of his investigation. He was capable of putting everyone around him into a deep freeze with a single laser-sharp look. Even before Tony had died, Miller had kept his emotions to himself, and he had to admit he'd played his cards even closer to his vest over the past few years.

He was aware of the speculation about his lack of close friends within the bureau, the whispered conversations that concluded he was incapable of emotion, devoid of compassion and humanity. After all, a man who so obviously didn't possess a heart and soul couldn't possibly feel.

Some of the younger agents would go well out of their way to avoid him. Hell, some of the *older* agents did the same. He was respected. With his record of arrests and successful investigations, he'd have to be. But he wasn't well liked.

Not that a robot would give a damn about that.

Daniel stepped farther into Miller's office. "Working on the Black Widow case?"

Miller nodded, gazing down at the open file on his desk. He'd been studying the photos and information from the latest in a string of connected murders before he'd fallen asleep.

And dreamed about Tony again.

He sat back down in his chair, grimacing at his stiff muscles. Christ, everything ached. Every part of him was sore. He desperately needed sleep, but the thought of going home to his apartment and sinking into his bed and closing his eyes was unbearable. The moment he closed his eyes, he'd be back outside that warehouse. He'd dream about the night that Tony died, and he'd watch it happen all over again. And for the four thousandth time, the choppers would never come. For the four thousandth time, Miller would arrive too late. For the four thousandth time, blowing Domino's ass straight to hell *still* wouldn't make up for the fact that Tony's brains were smeared across the concrete.

God, the stab of guilt and loss he felt was still so sharp, so piercing. Miller tried to push it away, to bury it deep inside, someplace from which it would never escape. He tried to put more distance between himself and this pain, these emotions. He could do it. He *would* do it. He was, after all, the robot.

Miller took a swig from a mug of now-cold coffee, trying to ignore the fact that his hand was still shaking. "The killer did her last victim about three months ago." The coffee tasted like something from a stable floor, but at least it moistened his mouth. "Which means she's probably preparing to make another go of it. She's out there somewhere, hunting down husband number eight.

At least we think it's number eight. Maybe there've been more we just don't know about."

"What if she's decided she's rich enough?"

"She doesn't kill for the money." Miller picked up the picture of Randolph Powers, knife blade protruding from his chest as he gazed sightlessly from his seat at the dinner table. "She kills because she likes to." And she was getting ready to do it again. He knew it.

"I haven't had time to look at this file," Daniel admitted, sitting down on the other side of the desk, pulling the report toward him. "Are we sure this is the same woman?"

"Exact M.O. The victim was found in the dining room, cuffed to the chair, with the remains of dinner on the table." Miller ran his fingers through his hair. God, he had a headache. "Opium was found in his system in the autopsy. The entire house was wiped clean of fingerprints. The only photo was a wedding portrait—and the bride's veil was over her face. It's her."

Daniel skimmed the report. "According to this, Powers married a woman named Clarise Harris two and a half weeks prior to his death." He glanced up at Miller. "The honeymoon was barely over. Didn't she usually wait two or three months?"

Miller nodded, rummaging through his desk drawers for his bottle of aspirin. "She's getting impatient." Jackpot. Miller twisted off the aspirin bottle's cap—empty. "Damn. Tonaka, do you have any aspirin in your desk?"

"You don't need aspirin, man. You need sleep. Go home and go to bed."

"If I wanted free advice, I would've asked for it. I think what I asked for was aspirin."

The deadly look Miller gave Daniel was designed to freeze a man in his tracks.

But Daniel just smiled as he stood up. "You know, I really hope we're partners for a good long time, John, because I cannot for the life of me imitate that look. I've tried. I practice every night in my bathroom mirror, but..." He shook his head. "I just can't do it. You have a real God-given talent there. See you later."

Daniel closed the door on the way out and Miller just sat, staring after him, wishing...for what?

If the kid had been Tony, Miller might have told him about the nightmares, about the fact that he was too damn scared even to try to sleep. If the kid had been Tony, Miller might have told him that this morning when he'd gotten on the bathroom scale, he'd found he'd lost twenty pounds. Twenty pounds, just like that.

But Daniel Tonaka *wasn't* Tony.

Tony was gone. He'd been dead and gone for years. Years.

Miller reached for the phone. "Yeah, John Miller. Put me through to Captain Blake."

It was time to get down to real work on this Black Widow case. Maybe then he could get some damned sleep.

GARDEN ISLE, GEORGIA, was the best kept secret among the jet set. The beaches were covered with soft white sand. The sky was blue and the ocean, although murky with mineral deposits, was clean. The town itself was quaint, with cobblestone streets and charming brick houses and window boxes that overflowed with brightly colored flowers. Most of the shops were exclusive, the restaurants trendy and four-star and outrageously expensive—except if you knew where to go.

And after two months on Garden Isle, Mariah Robinson knew exactly where to go to avoid the crowds. She loaded her camera and her beach bag into the front basket of her bike and headed toward the beach.

Not toward the quiet, windswept beach that was only several yards from her rental house, but rather toward the usually crowded, always happening beach next to the five-star resort.

Most of the time, she embraced the solitude, often reveling in the noise-dampening sound of the surf and the raucous calls of the seabirds. But today she felt social. Today, she *wanted* the crowds. Today, just on a whim, she wanted to use her camera to take photographs of people.

Today she was meeting her friend, Serena, for lunch at one of those very same four-star restaurants.

But she was more than an hour early, and she took her bike with her onto the sand. She set it gently on its side and spread her beach blanket alongside it. There was a reggae band playing in the tent next to the resort bar even this early in the morning, and the music floated out across the beach.

She sat in the sun, just watching the dynamics of the people around her.

Some sunbathers lay in chaise lounges, their noses buried in books. Others socialized, talking and flirting in large and small groups. Men and women in athletic gear ran up and down the miles of flat, hard sand at the edge of the water. Others walked or strolled. Still others paraded—clearly advertising their trim, tanned bodies, scantily clad in designer bathing suits.

Mariah took out her camera, focusing on a golden retriever running next to a muscular man in neon green running shorts. She loved dogs. In fact, now that she wasn't shut up in an office each day from dawn till dusk, she was thinking about getting one and—

"Fancy meeting you here this early."

Mariah looked up but the glare from the bright sun threw the face of the woman standing next to her into shadows. It didn't matter. The crisp English-accented voice was unmistakable.

"Hey," Mariah said, smiling as Serena sat down next to her on her blanket.

"I thought you'd sworn off the resort beach," Serena continued, looking at Mariah over the tops of her expensive sunglasses.

Serena Westford was older than Mariah had originally thought when they'd first met a few weeks ago— she was closer to forty than thirty, anyway. Her smile was young though. It was mercurial and charming, displaying perfect white teeth. Her hair was blond with wisps escaping from underneath the big straw hat she always wore, and her trim body was that of a twenty-four-year-old.

She was as cool and confident as she was beautiful. She was everything Mariah wished she could be. Everything Marie Carver wished she could be, Mariah corrected herself. But Marie Carver had purposely been left behind in Phoenix, Arizona. Mariah Robinson was here in Georgia, and Mariah was happy with her life. She went with the flow, calm and relaxed. No worries. No problems. No stress. No jealousy.

Serena was wearing a black thong bathing suit, covered only by a diaphanous short wrap that fluttered about her buttocks and thighs in the ocean breeze, leaving only slightly more than nothing to the imagination. Despite the fact that Serena Westford was no longer a schoolgirl, she was one of the minuscule percentage of the population who actually looked *good* in a thong bikini.

Mariah let herself hate her friend—but only for a fraction of a second. So what if Mariah was destined never to wear a similarly styled bathing suit? So what if Mariah was the exact physical opposite of petite, slender, golden Serena? So what if Mariah was just over six feet tall, broad shouldered, large breasted and athletically built? So what if her hair was an unremarkable shade of brown curls, always messy and impossible to control? So what if her eyes were brown? Light brown, not that dark-as-midnight intriguing shade of brown, or cat green like Serena's.

Mariah was willing to bet that behind Serena Westford's cool, confident facade, there lurked a woman with a thousand screaming anxieties. She probably worked out two hours each day to maintain her youthful figure. She probably spent an equal amount of time on her hair and makeup. She was probably consumed with worries and stress, poor thing.

"I just came down here to violate the photographic rights of these unsuspecting beachgoers," Mariah told her friend, unable to hide a smile.

The two women had first met when Mariah took Serena's picture here on the resort beach. Serena had been less than happy about that and had demanded Mariah hand over the undeveloped film then and there. What could have been an antagonistic and adversarial relationship quickly changed to one of mutual respect as Serena explained that while in the peace corps, she'd spent a great deal of time with certain tribes in Africa who believed that being photographed was tantamount to having one's soul kidnapped.

Mariah had surrendered the film, and spent an entire afternoon listening to Serena's fascinating stories of her travels around the world as a volunteer humanitarian.

They'd talked about Mariah's work for Foundations for Families, too. Serena had mentioned she'd seen Mariah getting dropped off by the Triple F van in the evenings. And they'd talked about the grassroots organization that used volunteers to help build affordable homes for hardworking, low-income families. Mariah spent three or four days each week with a hammer in her hand, and she loved both the work and the sense of purpose it gave her.

"Hey, I got a package notice from the post office," Mariah told her friend. "I think it's my darkroom supplies. Any chance I can talk you into picking it up for me?"

"If you had a car, you could pick it up yourself."

"If I had a car, I would use it once a month, when a heavy package needed to be picked up at the post office."

"If you had a car, you wouldn't have to wait for that awful van to take you over to the mainland four times a week," Serena pointed out.

Mariah smiled. "I like taking the van."

Serena looked at her closely. "The driver *is* a real hunk."

"The driver is happily married to one of the Triple F site supervisors."

"Too bad."

Serena's sigh of regret was so heartfelt, Mariah had to laugh. "You know, Serena, not everyone in the world is husband hunting. I'm actually very happy all by myself."

Serena smiled. "Husband hunting," she repeated. "The biggest of the big game." She laughed. "I like that image. I wonder what gauge bullet I'd need to bring one down…"

Mariah gathered up her things. "Let's go have lunch."

SHE WOULD KNOW HIM WHEN she saw him, but she simply hadn't seen him yet. He would have money. Lots of money. Enough so that when she asked for the funds for the down payment on a house, he wouldn't hesitate to give it directly to her. Enough so that he would open a checking account in her name—an account she would immediately start draining. She would transfer the money to dummy accounts out of state.

She had the system set up so that anyone following the paper trail would be stopped cold, left high and dry.

She'd sit on the cash for a week or two, then make the deposits into her Swiss bank accounts.

Three million dollars. She had three million dollars American already in her Swiss accounts.

Three million dollars, and nine locks of hair.

Yes, she'd know him when she saw him.

"GARDEN ISLE, GEORGIA," the agent named Taylor said as he looked around the table from Daniel Tonaka to Pat Blake, the head of the FBI unit, and finally to John Miller. "It's her. The Black Widow killer. It's got to be."

He slid several enlarged black-and-white photos

across the conference table, one toward Blake and the other toward Miller and Daniel. Miller sat forward slightly in his chair, picking it up and angling it away from the reflections of the overhead lights. He couldn't seem to hold it steady—his hands were shaking—and he quickly put it down on the table.

"She's going by the name Serena Westford," the young agent was saying. "She came out of nowhere. Her story is that she spent the past seven years in Europe— in Paris—but no one seems to know her over there. If she *was* living there, she wasn't paying taxes, that's for sure."

The photograph showed a woman moving rapidly, purposefully across a parking lot. She was wearing a hat and sunglasses, and her face was blurred.

Miller looked up. "What's your name again?"

The young man held his gaze only briefly. "Taylor. Steven Taylor."

"Couldn't you get a better picture than this, Taylor?"

"No, sir," he said. "We're lucky we even got this one. It was taken with a telephoto lens from the window of the resort. It's the best of about twenty that I managed to get at that time. Any other time I tried to take her picture, she somehow seemed to know there was a camera around and she covered herself almost completely. I have about five hundred perfect pictures where her face is nearly entirely obscured by enormous sunglasses or her hat. I have five hundred other perfect shots of the back of her head."

"Yet you're certain this woman is our Black Widow." Miller didn't hide his skepticism.

Daniel shifted in his seat. "I believe it's her, John. Hear him out."

Miller was usually unerringly accurate when it came to reading people. He knew for a fact that Patrick Blake disliked him despite his record of arrests. And he knew quite clearly that Steven Taylor was afraid of him. Oh, he was polite and respectful, but something about his stance told Miller clear as day that Taylor was going to request a transfer off this case now that he knew Miller was aboard.

Daniel Tonaka, on the other hand, had never been easy to read. He was unflappable, with a quirky sense of humor that surfaced at the most unexpected moments. As far as Miller could tell, Daniel treated every person with whom he came into contact with the same amount of courtesy and kindness. He treated everyone from a bag lady to the governor's wife with respect, always giving them his full attention.

Daniel had spoken up to say he had a hunch or a feeling about a suspect or a case only a handful of times, and all of those times he'd been right on target. But this time he'd used even stronger language. He *believed* Serena Westford was the Black Widow.

Miller looked expectantly at Steven Taylor, waiting for him to continue.

Taylor cleared his throat. "I, um, used the computer to search out the most likely locations the Widow would choose for her next target," the young man told him. "She prefers small towns with only one or two resorts nearby. I programmed the computer to ignore everything within two hundred miles of the places she either met or lived with her previous victims, and narrowed the list down to a hundred and twenty-three possibilities. From there, I accessed resort records and used a phone investigation to query the resort staff, searching for female guests under five feet two inches, traveling alone, staying for extended lengths of time.

"Frankly, there was a great deal of luck involved in finding Serena Westford. She'd arrived at the Garden Isle resort only two days prior to our call. When it became clear she was traveling under an alias, I went to Georgia myself to try to further identify the suspect." He shook his head ruefully. "But as you can see, in all of the pictures we have of the Black Widow, her face is covered."

"But her legs aren't," Daniel pointed out. "Steve got plenty of pictures of Serena Westford's legs."

"Her legs are visible in some of the other photos we found in the victims' houses," Taylor said. "We have no pictures of the Black Widow's face, but we have plenty of photos of her legs." He looked at Daniel and grinned. "Tonaka had the idea to take those pictures and *these* pictures and run a computer comparison. According to the computer, there's a ninety-eight percent chance that the Black Widow's legs and Serena Westford's legs are one and the same."

Miller glanced at Daniel. Damn, the kid was good at finding creative alternatives. "A computer match of legs won't hold up in a court of law as proof of identity," he commented.

"No kidding," Taylor said, quickly adding, "Sir. But it's enough to convince *me* that there should be a further investigation."

Miller passed the photograph to Captain Blake, and again his hands shook. The older man glanced at him, eyebrows slightly raised.

Miller turned back to Taylor. "Tell me more," he commanded.

"When Serena first arrived, she had traces of bruising beneath her eyes," Taylor continued. "I'd dare to speculate that that was from recent plastic surgery—probably a nose job to alter her appearance."

"We've been talking about the possibility of flying husband number seven's former housekeeper to Garden Isle," Pat Blake interrupted, "but if the Widow *has* had extensive plastic surgery, there's no way she could make a one hundred percent positive ID. I want no room for reasonable doubt. This one isn't going to walk away."

Miller nodded. What they needed was to catch the killer in the act.

"She's recently rented a beach house on Garden Isle," Taylor continued. "That's a clear indication that she's intending to stay, although at this point, I don't believe she's targeted her next victim. I've compiled a list of all of the people—both men and women—whom our suspect has had contact with over the past several weeks. Out of forty-seven people, twenty-eight have since left the island. They were there only on vacation, and they've gone home. Out of the other nineteen, one in particular stands out."

Taylor took a series of photos from his file, spreading them out on the table.

"Her name is Mariah Robinson," he said. "Or so she says. According to our files, no such person exists. We've identified her as Marie Carver, former CEO of Carver Software out of Phoenix, Arizona."

Miller leaned forward to look at the photographs. One was of a tall young woman with shoulder-length dark hair, wearing a bathing-suit top and shorts, seated on a beach blanket. Another bikini-clad woman was sitting next to her, her face obscured by a huge straw hat.

The woman in the hat had to be Serena Westford. Her barely there bikini was designed to make blood pressures rise, yet it was the woman sitting next to her that drew Miller's eyes.

"Marie Carver—or Mariah Robinson as she calls herself—lives alone in a rented house on the island," Taylor continued. "She spends most of her time on a private beach taking nature photographs. She has a darkroom in her cottage. Every few days, she goes off island—I don't know where. I haven't had the opportunity yet to follow her. She and Serena seem pretty tight."

Mariah Robinson was more than tall, Miller realized. She was an Amazon—a goddess. She had to be only an inch or two shorter than his own six feet two inches. She was as tall as a man, but built entirely like a woman. Her breasts were full and generously proportioned to the rest of her body. Her hips were appropriately wide—enough so that she was probably self-conscious, hence the shorts. Her legs were impossibly long and well muscled.

Another picture caught her riding an ancient bicycle. She was going up a slight hill and standing above the seat, muscles straining in her legs, breasts tight against the cotton of her T-shirt.

Christ, what a body. There was so damned much of her.

Serena Westford was their Black Widow suspect. She had allegedly lured seven men to their deaths with her searing sexuality. She was a femme fatale in the most literal sense.

Yet it was this other woman, Mariah Robinson, who made Miller stand at attention. Of course, he'd always been a breast-and-leg man. And from what he could see from these pictures, she had more than enough of both. Enough for a man to sink into and lose himself in for a solid year or two.

God, what was wrong with him? He didn't usually have this kind of reaction to the female suspects in a case. Apparently, it had been too long since his last sexual encounter. Way too long. Back even before Daniel came on as his partner. Miller couldn't even remember when it was, or even whom he'd been with.

Maybe that was why he wasn't sleeping. Maybe he *would* finally be able to sleep if a woman was in bed with him. Maybe all he needed was a little sexual relief.

Except the reason he *hadn't* had sex since forever was because none of the women he'd met during that time had managed to turn him on.

Yet here he was, having a definite physical reaction from surveillance photos of a murderess's best friend, who also happened to be living under an alias. What the hell was wrong with him?

And wasn't it just his luck that it wasn't going to be the goddess, but the murderess who was probably going to end up in his bed? And *that* sure as hell wasn't going to make him sleep any better.

Miller picked up the fifth photo. It was a close-up of Mariah Robinson's face.

She was pretty in a sweet, girl-next-door kind of way. Her face was heart shaped, with broad cheekbones and a strong, almost pointed chin. Her mouth was generous and wide. Her smile revealed straight white teeth and made dimples appear in her cheeks. Her eyes were light colored—Miller couldn't tell from the black-and-white photo if they were blue or light brown. But they sparkled with some secret amusement, as if she were laughing at him.

Miller felt a swirl of anticipation deep in his gut. It was sexual energy combined with something else, something deeper and far more complicated. Something that made his pulse quicken. Something he couldn't identify.

Captain Blake smoothed one hand along the top of his nearly bald head as he shuffled through his copy of the file. "How long do you think it'll take till we can get a cover in place for an agent to portray potential husband material?" he asked.

"A week," Taylor answered. "Two at the most. In order to match the profiles of the previous victims, we'd need to find an agent who could pose either as a much older man or a man in poor health. We'd need to provide fictional background, complete with financial records and heavily padded bank accounts. You can bet Serena will run a credit check on anyone she's considering targeting. We'll need to prep the agent, set up protection and a surveillance team—"

Miller sat forward. "I could be ready to go down to Garden Isle tomorrow."

Taylor stared at him, unable to hide his expression of surprise. "*You?* You're not old enough."

"Husband number three was only twenty-nine years old," Daniel pointed out mildly. "And husband six was in his mid-thirties."

"Both were in extremely poor health, one in a wheel-chair."

Miller took two copies of his file from his briefcase, handed one to Blake and tossed the other onto the table in front of Steven Taylor. "Meet Jonathan Mills," he said. "I'm thirty-nine years old. Recently in remission after a long struggle with Hodgkin's disease—that's a kind of cancer of the lymph system."

Taylor opened the file and quickly skimmed Miller's investigation summary. His eyes widened. "You actually intend to *marry* this woman…?"

"If I don't, she won't try to kill me."

"You're going to *be* her husband," Taylor said. "You're actually planning to *sleep* with her…?"

Even Daniel had a hint of curiosity in his dark brown eyes as he waited for Miller's answer.

Pat Blake shook his head. "Should I not be hearing this?"

"Don't worry, Captain, the marriage will be legal. She'll be my wife," Miller said. "And I'll make a point to practice safe sex." He smiled. "Of course, in *her* case, that means no knives in bed." He stood up, scooping the photos and files off the table, and looked at Blake. "Am I good to go?"

The older man nodded. "Let's do it."

Daniel and Steven Taylor got to their feet, and Miller turned to leave the room.

"One moment, if you don't mind, John," Blake said. He waited until the younger agents had left his office, then stood up and closed the door behind them. "You look like crap."

Miller knew Blake hadn't missed the fact that his hands were shaking. "Too much coffee," he said. "I'm fine, but thanks for your concern."

Blake nodded, clearly not buying it for one second. "I know we haven't exactly been friends down through the years, John. I've always just figured I'll stay out of your way, let you do what you do best, and you'll continue to give me the highest success record in the Bureau. But if you've got some kind of problem, maybe there's something I can do to help."

Miller met his superior's eyes steadily. "I just want to get to work."

"Do you have anyone at all you can talk to, Miller?"

"Will that be all, sir?"

Blake sighed. "I'm not supposed to give you a warning, but after this one's over, I'm bringing you in for a full psychological evaluation. So go on, get out of here. And try to spend a least *some* of your time on that resort island with your eyes closed and your head on a pillow."

Miller *had* to protest. "Over the past eighteen months my efficiency has *increased*—"

"Yeah, because you work twenty-two hours each day." Blake sighed again. "Go to Georgia, John. Catch this killer. Get the job done and make the world safe again for rich, dirty old men. But be ready to be stuck under a shrink's microscope when you get back."

Blake turned toward his desk, and Miller knew the conversation was over. He let himself out, aware that his pulse was racing, the sound of blood rushing through his veins roaring in his ears. Psych evaluation. Christ, he didn't stand a chance. Somehow, over the next few weeks, he was going to have to teach himself to sleep again—or face the new nightmare of a psychological evaluation.

God, he needed another cup of coffee.

He was halfway down the hall that led to the lounge when he heard voices coming from one of the tiny windowless cubicles assigned to the less experienced agents. He heard what's-his-name's voice. Taylor. Steven Taylor's voice.

"He's a time bomb, about to explode. You know that as well as I do. You wouldn't *believe* the rumors that are circulating about John Miller. Talk is that he's on the verge of some kind of breakdown."

"Do you always listen to rumors?" It was Daniel, and there was a hint of amusement in his voice.

"Not usually, no. But the man looks *terrible*—"

Daniel's voice was gentle now. "He's a living legend, Steve. He's the best there is. He looks terrible because he's got insomnia. It gets worse when he's between investigations. But believe me, he'll be fine. Don't request a transfer—you'll be able to learn a lot from this guy. Trust me on this one."

"Humph." Taylor didn't sound convinced. "Did you see the way his hands shook? No way do I want to be under the command of some flaky insomniac James Bond has-been who's on the edge. No, I'm outta here. Haven't you heard that his partners have a way of dying on him?"

Miller stepped into the room. "If you've got a problem with me, Taylor," he said coldly, "come and tell me to my face."

A flush of embarrassment darkened Taylor's cheeks as he gazed at him in surprise. His eyes lost their focus for a second or two, and Miller knew that he was replaying his words in his mind, recalling all the harsh things he'd said that Miller had no doubt overheard.

Time bomb. Flaky insomniac. James Bond has-been.

"Excuse me, sir," Taylor said, making a quick exit out of the room.

That was one agent *he* was never going to see again.

Miller turned to Daniel Tonaka. "Mind stepping into my office with me?"

Daniel didn't look perturbed, but then again, Daniel never did.

Miller went out into the corridor, leading the way back to his office. He went inside, then turned and waited for Daniel to join him.

"What's up?" Daniel asked evenly.

Miller closed the door and immediately lit into him. "If I hear you discussing my personal life with another agent ever again, you will be transferred off my team so fast, you won't know what hit you."

He'd truly caught Daniel off guard, and a myriad of emotions flashed across the young man's face. But he quickly recovered. "I was unaware that you believed your inability to sleep was a secret around here."

"I know damn well that it's no secret," Miller said coolly. "But it's not your business to discuss."

Daniel nodded and even managed to smile. "Okay. I can respect that, John. And I apologize for offending you."

Miller opened his office door. "Just be ready to leave first thing in the morning."

"I will." Daniel paused and smiled again before he went out the door. "I'm glad we had this little time to talk and straighten things out."

Miller didn't let himself smile until he'd closed his office door behind Daniel. *I'm glad we had this little time to talk...* Hell, other men would've wet themselves. *Taylor* sure as hell would've—it was just as well he wasn't going to be hanging around, getting in the way.

Miller tossed his briefcase onto a chair and the photos Taylor had taken onto his desk. The blurred picture of Serena Westford had been on top, but it slid off the pile, and Mariah Robinson's laughing eyes peeked out at him.

Tomorrow he was going to be in Garden Isle, Georgia, and he was "accidentally" going to bump into Mariah Robinson. For the first time in weeks, he felt wide-awake with the buzz of anticipation.

## CHAPTER TWO

THERE WAS A DOG ON THE beach, frolicking in the surf in the predawn light.

There was a dog—and a man.

It wasn't such a rare occurrence for a dog and its master to be on the beach outside of Mariah's cottage. The stretch of sand was nearly seven miles long, starting down by the resort, and ending at the lighthouse on the northernmost tip of the island. Ambitious runners and power walkers often provided a steady stream of traffic going in both directions.

No, finding a dog and a man on the beach wasn't odd at all, except for the fact that it wasn't yet even five o'clock in the morning.

Mariah had risen early, hoping to get some photos of the deserted beach at sunrise.

There was still time—she could ask them to move away, off farther down the beach. But the man was sitting in the sand, his back slumped in a posture of exhaustion, his head in his hands. And the dog was having one hell of a good time.

Mariah moved closer. The wind was coming in off the water, and neither dog nor man was aware of her presence. She settled herself on her stomach in the sand and propped her camera up on her elbows as she focused her lens on the dog.

It was a mutt and probably female. Mariah could see traces of collie in the animal, along with maybe a little spaniel and something odd—maybe dachshund. Her coat was long and shaggy—and right now almost entirely soaked. She had short legs and a barrel-shaped body, a long, pointed nose and two ears that flapped ungracefully around her head. She may not have been eligible to win any beauty contests, but Mariah found herself smiling at her expression of delight as she bounded in and out of the waves. She could swear the dog was full-out grinning.

Her master, on the other hand, was not.

He stood up slowly, painfully, as if every movement hurt. He moved as if he were a hundred years old, but he wasn't an old man. His crew-cut hair was dark without even a trace of gray, and the lines from the glimpse she saw of his face seemed more from pain than age.

As he straightened to his full height, Mariah saw that he was tall—taller even than she was by at least a few inches. He wore sweatpants and a windbreaker that seemed to fit him loosely, as if he'd recently lost weight or been ill.

Together, man and dog made a great picture, and Mariah snapped shot after shot.

The dog bounded happily up to the man.

"Hey, Princess. Hey, girl." His voice was carried on the wind directly to Mariah. "Time to go back."

His voice was low and resonant, rich and full.

Dog and master were silhouetted against the red-orange sky, making a striking picture. Mariah moved her camera up to snap another photo, and the dog turned toward her, ears up and alert. She launched herself in Mariah's direction, and the man turned, too.

"Stop," he commanded. He spoke softly, just one single word, but the dog pulled up. She backed off slightly, her entire backside wagging as she grinned at Mariah.

Mariah looked from the dog to the man.

The man was far better-looking—or at least he would be if he smiled.

His hair was dark and severely cut close to his scalp, almost as if it was growing in after he'd shaved his head. Despite the austerity of his crew cut, he was a strikingly handsome man. His features looked almost chiseled, the bone structure of his face more elegant than rugged. His eyebrows were thick and dark, and right now forming a rather intimidating scowl over eyes that she guessed were brown. His chin quite possibly was perfect, his lips generously full, but his nose was large and slightly crooked.

On closer scrutiny, Mariah realized that it was possible some people might not have found this man worthy of a second glance. Actually, he wasn't conventionally handsome—he'd certainly never grace the cover of a men's fashion magazine. But there was something about his looks that she found incredibly appealing.

Or maybe it wasn't his looks at all, Mariah thought with a smile, remembering how the young woman in the natural-food store on the mainland had spoken of cosmic reverberations and auras. Maybe as far as auras went, his was a solid ten.

As he stepped closer, she saw in the pale morning light that his face was lined with weariness and gray with fatigue. Still, despite that and his too-short hair, she found him to be remarkably attractive.

"Hi," Mariah said, sitting up and brushing the sand

off the front of her T-shirt. His eyes followed the movement of her hand, and she became self-consciously aware of the fact that she'd only thrown a pair of shorts on underneath the T-shirt she'd worn to bed. She wasn't wearing a bra and she didn't have the body type that allowed for such wardrobe omissions. The only times she didn't bother to put on a bra were mornings like this, when she was certain she would be alone.

But she'd been wrong. Right now, she most definitely was not alone.

"I'm sorry," she said, trying to fold her arms across her chest in a casual manner. "I didn't mean to intrude."

Dear God, would you listen to her? She was *apologizing* for being on her own stretch of beach.

She didn't have to apologize for that. And she certainly shouldn't bother to apologize for her missing bra. Despite the man's earlier scowl, it was clear from the way that his gaze kept straying in the direction of her breasts that he, for one, was not in the least put out by her lack of underwear.

He pulled his gaze away from her long enough to glance up at the cottage. "Is this your place?"

Mariah nodded. "Yeah," she said. "I'm renting it for the season."

"Nice," he said, but his eyes were back on her, sweeping along the lengths of her bare legs, skimming again across her body and face. "I hope we didn't disturb you. The dog can get loud—she's still young."

"No, I woke up to catch the sunrise on film."

He glanced up at the sky. The sun was already above the horizon and climbing fast. "I'm sorry," he said. "We were in your way."

"It's all right."

He held out one hand, offering to help her up.

Taking his hand meant she'd have to unfold her arms. But there was no way she'd be able to get to her feet with her arms folded anyway.

What the heck, Mariah thought, reaching up to clasp his hand. With a face like his, this man had no doubt seen a vast array of female bodies, and probably wearing far less than a worn-out T-shirt. She was nothing new, no big deal.

He, on the other hand, was a very, *very* big deal. He pulled her up from the sand, and she found herself standing much too close to him. But when she moved to back away, he steadied her with his other hand, his fingers warm against her elbow.

He was tall, with shoulders that went on forever and a broad chest that tapered down to a narrow waist and slim hips and... Embarrassed, Mariah quickly brought her eyes back to his face.

His eyes were blue. They were electric, brilliant, neon blue. And they sparked with the heat of attraction. Dear God, he found *her* attractive, too.

"Is it just you?" the man asked, and Mariah gazed up at him stupidly, wondering *what* he was talking about.

"Renting the house," he added, and she understood.

"Yes," she said, gently pulling free and putting some distance between them. "I'm here by myself."

He nodded. God, whoever he was, he was *so* serious. She'd yet to see him smile.

"How about you?" she asked. "Are you vacationing with your family?"

He shook his head. "No, I'm here alone, too." He motioned vaguely down the beach. "I'm staying at the resort, at least temporarily. I was thinking about renting one of the houses up on this part of the beach. I'm getting tired of room service—I'd like to have my own kitchen."

"It's a trade-off," Mariah told him. "Renting a house is more private, but you lose the benefits of having a hotel maid. And if you're not careful about cleaning up after yourself in the kitchen… Well, the variety of insect life you can attract is immense. You can't leave *any*thing out. Not even a plate with crumbs on it. You have to keep all the food in the refrigerator—or in plastic containers. But as long as you don't mind doing that, it's great."

He nodded. "Maybe I'll stick with room service for a while longer."

Princess the dog inched forward and pressed her cold nose against the back of Mariah's knee. "Yikes!" Mariah exclaimed.

"Princess, back," the man said sharply.

"She was just playing," Mariah protested as the dog immediately obeyed. "It's okay—she just startled me. I don't mind. She's…an unusual mix."

There was a glint of amusement in his eyes. "You're unusually tactful. But it's okay. She's not a mix of anything. She's a pure mutt, and she knows it. There's no ego involved—for either one of us."

"She does what you say," Mariah said. Princess gazed up at her, tongue lolling from her mouth, eyes sharp, ears alert, tail thumping slightly even though she was sitting down. She seemed to understand every word of the conversation. "That's worth more than a pedigree."

"She was well trained," he told her. "I…inherited her from a friend a few years ago."

He glanced out over the ocean as if trying to hide the sudden sadness in his eyes. Or maybe she only imagined she saw such an emotion there—when he looked back at her, it was gone.

He held out his hand. "I'm Jonathan Mills."

His fingers were warm and large and made her own hand seem slender and practically petite. "I'm..." She hesitated for a moment, uncertain of which name to give him. "...Mariah Robinson," she decided. It wasn't as if she were telling a lie. It had become true. Over the past two months, she'd acted less and less like Marie Carver and more and more like Mariah Robinson. At least more like the Mariah Robinson she'd heard about from her grandmother. The Mariah her own childhood nickname had come from.

He was still holding her hand, but his gaze had dropped to her breasts again.

"Are you here for the week?" she asked.

He looked up, and for half a second, Mariah thought she saw a flash of embarrassment in his eyes—embarrassment that he'd been caught staring. But it, too, was quickly gone. This man was a master at hiding his feelings.

"I'm here until my hair grows back in," he told her.

Mariah gently pulled her fingers free from his grip. "Well, that's one way to handle a bad-hair day."

Jonathan Mills almost smiled. Almost, but not quite. He ran one hand across his short hair. "Actually, today's a rather good hair day, if you want to know the truth."

God, had she insulted him? "I'm sorry, I didn't mean that your hair looks bad...or anything..." Her voice trailed off.

He finally smiled. "It's okay. I know exactly what

it looks like, and it looks much better than it did a few days ago."

He had a nice smile. It was only a small smile, barely playing about the corners of his elegantly shaped lips, but it was very nice just the same.

He looked down at the camera she was holding, its strap still encircling her arm. "Are you a professional photographer?" he asked.

Mariah shook her head. "No, no, I'm...not." God, what was her problem? It had been two decades since she was a seventh grader, so why was she suddenly acting like one? "It's a hobby."

Was it her imagination, or had Jonathan Mills just gone another shade paler?

"I've got a camera, too," he said, "though I've got to confess I'm not sure I can get it to work. I bought it a few years ago and don't use it much. Would you mind if I brought it over sometime? Maybe you could show me how it works."

Would she mind? "Of course not."

He looked down the beach in the direction of the resort. "I think I better go," he said.

He *was* more pale. And perspiration was beading on his upper lip. He wiped it away with the back of his hand. The morning sun was hot, but it wasn't *that* hot.

"Are you all right?" she asked.

He pressed his temples with both hands. "I'm not sure. I'm feeling a little...faint."

He was a stranger. Mariah knew she shouldn't invite him into her house. But it couldn't hurt to bring him up so he could sit for a minute in the shade on her deck, could it?

"Why don't you come up to the house and sit in the

shade?" she suggested. "I've got some iced tea in the fridge."

Jonathan nodded. "Thanks."

His entire face was slick with sweat as he followed Mariah up toward the cottage.

Even Princess was subdued, trailing after them quietly.

Mariah walked backward, watching him worriedly. "You're not, like, having a heart attack on me, are you?"

Whatever was happening, he was hurting. His lips twisted in a smilelike grimace. "My heart's fine."

Mariah could see that it took him some effort to speak, so she didn't ask any other questions. He staggered slightly, and she quickly moved to help him, unthinkingly supporting him by putting her arm around his back and his arm across her shoulders.

He was warm and he was solid and he was pressed against her side from her underarm all the way to her thighs. She may have reached for him unthinkingly, but now that she was in this rather intimate position, she could do nothing *but* think.

When was the last time she'd walked arm in arm with a man like this?

Never.

The thought flashed crazily through her mind as she misinterpreted her own silent question. She'd walked arm in arm with plenty of men—although not recently—but she'd never walked arm in arm with a man like this.

Jonathan Mills was different from all of the men she'd ever known. Including Trevor. Maybe especially Trevor.

"I'm really sorry about this," he murmured as they reached the stairs that led to her deck.

"Can you make it up here?" Mariah asked.

But he'd already started to lower himself down so that he was sitting on the third step. He shook his head. "Can you do me a favor?"

"I can try."

"Call my assistant at the resort. His name's Daniel Tonaka. Room 756. Will you ask him to come and please pick me up?"

"Of course."

Mariah took the steps up two at a time, leaving Princess sitting and worriedly watching her master.

It didn't take long to make the phone call. She woke Daniel Tonaka up, but he snapped instantly awake. She gave him directions, and he told her he was on his way. Mariah had to wonder. Did this happen often?

She poured a plastic tumbler of iced tea as she spoke on the phone, then carried it back to the deck. "It shouldn't take him much more than ten minutes to get over here from the resort...."

Jonathan Mills was no longer sitting on the stairs. He wasn't on the deck, and she would have seen him if he'd come into the house...

Down in the sandy yard, Princess barked sharply. Mariah went halfway down the stairs and then she saw Jonathan.

He was crumpled in the sand, out cold.

At first she thought he was dead, he was lying there so completely motionless. She set the glass of iced tea down on the stairs but knocked it over in her haste to get down to him as quickly as possible.

She found the pulse in his neck beating slowly and

steadily and she breathed a sigh of relief. His skin was warm and the stubble from his chin felt rough against her fingers. When was the last time she'd touched a man's face? Surely not an entire five years, back before Trevor finally left? Still, she honestly couldn't remember.

"John," she said softly, trying to rouse him but not wanting to shout in his ear.

He groaned and stirred, but didn't open his eyes.

Mariah could feel the early morning sun already beating down on her head and her back. "John," she said again, louder this time, touching his shoulder. "Come on, wake up. We've got to get you out of the sun."

He was a large man, but Mariah was no lightweight herself, and she was able to hoist him up by taking hold under both arms. As she dragged him toward the shade, he roused slightly, trying to help her. He opened his eyes, but quickly shut them, wincing against the brightness of the sun.

"God, what happened?"

"I think you fainted," she told him.

There was a bit of shade at the side of the house, and he sank to the ground.

"Can you sit up?" she asked.

He shook his head. "Still dizzy."

He lay on his back, right there on the sandy ground. His eyes were closed, and he had one arm thrown across them as if for added protection from the brightness. There were bits of gravel and sand stuck to the side of his face, and Mariah gently brushed them off.

"John, I'm going to go get some cold towels," she told him. "Don't try to stand up, all right?"

"Yeah," he managed to say.

Mariah dashed back up the stairs and into the house. She grabbed two hand towels from the linen closet, stopping only to dampen one with cool water in the kitchen sink.

Jonathan hadn't moved when she reached him, but he did open his eyes again at the sound of her footsteps. "I'm really sorry about this," he said. His eyes were so blue.

Mariah sat down next to him, lifting him slightly so that his head was off the hardness of the ground and resting instead in her lap. She pressed the cool towel against his forehead and he closed his eyes. "I really hope whatever this is, it's not contagious."

Another flash of blue as he looked up at her. "It's not. I'm…not contagious, I promise. I haven't been sleeping that well and… I'm really sorry about this," he said again.

*Someday their children would marvel at the story of the way they'd met....*

Where had *that* thought come from? It had simply popped into Mariah's mind. Their *children?* What was *that* about? Still, she had to admit, this made one heck of a good story. They meet on the beach, and he turns green and passes out. It certainly was different, at any rate.

"I don't know what happened," he admitted. "I was sitting on the steps, and I was positive I was going to get sick to my stomach, so I stood up and…" He laughed, but it was painful-sounding, embarrassed. "I don't think I've ever fainted before."

He seemed to want to sit up, so Mariah helped him. She could tell with just one touch that he was a mass of tension, a giant bundle of stress. She could feel it in his body, in his shoulders and neck, even see it in the tightened muscles in his face. Gently, she massaged his shoulders and back, wishing she had the power to teach this man in one minute all that she'd learned in the past two months, all the relaxation techniques and stress-reduction exercises that had helped her.

"God, that feels good," he breathed.

"There's a licensed masseur at the resort," Mariah told him. "You should definitely schedule some time with him. You're *really* tense."

He was starting to relax, the tightness in his shoulders melting down to a more tolerable level. He sighed and she saw that his eyes were closed as he sat slumped forward, forehead resting in his hands.

"Don't fall asleep yet," Mariah leaned closer to whisper. "I think your friend just pulled up in front of the house."

Her lips were millimeters away from the softness of his ear, and on a whim, she closed the final gap, brushing her lips gently against him in the softest of kisses.

His eyes opened again, and he turned to stare at her, as if she'd taken a bite out of him instead.

Mariah felt her cheeks heat with a blush. Obviously, she'd finally lost her mind. It was the only explanation she could come up with, the only reason she had for kissing this stranger who'd fainted in her yard.

But his eyes seemed to soften as he saw her blush, and with that softness came an almost haunting vulnerability.

That vulnerability was something she instinctively knew that he usually kept hidden. He kept a lot hidden, she knew that, too. There was quite a bit about this man that she recognized, that seemed familiar.

"Wow, John, are you okay?"

Daniel Tonaka was a man of slightly shorter than average height. But he was stronger than his lean build suggested. He leaned over and easily helped Jonathan to his feet.

Daniel looked at Mariah. "What happened?"

"I don't know." She shook her head, gracefully rising and helping Daniel support John as they headed toward his car. "He walked out here from the resort, along the beach. We were talking, and then suddenly, wham-o. He started to sweat and then he passed out."

"I just need some breakfast," John insisted as they helped him into the passenger seat. "I'm all right."

"Yeah, man, you look about as all right as roadkill."

Mariah reclined the seat slightly, then leaned across John to fasten his seat belt. Her breasts brushed his chest, and when she glanced down at him, his eyes were open again, and he was looking directly at her.

"Thank you," he said, giving her one of his almost smiles.

Mariah's mouth was dry as she backed out of the car and closed the door.

"Come on, Princess," Daniel said.

The dog jumped into the car, taking a surefooted stance on the back seat.

"Thank you very much, Miss…?" Daniel called to her. "I'm sorry, I've forgotten your name."

"Robinson," she told him. "Mariah Robinson."

Jonathan Mills lifted a hand in a weak wave as the car pulled away.

Mariah looked at her watch. It wasn't even 6:00 a.m. The day had barely just begun.

SHE SAW THEM THROUGH THE window of the resort health club.

She worked out for several hours early each morning—earlier than most other people used the resort facility. She was here only to tone and strengthen her body. She wasn't here to flash her spandex-clad reflection in the mirrors on the wall, to catch the attention of some healthy, weight-lifting, muscle-bound man.

No, the man she was looking for wasn't going to be found pumping iron.

A car pulled into the parking lot alongside the building—the only thing moving in the early-morning stillness. As she worked her triceps, she watched a young Asian man help another man out of that car and toward the wing that held the more expensive rooms. A dog trotted obediently behind them.

The older man was bent over, his shoulders stooped as if from fatigue or pain. His skin had a grayish cast. Yet there was still something about him that caught her eye.

She set down her weights and moved closer to the window, watching until they moved out of sight.

MARIAH ROBINSON belonged to him.

The game had begun early this morning, and already he'd gotten much further than he'd hoped.

John Miller pulled to a stop in Mariah's driveway. He took a deep breath, both amused and disgusted by the sensation of anticipation that was flowing through him.

This woman was his way to get closer to a suspected killer. No more, no less.

He tried to tell himself that the anticipation he was feeling was from being under cover, from closing in on the Black Widow. And those flowers he had on the car seat next to him were all part of his plan to make friends with a woman who was close to his suspect.

Miller had ordered a dozen roses yesterday—a thank-you gift for helping him—before he'd even met Mariah Robinson, as she was currently calling herself. But as he'd gone into the florist's to pick them up this afternoon, he'd spotted a display of bright yellow flowers—great big, round flowers that brought huge, colorful splashes of brilliance into the room.

He'd known instantly that Mariah would prefer wild-looking flowers like that over hothouse roses. On a whim, he'd canceled the roses and bought a huge bouquet of the yellow flowers instead, mixed together with a bunch of daisies and something delicate and white called baby's breath.

He should've stomped down his impulse and bought the damned roses. The roses were part of his plan. The roses said an impersonal thanks. But the yellow flowers echoed the memory of Mariah's gentle hands touching his face, her strong, slender fingers massaging his shoulders, her lips brushing lightly against his ear.

And that was trouble.

The yellow flowers had nothing to do with catching Serena Westford and everything to do with the unmistakable heat of desire that had flooded him as he'd gazed into Mariah's soft brown eyes.

She was everything her picture had shown and more.

And now he was going to walk into her house with these stupid flowers and lie to her about who he was and why he was here. But the biggest lie of all would be in denying the attraction that had flared between them. Jonathan Mills was only to become Mariah's friend. It was John Miller who wanted to take this woman as his lover and lose himself in her quiet serenity for the entire rest of the year.

It was John Miller who'd found himself unable to tear his eyes away from the soft cotton of Mariah's T-shirt as it clung revealingly to her body out on the beach that morning. He'd caught himself staring more than once, and he could only hope that she hadn't noticed.

But he knew damn well that she had. He'd seen the slight pink of her blush on her cheeks.

Miller got out of the car and, carrying the flowers with him, went to Mariah's front door and rang the bell.

There was no answer.

He knew she was home—Daniel had been out on surveillance all day and had just called saying that Mariah was back home after an afternoon of running errands in town. Sure enough, her bike was leaning against the side of the house.

Miller went around toward the back, toward the beach, and nearly ran smack into Mariah.

She'd come directly from the ocean. Her hair was wet, her dark curls like a cap against her head. Her skin glistened from the water, and her tank-style bathing suit was plastered to her incredible body. The sun sparkled on a bead of water caught in her eyelashes as her eyes widened in surprise.

"John! Hi! What are *you* doing here?"

God, she was gorgeous. Every last inch of her was

fantastic. But she wrapped her towel around her waist as if self-conscious of the way she looked in a bathing suit.

He held out the yellow flowers. "I wanted to thank you for helping me this morning."

She took the flowers, but barely looked at them. Her attention was fully on him, her gaze searching his face. "Are you all right? You didn't walk all the way out here, did you?"

"No, I drove."

"By yourself?" She looked over his shoulder at the car, parked in her drive.

"I'm feeling much better," he said. "It was just…I don't know, low blood sugar, I guess. I didn't have much dinner last night, and I didn't have anything to eat before I left the resort this morning. But I had some breakfast and even managed to catch a few hours of sleep after Daniel gave me a ride back to my room."

"Low blood sugar," she repeated her gaze never leaving his face.

She clearly didn't believe him. It was the perfect opening for him to begin to tell her Jonathan Mills's cover story. But the words—the lies—stuck in his throat, and for the first time in his life, he almost couldn't do it.

What was wrong with him? This was the part of being under cover that he always enjoyed—getting close to the major players in the game. He'd never thought of his cover story as lies before. It was, instead, the new truth. His cover became his new reality. He *was* Jonathan Mills.

But as he looked into Mariah's eyes, he couldn't push John Miller away. No doubt the fatigue and the stress of the past few years were taking their toll.

"Actually," he said, clearing his throat, "it was probably a combination of low blood sugar-and the fact that I've just finished a course of chemotherapy." He ran his fingers through his barely there hair as he watched realization and horror dawn in Mariah's eyes. He should have felt a burst of satisfaction, but all he felt was this damned twinge of guilt. He hardened himself. He was the robot, after all.

"Oh," she said.

"Cancer," he told her. "Hodgkin's. The doctors caught it early. I'm...I'm lucky, you know?"

She was looking down at the flowers now, but her gaze was unfocused. When she glanced back up at him, he could see that she had tears in her eyes. Tears of compassion, of sympathy. He knew he'd moved another step closer to his goal, but robot or not, he felt like a bastard.

"Would you be interested in that glass of iced tea I offered you this morning?" she asked, blinking back the tears and forcing a friendly smile.

Miller nodded. "Thanks."

Mariah led the way up the stairs to her deck, her hips swaying beneath her beach towel. Miller let himself look. Looking was all he was going to be able to do, God help him.

"These flowers are beautiful. I've never seen anything like them before." She gestured toward a round, umbrella shaded table, surrounded by cushioned chairs. "Why don't you sit down?"

"Thanks."

Mariah carried the flowers into the kitchen and set them down on the counter. Cancer. Jonathan Mills had cancer. He'd just finished a course of *chemotherapy*.

She gripped the edge of the counter, trying hard to keep her balance.

Talk about stress. Talk about pain. Talk about problems. Her own petty problems were laughable compared to having an illness that, left unchecked, was sure to kill him. And even with the treatment, there was still a pretty big chance that he wouldn't survive.

Cancer. God. And *he* was the one bringing *her* flowers.

Mariah took a moment to put them in water, gathering the strength she needed to go back out onto the deck and make small talk with a man who was probably going to die.

Taking a deep breath, she took two glasses from the cabinets and filled them with ice, then poured the tea. *Cancer.*

Somehow, she was able to smile by the time she carried the glasses back out to the deck.

But he wasn't fooled. "I freaked you out, didn't I?" John asked as she set the glass down in front of him. "I'm sorry."

Mariah sat down across from him, arranging her towel so that it covered most of her legs, grateful that he wasn't going to ignore the fact that he'd just told her he was so desperately ill. "Are you able to talk about it?" she asked.

He took a sip of his iced tea. "Sometimes it seems as if it's all I've talked about for the past year."

"If you don't want to, it's—"

"No, that's all right. I guess I...wanted you to know. I haven't always made a habit of doing nosedives into the sand at the drop of a hat." He took a deep breath and forced a smile. "So. I'll give you the *Reader's Digest* version. I was diagnosed with Hodgkin's disease, which is a form of cancer of the lymph nodes. Like I said, my doctors caught it early—I was stage one, which means the cancer hasn't metastasized. It hasn't spread. The survival rate is higher for patients with stage one Hodgkin's. So I took the treatments, did the chemo—which made me far sicker than the Hodgkin's ever did—and here I am, waiting for my hair to grow back in." He paused. "And to find out if I'm finally out of danger."

Mariah remembered the tension she'd felt in his shoulders. Was it any wonder this man was a walking bundle of nerves? He was waiting to find out if he was going to live or die. He looked exhausted, sitting there across from her, the lines in his face pronounced.

"No wonder you're not eating well. You're probably not sleeping very well, either," she said. "Are you?"

Something shifted in his eyes, and he looked out at the ocean, shimmering at the edge of the sand. He didn't answer right away, but she just waited, and he finally turned back to her. "No," he said. "I'm not."

"Is it that you can't fall asleep?" she asked. "Or after you fall asleep, do you wake up a few hours later and just lie there, thinking about everything, worrying…?"

"Both," he admitted.

"I used to do that," she told him. "Two hours after I fell asleep, I'd be wide-awake, lying in bed, suffocating underneath all these screaming anxieties…." She shook her head. "That's not a fun way to live."

"I have nightmares." Miller heard the words leave his mouth, and it was too late to bite them back. Jonathan Mills didn't have nightmares. The nightmares were John Miller's albatross. They belonged to Miller alone. He drank the last of his iced tea and stood up.

"I really didn't mean to stay long. I know you probably have things to do. I just wanted to thank you for... everything."

Mariah stood up, too. "You know, I have a book on stress-reduction techniques that I could lend you, if you want."

A book. She could lend him. How perfect was that? He could drop by to return it some afternoon—while Serena Westford just happened to be visiting. What a coincidence. Serena meet Jonathan Mills. John, this is Serena...

"Thanks," Miller said. "I'd like that."

With the swish of her towel against her legs, she disappeared into the darkness of the house. The book must've been right in the living room because she came out almost immediately.

He took it from her, glancing quickly at the cover, which read *101 Innovative Ways to Relieve Stress.* "Thanks," he said again. "I'll bring it back in a few days."

"Why don't you keep it," she said. "I've gotten pretty good at most of the exercises in there. Besides, I can always pick up another copy."

Miller had to laugh as his perfect plan crumbled. "Don't you get it? I *want* to return it. It gives me an excuse to come back out here."

Mariah's soft brown eyes got even softer, and John was reminded of the way she'd looked at him this morning after she'd gently kissed his ear. "You don't need an excuse to come over," she told him quietly. "You're welcome here. Anytime."

Miller tried to force a smile as he thanked her. What was wrong with him? he wondered again as he walked around to his car. He should be feeling triumphant. She liked him—that couldn't have been more obvious. This was working out perfectly.

Feeling like an absolute bastard, he put the car in gear and drove away.

## CHAPTER THREE

MARIAH WAS ON THE ROOF when she saw Serena's sports car pull up in front of the Foundations for Families building site.

"Hel-lo!" Her friend's bright English accent carried clearly up to her.

Mariah used the back of her hand to wipe the perspiration from her forehead. Tomorrow she was going to have to remember to bring a sweatband—the weather forecast had predicted more of this relentless heat. She was dirty and hot, with stinging salt and sunblock dripping into her eyes, and her back was starting to ache.

But she was surrounded by people who laughed and sang as they worked. Today she was driving nails alongside Thomas and Renee, the man and woman who would own this house, watching the pride they took in being able to help build the home that would shelter them and their two daughters—Jane Ann and Emma.

Foundations for Families started each day with a minute of silent meditation, of joining hands and closing their eyes, just taking a moment to touch base with the powers that be—God, or Mother Nature, or even Luke Skywalker's Force—it didn't matter which. Meals were something out of an old-fashioned barn raising with sandwiches and lemonade provided by volunteers. And each day, Thomas and Renee would call to Mariah and thank her by name—sometimes even enveloping her in an embrace as she left to go home.

Mariah couldn't remember ever being happier.

Down on the ground, Serena shaded her eyes to gaze up at her. "What time are you done here?"

Mariah rested her hammer against her work boot and unfastened her water bottle from her belt. She took a long swig before answering. "My shift ends at six," she said.

"Good. Then you can meet me at seven, at the resort," Serena decided. "We can eat at the grill out by the pool, then prowl the bars, husband hunting as you so aptly put it."

The resort. Where Jonathan Mills was staying. Except Mariah was almost certain he wasn't the type to hang out in a bar. Still, she was almost tempted to go over there. Almost.

She hooked her water bottle back onto her belt and hefted her hammer. "Sorry. Can't," she told her friend, glad she had an excuse. She wasn't the type to hang out in bars, either. They were noisy, crowded and filled with smoke and desperation. "I'm coming back out here tomorrow. I've got to be up early in the morning. Laronda scheduled a building blitz. We're gonna get this sucker watertight by sundown."

Serena looked at the rough plywood that framed the modestly sized house and skeptically lifted an elegant eyebrow. "You're kidding."

"Nope," Mariah said cheerfully. "Of course, we could always use more volunteers. I don't suppose you're interested…?"

"Not on your life." Serena snorted. "I did my share— in Africa fifteen years ago, with the peace corps."

The peace corps. Funny. Mariah knew Serena had spent nearly eighteen months with the peace corps—building roads and houses, working in a part of Africa where electricity hadn't found its way to this very day. They'd talked about it quite a bit, but Mariah *still* couldn't picture the elegant blonde actually getting her hands dirty digging latrines. Serena? No, she just couldn't imagine it. Still, why would the woman lie? And she spoke of her time in the corps with such authority.

"Sure I can't talk you into having some fun tonight?" Serena asked.

Mariah shook her head. "I'm having fun right now," she told her friend.

"You," Serena said, "are one seriously twisted woman." She called back over her shoulder as she headed toward her car, "Don't forget about my party Friday night."

"You know, Serena, I'm not really the party type..."

But Serena had already climbed behind the wheel, starting her car with a roar.

Mariah didn't want to go to any party. She'd been to several of Serena's affairs before and stood uncomfortably while Serena's chic resort friends talked about nothing of any substance. The weather. The stock market. The best place to rent jet skis.

Last time, she'd left early and vowed to make up an excuse if Serena ever invited her again. She'd have to think up something convincing...

But she wasn't going to think about it right now. She had a house to build. No worries. No problems.

Mariah got back to work.

MILLER WAS RUNNING on empty.

He'd awakened before dawn, after only a few hours of rest, jarred out of sleep by an ominous dream. It wasn't his usual nightmare, but it was a dream filled with shadows and darkness, and he knew if he fell back to sleep, he'd soon find himself outside that damned warehouse.

So he'd made himself a cup of coffee, roused Princess and headed down the beach, toward Mariah's cottage.

The first glimmer of daybreak had been lighting the sky when he'd reached the part of the strand where he'd met Mariah two mornings ago. And as he'd watched, the light in her beach house went off, and she came outside, shouldering a backpack.

She climbed on her bicycle and rode away, down the road toward town, before he was even close enough to call out to her.

He stayed for a while, hoping she would return, but she hadn't. Later, he'd found her bike, locked to a rack by the public library.

Having to wait for her to come back was frustrating, but Miller had been on stakeouts that had literally lasted for months, and he knew how to curb his impatience. He'd set up camp under the shade of a brightly colored beach umbrella, lathered himself with sunblock and waited.

He'd spent the first part of the morning reading that book Mariah had lent him. It was one of those touchy-feely books that urged the reader to become one with his or her emotions, and to vent—to talk or cry. Emotional release was necessary—according to the author, a Dr. Gerrard Hollis from California, of course—before the anxiety causing stress could be relieved.

Miller flipped through the chapters on breathing exercises and self-hypnosis techniques, focusing instead on the section about reducing stress through sex. There was nothing like regularly scheduled orgasmic release—according to the esteemed Dr. Hollis, whoever the hell he was—to counter the bad effects of stress on the human nervous system.

Each of the exercises outlined in the book—and this section went on for an entire detailed chapter—were designed to be both physically and emotionally relaxing. They were also designed to be done either by a couple, or by an individual. Women could make use of certain "assistive" devices if they so desired, Dr. Hollis pointed out.

Miller had gotten a hell of a lot of mileage out of thinking about Mariah performing those exercises, with or without assistive devices.

But she still hadn't returned by lunchtime, and Miller had gone back to the resort. He'd spent the afternoon helping Daniel fine-tune the surveillance equipment the younger man had planted in Serena Westford's rented house. Yesterday, around noon, their suspect had gone off island. Instead of following her, assuming that if she was going over the causeway to the mainland she was planning to stay for a while, Daniel had used the opportunity to hide miniature microphones in key spots in Serena's home.

Their surveillance system was up and running.

And now Miller was back outside Mariah's house, watching the sun set, wondering where she had gone, feeling slightly sick to his stomach from fatigue.

He heard the squeak of her bicycle before he saw her. As he watched, she turned up her driveway, getting off her bike and pushing it the last few feet up the hill. She put down the kickstand, but the sandy ground was too soft to hold it up, and she leaned it against the side of the house instead.

She slipped her arms out of her backpack and tossed it down near the foot of the stairs leading up to her deck. And then, kicking her feet free from a pair of almost ridiculously clunky work boots, she pulled her T-shirt over her head and headed directly toward the ocean.

As Miller watched, she dropped her shirt on the sand and crash-dived into the water. She didn't notice him until she was on her way back out. And then she saw Princess first.

Mariah's running shorts clung to her thighs, their waistband sagging down across her smooth stomach, the pull of the water turning them into hip huggers. The effect was incredibly sexy, but she quickly hiked her shorts up, pulling at the thin fabric in an attempt to keep it from sticking to her legs.

"John," she said, smiling at him. "Hi."

She was wearing some kind of athletic bra-type thing, the word "Champion," emblazoned across her full breasts. There was nothing she could do to keep *that* wet fabric from clinging, but she seemed more concerned with keeping her belly button properly concealed.

And Miller couldn't think of anything besides the exercise that Dr. Hollis called "Releasing Control." And the one the good doctor called "Pressure Cooker Release." And something particularly intriguing that was cutely labeled "Seabirds in Flight." It was a damned good thing *his* shorts weren't wet and clinging to *his* body.

"Hey." Somehow he managed to make his voice sound friendly—and as if he *wasn't* thinking about how incredible it would be to reenact that famous beach scene in *From Here to Eternity* with this woman right here and now. "Where've you been all day?"

"Were you looking for me?" She couldn't hide the pleasure in her voice or the spark of attraction in her eyes.

Miller felt that same twinge of something disquieting and he forced it away. So she liked him. Big deal. "I came by this morning," he told her.

The waves tugged again at her shorts, and she came all the way out of the water to stand self-consciously, dripping on the sand. She had no towel to cover herself this time, and she was obviously uncomfortable about that. But she leaned over to greet Princess, enthusiastically rubbing the dog's ears.

"I went over to the mainland," she told Miller, rinsing her hands in the ocean. "I volunteer for Foundations for Families, and I was working at a building site. We got the vinyl siding up today."

"Foundations for Families?"

She nodded, squeezing the water out of her ponytail with one hand. "It's an organization that builds quality homes for people with low incomes. The houses are affordable because of the low-interest mortgages Triple F arranges, and because volunteers actually build the houses alongside the future home owners."

Miller had heard of the group. "I thought you had to

be a carpenter or an electrician or a professional roofer to volunteer."

She narrowed her eyes at him. "And how do you know I'm not one?"

Miller covered his sudden flare of alarm with a laugh. She wasn't challenging him or questioning him. She hadn't suddenly realized he knew all about her background through his FBI files. She was teasing. So he teased her back. "Obviously because I'm a sexist bastard who archaically thinks that only men can be carpenters or electricians or roofers. I apologize, *Miz* Robinson. I stand guilty as charged."

Mariah smiled. "Well, now that you've confessed, I can tell you that I'm *not* a carpenter. Although I *am* well on my way to being a professional roofer. I've helped do ten roofs since I got here a couple of months ago. I'm not afraid of heights, so I somehow always end up working there."

"How many days a week do you do this?"

"Three or four," she told him. "Sometimes more if there's a building blitz scheduled."

"A building *blitz?*"

"That's when we push really hard to get one phase of the project finished. Today we blitzed the siding. We've had weeklong blitzes when we start and finish an entire house inside and out." She glanced at him. "If you're interested, you could come along with me next time I go. I've got tomorrow off, but I'm working again the day after that."

"I'd like that," he said quietly. The uneasiness was back—this time not because he was deceiving her, but because his words rang with too much truth. He *would* like it. A lot.

Means to an end, he reminded himself. Mariah Robinson was merely the means to meeting—and catching—Serena Westford.

But Mariah smiled almost shyly into his eyes and he found himself comparing them to whiskey—smoky and light brown and intoxicatingly warming.

"Well, good. I leave early in the morning—the van picks me up at six. You could either meet me here or downtown in front of the library." She looked away from him and glanced up at the sky. The high, dappled clouds were streaked with the pink of the setting sun. "Look at how pretty that is," she breathed.

She was mostly turned away from him, and he was struck by the soft curve of her cheek. Her skin would feel so smooth beneath his fingers, beneath his lips. Her own lips were slightly parted as she gazed raptly out at the water, at the red-orange fingers of clouds extending nearly to the horizon, lit by the sun setting to the west, to their backs.

And then Miller followed her gaze and looked at the sky. The clouds were colored in every hue of pink and orange imaginable. It *was* beautiful. When was the last time he'd stopped to look at a sunset?

"My mother loved sunsets," he said, before he even realized he was speaking. God, what was he telling her? About his *mother...*?

But she'd turned to look at him, her eyes still so warm. "Past tense," she said. "Is she...?"

"She died when I was a kid," he told her, pretending that he had only said that because he was looking for that flare of compassion he knew was going to appear in her eyes. Serena Westford, he reminded himself. Mariah was a means to an end.

Jackpot. Her eyes softened as he knew they would. She was an easy target. He was used to manipulating hardened, suspicious criminals. Compared to them, Mariah Robinson was laughably easy to control. One mention of his poor dead mother—never mind that it was true—and her eyes damn near became filled with tears.

"I'm so sorry," she murmured. She actually reached for his hand and gently squeezed his fingers before she let him go.

"She always wanted to go to Key West," Miller said, watching her eyes. "She thought it was really great that the people on Key West celebrate every single sunset— that they stop and watch and just sit quietly for a few minutes every evening. God, I haven't thought about that in years."

Mariah gave him another gentle smile, and he knew he was lying to himself. He was doing it again. This was *his* background, *his* history, not Jonathan Mills's cover story. He was telling her about his mother because he wanted to tell her. He'd known Tony for nearly two decades, and the topic had never come up in their conversations. Not even once. He knew this girl, what? Two days? And he was telling her about his mother's craziest dream.

They'd planned to rent a car and drive all the way from New Haven down to Key West. But then she'd gone and died.

Mariah was silent, just watching the sky as the last of the light slipped away. Who was controlling whom? Miller had to wonder.

"Do you have plans for this evening?" he asked.

She turned to scoop her T-shirt up off the sand. "A

friend wanted me to go barhopping, but I turned her down. That's not exactly my idea of fun. Besides, I'm beat. I'm going to have a shower, a quick dinner, and then sit down with a good book with my feet up."

"I should go," Miller murmured. He definitely had to go. Serena Westford was probably that friend, and if she was out, she probably wasn't going to be dropping by tonight. He'd come back in the morning when the sun was up, when the soft dusk of early evening wasn't throwing seductive shadows across everything.

"Oh, I almost forgot," Mariah said. "I picked something up for you on the mainland this morning."

She hurried back up the beach toward the backpack she'd left at the bottom of the stairs. Miller followed more slowly. She'd picked something up for him?

"Wait a sec," she said, bounding up the stairs, carrying the heavy-looking backpack effortlessly. "I want to turn on the deck light."

Princess followed her up the stairs.

"Hey, what are you doing?" he heard Mariah say to Princess. "You can't go in there. My rental agreement distinctly says no dogs or cats. And I hate to break it to you, babe, but you're definitely a dog. I know you don't believe me...."

The light came on as Miller started up the stairs. It was one of those yellow bug lights, easy on the eyes. It cast a golden, almost fairy-tale-like glow on the deck.

Mariah had her backpack on the table as she unzipped one of the compartments. He stopped halfway up the stairs, afraid to get too close, fighting the pull that drew him toward her. Means to an end, he reminded himself.

"There's a Native American craft shop on the mainland," she told him as she drew a heavy tool belt out and set it on the table. "I love going in there—they've got some really beautiful jewelry and some fabulous artwork. But when I went past this morning, I was thinking about you and I went in and bought you *this*." She pulled a bag out of her pack and something out of that bag.

It was round and crisscrossed with a delicate string of some kind, intricately woven as if it were a web. A feather was in the center, held in place by the string, and several other longer feathers hung down from the bottom of the circle.

Miller didn't know what the hell it was, but whatever it was, Mariah had bought it for *him*. She'd actually bought him a *gift*.

"Wow," he said. "Thanks."

She grinned at him. "You don't have a clue what this is, do you?"

"It's, um, something to hang on the wall?"

"It's something to hang on the wall by your bed," she told him. "It's a dream catcher. Certain Southwestern Native American tribes believed having one near while you slept would keep you from having nightmares." She held it out to him. "Who knows? Maybe they're right. Maybe if you hang it up, you'll be able to sleep."

Miller had to climb the last few steps to take the dream catcher from her hands. He wasn't sure what to say. He couldn't remember the last time anyone had bought him anything. "Thank you," he managed. She had been thinking about him today. They'd only met twice, and she had been thinking about him....

That was good for the case, he tried to tell himself,

but he knew the real truth. It had nothing to do with Serena Westford and everything to do with this sudden ache of desire he couldn't seem to ignore.

For the briefest, wildest moment, he actually considered following through on his urges to make his relationship with Mariah a sexual one. But even he couldn't do that. Even he wasn't enough of a son of a bitch to use her that way.

Still, when Miller opened his mouth to take his leave, he found himself saying something else entirely. "I haven't had dinner yet. Can I talk you into joining me? There's a fish place right down the road…?"

"I'm really not up to going out," Mariah told him. "But I've got a swordfish steak in the fridge that I was going to throw on the grill. I'd love it if you'd join me." She didn't give him time to respond. "I've *got* to take a shower," she said, pushing open the sliding door that led from the deck into the house. "I'll be quick—help yourself to a beer or a soda from the kitchen."

She was inside the house before he could come up with a good reason why he *shouldn't* stay for dinner. But there were plenty of reasons. Because eating here, in the seclusion of her cottage, was too intimate. Because he wasn't sure he'd be able to maintain this pretense of wanting to be only friends. Because the thought of her in the shower while he was out here waiting was far too provocative. Because he didn't trust himself to keep his distance.

But Miller didn't say anything.

Because, despite the fact he knew he was playing with fire, he wanted to stay here with Mariah Robinson more than he'd wanted anything in years.

"CAR ALARMS," JOHN SAID as he helped Mariah carry the last of the dishes back into the kitchen. "The company makes car alarms, and in the late eighties the business boomed. I took over as CEO when my father retired. I've been gone too long—I need to get back to work in a month or two."

Mariah leaned back against the sink. "How have the sales figures been since you've left?"

He shrugged. "Holding steady."

"Then you don't *need* to do anything," she told him. "Particularly not throw yourself back into the rat race before you're physically ready. Give yourself a break."

He smiled very slightly. "I still look pretty awful, huh?"

"Actually, you look much better." Over the past few days, his hair had grown in quite a bit more. Mariah figured he must be one of those men who needed a cut every two weeks or so because his hair grew so quickly. It was dark and thick and he now looked as if he'd intentionally gotten a crew cut rather than as if he'd been attacked by a mad barber with an electric razor.

His skin looked a whole lot less gray, too. He actually had some color, as if he'd been out in the sun for part of the day.

His eyes were a different story. Slightly bloodshot and bleary, he still looked as if he hadn't slept in weeks.

"Did you get a chance to look at that book I gave you?" she added.

"Yeah." He couldn't hide his smile. "It was…educational. Particularly the chapter about stress reduction through sex."

Mariah felt her cheeks heat with a blush. "Oh, God," she said. "I forgot all about that chapter. He *does* go into some detail, doesn't he? I hope you didn't think I was—"

"I didn't think anything," he interrupted her. "It's all right. I was just teasing."

She laughed giddily. "And I was just going to ask you into the living room to try out one of my favorite stress-relieving exercises, but now I'm not sure how you'll take that invitation."

"It wouldn't happen to be the exercise called "Pressure Cooker Release," by any chance?" he asked.

She knew exactly which one he was talking about, and she snorted, feeling her face turn an even brighter shade of red. "Not a chance." But maybe after she got to know him quite a bit better…

He smiled as if he was following the direction of her thoughts. Jonathan Mills had the *nicest* smile. He didn't use it very often, but when he did, it softened the harsh lines of his face and warmed the electric blue of his eyes.

She found herself smiling back at him almost foolishly.

He broke their gaze, glancing away from her as if he were afraid the heat that was building in both of their eyes had the potential to burn the house down.

Pressure cooker release indeed.

Mariah waited for a moment, but he didn't look back at her. Instead, he poured himself another mug of decaf, adding just a touch of sugar, no milk.

The conversation had been heading in a dangerously flirtatious and sexually charged direction. John had started it, but then he'd just as definitely ended it. He'd stopped them cold instead of continuing on into an area peppered with lingering looks and hot sparks that could jolt to life a powerful lightning bolt between them.

Mariah didn't know whether to feel disappointed or relieved.

Jonathan Mills had proven himself to be the perfect dinner guest. He'd started the gas grill while she was in the shower and had even put together a salad from the fresh vegetables she'd had in the refrigerator.

He was clearly good at fending for himself in a kitchen. He had to be—he'd told her over dinner that he'd never been married. He'd told her quite a bit more about the successful business he'd inherited.

What she couldn't figure out was why no woman had managed yet to get her hooks into such an attractive and well-to-do man.

Not that Mariah was looking to get involved on any kind of permanent basis. She wasn't like Serena, eyeing every man who came her way for eligibility and holding a checklist of whatever characteristics she required in a husband. Money, Mariah thought. Serena wouldn't want a man if he didn't have plenty of money. John had that, but he also had cancer. Serena probably wouldn't be very interested in acquiring a man who was fighting a potentially terminal illness.

Nobody would.

Who would want to risk becoming involved with a man who had Death, complete with black robe and sickle, hovering over him?

Mariah cleared her throat. "Well," she said, "if you're interested in giving it a try, the relaxation exercise I'm thinking about is one I found extremely effective and..."

He looked a little embarrassed. "I don't know. I've

never been very good at that kind of thing. I mean, it's never worked for me in the past and—"

"What can it hurt to try?"

John met her eyes then. He laughed halfheartedly, sheepishly. "I really don't have much patience for doing things like lying on your back and closing your eyes and having someone tell you to imagine you're in some special place with a waterfall trickling and birds singing. I've never been to a place like that and I can't relate at all and—"

Mariah held out her hand. "Just try it."

He looked from her face to her hand and back, but didn't move. "I should just go."

She stepped closer and took his hand. "I promise it won't hurt," she said as she led him into the living room.

Miller knew he shouldn't be doing this. This kind of touchy-feely stuff could lead to actual touching and feeling. And as much as he wanted that, it wasn't on his agenda.

He was here to catch a killer, he reminded himself. Mariah was going to provide his introduction to that killer. Her role was to be that of a mutual friend. A *friend,* not a lover. A means to an end.

As Mariah passed a halogen lamp, she turned the switch, fading the light to an almost nonexistent glow. It was a typical rental beach house living room. Sturdy furniture with stain-resistant slipcovers. Low-pile, wall-to-wall carpeting. Generic pictures of lighthouses and seabirds on the walls. A rental TV and VCR all but chained to the floor. White walls and plain, easy-to-clean curtains.

But Mariah had been here for two months, and she'd added touches of her own personality to the room.

A wind chime near the sliding glass doors, moving slightly in the evening breeze. Books stacked on an end table—everything from romances to military nonfiction. A boom box and a pile of CDs on another end table. A crystal bird on a string in front of a window, sparkling even in the dim light. A batik-print throw across the couch. The bouquet of bright yellow flowers he'd brought her just a few mornings ago.

She released his hand. "Lie down."

"On the floor?" God, he hated this already. But he did it, lying on his back. "And close my eyes, right?"

"Mmm-hmm."

As he closed his eyes, he heard her sit on the couch, heard her sandals drop to the floor as she pulled her long legs up underneath her.

"Okay, are your eyes closed?"

Miller sighed. "Yeah."

"Okay, now I want you to picture yourself lying in a special place. In a field with flowers growing and birds flying all around and a waterfall in the distance…"

Miller opened his eyes. She was laughing at him.

"You should see the look on your face."

He sat up, rubbing his neck and shoulders with one hand. "I'm glad I entertained you. Of course, now my stress levels are so high I may never recover."

Mariah laughed. It was a husky, musical sound that warmed him.

"Lie down here on the couch," she said, moving out of his way and patting the cushions. "On your stomach this time. I'll rub your back while we do this, get those stress levels back down to a more normal level—which for you is probably off the scale, right?" She stopped, suddenly uncertain. "What I meant to say was, I'll rub your back if you *want*..."

Miller hesitated. Did he want...? God, yes. A back rub. Mariah's fingers on his neck and shoulders... He moved up onto the couch. Surely he was strong enough to keep it from going any further.

"Thanks," he said, resting his head on top of his folded arms.

"It'll be easier if you take your shirt off," she told him, "but you don't have to if you don't want to," she added quickly.

Miller turned to look up at her. "This is just a back rub, right?"

She nodded.

"You're doing me a favor. Why wouldn't I want to make it easier for you?"

Mariah was blunt. "Because people sometimes misinterpret removing clothes as a sign that something of a sexual nature is going to follow."

He had to smile. "Yeah, well, that's mostly true, isn't it?"

She sat down next to him, on the very edge of the couch. "If I was going to come on to you, I would be honest about it. I would tell you, 'Hey. John, I'm going to come on to you now, okay?' But that's not what I'm doing here. Really. We just met. And if *that* weren't enough, you have issues. *I* have issues."

"You have issues?" he asked. Did they have something to do with the reason why she'd traveled more than halfway across the country to live under an assumed name?

"Not like yours. But yeah. I do. Doesn't everyone?"

"I guess."

She was remarkably pretty, sitting there above him like that, her clean, shiny hair falling in curls and waves down to her shoulders.

She'd put on a pair of cutoff jeans and a tank top when she came out of the shower. She smelled like after-sun lotion, sweet and fresh.

Miller pulled his T-shirt over his head, rolling it into a ball and using it, along with his arms, as a pillow. As he shifted into position, he could feel Mariah's leg pressed against him. It felt much too good, but she didn't move away, and he was penned in by the back of the couch. He had nowhere to go.

But then she touched him, her fingers cool against the back of his neck, and he forgot about trying to move away from her. All he wanted was to move closer. He closed his eyes, gritting his teeth against the sweet sensation.

"This is supposed to make you relax, not tighten up," Mariah murmured.

"Sorry."

"Make a fist," she told him.

Miller opened his eyes, lifting his head to look back at her. "What?"

She gently pushed his head back down. "Are you right-or left-handed?"

"Right-handed."

"Make a fist with your right hand," she said. "Hold it tightly—don't let go."

"Am I allowed to ask why?"

"Yeah. Sure."

"Why?"

"Because I'm telling you to. You agreed to do this

exercise, and it won't work unless you make a fist. So do it."

"I never agreed to do anything," he protested.

"You gave your unspoken consent when you lay down on this couch. Make a fist, Mills." She paused. "Or I'll stop rubbing your back."

Miller quickly made a fist. "Now what?"

"Now relax every other muscle in your body—but keep that fist tight. Start with your toes, then your feet. You've surely done that exercise where you relax every muscle, first in your legs and then your arms and then all the way up to your neck?"

"Yeah, but it doesn't work," he said flatly.

"Yes, it does. I'll talk you through it. Start with your feet. Flex them, flex your toes, then relax them. Do it a couple of times."

She ran her fingers through his hair, massaging the back of his head and even his temples. Christ, it felt heavenly.

"Okay, now do the same thing with your calves," she told him. "Tighten, then relax. You know, this is actually an exercise from a Lamaze childbirthing class. The mothers-to-be learn to keep the rest of their bodies relaxed while one muscle is tensed and working hard. Of course they can't practice with the actual muscle that's going to be contracting, so they contract something else, like a fist." Her voice was soft and as soothing as her hands. Despite himself, he felt his tension draining away. He actually felt himself start to relax. "Okay, tighten and relax the rest of your legs. Are you doing it? Are you loose?"

He felt her reach down with one hand and touch his legs, shaking them slightly.

"That's pretty good, John. You're doing great. Relax your hips and stomach…and your rear end. And don't forget to breathe—slow it down, take your time. But keep that fist tight."

Miller felt as if he were floating.

"Okay, now relax your shoulders and your arms. Relax your left hand—everything but that right fist. Keep holding that."

He could feel her touching him, her hands light against his back, caressing his shoulders and arms.

"Relax the muscles in your face," she told him softly. Her husky, musical voice seemed to come from a great distance. "Loosen your jaw. Let it drop open.

"Okay, now relax your right hand. Open it up as if you're setting everything free—all of your tension and stress. Just let it go."

Let it go.

*Let it go.*

Miller did as she commanded, and before he could stop himself, he sank into a deep, complete, dreamless sleep.

# CHAPTER FOUR

MARIAH WOKE UP, heart pounding, sure she'd been dreaming.

But then she heard it again. A strangled, anguished cry from the living room. She nearly knocked over the lamp on her bedside table as she lunged for it, using both hands to flip the switch.

Four fifty-eight. It was 4:58 in the morning.

And that was Jonathan Mills making those noises out in her living room.

He'd fallen asleep on her couch. He'd lain there motionless, as thoroughly out cold as if he'd been hit over the head with a sledgehammer. Mariah had stayed up reading for as long as she could, but had finally given in to her own fatigue. She hadn't had the heart to wake him and send him home.

She'd put an old blanket under the patio table for Princess to curl up on and covered John with a light sheet before she went to bed herself.

He cried out again, and she went out into the hall, turning on the light.

He was still asleep, still on the couch. He'd thrown off the sheet, shifting onto his back. Perspiration shone on his face and chest as he moved restlessly.

He was having a nightmare.

"John." Mariah knelt next to him. "John, wake up."

She touched him gently on the shoulder, but he didn't seem to feel her. His eyes opened, but he didn't even seem to see her. What he *did* see, she couldn't imagine—the look of sheer horror on his face was awful. And then he cried out, a not quite human sounding "No!" that ripped from his throat. And then the horror turned to rage. "No!" he shouted again. *"No!"*

He grabbed her by the upper arms, and Mariah felt a flash of real fear as his fingers bit harshly into her. For one terrifying moment, she was sure he was going to fling her across the room. Whoever it was he saw here in her place, he was intending to hurt and hurt badly. She tried to pull away, but he only tightened his grip, making her squeal with pain.

"Ow! John! God! Wake up! It's me, Mariah! Don't—"

Recognition flared in his eyes. "Oh, *God!*"

He released her, and she fell back on the rug on her rear end and elbows. She pushed herself away from him, scooting back until she bumped into an easy chair.

She was breathing hard, and he was, too, as he sat, almost doubled over on the couch.

The shock in his eyes was unmistakable. "Mariah, I'm sorry," he rasped. "What the hell happened? I was... God, I was dreaming about—" He cut himself off abruptly. "Did I hurt you? God, I didn't mean to hurt you...."

Mariah rubbed her arms. Already she could see faint bruises where his fingers had pressed too hard in the soft underside of her upper arms. "You scared me," she admitted. "You were so *angry* and—"

"I'm sorry," he said again. "Oh, God." He stood up. "I better go. I'm so sorry...."

As Mariah watched, he turned to search for his T-shirt. He couldn't find it and he had to sit down on the couch again for a moment because he was shaking. He was actually physically shaking.

"You don't ever let yourself get good and angry," Mariah realized suddenly. "Do you?"

"Do you have a shirt I can borrow? Mine's gone."

"You don't, do you?" she persisted.

He could barely meet her eyes. "No. Getting angry doesn't solve anything."

"Yeah, but sometimes it makes you *feel* better." She crawled back toward him. "John, when was the last time you let yourself cry?"

He shook his head. "Mariah—"

"You don't cry, either, do you?" she said, sitting next to him on the couch. "You just live with all of your fear and anger and grief all bottled up inside. No wonder you have nightmares!"

Miller turned away from her, desperate to find his shirt, desperate to be out of there, away from the fear he'd seen in her eyes. God, he could have hurt her so badly.

But then she touched him. His hand, his shoulder, her fingers soft against the side of his face, and he realized there was no fear in her eyes anymore. There was only sweet concern.

Her face was clean of any makeup and her hair was mussed from sleep. She was wearing an oversize T-shirt that barely covered the tops of her thighs, exposing the full length of her statuesque legs. Her smooth, soft skin seemed to radiate heat.

He reached for her almost blindly, wanting only… what? Miller didn't know what he wanted. All he knew was that she was there, offering comfort that he couldn't keep himself from taking.

She seemed to melt into his arms, her face lifted toward his, and then he was kissing her.

Her lips were warm and soft and so incredibly sweet. He kissed her harder, drinking of her thirstily, unable to get enough.

Her body was so soft, her breasts brushing against his chest, and he pulled her closer. She fit against him so perfectly, the room seemed to spin around him. He wanted to touch her everywhere. He wanted to pull off her shirt and feel her smooth skin against his.

He pulled her back with him onto the couch and their legs intertwined. Not for the first time that night, Miller wished he'd worn shorts instead of jeans.

He shifted his weight and nestled between the softness of her thighs, nearly delirious with need as he kissed her harder, deeper.

*This was one hell of a bad mistake.*

She pushed herself tightly against him, and he pushed the thought away, refusing to think at all, losing himself in her kisses, in the softness of her breast cupped in his hand.

She was opening herself to him, so generously giving him everything he asked for, and more.

And he was going to use her to satisfy his sexual desires, then walk away from her without looking back the moment she introduced him to Serena Westford— her friend, his chief suspect.

He couldn't do this. How could he do this and look himself in the eye in the mirror while he shaved each morning?

But look where he was. Poised on the edge of total ecstasy. Inches away from paradise.

He pulled back, and she smiled up at him, hooking her legs around him, her hands slipping down to his buttocks and pressing him securely against her.

"John, don't stop," she whispered. "In case you haven't noticed, I *am* coming on to you now."

"I don't have any protection," he lied.

"I do," she told him. "In my bedroom." She reached between them, her fingers unfastening the top button of his jeans. "I can get it…."

Miller felt himself weaken. She wanted him. She couldn't be any more obvious about it.

He let her pull his head down toward hers for another kiss, let her stroke the solid length of his arousal through the denim of his jeans, all the while cursing his inability to keep this from going too far.

He was a lowlife. He was a snake. And after all was said and done, she would hate him forever.

Somehow, Miller found the strength to pull back from her, out of her arms, outside the reach of her hands. "I can't do this," he said, nearly choking on the words. He sat on the edge of the couch, turned away from her, running his shaking hands through his hair. "Mariah, I can't take advantage of you this way."

She touched his back gently, lightly. "You're not taking advantage of me," she said quietly. "I promise."

He turned to look at her. Big mistake. She looked incredible with her T-shirt pushed up and twisted around her waist. She was wearing high-cut white cotton panties that were far sexier than any satin or lace he'd ever seen. She wanted to make love to him. He could reach for her and have that T-shirt and those panties off of her in less than a second. He could be inside of her in the time it took to go into her bedroom and find her supply of condoms.

He had to look away before he could speak.

"It's not that I don't want to, because I do," he told her. "It's just…"

Miller could feel her moving, straightening her T-shirt, sitting up on the other end of the couch. "It's all right. You don't have to explain."

"I don't want to rush things," he said, wishing he could tell her the truth. But what *was* the truth? That he couldn't make love to her because he was intending to woo and marry a woman she considered one of her closest friends?

He had to stop thinking like John Miller and start thinking like Jonathan Mills. He had to *become* Jonathan Mills, and his reality—and the truth—would change, too. But he'd never had so much trouble taking on a different persona before.

"I'm not ready to do more than just be friends with you, Mariah. I just got out of the hospital, my latest test results aren't even in and…" He broke off, staring out the window at the dawn breaking on the horizon, Jonathan Mills all but forgotten. "It's morning."

As Mariah watched, John stood up, transfixed by the smear of color in the eastern sky.

"I slept until morning," he said, turning to look at her. He smiled—a slight lifting of one side of his mouth, but a smile just the same. "Whoa. How'd *that* happen?"

She smiled back at him. "I guess you're going to have to admit that my silly relaxation exercise worked."

He shook his head in wonder, just gazing at her. She

could still see heat in his eyes and she knew he could see the same in hers.

He looked impossibly good with his shirt off and the top button of his jeans still unfastened. He was maybe just a little bit too skinny, but it was clear that before his illness he'd been in exceptionally good shape.

She could guess why he didn't want to become involved with her. He was just out of the hospital, he'd said. He didn't even know if he was going to live or die. And if he thought he was going to die…

Another man might have more of a live-for-today attitude. But John refused to take advantage of her. He was trying to keep her from being hurt, to keep her from becoming too involved in what could quite possibly be a dead-end relationship in a very literal sense.

But it was too late. She already was involved.

It was crazy—she should be pushing to keep her distance, not wanting to get closer to him. She didn't need to fall for some guy who was going to go and die. She should find his shirt for him, and help him out the door.

But he found his shirt on his own, on the floor next to the couch. He slipped it on. "I better go."

He didn't want to leave. She could see it in his eyes. And when he leaned over to kiss her goodbye—not just once, but twice, then three times, each kiss longer than the last—she thought he just might change his mind.

But he didn't. He finally pulled away, backing toward the door.

"I'd love it if you came over for dinner again tonight," she told him, knowing that she was risking everything—*every*thing—with her invitation.

Something shifted in his eyes. "I'm not sure I can."

Mariah was picking up all kinds of mixed signals from him. First those lingering goodbye kisses, and now this evasiveness. It didn't make sense. Or maybe it made perfect sense. Mariah wasn't sure which—she'd never been this intimate with someone dealing with a catastrophic illness before.

"Call me," Mariah told him, adding softly, "if you want."

He looked back at her one more time before going out the door. "I want. I'm just not sure I should."

SERENA WENT THROUGH the sliding glass doors, past the dining table and directly into the kitchen, raising her voice so that Mariah could hear from her vantage point on the deck. "Thank God you're home. I'm so thirsty, I was sure I was going to die if I had to wait until I got all the way to my place."

"Your place is not *that* much farther up the road." Mariah glanced up from the piles of black-and-white photographs she was sorting as Serena sat down across from her at the table on the deck, a tall glass of iced tea in hand.

"Three miles," Serena told her after taking a long sip. "I couldn't have made it even one-*tenth* of a mile. Bless you for keeping this in the icebox, already chilled. I was parched." She leaned forward to pull one of the pictures out from the others, pointing with one long, perfectly manicured fingernail. "Is that me?"

Mariah looked closely. Ever since her initial meeting with Serena, she had tried to be careful not to offend her friend by taking her picture. Or rather, she had tried not to offend Serena by letting her *know* her picture was being taken. Mariah had actually managed to get several excellent photographs of the beautiful English-woman—taken, no less, with one of those cheap little disposable cameras. Serena was incredibly photogenic, and in color, even on inexpensive film, her inner vibrance was emphasized. Mariah was careful to keep those pictures hidden.

But yes, that was definitely Serena, caught in motion at the edge of a particularly nice shot of the resort beach, moments before a storm struck. "You must've walked into the shot," Mariah said.

Serena picked it up, looking at it more closely. "I'm a big blur—except for my face." She lifted her gaze to Mariah. "Do you have any copies of this?"

Mariah sifted through the pile that photo had been in. "No, I don't think so."

"How about the negative? You still have that, right?"

Mariah sighed. "I don't know. It might be down in the darkroom, but it might've been in the batch I just brought over to B&W Photo Lab for safekeeping."

"Safekeeping?" Serena's voice rose an octave in disbelief. "Forgive me for being insensitive, but, Mariah sweetheart, no one's going to want to steal your negatives. You know I love you madly, dearest, but it's not as if you're Ansel Adams."

Mariah laughed. "I bring them to B&W for storage. I don't have air-conditioning here, and the humidity and salt air are hell on film."

Serena slipped the photo in question into her purse. "You realize, of course, that I'm going to have to kill you now for stealing my soul," she said with a smile.

"Hey, you were the one who stuck your soul into my shot," Mariah protested. "Besides, I'll get the negative next time I'm over at B&W. You can have it, and your soul will be as good as new."

"Do you promise?"

"I promise. Although it occurs to me that you might want to get yourself a more American approach to having your picture taken. You're not living in Africa anymore."

"Thank God." Serena took another sip of her drink. "So. How are you?"

"Fine." Mariah glanced suspiciously at the other woman. "Why?"

"Just wondering."

"Don't I look fine?"

Serena rested her chin in the palm of her hand, studying Mariah with great scrutiny. "Actually, you don't look half as fine as I would have thought."

Mariah just waited.

"You're not going to tell me a thing, are you?" Serena asked. "You're going to make me ask, aren't you? You're going to make me pull every little last juicy detail out of you."

Mariah went back to work. "I don't know what you're talking about."

"I'm talking about the man."

"What man?"

"The one I saw leaving your house at five-thirty this morning. Tall, dark and probably handsome—although I'm not certain. I was too far away to see details."

Mariah was floored. "What on earth were *you* doing up at five-thirty in the morning?"

"I get up that early every morning and go over to use the resort health club," Serena told her.

"You're kidding. Five-thirty? *Every* morning?"

"Just about. This morning the tide was low, so I rode my bike along the beach. And as I went past your place, I distinctly saw a man emerging from your deck door. I'm assuming he wasn't the refrigerator repairman."

"No, he wasn't." Mariah didn't look up from her photos.

"Well...?"

"Well what?"

"This is the place in the conversation where you tell me who he is, where you met him, and any other fascinating facts such as whether he was any good in bed, and so on and so forth?"

Mariah felt herself blush. "Serena, we're just friends."

"A friend who happens to stay until dawn? How modern of you, Mariah."

"He came over for dinner and fell asleep on my couch. He's been ill recently." Mariah hesitated, wanting to tell Serena about Jonathan Mills, but not wanting to tell too much. "His name is John, and he's very nice. He's staying over at the resort."

"So he's rich," Serena surmised. "Medium rich or filthy rich?"

"I don't know—who cares?"

"*I* care. Take a guess."

Mariah sighed in exasperation. "Filthy rich, I think. He inherited a company that makes car alarms."

"You said he's been ill? Nothing serious, I hope."

Mariah sighed again. "Actually, it *is* serious. He's got cancer. He's just had a round of chemotherapy. I think the prognosis is good, but there's never any guarantees with something like this."

"What did you say his name was?"

"Jonathan Mills."

"It's probably smart to keep your distance. If you're not careful, you could end up a widow. Of course, in his case, that means you'd inherit his car alarm fortune, so it *could* be worse—"

*"Serena!"* Mariah stared at her friend. "Don't even *think* that. He's *not* going to die."

The blonde was unperturbed. "You just told me that he might." She stood up. "Look, I've got to run. Thanks for the tea. See you later tonight."

Mariah frowned. "Later...tonight?"

"My party. You've forgotten, haven't you? Lord, Mariah, you're hopeless without your date book."

"No, I'm *relaxed* without my date book. Oh, that reminds me—can I borrow your car this afternoon? Just for an hour?"

Serena looked at her watch. "I'm getting my hair done at half past two. If you want to drive me to the salon, you can use the car for about an hour then."

"Perfect. Except I'm not sure I can make it to the party—I'm tentatively scheduled to have dinner again with John." Except she wasn't. Not really. She'd asked, but he'd run away.

"Bring him. Call him, invite him to my party, and bring him along with you. I want to meet this *friend* of yours. No excuses," Serena said sternly as she disappeared down the deck steps.

Mariah gazed after her. Call him. Invite him to the party. Who knows? Maybe he'd actually agree to go. HE WAS THE ONE. THE gray-faced man from the resort.

She'd recognized him right away.

The fact that he'd spent the night with that silly cow only served to make him even more perfect.

Tonight she would begin to cast her spell.

Tonight she would allow herself to start thinking about the dinner she would serve him.

Oh, it was still weeks away—maybe even months. But it was coming. She could taste it.

And tomorrow morning, she would go shopping for the perfect knife.

THE MESSAGE LIGHT ON HIS telephone was blinking when Miller returned to his suite of rooms after lunch.

Daniel had the portable surveillance equipment set up in the living room. The system was up and running when Miller came in. Daniel was wearing headphones, listening intently, using his laptop computer to control the volume of the different microphones they'd distributed throughout Serena Westford's house. The DAT recorder was running—making a permanent record of every word spoken in the huge beach house.

"Lots of activity," Daniel reported, his eyes never leaving his computer screen. "Some kind of party is happening over at the spider's web tonight."

"I know." Miller picked up the phone and dialed the resort desk. "Jonathan Mills," he said. "Any messages?"

"A Mariah Robinson asked to leave voice mail. Shall I connect you to that now, sir?" the desk clerk asked.

"Yes. Please."

There was a whirr and a click, and then Mariah's voice came on the line.

"John. Hi. It's me, Mariah. Robinson. From, um, last night? God, I sound totally lame. Of course you know who I am. I just… I wanted to invite you to a party that a friend is having tonight—"

"Jackpot," Miller said.

Daniel glanced in his direction. "Party invitation?"

Miller nodded, holding up his hand. Mariah's message wasn't over yet.

"…going to start at around nine," her voice said, "and I was thinking that maybe we could have dinner together first—if you're free. If you want to." He heard her draw in a deep breath. "I'd really like to see you again. I guess that's kind of obvious, considering everything that happened this morning." She hesitated. "So, call me, all right?" She left her phone number, then the message ended.

Miller really wanted to see her again, too. *Really* wanted to see her again.

Daniel glanced at him one more time, and Miller realized he was standing there, staring at nothing, listening to nothing. He quickly hung up the phone.

"Everything all right?" Daniel asked.

"Yeah." He was well aware that Daniel had said not one word about the fact that Miller hadn't come back to the hotel last night until after dawn. The kid hadn't even lifted an eyebrow.

But now Daniel cleared his throat. "John, I don't mean to pry, but—"

"Then don't," Miller said shortly. "Not that it's any of your business, but nothing happened last night." But even as he said the words, Miller knew they were a lie. Something *had* happened last night. Mariah Robinson had touched him, and for nearly eight hours, his demons had been kept at bay.

Something very big had happened last night.

For the first time since forever, John Miller had slept.

MARIAH WAS DRESSING UP.

She couldn't remember the last time she'd worn anything besides shorts and a T-shirt or a bathing suit. She'd gone to Serena's other parties in casual clothes. But tonight, she'd pulled her full collection of dresses—all four of 'em—out of the back of her closet. Three of them were pretty standard Sunday-best, goin'-to-meeting-type affairs, with tiny, demure flowers and conservative necklines.

The fourth was black. It was a short-sleeved sheath cut fashionably above the knee, with a sweetheart neckline that would draw one's eyes—preferably Jonathan Mills's eyes—to her plentiful assets. Her full breasts were, depending on her mood, one of her best features or one of her worst. Tonight, she was going to think positively. Tonight they were an asset.

She briefly considered sheer black stockings, but rejected them in place of bare legs and a healthy coating of Cutter's—in consideration of the sultry evening heat.

Usually when she went out with a man, she wore flats, but Jonathan Mills was tall enough for her to wear heels. They might make her stand nose to nose with him, but she *wouldn't* tower over him.

Since the moment he'd called to tell her that he wasn't available for dinner but he'd love to go to the party with her, Mariah had been walking on air. She was ridiculously excited about seeing him again—she'd thought about almost nothing else all afternoon.

She couldn't remember the last time she'd felt this

way. Even in college, when she was first dating Trevor, she hadn't felt this giddy.

Even the dark cloud of anxiety cast by John's potentially terminal illness didn't faze her tonight. They'd caught the cancer early, he'd told her. The survival rate for this type of cancer was high. He was going to live. Positive thinking.

Mariah felt another surge of anticipation as she slipped into her shoes and stepped back to look at herself in the mirror.

She looked…sexy. She looked…well proportioned. It was true that those proportions were extra large, but they had to be to fit her height. And in this case, she was using her body to her advantage. In this dress, with this neckline, she had cleavage with a capital *C*. All that without a WonderBra in sight.

The doorbell rang, and she smoothed the dress over her hips one last time, leaning closer to check her lipstick.

Ready or not, her date had come.

Praying that she wasn't coming on too strong, what with the attack of the monster cleavage and all, Mariah opened her front door.

"Hi," she said breathlessly.

John's eyes skimmed down her once, then twice, then more slowly, before coming back to rest on her face as he smiled. "Wow. You look…incredible."

She stepped back and opened the door wider to let him in.

"Incredibly tall," he added as he noted the heels that put them eye to eye.

Was that a compliment? Mariah took it as one. "Thank you," she said, leading the way into the kitchen.

"I'm ready to go, but I wanted to show you something first."

He was dressed a whole lot more casually than she, in a faded pair of jeans, time-softened leather boat shoes and a sport jacket over a plain T-shirt.

"I think I might be underdressed," he said.

"Don't worry about it. Knowing Serena's friends, there'll be an equal mix of sequined gowns and tank tops over swimsuits." Mariah opened the door to the basement.

"Serena?" he asked.

"Westford," she told him, turning on the switch that lit the stairs going down. "She lives a little more than three miles north, just up the road."

"Is she one of the Boston Westfords? Funny, maybe I know one of her brothers."

Mariah shook her head, poised at the top of the stairs. "She hasn't talked about Boston. Or any brothers. When we met, she *did* give me a business card with a Hartford hotel, but I think that was only a temporary address. I think she lived in Paris for a few years." She started down, careful of the rough wooden steps in her heels. "Aren't you coming?"

"Into the basement? Is your darkroom down there?"

"My darkroom's down here," Mariah told him, "but that's not what I want to show you."

She turned on another light.

The ceiling was low, and both she and John had to duck to avoid pipes and beams. But it was a nice basement, as far as basements went. The concrete floor had been painted a light shade of gray and it had been carefully swept. Boxes were neatly stacked on utility shelves that lined most of the walls.

A washer and dryer stood in one corner, along with a table for folding laundry. Another corner had been walled off to make the darkroom.

But she led him to the open area of the basement, where an entire concrete-block wall and the floor beneath it had been cleared. Only one box sat nearby, in the middle of the room on top of a broken chair.

Mariah reached inside and pulled out one of the plates she'd bought dirt cheap at a tag sale that afternoon, when she'd borrowed Serena's car. It was undeniably one of the ugliest china patterns she'd ever seen in her life. She handed it to John.

He stared at it, perplexed.

"It occurred to me this morning that you probably never give yourself the opportunity to really vent," she explained.

"Vent."

"Yes." She took another plate from the box. "Like this." As hard as she could, she hurled the china plate against the wall. It smashed into a thousand pieces with a resounding and quite satisfying crash.

John laughed, but then stopped. "You're kidding, right?"

"No." She gestured to the plate in his hands. "Try it."

He hesitated. "Don't these belong to someone?"

"No. Look at it, John. Have you ever eaten off something that unappetizing? It's begging for you to break it and put it out of its misery."

He hefted it in his hand.

"Just do it. It feels...liberating." Mariah took another plate from the box and sent it smashing into the wall. "Oh, *yeah!*"

John turned suddenly and, throwing the plate like a Frisbee, shattered it against the wall.

Mariah handed him another one. "Good, huh?"

"Yeah."

She took another herself. "This one's for my father, who didn't even *ask* if I wanted to spend nearly seven years of my life working eighty-hour weeks, who didn't even *try* to quit smoking or lose weight after his doctor told him he was a walking heart attack waiting to happen, and who died before I could tell him that I loved him, the bastard." The plate exploded as it hit the wall.

John threw his, too, and reached into the box for another before she could hand him one.

"This one's the head of the bank officer who wouldn't approve the Johnsons' loan for a Foundations for Families house even when the deacons of their church offered to co-sign it, all on account of the fact that she's a recovering alcoholic and he's an ex-con, even though they both have good, steady jobs now, and they both volunteer all the time as sponsors for AA."

The two plates hit the wall almost simultaneously.

"We only have time for one more," Mariah said, breathing hard as she prepared to throw her last plate of the evening. "Who's this one for, John? You call it."

He shook his head. "I can't."

"Sure you can. It's easy."

"No." He glanced at the plate he was holding loosely in his hands. "It gets too complicated."

"Are you kidding? It simplifies things. You break a plate instead of someone's face."

"It's not always that easy." He gazed searchingly into her eyes as if trying to find the words to explain.

But he gave up, shaking his head. Then he swore suddenly, sharply. "This one's for me." He threw the plate against the wall so hard that shards of ceramic shot back at them. He moved quickly, shielding her.

"Whoa!" Mariah said. She wasn't entirely sure what he meant by that, but he was catching on.

"I'm sorry. *God—*"

"No, that was *good,*" she said. "That was *very* good."

He had a tiny piece of broken plate in his hair, and she stepped toward him to pull it free.

He smelled delicious, like faintly exotic cologne and coffee.

"We should get going," he murmured, but he didn't step back, and she didn't, either, even after the ceramic shard was gone.

As Mariah watched, his gaze flickered to her mouth and then back to her eyes. He shook his head very slightly. "I shouldn't kiss you."

"Why not?" He'd shaved, probably right before he'd come to pick her up, and his cheeks looked smooth and soft. Mariah couldn't resist touching his face, and when she did, he closed his eyes.

"Because I won't want to stop," he whispered.

She leaned forward and brushed his lips with hers. With her heels on, she didn't even need to stand on her toes. She kissed him again, as softly and gently as before, and he groaned, pulling her into his arms and covering her mouth with his.

Mariah closed her eyes as he kissed her hungrily, his tongue possessively claiming her mouth, his hands claiming her body with the same proprietary familiarity.

But just as suddenly as he'd given in to his need to

kiss her, he pulled himself away, holding her at arm's length. "You're dangerous," he gasped, half laughing, half groaning. "What am I going to do with you?"

Mariah smiled.

"No," John said, backing even farther away. "Don't answer that."

"I didn't say anything," she protested.

"You didn't have to. That wicked smile said more than enough."

Mariah started back up the stairs. "What wicked smile? That was just a regular smile."

When she reached the top of the stairs, she realized he wasn't behind her.

"John?" she called.

From the basement, she heard the sound of a shattering plate.

"Did that help?" she asked with a smile, as he came up the stairs.

He shook his head. "No." His expression was so somber, his eyes so bleak, all laughter gone from his face. "Mariah, I'm…I'm really sorry."

"Why, because you want to take some time before becoming involved? Because you're trying to deal with a life-threatening illness? Because it's so damn unfair and you're mad as hell? Don't be sorry about that." She gazed at him. "We don't have to go to this party. We can stay here and break some more plates." She paused. "Or we could talk."

He tried to smile, but it didn't quite cancel out the sadness in his eyes. "No, let's do it," he said. "I'm ready to go." He took a deep breath. "As ready as I'll ever be."

## CHAPTER FIVE

SERENA WESTFORD. SHE WAS small and blond and green-eyed with a waist Miller could probably span with his hands. Her fingernails were perfectly manicured, her hair arranged in a youthful style. She was trim and lithe, dressed in a tight black dress that hugged her slender curves and showed off her flat stomach and taut derriere to their best advantage. She had sinewy muscles in her arms and legs that, along with that perfect body, told of countless hours on the Nautilus machine and the StairMaster.

She was beautiful, with a body that most men would die for.

But Miller knew more than most men.

And even if she wasn't his only suspect in a string of grisly murders, he *still* wouldn't have wanted to give her more than a cursory glance.

But she *was* his suspect, and even though he didn't want to look at anyone but Mariah, he smiled into Serena's cat green eyes. He'd come into this game intending to do more than smile at this woman. He was intending to marry her. Until death—or attempted murder—do us part.

Of course, his plan depended quite a bit on Serena's cooperation. And it was entirely possible that she wouldn't hone in on what Mariah was clearly marking as her territory with a hand nestled into the crook of his elbow. Serena was probably a killer, but Miller's experience had taught him that even killers had their codes. She may not hesitate to jam a stiletto into a lover's heart, but hitting on a girlfriend's man might not be acceptable behavior.

And that would leave Miller out in the cold, forced to bring in another agent to do what? To play the part of his even more terminally ill friend? A buddy he'd met in the oncology unit of the hospital?

God, if Serena wouldn't take his bait, the entire case could well be lost. Still, he found himself hoping...

But Serena smiled back at him and held his hand just a little too long as Mariah introduced them, and Miller knew that he was looking into the eyes of a woman who had no kind of code at all. If she was interested, and he thought that she was, she would do what she wanted, Mariah be damned.

"Look at us," the blond woman said, turning back to Mariah. "We're wearing almost exactly the same thing tonight. We're twins." She flashed a glance directly into Miller's eyes, just so that he knew she was well aware of the physical differences between the two women.

Miller forced himself to smile conspiratorially back at Serena, knowing that Mariah was going to see the exchange, knowing that she was going to interpret it as friendliness. At first.

Later, when she'd had time to think about it, Mariah would realize that he'd been flirting with her friend right from the start.

"You wouldn't happen to be from the Boston area, would you?" he asked Serena. "I know a Harcourt

Westford from my Harvard days—his family came from...I think it might've been Belmont."

"No, as a matter of fact, I've never even been to Boston."

She was lying. She'd met, married and murdered victim number six in Hyannisport, out on Cape Cod. The victim's sister had told investigating officers that her brother and his new wife—she was using Alana as an alias back then—frequently went into Boston to attend performances of the BSO.

"Help yourself to something from the bar," Serena directed them. "And the caterer made the *best* crab puffs tonight—be sure you sample them."

As Serena moved off to greet other arriving guests, she glanced back at Miller and blew him a kiss that Mariah couldn't see.

"Are you okay?" Mariah's fingers gently squeezed his upper arm. "You look a little pale."

He met her eyes and forced a smile. "I'm fine."

"Why don't you sit down and I'll get us something to drink?"

"You don't have to do that." He didn't want her to go. He didn't want to have to use the opportunity to watch Serena, to smile at her when he caught her eye.

"I don't mind," Mariah told him. "What can I get you?"

"Just a soda."

"Be right back."

Miller couldn't stop himself from watching her walk away, knowing that by the time she came back, he'd be well on his way toward destroying the easy familiarity between them.

There were chairs along the edge of the deck, but

he didn't sit down. If he sat down there, he wouldn't be able to see Serena Westford where she was standing on the other end of the wide deck, at the top of the stairs that led down to the beach.

He made his way to one of the more comfortable-looking lounge chairs instead. He'd have a clear view of Serena from there.

Serena was watching him. He could feel her glancing in his direction as he gingerly lowered himself into one of the chairs. From the corner of his eye, he saw her lean closer to the man she was talking to. The man turned to look over at the bar and nodded. As he walked away, Miller sensed more than saw Serena heading in his direction.

His cover flashed through his mind like words scrolling down a computer screen. He was Jonathan Mills. Harvard University, class of '80. M.B.A. from NYU in 1985. Car alarms. Hodgkin's. Chemotherapy. Never married. Facing his own mortality and the end of his family line.

Forget about Mariah. God knows she'd be better off without a man like him in the long run. He was "The Robot," for God's sake. What would a woman who was so incredibly warm and alive want with a man rumored to have no soul?

"Are you feeling all right?" Serena's cool English voice broke into his thoughts. He glanced over to find her settling onto the chair next to his. "Mariah was telling me how you've recently been ill."

There was an unmistakable glint of interest in her eyes.

Miller nodded. "Yeah. I have been." Across the deck he could see Mariah, a glass of something tall and cool in each hand, held in conversation by the same man who'd been talking to Serena earlier. She glanced at him, but he looked away before she could meet his eyes.

"How awful," Serena murmured.

"Mariah didn't tell me anything at all about *you*," Miller countered, knowing that everything she was about to tell him about herself would be a lie.

In the past, this game of pretend had had the power to excite him, to invigorate him. She would lie to him, and he would lie to her, and the game would go on and on and on until one of them slipped up.

It wouldn't be him. It never was him.

But tonight he didn't want to play. He wanted to turn back the clock and spend the next one hundred years of his life reliving this morning's dawn, with Mariah in his arms, the taste of her kisses on his lips.

"I think our Mariah has something of a crush on you," Serena told him. "I don't think she was eager for you to meet me."

Meaning that it was an indisputable fact that the moment Miller met Serena, he would turn away from Mariah, and—in Serena's opinion—rightly so.

This woman's self-confidence and ego were both the size of the Taj Mahal.

Miller leaned closer to Serena, feeling like Peter in the Garden of Gethsemane. "I don't really know her— not very well. We just met a few days ago, and…I know we're here together tonight, but we're really just friends. She seems very nice, though."

Meaning, he hadn't made up his mind about anything.

"Tell me," Miller said, "what's a woman like you doing on Garden Isle all by yourself?"

Meaning Serena was definitely interesting and attractive to him with her petite, aerobicized body and her gleaming blond hair and killer smile.

Serena smiled.

The game had moved into the next round.

MARIAH FELT LIKE A GIANTESS. Standing next to Serena, she felt like a towering football linebacker despite the dress and heels. Maybe *because* of the dress and heels. She felt as if she'd dressed up like this in an attempt to fool everyone into thinking she was delicate and feminine, but had failed.

Miserably.

John and Serena were deep in a conversation about Acapulco. Mariah had never been to Acapulco. When had she had the time? Up until just a few months ago, she hadn't gone anywhere besides the office and to the occasional business meeting up in Lake Havasu City or Flagstaff.

Feeling dreadfully left out, but trying hard not to let it show, Mariah shifted her weight from one Amazon-sized leg to another and took a sip of her wine, wishing the alcohol would make her feel better, but knowing that drinking too much would only give her a headache in the morning.

This evening was *so* not what she'd hoped. Silly her. She'd never even considered the fact that Jonathan Mills would take one look at Serena and be smitten. But he was obviously infatuated with Mariah's friend. He'd watched the blond woman constantly, all evening long. The few times Mariah had been alone with him, he'd talked only about Serena. He'd asked Mariah questions about her. He'd commented on her hair, her house, her party, her shoes.

Her *tiny* shoes. Oh, he didn't say anything about size, but Serena's feet were small and feminine. Mariah hadn't worn shoes that size since third grade.

All those signals she'd thought she'd picked up from him were wrong. Those kisses. Had he kissed her first, or had she kissed him? She couldn't remember. It was entirely possible that she had made the first move this morning on the couch. She *knew* she'd made the first move down in the basement.

And each time she'd kissed him, he'd told her in plain English that he thought they should just be friends.

But did she listen? Nope, not her. But she was listening now. It was all that she could do—she had nothing worth adding to the conversation. Acapulco. Skiing in Aspen. John and Serena had so much in common. So much to talk about. Art museums they'd both been to in New York…

Serena seemed just as taken with John as he was with her. In spite of the fact that she herself had warned Mariah about becoming involved with a man who could very well die, Serena looked for all the world as if she was getting ready to reel John in.

Some friend.

Of course, Mariah had told Serena that she and John were just that—friends. Still, Mariah had the sense that even if she'd told her friend that she was already well on her way to falling in love with this man, Serena wouldn't have given a damn.

Neither John nor Serena looked up as Mariah excused herself quietly and went back to the bar.

The hard, cold fact was that Mariah didn't stand a chance with John if Serena decided that she wanted him for her own. And it sure seemed as if she wanted him.

Disgusted with all of them—herself included—Mariah set her empty glass down on the bar, shaking her head when the bartender asked if she wanted a refill. No, it was time to accept defeat and beat a retreat.

The bartender had a pen but no paper, so Mariah quickly wrote a note on a napkin. "I'm partied out, and I've got to be up early in the morning. I've gone ahead home—didn't want you to feel obligated to drive me. Enjoy the rest of party. Mariah."

She folded the napkin in half and asked the bartender to bring it to John in a minute or two.

Chin up, she silently commanded herself as she took off her shoes and went barefoot down the stairs that led to the beach. Jonathan Mills wasn't the man she'd thought he was anyway. He was just another member of the jet set, able to talk for hours at a time about nothing of any importance whatsoever. Frankly, she'd expected more of him. More depth. More soul. She'd thought she'd seen more when she'd looked into his eyes.

She'd thought she'd seen a lover, but she'd only seen the most casual of acquaintances.

She headed down the beach, toward home, determined not to look back.


"JOHN." THERE WAS THE briefest flare of surprise in Daniel Tonaka's eyes as he opened the door to his hotel room and saw Miller standing on the other side. "Is there a problem?"

Miller shook his head. What the hell was he doing here? "No. I..." He ran his hand through his too short hair. "I saw that your light was still on and..." And what? "I couldn't sleep," he admitted, then shrugged. "What else is new?"

What was new was his admitting it.

Daniel didn't comment, though. He just nodded, opening the door wider. "Come in."

The hotel suite was smaller than Miller's room, but decorated with the same style furniture, the same patterned curtains, the same color rug. Still, it seemed like another planet entirely, strange and alien. Miller stood awkwardly, uncertain whether to sit or stand or beat a quick exit before it was too late.

He remembered the way he used to go into Tony's room without even knocking, the way he'd simply help himself to a beer from Tony's refrigerator. He remembered the way they'd pick apart every word spoken in the course of the night's investigation, hashing it out, searching for the hidden meanings and subtle clues, trying to figure out from what had—or hadn't—been said, if their cover had been blown.

They'd done the same thing in high school, except back then the conversation had been about girls, about basketball, about the seemingly huge but in retrospect quite petty troubles they'd had with the two rival gangs that ruled the streets of their worn-out little town. They'd often been threatened and ordered to choose sides, but Tony had followed Miller's lead and remained neutral. They were Switzerland, for no one and against no one.

Switzerland. God, Miller hadn't thought about *that* in ages.

"Can I get you something to drink?" Daniel asked politely. "A beer?"

"Are you having one?"

Daniel shook his head. "I don't drink." He paused. "I thought you knew that."

Miller gazed at him. "I knew that when you were around me, you chose not to drink. I didn't want to assume that held for all the times you *weren't* with me."

"I don't drink," Daniel said again.

"I shouldn't have bothered you. It's late—"

"Be careful about coming on too strong with the suspect," Daniel warned him.

Miller blinked. "Excuse me?"

The kid's lips curved slightly in amusement. "I figured that's why you came over here, right? To ask my opinion about where you stand with Serena Westford?"

Miller didn't know why the hell he was here. He turned toward the door. "I'll let you get back to whatever you were doing."

"John," Daniel said, "sit down. Have a soda." He unlocked the little self-service refrigerator and crouched down to look inside. "How about something without any caffeine?"

Miller found himself sitting down on the edge of the flower-patterned couch as Daniel set a pair of lemon-lime sodas on the coffee table.

Daniel sat across from him and opened one of the cans of soda. "I listened in on most of your conversations," he said. "I think it went well—Serena kept talking about you even after you left. She was asking people if they knew you. She's definitely interested. But she kept referring to you as Mariah's friend, John, and it was more than just a way to identify you. I got the feeling that she's getting off on the idea of stealing you away from her friend."

Miller gazed at his partner. He'd never heard Daniel talk quite so much—and certainly not unless his opinion had been specifically solicited. "Yeah, I got that feeling, too," he finally said.

"What are you going to do about it?" Daniel asked.

"What do *you* think I should do?"

It was clear that Daniel had already given this a great deal of thought. "The obvious solution is for you to see the friend again. Play Serena's game. Hook her interest even further by making it seem as if you're not going to be an easy catch." The kid gazed down at the soda can in his hands as if seeing the bright-colored label for the first time. "But that doesn't take into consideration other things."

Other things. "Such as?"

Daniel looked up, squarely meeting Miller's gaze. "Such as the fact that you really like this other lady. Mariah. Marie. Whatever she wants to call herself."

Miller couldn't deny it. But he could steer the conversation in a slightly different direction. "Mariah invited me to go out to the Triple F building site tomorrow morning." Of course, that had been *before* he'd ignored her so completely at Serena's party.

Daniel nodded. "What are you going to do?"

"I don't know."

Miller had never hesitated over making this kind of a decision before. If he had a choice to do something that would further him in his case, by God, he'd do it. No questions, no doubt. But here he was wavering for fear of hurting someone's feelings.

It was absurd.

And yet when he closed his eyes, he could still see Mariah, hurt enough to leave the party without him, but kind enough to write a note telling him she was leaving. He could see her, head held high as she went down the stairs to the beach.

He'd left the party soon after and followed her to make sure she'd arrived home safely. He'd sat in his car on the street with his lights off and watched her move about her house through the slats in her blinds. He watched her disappear down the hall to her bedroom, unzipping the back of that incredible dress as she went.

She'd returned only a moment later, dressed in the same kind of oversize T-shirt that she'd worn to bed the night before. When she'd curled up on the couch with a book he'd driven away—afraid if he stayed much longer he'd act on the urge to get out of the car, knock on her door and apologize until she let him in.

And once she let him in, he knew damn well he'd end up in her bed. He'd apologize and she'd eventually accept. He'd touch her, and it wouldn't be long until they kissed. And once he kissed her, there'd be no turning back. The attraction between them was too hot, too volatile.

And then she would *really* be hurt—after he slept with her, then married her best friend.

So he'd make damn sure that he wouldn't sleep with her.

He'd show up in front of the library tomorrow at 6:00 a.m. He'd see her again—God, he wanted to see her again—but in public, where there'd be no danger of intimacies getting out of hand. Somehow he'd make her understand that their relationship was to be nothing more than a friendship, all the while making Serena believe otherwise. Then Serena could "steal" him from Mariah without Mariah getting hurt.

Miller stood up. "I'm going to do it. Figure I'll be out of the picture all day tomorrow."

Daniel rose to his feet, too. "I'll stay near Serena." Miller turned to leave, but Daniel's quiet voice stopped him. "You know, John, we could do this another way."

His cover was all set up. He was here, he was in place. And all of his reasons for not going ahead would be purely personal. He'd never pulled out of a case for personal reasons before and he sure as hell wasn't about to start now.

"I haven't come up with a better way—or a quicker way—to catch this killer," he flatly told his partner. "Let's do this right and lock her up before she hurts anyone else."

## CHAPTER SIX

MARIAH SAW HIM AS soon as she rounded the corner.

Jonathan Mills was sitting on the steps to the library, shoulders hunched over, nursing a cup of coffee.

He couldn't have been waiting for her—not after last night. Not after he'd been visibly dazzled by Serena.

And yet she knew there was no one else he could have been waiting for. She was the only one on all of Garden Isle who regularly volunteered for Foundations for Families. Occasionally there would be a group of college students on vacation, but the Triple F van would pick them up over by the campground.

Mariah briefly considered just riding past. Not stopping. Flagging the van down near the drugstore or the post office. Leaving her bike…where? This bike rack in front of the library was the only one in town.

Maybe if she ignored him, he'd go away.

But Mariah knew that that, too, wasn't any kind of solution, so she nodded to him briefly as she braked to a stop.

He stood up as if every bone in his body ached, as if he, too, hadn't had an awful lot of sleep last night.

"I realized as I was getting ready to meet you here that I don't have a tool belt," he told her.

Her own belt was in her backpack, weighing it down, and she slid it off her shoulders and onto the sidewalk as she positioned her bike in the rack. She didn't know what to say. Was he actually serious? Did he really intend to spend the day with her?

Her cheeks still flushed with embarrassment when she thought about last night. And the night before. She'd actually thought he was as attracted to her as she was to him. She'd gone and thrown herself at him and…

She could think of nothing worse than spending the entire day with this man, yet she couldn't simply tell him to go home. She couldn't bring herself to do it. Yes, she'd resolved last night that she'd have nothing more to do with him. Yes, she'd come to the conclusion that he was far more shallow and self-absorbed than she'd previously thought. Still, she couldn't tell him to go away.

"I couldn't sleep again last night," he told her, "and I was lying there in bed, listening to the radio. I had it tuned in to that college station on the mainland, and they were playing this song—these two women singing with guitars, it was really nice. But it was the words that got to me. There I was, listening to the lyrics of this song, something about getting out of bed and getting a hammer and a nail or something like that, and I couldn't stop thinking about you. It was as if they wrote this song about you."

Mariah turned and really looked at him for the first time. He was dressed in jeans, sneakers and a T-shirt. He looked as if he'd climbed out of bed without a shower or a shave. His chin was rough with his morning beard, and he wore a baseball cap on his head, covering his hair. It was silly, actually. His hair was still too short to be rumpled from sleep.

But she knew the song he was talking about. It was

a wonderful song, a thoughtful song, a not-at-all shallow song. "That was the Indigo Girls," she said.

"Was that who they were? It was good. I liked them. I never used to listen to music…you know, *before*."

Before he'd been diagnosed with cancer. Cancer— the reason she couldn't just tell him to go away. He could very well be living the last of his days right now. Who was she to tell him he couldn't spend his time doing exactly as he pleased?

"Mariah, I'm really sorry about last night. I didn't realize I was neglecting you, and then you were gone and—"

"I think my expectations were too high," she admitted. "You had no way of knowing."

"I really want to be your friend," he said quietly.

Mariah turned and looked at him. He'd told her point-blank that he wanted to be her friend before, too. Was it his fault that she hadn't listened? Was it his fault that her feelings already were much stronger than mere friendship?

"Please let me come with you today," he added.

Mariah could see the Triple F van approaching, and she shouldered her backpack.

"All right," she said, knowing that she was a sucker. *He* wanted to be friends. So she'd spend the day with him because *he* wanted to be friends, never mind the fact that every moment she was with him made her like him even more. Want him even more. As more than just a friend.

The really stupid thing was that she would have turned another man down. But for Jonathan Mills, with his sad smile, his startlingly heaven-blue eyes and his catastrophic illness, she was ready to cut a great deal of slack.

Even though she knew damn well she was going to live to regret it.

MILLER WAS GETTING INTO THE rhythm. Take a nail, tap it gently, then drive it in.

He'd never really had much of an opportunity to work with a hammer before. It fitted well in his hand, though. Almost as well as his gun did.

Mariah glanced over at him, wiping ineffectively at a river of sweat that streamed down her face despite the sweatband she wore. "Tired yet?"

"I'm fine."

When they'd first arrived, she'd set him up in a lawn chair in the shade, like some kind of invalid. Like the invalid he was *supposed* to be.

But he'd been unable to sit and watch. Even though it jeopardized his cover as a weak and ailing man, it hadn't been long before he'd begged an extra hammer and was working alongside Mariah.

They were inside the little house, putting plaster-board up, turning the framed-off and already electrically wired areas into real rooms. They'd completed the living room, with several more experienced members of the volunteer building crew cutting out the holes for the electrical outlets and the light switches. They'd worked their way down the hall and into the larger of two bedrooms. The place was starting to look like a home. Sure, the seams had to be taped, and the tape and the nail heads covered with spackle, then sanded before the rooms could be painted, but all of its promise gleamed through.

The owners of the house, a tall black man named Thomas and a slender, proud-looking woman named Renee, kept wandering through every time they took a break, holding hands like a pair of wide-eyed school-children, going from room to room.

"Glory be," Thomas kept saying, tears in his eyes. He'd never owned his own home before, never thought he'd be able, he kept saying. He'd even stopped at one point to pull Miller into his arms, giving him a heart-felt hug of thanks.

Miller knew why Mariah liked this work. He'd caught her with a tear or two in her own eyes more than once. And when everyone on the work crew wasn't busy fighting back tears of joy, they were singing. They sang anything and everything from current pop tunes to spirituals as the radio's dial got moved back and forth, depending on who was in control at the moment. Miller even found himself joining in once or twice when the Beatles came on. He remembered the Beatles from when he was very young. To his surprise, he still knew almost all of the words to their songs.

But as the sun was rising in the sky, the little house was starting to heat up. Miller had long since pulled his shirt off. He wished to hell he'd worn shorts instead of these jeans. It had to be near ninety—and the mercury was climbing.

Mariah set down her hammer and took off her T-shirt. She was wearing another athletic bra—a sweat-shirt-colored gray one this time. She used her shirt to mop her face and then hung it over her tool belt.

Miller tried not to watch her, but it was damned hard. He drove another nail into the wall, narrowly missing hitting his thumb.

In the other bedroom, someone turned the radio to a classical station.

"Mozart," Miller said, barely aware he'd spoken aloud. He looked up to find Mariah watching him. "His clarinet concerto," he continued, giving her a half smile. "My mother loved this piece. She swore that listening to Mozart would make you smarter."

"I've heard that, too," Mariah said. "The theory being that the complexity of the music somehow expands your ability to reason."

"Lemonade break," Renee said cheerfully, carrying two tall glasses into the room.

Mariah put down her hammer and took one of the plastic glasses as John took the other. He nodded his thanks to Renee, then sat down next to Mariah on the dusty plywood floor.

Mariah drained half her glass in one long drink. "God," she gasped, catching her breath, "what I *really* need is a hosing down. Can it get any hotter?"

"Yes."

Mariah laughed. "That was *not* the correct answer." She leaned her head back against the newly erected plasterboard and pressed the cool plastic against her neck as she closed her eyes.

Miller let himself stare. As long as her eyes were closed, he could take the opportunity to drink her in. Her eyelashes were about a mile long. They rested, thick and dark, against her sun-kissed cheeks. She had a sprinkling of freckles on her nose. Freckles on her shoulders and across her chest, too.

He looked up to find her eyes had opened. She'd caught him doing all but drooling. Perfect.

But she didn't move away. She didn't reprimand him.

"Thomas and Renee can't wait to move in."

It took him a moment to realize what she was talking about.

"This is a really nice little house," Mariah continued. "It's a popular one—I've helped build at least seven just like it."

Miller nodded. "I lived in a house with a layout almost exactly like this when I was a kid."

Mariah pulled her knees up to her chest, her eyes sparking with interest. "Really?"

"Yeah, it's almost weird walking through here." He pointed down the hall. "That was my bedroom, next to the bathroom. This one was my mother's."

Mariah was watching him, waiting for him to tell her more. He knew that once again he'd already said too much, but her eyes were so warm. He didn't want her to stop looking at him that way.

Besides, he'd figured out a way to make it work— this odd blending of his background and the Jonathan Mills cover story. As Mills, he would have the same background as Miller, except when he was eleven, when his mother died, he hadn't gone into foster care. He— Mills—had gone to live with his fictional estranged father, the king of the car alarms. It would work.

"I can still remember how the kitchen smelled," he told Mariah. "Ginger and cinnamon. My mother loved to bake." He glanced up at the white plasterboard they'd just used to cover the wall opposite the closet, gesturing toward it. "She also loved books. That whole wall was covered with bookshelves and *filled* with books. Everything and anything—if it was any good, she read it." He smiled at Mariah. "She was kind of like you."

As he said the words, he realized how accurate

they were. Physically, Mariah looked nothing like his mother. His mother had been average height and willow thin. But their smiles had the same welcoming glow, the same unconditional acceptance. When he was with Mariah, he felt accepted without question. It was something he hadn't felt in years.

"She worked as a secretary," he told Mariah. "Although she swore she was four times smarter than her boss. I remember, even though it was expensive, we kept the house heated well past seventy degrees all winter long. She would get so cold. I used to walk around in T-shirts and shorts, and she'd be wearing a sweater and scarf." He smiled, remembering. "And then there was the year she let me pick the color we were going to paint the living room. I must've been six, and I picked yellow. Bright yellow. She didn't try to talk me out of it. People's eyes would pop out of their heads when they came into the house."

"When did she die?" Mariah asked softly.

"A few days before I turned eleven."

"I'm sorry."

"Yeah, I was, too."

"You talk about your mother, but you've never said anything about your father," she said quietly.

Miller's real father had died in Vietnam. He was a medic who'd been killed evacuating a bombed Marine barracks, two weeks away from the end of his tour of duty.

He shrugged. "There's not much to say. He and my mother were divorced," he lied. "I went to live with him after she died." He shifted his weight, changing the subject. "We always talk about me. You've never really told me about yourself."

"My life has been remarkably dull."

"You mentioned your father dying of a heart attack," he pointed out. "And at dinner the other night, you told me you'd once been married, but you didn't go into any detail."

"His name was Trevor," she told him. "We were married right out of college. We parted due to irreconcilable differences in our work schedules, if you can believe *that*. He wanted kids and I couldn't schedule them in until late 1999. So he left."

Miller was quiet, just waiting for her to say more.

"He married again about six months after we split," she said. "I ran into him downtown about a year ago. He had two little kids with him. His new wife was in the hospital, having just delivered number three."

She was silent for a moment.

"I looked at Trevor and those kids and I tried to feel really bad—you know, that could have been my life. Those could have been my cute little kids. Trevor still could've been my husband...."

"But..." he prompted.

"But all I could feel was *relieved*. And I realized that I had married Trevor because I couldn't really think of a good reason *not* to marry him. I loved him, but I'm not sure I was ever really *in* love with him. I never felt as if I'd die if he didn't kiss me...."

She trailed off, and Miller found himself staring at her, memorizing her face as she in turn stared down at the empty glass in her hands.

"If I ever get involved with anyone again, it's going to be because I find someone I can't live without. I want to find the kind of passion that's overpowering," she told him. "I want to lose control."

Lose control. Overpowering passion.

The kind of passion that started wars and crumbled empires. The kind of passion that made it difficult even for a hardened expert like Miller to do his job. The kind of passion that made him want to break every rule and restriction he'd set for himself and pull this woman into his arms and cover her mouth with his own.

She was talking about the kind of passion that flared to life between them even when they did no more than sit and quietly talk. It was a one-of-a-kind thing, and Miller hated the fact that he couldn't take it further— push it to see where it would lead.

Mariah was quiet, lost in her own thoughts.

Miller tried not to watch her. Tried, and failed.

"Mariah!" One of the little girls—one of Thomas and Renee's young daughters—came skidding into the room. "Jane Ann climbed way, *way* up into the big ol' tree in the backyard and now she can't get down!" the girl wailed. "Papa says he's too big—the branches up that high won't hold him. And Mama's got no head for heights. And Janey's crying cause she can't hold on much longer!"

Mariah scrambled to her feet and ran.

Miller was right behind her.

A crowd had gathered beneath the shade of the monstrously large tree that dominated the quarter-acre plot. It was a perfect climbing tree, with broad, thick branches growing well within even a child's reach of the ground. But the branches became narrower as they went up the trunk. And up where Janey was sitting and howling like a police siren, way up near the top of the tree, the branches were positively delicate-looking.

Mariah moved quickly, navigating her way up

through the branches effortlessly and efficiently. But she was no lightweight herself. Despite the fact that she'd told him she was good with heights, good at climbing, this was going to be tricky.

"Mariah!" Miller called. "We can call the fire department for help."

She only glanced down at him very briefly. "I think Jane Ann wants to come down right now, John," she told him. "I don't think she wants to wait for the fire truck to arrive."

He didn't know what to do—whether to climb up after her, or wait there on the ground, hoping that if she or the child slipped, he could somehow cushion their fall. He turned to the girl's father.

"Thomas, didn't I see some kind of tarp out front? Thick plastic—it was blue, I think—the kind of thing you'd use to cover a roof that's not quite watertight, in the event of rain?"

Thomas didn't understand.

"If we stretched it tight, it could break the girl's fall," he explained. "We could try to catch her if she slips."

Thomas gave a curt order and two teenaged boys ran quickly to get the tarp.

Miller looked up into the tree. Mariah was moving more slowly now, more carefully. He could hear the soothing rise and fall of her voice as she spoke to the little girl, but he couldn't make out the words. But the girl was finally quiet, so whatever Mariah was saying was working to calm her.

The boys came back with the tarp, and everyone but Miller took an end, pulling it taut, ready for disaster. Miller, instead, started up into the tree.

Mariah had climbed as far as she dared and she held

out one hand to the little girl. Her other arm was securely wrapped around the rough trunk of the tree. Miller knew she was willing the child to move closer, just a little bit closer, so that she could grab hold of her.

Slowly, inch by inch, Jane Ann began to move.

There was an audible sigh of relief from the ground as Mariah pulled the child close to her and the girl locked her arms around Mariah's neck.

But the worst was not yet over. Mariah still had to get back down—this time with the added weight of an eight-year-old girl threatening her balance.

Mariah stepped down, one branch at a time, testing its strength before she put her full weight upon it.

And then it happened.

Miller saw the branch give before he heard the rifle-sharp snap. In nightmarish slow motion, he saw Mariah grab for the branch above her, holding them both with only one hand, one arm. He could see her muscles straining, see her feet searching for a foothold.

And then he saw her fingers slip.

"Mariah!" The cry ripped from his throat as she began to fall.

But somehow, miraculously, she didn't fall far. She jerked to a stop, still holding tightly to the little girl in her arms.

Her tool belt. Somehow the back of her belt had gotten hooked upon the stub of a branch—a branch sturdy enough to hold both of them. They hung from the tree, facing out, dangling like some kind of Christmas ornament.

Miller raced up the tree, the bark rough against his hands and sharp against his knees, even through his jeans.

As he drew closer, he could see that Mariah's elbow was bleeding. Her knees, too, looked scraped and the worse for wear. The belt was holding her not around the waist, but rather around the ribs. Still, she managed to smile at Miller. "That was fun," she whispered.

"Are you all right?" He saw them then—bruises on the insides of her upper arms. The tree hadn't done that to her—*he* had. That night that he'd fallen asleep on her couch. He'd grabbed her, thinking she was Domino. God, he could have killed her. The thought made him feel faint and he brought himself back to here and now. He'd have enough time to feel bad about Mariah's bruises *after* he got her down from this tree.

"I think I may have rearranged a rib," she told him. "I had the breath knocked out of me, too. Take Janey. Please? Jane Ann, this is John. He's going to take you down to your mommy and dad, okay?"

The little girl looked shell-shocked. Mariah gave her a kiss on the cheek and Miller lifted her out of Mariah's arms without a fuss. "Let me get you down from there," he said to Mariah.

"Take Janey down first," she told him, still in that odd, whispery voice. "I think you're going to need two hands for me."

Miller nodded, moving as quickly down the tree with the child as he dared. He looked back at Mariah, but she'd closed her eyes. Rearranged a rib. He knew she'd put it that way so as not to frighten Jane Ann. Her tool belt had slammed into her ribs with the full weight of her body against it. And it wouldn't take much for a broken rib to puncture a lung.

Miller felt a flash of fear as he glanced back up at

Mariah. Had she simply closed her eyes or had she lost consciousness?

He practically threw Jane Ann into her father's waiting hands, then swiftly climbed back up to where Mariah was still hanging by her belt.

She opened her eyes as he approached, and he nearly fell out of the tree from relief.

"Ouch," she said. "Can I say ouch now?"

Miller nodded, looking hard into her eyes for any sign of shock. "Can you breathe? Are you having trouble breathing?"

She shook her head. "I'm still a little…squashed."

"Can we unfasten your belt?" he asked.

She shook her head. "I already thought of that, but the buckle seems to be in the back. And it's not easy to undo even in the best of circumstances."

They were going to have to do this the hard way.

Miller braced each foot on a separate branch, pressing his body up close to Mariah's. "Hold on to me," he ordered her. "I'm going to lift you up and get your belt free."

She hesitated.

"I'm a little sweaty," he apologized. "I'm sorry. There's not a lot I can do about that. Lock your legs around my waist."

"Maybe I should wait for the fire department."

"Put your legs around my waist," he said again. "Come on, Mariah. Just do it."

She did it.

Miller refused to think about anything but getting her down from there. Yes, she was soft, she was warm, and yes, she smelled delicious. Yes, she was everything he remembered from that night on her couch, but she was also in danger of falling and breaking her neck.

"Hold me tighter," he commanded as he tried to shift her up, one hand reaching behind her, searching for the stub of the branch that had hooked her tool belt and saved her and Janey's lives.

He found it. He found the wetness of blood, too—Mariah's blood—where the sharp edge of the branch had scratched and scraped and stabbed into her back. Her ragged intake of breath told him how much it hurt.

"Try to lift yourself up," he told her. "Help me get you free."

Her legs tightened around him as he pushed her up, every muscle straining. His head was pressed against the soft pillow of her breasts, but there was nothing he could do about that.

Finally, *finally,* with a strength he didn't even know he possessed, he got the tool belt free. His muscles tensed as he held Mariah's full weight. She clung to him now, more tightly than he'd ever dreamed she'd hold him.

"I'm not feeling very secure here," she told him.

"I've got you," he said. "I won't let go."

And he wouldn't. At least not until they reached the solidness of the ground.

He helped her find her footing, helped her down to the larger, sturdier branches, but still she held on to his hand.

Her face was still mere inches from his, and her eyes were swimming with unshed tears.

"I think I have to cry," she told him.

"Can you wait just a few minutes more?" he asked. "Until we get you down onto the ground?"

She forced a wavery smile. "Yeah."

One branch at a time, they moved slowly down the tree. When they got to the bottom, Miller knew he was going to have to let her go.

Sure enough, Renee and Thomas were there, reaching out to help her, along with the entire rest of the site crew.

But she still didn't cry. She smiled at them. She made light of her scrapes and scratches. She pooh-poohed the angry-looking cut on her back. And when Jane Ann and the other little girl, Emma, leaped at her, nearly knocking her over, she hugged them back, hiding the fact that she was wincing.

Miller approached Laronda, the site coordinator. "I want to take Mariah over to the hospital," he told her quietly. "I think she might've broken a rib and she'll probably need stitches for that cut on her back. Can someone give us a lift, or do you want to give me the keys to the van?"

"I was going to have Bobby take her over, but if you're thinking about going, too..."

"I *am* going. Definitely."

Laronda nodded. "Show me your driver's license, Mr. Mills, and I'll let you take the van."

Miller took out his wallet and within moments had the keys to the van in his pocket. He briefly went inside to get his T-shirt. Pulling it over his head, he intercepted Mariah. He took her arm and led her toward the van.

She protested. "I want to wash up."

"You can wash up at the hospital."

Mariah nodded. "All right."

The fact that she didn't protest further was not a good sign. She *was* hurt worse than she was letting on.

Miller helped her up onto the hot vinyl of the bench seat in the front of the van, then went around and climbed behind the wheel. He started the engine and pulled onto the street, moving carefully over the potholes so as not to jar Mariah.

He glanced at her as he pulled up to the stop sign at the end of the street. She was sitting very still, with her eyes closed, arms wrapped around herself.

"You can cry now," Miller said softly. "No one's here but me."

She opened her eyes and looked at him and he put the van in park. It was crazy and he knew he shouldn't do it, but he held out his arms and she reached for him as she burst into tears.

"I thought that little girl was going to fall," Mariah sobbed as she clung to him. "I was sure that I'd killed her—and myself, too."

"Shhh," Miller whispered into her hair, holding her as close and as tightly as he dared. "It's all right. It's all right now."

What was he doing? This was sheer insanity. Holding her this way, giving her this kind of comfort... His body responded instantly to the sensation of her in his arms, his wanting all but overpowering his sense of right and wrong.

He couldn't kiss her. He *would not* kiss her.

"I'm sorry," she said, half laughing, half crying as she lifted her head to look up at him. "I'm getting your shirt all wet."

He wanted to kiss her. Her mouth was right there,

inches away from him. Her lips would taste so soft and sweet….

Miller clenched his teeth instead. "Don't worry about my shirt."

A new flood of tears welled in her eyes. "I don't think I've ever been so afraid. But I didn't drop her. Even when all the air was knocked out of me, even when it felt like that branch went into my back like a knife, I didn't let go."

Miller smoothed her hair back from her face, knowing that he shouldn't touch her more than was necessary. Except, this felt very necessary. "You did great," he told her. "You were amazing."

"I was stupid not to wait for the fire department."

"You were brave—and lucky."

She nodded. "I *was* lucky, wasn't I? Oh, God, when I think about what might've happened…"

She held him tighter, and he felt his arms closing around her, too.

*Think about what might've happened…* He couldn't think about anything else—except maybe how much he wanted to kiss this woman.

It was not the right thing to do. He knew that, but he did it anyway.

She met his lips eagerly as if she, too, was as starved for his kisses as he was for hers.

God, it was heaven.

And it was hell, because he knew it had to end.

He forced himself to lift his head. He made himself pull back as he gazed into Mariah's whiskey-colored eyes.

"I need to get you to the hospital." His voice didn't come out more than a whisper.

She nodded, a flare of embarrassment in her eyes. "I'm sorry. I'm...doing it again, aren't I?"

"Doing what?"

She pulled away, moving back to her side of the bench seat. "Kissing you," she told him with her usual blunt honesty. "I seem to be unable to keep myself from kissing you." She wiped her face with her hands, pushing away her tears. "Come on. The hospital's not far from here. I drove José over a few weeks ago when he stepped on a nail."

Miller put the van into gear, uncertain of how to respond. He'd made another mistake by kissing her, yet she seemed to think it was *her* mistake.

He took a left out onto the main road, wishing not only that he'd been strong enough to keep from kissing her again, but that he was weak enough to be kissing her still.

JOHN WAS WAITING FOR MARIAH as she came out of X ray.

He looked sweaty and hot, and with that unshaved stubble and covered with the grime of a full morning's worth of construction work, he looked dangerously sexy. He also looked as worried as hell.

"I'm okay," she told him. "Nothing's broken. Not even cracked. Just bruised."

He smiled then, one of his crooked half smiles. "Good." He looked up at the nurse who was wheeling Mariah's chair. "What's next?"

"She's got a cut on her back that's going to need a stitch or two," the nurse told him. "Unfortunately, she's going to have to wait for the doctor."

"May I sit with her?" John asked.

"Of course."

"I mean, if she wants me to," he added, glancing down at Mariah.

"Thanks," Mariah said, feeling strangely shy as she briefly met his eyes. "I'd like that."

The nurse brought them back into one of the emergency rooms. There were six beds in this one, each with a curtain on runners that could be pulled around to give them some privacy.

John helped Mariah up onto the bed. During her X ray, she'd taken off her athletic bra, and now she wore only a hospital gown over her shorts. It was tied loosely at her neck, and she could feel the coolness from the air conditioner blowing against her exposed back.

It was the front of the gown that made her self-conscious, though. The cotton was thin, and every time she moved, it seemed to cling provocatively to her breasts, outlining every detail, every curve. She pulled it up at her neck, wishing there was some way to ensure that it wouldn't fall off.

Her movement made the short sleeves of the gown ride up, and John reached for one of her arms, pushing the sleeve even farther up. He turned her arm over, exposing the bruises she had there. There were five of them—little oval finger-and thumb-shaped bruises. She had a similar set on her other arm.

He looked into her eyes. "I'm so sorry about this."

"I know." She held his gaze. "What were you dreaming that night?"

He didn't look away, but he didn't speak for several long moments, as if he was deciding what to tell her. "Tony, my best friend, was…an officer of the law," he finally said. "He was executed by a drug runner's gang. Shot in the head."

"Oh, my God." Mariah couldn't believe what he was telling her. "Were the people who killed him caught?"

John nodded. "Yeah. They were caught. That doesn't keep me from dreaming about them, though. I see their faces and…" He broke off, turning away. "I shouldn't be telling you this. I must be insane."

"Did you know the men who did it?"

For a moment, she thought he wasn't going to answer.

"One of the guys working for the drug lord went to high school with Tony and me." He shifted his weight, looking away from her. "I keep wondering if his bullet killed Tony. I keep thinking I should've beaten the hell out of him—and put the fear of God in him—in high school, when I had the chance."

"That's where you got Princess," she guessed. "Tony was the friend that you inherited her from."

He nodded. "Yeah. She still misses him." He glanced back at her. "I do, too."

"So you dream about him dying. Were you there when it happened? God, you didn't see it, did you?"

He shook his head, his voice bitter. "No. I got there too late." He changed the subject. "Mariah, I'm sorry that I hurt you."

He was talking about the bruises on her arms, but for a moment, she could have sworn he was talking about the way he'd treated her at Serena's party.

"And I'm sorry about your friend." She paused. "You knew him—Tony—since high school?"

Miller pulled a chair closer to her bed and sat down. God, why had he told her about Tony? Tony hadn't been friends with high-class Jonathan Mills. At age six-

teen, Tony had befriended John Miller, the new kid in
school—the poor kid, the *foster* kid, the troublemaker.
Tony had accidentally broken a window, and Miller
willingly took the fall. It hadn't been hard to fool everyone—everyone expected that the troublemaker in
foster care was the kid who'd broken the glass, anyway.

He'd been living with his current foster family long
enough to know that he would be preached-at to death,
but he wouldn't be hit. Tony, on the other hand, had a
brute of a stepfather who didn't care enough even to
keep his blows from marking the boy's face.

Miller had stepped forward, confessed to a crime he
hadn't committed, and in return had won Tony's undying loyalty. Not that Miller had wanted it. Not at first.
But eventually, Tony had pushed his way past Miller's
hardened shell and the two boys became friends.

There was no way in hell he could tell Mariah any
of this—foster families and stepfathers with iron fists
didn't fit in with Jonathan Mills's world of yacht clubs
and tennis lessons and stock dividends.

"How many stitches do you think I'm going to
need?" Mariah asked, changing the subject after his
silence had dragged on and on and on.

Miller shook his head. "I don't know."

Silence again. Miller could feel her watching him.
"How are *you?*" she finally asked. "In all the excitement, I forgot that just a few days ago you were feeling ill enough to faint on the beach. And here you are,
suddenly building a house and climbing up and down a
tree…" She was still gazing at him, her eyes questioning now. Wondering. "Carrying Janey. Carrying me. If
you're this strong now, how strong did you *used* to be?"

"I'm feeling pretty tired," he said, hoping she wouldn't notice that he hadn't answered her question. He prayed that she wouldn't think too long or too hard about the fact that he *had* moved up and down that tree with the balance and strength of a man who couldn't possibly have just completed a crippling round of chemotherapy. He knew one way to get her mind off this topic and fast. "Mariah, about before...in the van...?"

She blushed, but she met his gaze steadily. "John, I'm really sorry about that. I know—you just want to be friends. It's taking a while to sink in, but I'm finally starting to get it and—"

"I wanted to apologize to you."

"To me? But—"

"I kissed you," he told her. "You didn't kiss me until after I kissed you, and I shouldn't have, so I'm sorry."

She was gazing at him, wide-eyed. It was all he could do not to kiss her again. "It *wasn't* me."

Miller shook his head. "I couldn't resist."

"I don't get it," she said. "If you can't resist kissing me, and *I* can't resist kissing *you,* then why aren't we doing a whole heck of a lot more kissing?"

The doctor came in, saving Miller from even attempting to answer her. He stood up, grateful for the escape. "I'll wait outside."

"John."

He stopped and looked back at her.

"Forget I ever said that, okay? We're friends. That's enough—it's okay with me."

Miller nodded and went out the door. He just wished he could close his eyes and fall asleep and wake up in a place where simply being friends with Mariah Robinson was okay with him, too.

HE WAS SEEING HER, TOO.

He was still seeing her. They were gone all day, and she realized he must have gone to that silly house-building.

She found it amusing, but nothing to worry about.

When it was time to make a choice, he would choose correctly. There was no doubt about it.

## CHAPTER SEVEN

TWO STITCHES. TWO TINY little stitches, and she had to stay out of the water and away from Foundations for Families for another unknown quantity of days.

It wouldn't be so bad if she knew precisely how long it was going to be before she could get back to her routine. Two days? Two weeks? Two *months?* Nobody would give her any definite answers, and meanwhile, her entire life was on hold.

All for two little stitches.

She was working hard to control her impatience. But Foundations for Families was counting on her. She'd already missed too many of her shifts. She needed to get back and...

Mariah did one of her breathing exercises. She sounded like Marie. This was not Mariah, with her no-worries, no-stress attitude. Mariah would take these imposed days off as a gift. A chance to lie on the beach and catch up on her reading. A chance to sleep late, to take the time to cook herself delicious, healthful dinners, to watch the sunset and see the stars come out at night.

The first few days actually had been fun. Jonathan Mills had dropped by once a day, bringing her things to eat and books to read, videotapes to watch and tacky little toys from the souvenir shop to amuse her. A goofy-looking duck made from seashells glued together. A Garden Isle coloring book and a thirty-six-pack of crayons. A booklet of Mad-Libs.

Funny things. Silly things. The kind of things one friend would give another.

John's visits were nothing but friendly. In fact, he seemed to take special care that they never touched—that they never got close enough even to brush against one another by accident.

Their conversations were safe, too. They talked about books and movies and newspaper headlines. They talked about Foundations for Families and the best place on the island to get an omelet.

Mariah wasn't certain when John's latest medical test results would be coming in, but she was more than ready for him to receive a clean bill of health. From things he'd said, little hints he'd dropped, she had to believe that he'd be getting word soon. Maybe then he'd let himself give in to the attraction she still saw simmering in his eyes whenever he thought she wasn't looking.

Of course, it was entirely possible that when he wasn't looking at her, he was looking at Serena with the exact same heat in his eyes. Serena didn't come to visit, not even once, and Mariah couldn't bring herself to call her. She suspected, though, by John's notice-able absence at dinnertime, that the two of them were together. She suspected, but she hoped it was only her too-vivid imagination, fueled by jealousy, rearing its ugly little head.

She tried to stomp it back into place, but it peered at her from dark corners. She tried to bring it out into the light. So what if John was seeing Serena? He'd made it clear to Mariah that he and she were no more than friends. She could be happy with his friendship. She could be content to keep their relationship on that level.

And her Aunt Susan was the pope.

The truth was always there—a tiny voice that never failed to remind her of how she'd felt when John had kissed her. The voice reminded her of the way she'd been so ready to give herself to him in every way imaginable. The voice was always there to point out just how much she wanted this man, even despite his rejection.

She was a fool, yet every time he came to her door, she let him in. She knew damn well that in her case, being friends *wasn't* better than nothing, but she couldn't get past his illness.

What if she shut him out, what if she turned him away, refused his friendship, and he died?

He was comfortable with her. She could see him visibly relax as they sat and talked. How could she deny him that?

She was a sucker, too kind for her own good, but at least she knew it.

As of this morning, it had been nearly a day and a half since John had last stopped in.

Afraid to overstep the bounds of friendship, Mariah hadn't even called. She'd picked up the phone more than once. She'd even dialed the resort. She'd gone as far as inquiring if Mr. Jonathan Mills was still staying there. He was. But she didn't leave a message, fearful of her tendency to want too much where John was concerned.

She more than missed him. She worried about him. Was he feeling sick? Was he relapsing? Where the heck *was* he?

A dog was barking, down on the beach.

Mariah looked up from the book she was trying her best to concentrate on, hoping it was Princess. And John.

It was Princess all right, but John was nowhere in sight. The funny-looking little dog was dancing in and out of the water, barking at the seagulls. There was no one around her for quite some distance in either direction.

Mariah laid her book aside and went down onto the beach. She whistled and the little dog looked up, ears alert. "Princess!"

Princess seemed almost to grin as she trotted toward Mariah.

"Hey," Mariah said to her, "what are you doing out here all by yourself? Where's John? Where's your master?"

The dog, of course, didn't answer.

Mariah was under doctor's orders to take it easy, but a nice, slow walk down the beach...? Now, that couldn't hurt, could it?

"Come on, Princess," Mariah said. "Let's get you something to drink and let me grab some shoes and we'll go find John."

Returning his wandering dog was clearly a friendly gesture. It was neighborly—something even just a casual acquaintance would do.

It was also the best idea she'd had all day.

SERENA WESTFORD WAS WAITING for him in the most elegant of the resort's lounges.

Miller went slowly inside, letting his eyes adjust. Even at this time of the morning, the room was barely lit. In small bits and pieces, light filtered in through the heavy curtains that covered the windows, giving the room an odd, almost smoky feel.

Serena sat in the corner, sipping a cup of coffee, her perfect legs gracefully crossed, her dress an angelic shade of white.

Miller felt a sense of dread as he approached her. They'd met for dinner two nights ago. He'd gone directly from Mariah's house to pick her up, and he'd been late. He hadn't wanted to leave.

He'd been far too comfortable at Mariah's, far too at home, and he'd cursed himself soundly even for going there in the first place. He'd visited her for several days running—well above and beyond the call of duty. The truth was, duty had nothing to do with his visits. They were for pure pleasure—his own pleasure as well as Mariah's.

Mariah. She'd been unable to hide the flare of happiness in her eyes whenever he arrived. It was addictive, and he'd found himself visiting her more often than he should.

He'd been careful to keep his distance since their kiss in the Triple F van. But the minimum distance he *should* have maintained was at least several miles wide. The truth was, he should have stayed at the resort.

But he couldn't do it. He couldn't stay away.

And two nights ago when he'd left to pick up Serena, it had been all that he could do not to pull Mariah into his arms and tell her everything. He wanted to tell her who he really was and *what* he really was. And he wanted to kiss her until they melted into one, kiss her until time itself stood still.

Instead he'd left to meet Serena. He'd spent yes-

terday afternoon with Serena, too, purposely staying away from Mariah's house. They'd shared another
early dinner and he'd sat in the resort restaurant, and
thought about Mariah while Serena told him about her
fictional past, working for the peace corps in Africa.
He'd been far less attentive than he should have been.
After dinner, they had a drink out on the restaurant's
veranda, and he found Serena gazing at him, waiting
for him to respond to some question she'd asked.

He hadn't had a clue what they had just been talking
about, and that scared him. He hadn't kept his mind on
his job. He'd been standing there thinking about how
badly he wished he was with Mariah.

The power Mariah had over him scared him to death,
and at the time he did the only thing he could think
of—he took Serena into his arms and he kissed her.

He'd kissed her hard, trying to banish the ghost of
Mariah that seemed to hover permanently in his subconscious. He'd tried to call up some degree of passion,
but even though Serena had pressed her sinewy, lithe
body against him, even though she'd responded enthusiastically, Miller had been left feeling bitterly cold—
and thinking once again of the fire Mariah could start
within him with just one look.

He hadn't liked kissing Serena Westford, but she
hadn't seemed to notice. As he approached her now, he
hoped to God he wouldn't have to kiss her again.

But Serena only lifted her cheek for him to brush
with his lips, and as he sat down next to her, she poured
him a cup of steaming coffee from a silver coffeepot.

"Good morning," she said. He knew the English
accent was a fake, but unlike most Americans who
slipped into unauthentic-sounding British accents,

Serena clearly had listened quite carefully to tapes, almost as if she was learning an entirely new language. "Did you sleep well last night?"

"Like a child," he lied. In fact, he'd stared at the ceiling for hours…thinking of Mariah. And when he finally *had* fallen asleep, it was not his nightmare that had jerked him awake before dawn, but rather an all too realistic erotic dream. He and Mariah, tangled together on her couch, clothing melted away as she opened herself to him and…

He'd awakened, disoriented, reaching for her, aching with need. But, of course, she wasn't there.

Serena was gazing at him, her cat green eyes watching him closely. He managed a smile. It was time to move this game up to a new level. "I spoke to my doctor today," he told her, mentally bracing himself, knowing that upon receiving his "good news" Serena was going to kiss him again. "He had the results from my most recent blood test. So far, it looks as if I'm not going to die."

"Oh, John, that's such wonderful news," Serena said. Sure enough, she leaned forward to kiss him.

And sure enough, Miller wished he was kissing Mariah instead.

THERE WAS AN AMBULANCE waiting outside the resort. The moment Mariah saw it, her heart began to pound, and her mind flashed to the worst-case scenario. The paramedics had come because of John. He'd fallen ill again. He was dying. He was already dead.

She stopped herself cold. That was ridiculous. It was extremely unlikely. Thinking that way wasn't going to do her one bit of good. Still, she went quickly toward the front desk, holding tightly on to Princess's collar. Through the window, she could see the ambulance pulling away. "Excuse me, can you please tell me which room Jonathan Mills is in?"

The desk clerk was cheerfully apologetic. "I'm sorry, we can't give out room numbers. But we can ring a guest's room for you, if you like."

"Yes, please. Jonathan Mills."

The clerk handed her the telephone. It rang. And rang. And rang. No answer.

The fear was returning, lodging in her throat, when Princess pulled free.

"Hey!" Mariah tossed the phone back to the clerk with a quick thanks and ran after the dog. Just because John wasn't in his room, she told herself, didn't mean that he was inside that ambulance.

Princess slipped out the doors that led to the deck by the pool, and Mariah followed. She hurried down the steps and ran nearly smack into Jonathan Mills.

He caught her elbows to hold her steady. "Mariah?"

"John!" She threw her arms around his neck. "Thank God!" He felt so warm and solid and he smelled so good—like sunblock and coffee. He always smelled like coffee. Maybe if he stopped drinking so much coffee, she thought inanely, maybe then he'd be able to sleep.

He pulled her even closer, held her even tighter for just a fraction of a second. It was so brief, she wondered if she'd imagined it, but she knew she hadn't. He'd held her like that before—almost desperately— all those mornings ago, on her couch. But instead of kissing her, the way he'd done that morning, he quickly moved back, away from her.

And that was when she saw Serena.

Looking cool and impossibly young and pure in a white sundress and hat, Serena moved to rest her hand possessively on John's arm. "Mariah," she said. "What a surprise."

Daniel, John's assistant—the slender young Asian man Mariah had met the day John had fainted on the beach—was also standing nearby. At a nod from John, he took Princess by the collar and led the dog away.

"We were…uh, we were just going to have lunch out here by the pool," John told Mariah. "Would you, um, care to join us?"

"Mariah's on some kind of macrobiotic diet," Serena told him. "There's nothing on the menu here that she could possibly want."

John and Serena. They were standing there, looking very much like a couple. Although the truth was that she was too short for him—they didn't look quite right together. Still, there they were. About to have lunch. Together.

Mariah could easily imagine them having spent the morning together. The morning—and maybe even longer. Maybe even the night before. When *had* she seen John last?

Mariah cleared her throat, gazing up into his eyes, knowing that he could clearly see her hurt, knowing she had no right to feel hurt, but unable to hide it. "I found Princess on the beach. Alone. I haven't seen you in a few days, so I was worried. I thought maybe you were sick or hurt or…and I can see right now that you're definitely not, so I guess I'll just…go."

She backed away.

"Did you hear the good news?" Serena asked as if she was totally unaware of the tension that seemed to leap and crackle between Mariah and John. "Jonathan got the first of his test results this morning. His doctor is almost certain the cancer's gone." She smiled up at John. "He's going to live to a ripe old age, aren't you, darling?"

This morning. He'd known this morning and he hadn't even bothered to call. "That's such good news," Mariah managed to say. She even managed a smile, despite the tears in her eyes. "John, I'm so glad for you."

True, she'd imagined him getting the news and coming to *her,* not Serena. Still, that didn't make the news any less wonderful. But now he was going to have lunch with Serena, and Serena had made it clear that their table was only for two.

"I better go," she said. She gazed into John's eyes for just a moment longer. "I'm *so* glad."

Miller couldn't believe it. Despite his careful talk of friendship, Mariah clearly had had expectations that were now dashed upon seeing him here like this with Serena. Yet her words were sincere and heartfelt. He'd hurt her, probably badly, yet she was honestly happy for him.

She looked out of place at the resort grill, dressed the way she was in cutoffs and a T-shirt. Her hair was windblown—her soft curls tumbling down to her shoulders. Her eyes were filled with tears—still she was smiling.

"So glad," she whispered again.

As Miller watched, she turned and walked away.

He wanted to follow her. He was dying to follow her. But he couldn't. He couldn't even take a moment and feel like crap for hurting her this way because Serena was watching him. He had to smile and pretend that the expression he'd seen on Mariah's face wasn't making his heart ache.

His heart *was* aching.

A surprising turn of events for a man who wasn't sure he even had a heart just a few short weeks ago.

"Shall we have lunch?" Serena murmured.

Miller nodded and gave her another smile. Tonight he was planning to ask her to marry him, and sometime in the next few weeks, she would try to stick a knife into his heart.

Even if she succeeded, he suspected it would not be a new sensation.

"HI, IT'S ME. IS THIS A GOOD time to talk?" Mariah asked.

There was a brief silence on the other end of the line, then Serena's cool voice answered, "If you're wondering if I'm alone, yes, I am. But I'm a little busy right now. I'll call you back."

The line went dead, and Mariah stared for a moment at the phone in her hand. Instead of hanging up, she pressed redial. But this time, Serena didn't answer. This time, her answering machine didn't even come on.

That was odd. Serena was nearly obsessive about getting her phone messages. Why she should leave the house without turning her machine on was a mystery.

But the phone rang before Mariah even started clearing her lunch dishes off the table. She picked it up. "Hello?"

It was Serena. "Sorry—I had to get *out* of there. I'm calling from the pay phone in front of the Northbeach pizza parlor. My place is *crawling* with bugs. I've had an infestation of some kind of disgusting cockroaches. *Awful.* I'm going off island for the rest of the afternoon and evening. To Atlanta—I have some business to take care of. Can I get you anything from the real world?"

She didn't let Mariah answer. "God, I can still see those nasty little bugs when I close my eyes. There were so *many* of them. The exterminator came and said they had to spray some awful poison, and even then, they'd need to come back every few days or so to spray again. I told the rental office that I *wouldn't* be coming back. Not to *that* cottage."

"Will you be coming back?" Mariah asked, hardly daring to hope.

"Of course. I'll probably stay at the resort for a few days until I can find something less populated by the native insect life."

The resort. That would put Serena closer to John. How convenient.

Mariah took a deep breath. "Serena, I wanted to talk to you about John."

"Jonathan Mills?"

"Yes."

"He was *so* excited when he received those favorable test results," Serena told her. "Just like a little boy. Of course, one set of favorable tests doesn't necessarily mean he's in remission or whatever. He still could die."

"If you think that, then what are you doing with him?" Mariah asked. "You want a husband who's alive, don't you?"

Serena laughed. "A husband? Who said anything about a husband?" Her voice changed. "Has Jonathan mentioned anything to you about wanting to get married?"

"No."

"Well, see? We're just friends. You're his friend. Can't *I* be friends with Jonathan, too? Really, Mariah, it's nothing serious. The man hasn't done more than *kiss* me," Serena pointed out. "He's had plenty of opportunities to come home with me or take me back to his place, but he hasn't." She paused. "Yet."

John had kissed Serena. Mariah closed her eyes as she fought the wave of jealousy and hurt that threatened to consume her. "It might be nothing serious for you, but..." She knew John pretty well by now. "John's *always* serious. And he's fragile in a lot of ways. His cancer has made him vulnerable. And he has those awful nightmares."

"Are you trying to scare me away—or give me instructions on how to hold his hand and warm his milk for him at night when he has a bad dream?"

"These aren't bad dreams. These are violent nightmares. Hasn't he told you?"

"Maybe he's afraid he'll scare me away if he tells me all of his dark secrets," Serena said.

Or maybe when he was with Serena, he didn't spend any time talking.

"He should realize that I don't scare easily," Serena added. "What are the nightmares about? Being sick?"

"No," Mariah told her. "A friend of his was a police detective and he was killed in the line of duty. It haunts him."

"Isn't that interesting," Serena mused. "A police detective, you said?"

"Actually, John said his friend—Tony—was a cop. Tony was killed on the orders of an organized-crime boss."

"Well, that certainly adds a new dimension to the game."

"Serena, if this is just a game to you—"

"Life is a game," Serena said. "You play it, and then you die. No matter what rules you play by, dying is the one given. Everyone dies sooner or later. Some, sooner. If the cancer doesn't kill Jonathan—who knows—maybe he'll be hit by a bus."

"That's a terrible thing to think!"

"Oh, please, Mariah," Serena said. "The Pollyanna act gets old after a while."

"Maybe when you leave today, you shouldn't come back."

Serena laughed. "Maybe I won't." She paused. "Was that really the most awful thing you could think of to say to me?"

Mariah gazed out over the ocean, curbing her impulse to say the words that were really on her lips. "No," she admitted. "But we're friends. I don't want to say anything that—"

"Did you get that negative back from the photo lab?" Serena interrupted.

"No. I haven't been off—"

"Now I've *got* to come back." Serena sounded annoyed. "Have it ready for me tomorrow, please. I'll come by to pick it up."

"Tomorrow? I'm sorry, I can't—"

The line was dead. Serena had hung up without even saying goodbye.

## CHAPTER EIGHT

A LIGHT WAS ON IN Mariah's cottage.

Miller stood on the beach, gazing up at the house, wishing he'd been able to sleep. He wished he hadn't given up and climbed out of bed. He wished he hadn't roused Princess and brought her out onto the beach. He wished he'd walked in the other direction.

Most of all, he wished he could erase the memory he had of Mariah's face as she turned away at lunch. But the hurt and disappointment in her eyes had been burned into his brain. There was no escaping it.

He shouldn't have come out here.

But something had pulled him in this direction. Something strong. Something he couldn't resist.

Nothing had gone right tonight. He'd planned to take Serena to dinner and ask her to marry him. But she'd called and left a message, canceling their date. She hadn't told him where she was going or when she'd be back—just that she had to go to the mainland to take care of business and that she'd be back soon.

His first thought was that she was on to him. Somehow, she'd made him. She knew he was FBI.

She was dangerously smart, and he had screwed up all over the place with this case, starting with his obsession with Mariah and continuing with his failure to stick to his cover story and play the part of the invalid at the Foundations for Families building site. He knew what chemotherapy did to a person, and it was highly unlikely that, had he had the treatments he was pretending to have had, he would've been able to rescue that eight-year-old from the tree, let alone Mariah.

Yeah, and then there was his telling Mariah about Tony. That was a real stroke of genius. He'd actually told Mariah that Tony was a *cop*. What had he been thinking?

He *wasn't* thinking. He was reacting. He was feeling. He was wanting. He was leading with a part of his anatomy that didn't have a very high IQ.

And that was how agents got themselves and their partners killed. And God help him, he may not give a damn about his own life, but he would not—*would not*—bury another partner.

He gazed out at the horizon, squinting to make out where the sky ended and the ocean began. A light haze obscured all but the brightest of the stars, and a steady breeze blew off the water, carrying with it a salty mist. It was almost cold.

He was exhausted, bone weary, yet he still couldn't sleep. He couldn't sleep because he was afraid to sleep. He was afraid to fall into his nightmare. Afraid to gaze down into Tony's sightless eyes. Afraid to hear Tony's voice, tight with fear. Afraid to face his own guilt.

Princess was halfway up the path that led to Mariah's, looking back at him with a quizzical expression on her fuzzy face. *Aren't you coming?*

"No," Miller said, softly but firmly. "Come back here, Princess. *Now.*"

But the dog either couldn't hear him over the wind

and the surf, or maybe she simply chose not to hear. She trotted steadily toward the shelter of Mariah's deck.

Miller went after her, breaking into a run, but she was too far ahead. As she started up the wooden steps of the deck, she barked sharply. Once. Twice.

*Damn.* That was all he needed—for Mariah to know he was here, skulking around outside her house, hoping for what? To get a glimpse of her? To talk to her? To kiss her? To fall back with her onto her bed? To lock her bedroom door and never come out?

All those things. *Dammit,* he wanted *all* those things.

"Princess, get your butt down here," he hissed, starting up the stairs after her.

The door slid open. "Hey, what are *you* doing here?" Mariah greeted his dog. Her voice was not so friendly when she turned and spotted him, frozen on his way up the stairs. "John?"

He climbed up the last few steps, silently cursing Princess, silently cursing himself. "Hi. Yeah, it's me. I'm sorry—I didn't mean to bother you, but the dog has a mind of her own."

Mariah looked incredible. She was wearing those same cutoffs she'd had on at lunchtime, the same clingy T-shirt. Her legs were long and tanned and looked as if they'd be deliciously smooth to touch. She'd pulled her hair up and off her neck, holding it in a messy bundle on top of her head with one of those giant bear-trap-type clips.

But she also looked tired—her normally sparkling eyes were shadowed. She looked wary and leery and not at all happy to see him.

As he watched, she took a breath, and the slight movement made her breasts strain against the cotton of her shirt. God, what he wouldn't have given to pull her into his arms.

She glanced back inside the house, twisting slightly to look at the clock on the wall. "It's after one. Couldn't you sleep?"

Miller shook his head. "No. I never can. Sleep, I mean. Except for that one time here…"

She was silent for several long moments, just gazing at him. He couldn't read her eyes, couldn't read her body language. He had absolutely no idea what she was thinking.

"It's cold tonight," she finally said. "Why don't you come inside?"

She turned and went in, not waiting for him to answer.

Miller knew he should take Princess and go. But he'd left everything he knew he should do behind a long time ago. And Princess was already curled up in the dry, protected corner of the deck. So instead, he followed Mariah into the house and closed the door tightly behind him.

It was outrageously bright in there after the darkness of the beach. Mariah had brought most of the lamps from other rooms over to the dining table near the sliding doors, and that part of the house seemed to glow. He stepped past the lights and into the dimness of the living room.

"How's your back?" he asked awkwardly, wishing that she would ask him to leave. It would make everything so much easier if she just kicked him out.

"It's fine." She was standing in the middle of the room, arms folded across her chest, watching him.

"What are you doing…you know, up so late?"

"I couldn't sleep, either," she admitted. "I thought I'd put some of my pictures in albums. I've been trying to organize them." She gestured back toward the dining-room table. Photos of all shapes and colors were spread across its surface, along with albums of all sizes.

Music was playing softly in the background. It wasn't soft music; it was just turned down low, as if she'd adjusted the volume when she heard Princess out on the deck. A slide guitar wailed over a heavy country backbeat. Vocalists in tight harmony came in—singing about a girl with a tattoo in the shape of Texas. Miller had to smile.

"You know, I always pictured you as being so serene, with your stress-reduction exercises and your crystals," he told her. "I guess I always imagined that when you were alone you'd listen to New Age music—not kick-ass country."

She smiled very slightly. "Oh, please. I thought you knew me better than that. New Age music puts me to sleep."

"Maybe we should both try listening to it, then."

Mariah turned away from him and sat on the end of the couch, her legs underneath her, tailor-style. It was dim in the living room, with all the lights moved into the dining area. She looked mysterious sitting there, shadows falling across her face. "Tell me about the test results."

Miller stepped away from the table and farther into the darkness of the living room. He sat down in the rocking chair opposite her and cleared his throat before he told her a lie. Another lie. There had been so many, yet at the same time, he'd told her more about himself than he'd ever told anyone. All those memories of his mother...

"There's not much to tell. My blood tests show vast improvements. If it keeps going like this, I'm going to be considered in remission. If the cancer doesn't recur in five years, I'm going to be considered cured."

He sounded bitter. He *was* bitter. He knew so much about Hodgkin's disease and about the so-called survival rate because his mother had been one of the ones who hadn't survived. She'd been in remission. She'd even been pronounced cured. And still, she'd relapsed and the second time around, the cancer had won. She'd died.

"Five *years*...?" Mariah leaned forward. "John, you've got to stop worrying about it. You can't not sleep for five years." She sighed. "Have you considered going into therapy?"

He wanted to sit next to her on the couch. God, he wanted her so badly he could barely speak.

Why was he here? What was he doing here? There was nothing—absolutely nothing—good that could possibly come of this. Nothing but a few brief moments of comfort, a temporary respite from the hell his life had become. Mariah could give him that. But what about her? What about all that he'd be taking away from her in return?

"I know you don't think so, but I'm okay about the Hodgkin's. It's not even real to me." Miller stood up swiftly, aware that he was saying the wrong thing again. What was he telling her now? Damn right the cancer wasn't real to him, because it *wasn't* real. But it *was* real to Jonathan Mills.

Except he *wasn't* Jonathan Mills. He was John

Miller. John Miller was the one who couldn't sleep, the one with the terrible nightmares. He was the one with all the guilt, all the suffocating blame. He was the one who had come here tonight, seeking her out.

Mariah stood, too, looking at him, her eyes wide. "John, are you all right?"

He shook his head. "No. I have to…" What? What did he have to do? Run away. God, he never thought he'd ever run away from anything. But here he was, forced to run from the one person who maybe could save him, given the chance.

But he couldn't give her—or himself—any kind of a chance.

She was moving toward him slowly, the way someone would approach a frightened animal. "John, when was the last time you slept?"

He shook his head. "I don't know." But that was another lie and he was tired of lying to her. He knew damn well when he'd last slept. "It was here," he said. "That time I was here."

Her eyes widened. "That was over a week ago!"

"I've had some naps since then, but…" He shook his head.

"But you wake up with that nightmare, and then you can't—or won't—go back to sleep, right? My God, you're shaking!"

He was. He jammed his shaking hands into the front pockets of his jeans and turned toward the door. "I have to go."

Mariah blocked his path. "Let me call Daniel to come and get you."

"No, I'm fine."

"You are so *not* fine. Look, just sit down. On the couch."

Miller didn't move.

"Please? John?"

He sat.

She sat down next to him. All he could think about was how badly he'd wanted to sit next to her. Well, now here he was.

"Talk to me," she said quietly. "Tell me about Tony. Why do you blame yourself for his death? What really happened, John?"

Miller turned to look at her, and with a flash of clarity that nearly pushed him down onto the floor, he knew why he wanted to be here, why he wanted to be with Mariah so desperately.

*Why do you blame yourself for his death?*

He did. He blamed himself. And yet he knew that Mariah would forgive him. He knew that without a doubt. Mariah would tell him that even if it *was* his fault that Tony had died, even if he *had* been to blame, even if there was something he could have done to save his partner and best friend, she would *still* forgive him.

He should have gotten out of the van sooner. He should have known there would be a snafu with the backup. He should have anticipated the fact that the choppers wouldn't arrive. His list of recriminations went on and on, but regardless of its length and content, the bottom line was the same.

He'd failed.

But Mariah, with her gentle smile and warm eyes, would forgive him for failing. She would forgive him his mistakes, forgive him for being human.

God help him, he wanted that forgiveness. He

wanted to hear her say it. And he knew with that same flash of clarity, brighter than all the lights gathered around the dining-room table, that he had to get out of here, and soon, or he'd break down in tears, crying like a baby. Crying for Tony, and crying for himself—for everything that he'd lost that awful night two years ago. Crying because the one time it had really mattered, the one time his reputation of never failing, of not accepting the word "impossible," of being "The Robot" with his superhuman ability to get the job done—the one time that would have really made a difference, reality had stepped in and Tony had died.

He knew he had to get out of there, but Mariah reached out and took his hand, and he couldn't move.

"I couldn't save him," he told her, his voice hoarse.

She touched his face. "But you tried, didn't you? You *were* there."

Miller had to close his eyes to keep his tears from escaping. "I didn't see it. But I heard them kill him. God, I heard him die!" He turned away as more than two years of pain and grief and rage erupted in an emotional cataclysm. His tears burned his face and his lungs ached for air and his body shook as he broke down and wept. "I was too late. I got there too late."

Miller felt Mariah's arms around him and he tried to pull away, tried to stop his tears, tried to shut himself off and push everything he felt back down inside him. He might've succeeded had she not held on to him so tightly.

"What if you'd gotten there earlier?" she asked, her voice as soothing as the gentleness of her hands in his hair. "How could you have stopped them from killing him? What would you have done?"

He knew the answer—and he knew that she knew it, too.

"You probably would've been killed, as well, wouldn't you?" she asked quietly.

"Yes." Not probably. Definitely. He would've died. It was only because he'd arrived after most of Domino's men had emptied their bullets into Tony's head that he'd managed to take them all out without being killed himself. If he'd shown up any sooner, he would've been lying on that concrete floor, just as dead as Tony.

"John, you've got to forgive yourself for not dying with your friend."

That was why he'd come here, wasn't it? For absolution. For the relief of his soul. But he wanted relief for his body, too. He wanted it so badly he was afraid he'd give in to the temptation. God, it wouldn't take much to push him over the edge.

He tried to pull free from her hands, well aware that her touch was giving him far more than comfort. Her touch was lighting him on fire, reminding him of the sweet oblivion that awaited him if only he gave in. He had to get out of here.

But she wouldn't let him go. "It's all right," she murmured, her hands in his hair, on his face, soothing his shoulders and back. "Let it out, John. Let it go. It's okay to feel angry and hurt. It's okay to grieve. If you don't, it'll poison you. Just let it all go."

Miller couldn't stop himself. Mariah held him even more tightly as he clung to her desperately. Please, God, don't let her kiss him. If she did, he'd be lost.

He closed his eyes as she began talking to him soothingly, softly, walking him through that same relaxation exercise she'd helped him with last week. And once again, like last week, his exhaustion crashed down upon him.

He was barely conscious as she pulled him back onto the couch with her, her arms tightly around him, his back pressed against her front.

"Forgive yourself," she murmured. "I'm sure Tony does."

MARIAH COULDN'T SLEEP.

The couch wasn't meant to hold two people lying down—especially not two people her and John's size. But she wasn't uncomfortable. In fact, she liked the sensation of John's body pressed against hers, their legs intimately intertwined.

She liked it too much.

She listened to the steady, quiet rhythm of his breathing and cursed herself for being a fool.

At least she hadn't had sex with him. Although, that was really only because he hadn't asked. If he'd wanted to, she probably wouldn't have been able to turn him down.

God, what had happened to her since that first morning she'd set eyes on this man? Where on earth had Jonathan Mills gotten the power to transform her so totally into some kind of doormat?

He stirred slightly, and she took the opportunity to pull her arm out from underneath him.

It was the cancer thing. The idea that this man had faced—and was still facing—the very real possibility of his imminent death did her in. His plight reduced her to a quivering mass of emotions and reactions.

It had to be that. Because she'd fallen in love before without losing her sense of self, her strength and…

Fallen in love.

She looked down at John's face. He looked impossibly young, improbably innocent, his lips slightly parted in sleep.

She was in love with him.

Mariah knew in that instant that her doormat days were done. She was in love, and yet she was more unhappy than she'd ever been in her entire life. She hadn't felt this bad even while she was going through her divorce from Trevor.

She couldn't do this to herself anymore.

She wasn't crazy. And yet here she was, holding John while he slept when she knew for a fact that he'd been sharing more than meals with Serena. From now on, he was going to have to go to Serena for the comfort he needed to get him through the blackest hours of the night.

Mariah peeled herself away from him, climbing off the couch. He stirred again, but he didn't wake up as she stood there, looking down at him.

She should have felt better. Pushing him away from her like that should have been empowering.

But without his body next to hers, warming her, all Mariah felt was cold.

SHE CAME BACK TO THE HOTEL quite late. She'd closed the bar down, drinking and dancing.

Her dress smelled of smoke and sweat, and she peeled it off, letting it fall in a heap on the soft, expensive carpeting. She wouldn't take it with her when she left in the morning.

She was going to have to go back. She needed that

negative. Except the stupid cow hadn't sounded as if she was going to go out of her way to get it back from…

Where was it she kept her negatives? B&W Photo Lab. Just over on the mainland from Garden Isle. It would be easy enough to find, easy enough to walk in there and get hold of her entire collection of negatives.

She caught sight of herself in the mirror and stopped for a moment to admire her body, her face.

She'd had plastic surgery to remove all but one of her scars. One she kept—a little one, just along the line of her left eyebrow.

The first one had done that to her. The first one had given her all her scars—at least all the scars that her father before him hadn't given her.

She closed her eyes, remembering the thrill she had felt when the policeman had come to her door, waking her in the middle of the night to tell her that the first one was dead. A car accident. He'd drunk himself into a stupor, and instead of coming home and beating her to a pulp, he'd driven his car into a tree.

The undertaker's wife, mistaking her round-the-clock vigilance at his coffin for grief, cut her a lock of his hair to remember him by.

But it hadn't been grief keeping her there—it had been fear. Fear that unless she watched him, unless she made damn sure he stayed right there in that wooden box until they nailed it shut, he might somehow escape. He might jump up and run away and come back to haunt her.

She'd nearly thrown the hair into the toilet, but on second thought, she'd kept it, wrapped in cellophane, at the bottom of her jewelry box.

The insurance money, along with a stash she'd found

in a suitcase in the garage, had been enough to get her to St. Thomas. She'd picked herself a new name, afraid that whoever owned the money that had been in that suitcase would come looking for her.

That was when she'd met the second one.

He was rich and old and nearly as mean as the first one. Except the abuse *he* dished out wasn't physical. And when a piece of chicken caught in his throat during dinner, she had stood by and watched him choke.

She didn't call for help. She just watched—watched the look in his eyes as he knew she would do nothing to save him, watched as he realized he was, indeed, going to die. She'd liked it—liked the power, liked the feeling of control.

The third one she'd married with the intention of killing.

It had been laughably easy. She was so much smarter than all of them.

Smarter than Jonathan Mills, who wasn't really named Jonathan Mills.

She knew that sooner or later the police would try to trap her. She'd been watching for them. She'd been ready. And when she'd found their clumsily hidden microphones all over her house, she knew that Jonathan Mills had been sent to stop her.

Instead, she'd escaped.

She climbed between the crisp hotel sheets, feeling a flare of regret.

She would have liked pushing her knife blade into Jonathan Mills's heart.

## CHAPTER NINE

MILLER OPENED HIS EYES to the sound of the telephone ringing.

It was daylight. Bright, gleaming morning. The sun had been up for at least an hour and he simply lay for a moment on the couch, staring up at the light playing across the ceiling, hazily wondering why that should seem such an amazing thing.

"Yes." He heard a soft voice from the other room. "Yes, he's here. I'll see if he's awake."

Then he heard the sound of footsteps coming into the living room, and he sat up, automatically raking his hair back with one hand, pushing it from his forehead. Except the hair his fingers connected with was shockingly short, and he remembered instantly both where he was and who he was supposed to be.

Dear God, he'd slept all night again. This time, without even a trace of his nightmare.

"Phone's for you," Mariah said quietly, handing him a cordless telephone.

She didn't meet his gaze. She hardly looked at him at all.

Miller quickly played back the previous evening in his mind. God knows he had plenty to be embarrassed about, what with breaking down and crying the way he'd done. But he couldn't recall a single thing Mariah had done that should make her so uncomfortable.

She hadn't even kissed him.

God help him—he'd somehow managed to spend all that time here last night without ever kissing Mariah. Although he had a very definite memory of falling asleep cradled in the softness of her arms.

He brought the telephone to his ear, still watching Mariah as she opened the sliders to let in the fresh morning air. Last night's coolness remained, but it wouldn't for long, not in the heat from the sun. She stayed for a moment, just looking out at the ocean, her fatigue evident in the way she stood, in the set of her shoulders.

He might have slept well last night, but she clearly hadn't.

"Yeah?" Miller said into the phone.

"John, it's Daniel. I'm sorry to have to call you there, but Serena appears to have gone for good."

Miller didn't move a muscle. He just sat and watched Mariah watch the ocean. "Based on...?"

"Based on the fact that yesterday she notified her rental agent that she was terminating her lease agreement. Her place is empty, John. All her things are cleared out. I went over there early this morning. All the surveillance microphones are still in place—it doesn't look as if she touched any of them, but that doesn't mean anything. I've got to believe she found 'em, got spooked and ran."

Miller swore sharply. Mariah glanced back at him, but quickly looked away. "Call Pat Blake," he told Daniel. "Advise him of the situation and then get back to me."

He should've proposed marriage to Serena yesterday at lunch, when he'd had the chance. But he'd hesitated, and now she was gone. And in his experience, when a suspect fled, that suspect was gone for good.

The case was over—at least this stage of it was— with the suspect still at large. But other than that first sharp flash of annoyance, all Miller felt was relief. Because, for the first time in his life, he had found something that he wanted even more than he wanted to solve this case.

He'd found Mariah.

He pushed the button to disconnect the phone, then set it on the end table. He stood up stiffly, stretching out his legs and back. "Mind if I use your bathroom?"

Mariah turned to face him. "No, of course I don't," she said stiffly, politely. "But afterward, I think you should leave."

He froze mid-stretch. Leave?

He'd found Mariah—who wanted him to leave.

She turned swiftly, disappearing into the kitchen.

It was too damned ironic. For the first time since he'd met her, Miller finally felt free. True, the case wasn't officially over. He couldn't tell her who he was or what he'd been up to—not yet anyway. But he could pull her into his arms and kiss her without knowing for damn sure that she was going to end up hurt.

Miller didn't believe in happily ever after. He had no misconceptions regarding his ability to make Mariah happy in the long run. He knew damn well that kind of future wasn't in his cards. But he was sure that he could make her smile in the short term. He was *very* sure of that.

He went into the bathroom, relieved himself, then

washed up. As he splashed cold water on his face, he caught sight of himself in the mirror. Despite the sleep he'd gotten, he still looked tired. For the first time in years, he found himself longing to crawl back into bed. For the first time in years, sleep beckoned invitingly instead of looming over him dangerously, like some snarling, vicious beast.

With Serena out of the picture, he had nothing to do, nowhere to go—at least not until Daniel contacted Pat Blake. Knowing Blake, he'd call a meeting, maybe even come down here himself to inspect the scene of the disaster firsthand. But that wouldn't be for hours, maybe even days.

Mariah wanted him to leave, but Miller wanted to stay. And for the first time, he *could* stay.

He took a deep breath before he opened the bathroom door. Mariah was in the kitchen. He could hear the sound of water running.

"I gave Princess some water," she told him without even looking up as he paused in the doorway.

"Thanks," he said. He hesitated, suddenly oddly embarrassed, a picture of the way he'd wept last night flashing into his head. "And thanks...for last night, too. I feel..." He smiled crookedly. "I feel *okay*."

Mariah turned to face him then. "You slept for a long time."

He nodded. "First time in over two years I've slept through the sunrise."

"You never let yourself grieve for him before, did you?" she asked quietly, talking about Tony.

Miller squinted slightly as he looked out the window at the brightness of the day. "No."

"It wasn't your fault that he died."

He shook his head very slightly. "No. No, it wasn't." He laughed very softly. "I know it wasn't. Logically. Rationally. I guess I just don't quite *believe* it wasn't." He paused, gazing at her, feeling that familiar ache of longing. He wanted to pull her into his arms, but she was sending out all kinds of signals warning him to keep his distance. "Maybe you could help me work on that."

"Gee, I'm sorry, but I can't." She took a deep breath. "I don't want to be your therapist anymore, John," she said bluntly. "What you're dealing with isn't going to be solved by breaking plates or silly little relaxation exercises. You need to find someone professional who can really help you. And I…" Her voice broke. "I need you to stay away from me. I can't pretend to be your friend anymore. Maybe that's petty of me, because I know you really need me as a friend, but I can't do this anymore. I respect myself too much to play this crazy game with you. Do you want me or don't you? Every time I think that you do, you back away. And just when I'm convinced that you don't, you look at me like…like… *that*. Don't look at me like that, dammit, because I'm not going to play anymore. I want you to leave."

He stepped toward her. "Mariah—"

Mariah lifted her chin, folding her arms across her chest, holding her ground despite the tears that filled her eyes. "The door's in the other direction."

John stopped moving toward her, but he didn't retreat, either. He just gazed at her. In spite of his long, quiet sleep, he still looked weary, his chiseled features in high relief. His chin was covered with dark stubble, making him look doubly dangerous. But it was the bright blue of his eyes that caught her and held her in place. Beneath the heat of desire that nearly always simmered there, his eyes were filled with apology and darkened with a haunting vulnerability.

"Whatever you do, don't think that I don't want you," he whispered. "Because I do. I've wanted you right from the start—and every minute from then till now."

She couldn't believe what she was hearing. She laughed, but it came out sounding more like a sob. "Then why have you been kissing Serena?"

He didn't seem surprised that she knew—and he didn't try to deny it. "I can't... I can't explain that."

"Try."

John just shook his head.

He was blocking the only way out of the room, but Mariah couldn't stand to be there a moment longer. She tried to push past him, but he caught her arm, his fingers locking around her wrist. "Mariah, wait—"

"Let *go* of me!"

Miller let go. No way was he going to risk hurting her again. Seeing those bruises on her arms had made him sick to his stomach. "I kissed her because I hoped it would make me stop wanting *you*." That was only part of the truth, but he hoped it would be enough.

She turned to look back at him, her eyes filled with anger, her lips tight with disgust. "You are so full of—"

Miller kissed her. He knew it wasn't playing fair, but he didn't give a damn. He knew kissing her would melt her anger and ignite her passion, leaving the arguments and harsh words far behind. He knew he was good at word games, but Mariah had told him point-blank that she didn't want to play games anymore.

This kiss would eliminate everything but the most basic of truths—that he wanted her and she wanted him.

And yes, she still wanted him.

He tasted it in the fire of her kiss, in the heat of her melting embrace. He kissed her harder, sweeping his tongue deeply into her mouth, and she met him with a fierceness that took his breath away. She pulled him closer, her hands gliding up his back, her fingers on his neck, in his hair, even as his own hands explored the softness of her body, cupping the fullness of her breasts.

"Make love to me, Mariah," he whispered, kissing her again. Her response was clear from the strength of her answering kiss.

She pulled back slightly, and he could see molten desire in her eyes. "If I do, I'm going to regret this, aren't I?" she said huskily.

"No," he said. "This is going to be too good to regret."

Her smile was tinged with sadness. "I just made up my mind to stay away from you, and now you go and totally mess me up. I mean, God! Give me one good reason why I shouldn't kick you out right here and now."

He couldn't. There was no reason, other than he wanted to stay, and she wanted him to stay, too. He leaned forward to kiss her again, but she stopped him with a finger against his lips.

"I don't know, maybe I haven't made this totally clear, but I'm emotionally involved here. Taking you into my bedroom and getting naked with you is going to be more than just great sex to me. It's going to be making love. Love, John—do you understand what

I'm trying to say to you?" Mariah took a deep breath and let it all out in a rush. "In plain English, I'm in love with you. So if you're going to get all freaked out and scared about that, maybe you should just run away now—*before* you tear my heart out."

Miller couldn't move. He couldn't speak. He couldn't breathe. Mariah was in love with...*him?*

He gazed down into her eyes, unable to look away, feeling an odd tightness in his chest. "That sounds like a good reason for me to stay," he whispered.

He wanted to be loved. God, how he wanted that. He was shaken by how badly he wanted that, wanted more than just lust, more than physical gratification. He wanted to be cared for, to be cherished. In the past, he'd run away from such emotions, but as he looked into Mariah's eyes, he only wanted to move closer. He wanted her to love him. He wanted *her.* And somehow she knew. He could see in her eyes that she knew.

Still, it wasn't quite enough.

"I need you to promise me something," she told him.

"Mariah, I can't promise much—"

"I'm not looking for any major commitment or anything like that," she countered. "Just..." She had to start again. "Don't sleep with Serena, okay?"

That was easy. "I won't," he said. "I promise."

That was all she needed. Taking his hand, she led him to her bedroom.

The morning sun shone through green curtains, giving the room a greenish tint. The ocean breeze made the curtains move, and the light seemed to shift and dance across the ceiling. It was like being underwater. Or maybe up in heaven.

Mariah's bed was in the center of the small room,

the headboard pushed against the wall. It was rumpled, unmade, the white sheets exposed beneath a green spread. Miller knew that Mariah had spent much of the night in here, unable to rest while he'd been fast asleep on the couch.

Mariah kissed him, and he knew his second assessment was right. This was definitely heaven.

She kissed him slowly, deeply, shifting her body against his in a way that made him groan. He knew from the burst of heat in her eyes that she liked the involuntary sound of his desire.

Her hands slid up underneath his T-shirt, traveling slowly up his back, and Miller closed his eyes.

This was too good, too intense, and too damn slow. But if she wanted it like this, dammit, he was going to curb his raging impulses and make love to her slowly.

He knew without a shadow of a doubt that he'd go to superhuman degrees to give her anything she wanted, anything at all.

She tugged at his T-shirt and he helped her pull it up and over his head. But when he reached for her shirt, she stopped him.

"Have you noticed that when it comes to sex, guys don't like to get naked first?" she said, kissing his shoulders, his neck, his chest. Her fingers moved down to the waistband of his jeans, lightly brushing against his stomach as she unfastened the top button. "It's a dominance thing," she added, smiling up at him as she slowly unzipped his pants, "a power thing. It makes sense, doesn't it? The person still dressed has a certain amount of power over the person who's naked."

"Are you, um, into that?" Miller asked.

She pushed him back onto the bed, pulling his

jeans down his thighs. "And then there's the female thing," she continued as if she hadn't heard his question. "Women tend to be afraid to take the lead for fear of coming on too strong. Socially, we're taught to lie back—let the man take off our clothes. Let him set the pace. Let him choose the time and place and position. Let him do the work. Hence the passive phrase 'to be made love *to*.' I much prefer 'making love *with*.'" She tossed his jeans onto the floor. "*That's* what I'm into."

He reached for her, pressing her back on the bed with the force of his kiss. But then he moved away, suddenly remembering. "Your back—is it all right?"

"It's fine." She pulled him toward her for another kiss, molding herself against him.

The sensation of the smoothness of her legs intertwined with his nearly overwhelmed him. He pulled her T-shirt up, over her head, and this time she didn't protest.

He gazed down at her and she smiled back at him, just letting him look. She was impossibly sexy, lying there like that. Her bra was white, covering her full breasts with some kind of stretchy lace material that allowed him tantalizing glimpses of dark pink nipples. He covered her breasts first with his hands, then with his mouth, suckling her through the lace of the bra, tugging on the desire-hardened tips with his lips, with his tongue.

She moaned, opening herself to him, cradling his swollen sex against the heat between her legs.

Miller reached for the button on her shorts, and she let him unfasten them and pull them down her legs. They soon joined his jeans on the floor.

Mariah closed her eyes. For all her liberated talk, she

was lying there, letting him undress her. And cringing because she was nearly naked—and afraid he wouldn't like her because she didn't have the body of a Barbie doll.

She felt John's hands skimming her body. She knew he was looking at her.

"God, you're incredible," he breathed.

About to protest, she opened her eyes, but then she saw the fire in his gaze, the sheer admiration on his face. He was serious. He honestly liked what he saw.

He wasn't one of those men who went for boyishly figured women like Serena. He wasn't like Trevor, who had been forever trying to get her to go on a diet, to lose weight, to shrink herself down to his height.

No, John clearly liked *women*. Real women. And maybe especially women who were six feet tall, and generously—and appropriately—proportioned for their height.

As Mariah watched John's face, her shoulders were no longer too broad. Her thighs weren't too big, her legs too thickly muscled. Her hips weren't too wide, or her breasts too full.

Mariah sat up and unfastened the front clasp of her bra—for the first time in her life voluntarily exposing herself to the eyes of a man without hiding in the cover of the darkness of night.

The look in John's eyes was well worth the risk. He smiled, a short, hot smile that nearly scalded her, as he pulled her up toward him.

The sensation of the hard muscles of his chest pressed against her bare breasts and his rock-solid arousal against the softness of her stomach was diz-zying as she knelt with him, there on her bed. His kiss made her sway, and she clung to him as he slipped one hand beneath the lace of her panties, his exploring fingers touching her lightly, intimately.

She reached between them, too, finding him hard and sleek and hot.

He groaned. "Mariah…"

She opened her eyes to find herself gazing directly into his. The connection was just as physical as his touch.

"You said you had protection," he said.

At just the same moment, she asked, "Will you put on a condom?"

They both laughed.

"I'll get one," Mariah said, pulling free from his grasp.

She rummaged through her bedside-table drawer, searching for the packet of condoms that her aunt had given her, complete with a note telling her to have a *very* good vacation. Mariah had rolled her eyes and tossed the box into her suitcase, hardly expecting to find call to use it. As she found the box, way down at the bottom of the drawer, John came to stand behind her, pressing himself intimately against her, covering her breasts with his hands and kissing her neck. It felt delicious—a hard promise of things to come.

And Mariah knew that she didn't want to wait a moment longer. He'd taken off his briefs and now he slipped her panties down her legs, as well, as she turned to face him.

They were both naked, but she was more so—because she'd told him that she loved him.

This should have been strange—standing here like this, just looking at this beautiful, naked man, letting him look at her. But it wasn't strange at all, despite the fact that it had been years since she'd been with a man this way. She'd been attracted to John from the first moment she'd laid eyes on him. She'd liked him from the first time they'd talked. And somewhere between then and now, she'd fallen deeply in love with him, too. And it was that love she felt that kept this from being strange, that instead made this moment perfect.

She knew he didn't love her—she didn't try to kid herself about that. But he liked her. She knew he really liked her. And on many levels, she preferred that steady, milder emotion to the short, hot, quick-burning flash of infatuation that many people mistook for love.

She pressed one of the condom packets into his hand. "Put this on," she told him. "Then lie down and close your eyes."

John laughed softly. "What are we doing? Pressure Cooker Release? Seabirds in Flight?"

Mariah gently pushed him onto the bed, unable to hide her smile. "You'll see." She was going to make this an experience he'd never forget. "I'll be right back."

She pulled on her robe and went quickly into the living room. She unplugged her boom box from the wall, found the CD she wanted, then carried both back into the bedroom.

John was on the bed, as she'd asked. He was gorgeous—all dark hair and sleek, hard muscles beneath his tanned skin. Lying there against the white sheets, he looked impossibly healthy. How could this physically perfect man have been in a hospital fighting for his life just a few weeks ago?

He was up on one elbow, watching her as she set the CD player on her dresser and plugged it in.

Miller's blood was burning with anticipation. He'd barely been able to get the condom on, he was so aroused. And now Mariah was putting a CD into her portable player, her brightly colored silk robe hanging open, revealing tantalizing glimpses of her incredible body.

When he'd first seen her picture, he'd thought of her as a goddess. He'd had no idea how completely right he had been.

With a swirl of turquoise silk, she turned to face him. "One more thing," she said, giving him a smile that put dimples of mischief and amusement in her cheeks. A small square that looked something like a speaker sat on the bedside table. She touched it, adjusted it, and the sound of flowing water filled the room. "A waterfall," she said. She smiled at him again as she let her robe flutter to the ground. "Close your eyes."

Miller didn't want to. He wanted to look at her—he'd never tire of looking at her.

She moved back to the CD player and turned it on, too, adjusting the volume.

It wasn't music that came on. Miller listened closely, trying to identify the sounds that were playing over the high-quality speakers.

Birds.

They were birdcalls. Sweetly melodic chirping and tweeting.

Mariah sat next to him on the bed, leaning forward to kiss him. "Close your eyes," she said again.

Miller closed them.

He felt her straddle him, felt her kiss him again, her stomach pressed against his erection, the tight beads of her nipples brushing erotically against his chest. He was on fire, but he wanted to please her, so he did what she asked. He stayed on his back and kept his eyes closed. But he couldn't keep from touching her, his hands sweeping down the softness of her skin. He filled his palms with her breasts, loving the sound of her breath catching in her throat.

And then she moved her hips, covering him with her soft heat, and he couldn't help himself. He pressed himself up, wanting more, needing to feel himself inside her. Now. *Now.*

She kissed him again and he groaned. "Mariah, please…"

She shifted her hips again, granting him access, and with one velvet-smooth thrust, he was ensheathed by her.

He held on to her hips, pressing himself more tightly inside her, praying that she wouldn't move even the slightest bit, sure that if she did, he would lose control. Too soon. It was too soon.

But she didn't move. She kissed him instead, her lips gentle against his mouth, his cheek, his chin and jaw, his ear.

"You are now in a very special place," Mariah said softly, laughter in her voice, her breath warm against his ear, "with birds singing and a waterfall trickling…."

Miller opened his eyes to find her smiling down at him, amusement dancing in her whiskey-colored eyes.

"The next time someone tells you to close your eyes and picture yourself in your special place," she continued, "you'll have no problem imagining yourself *right* here. And I mean right here." She moved her hips for emphasis.

Miller had to laugh. And then he had to kiss her. As he claimed her mouth, she began to move slowly on top of him. Each stroke was sheer heaven as she took her sweet time.

She was driving him mad, and she knew it, too. He could tell from the little smile she gave him as she sat up above him.

He reached for her, pulling her down against him, drawing her breasts toward his hungry mouth, pulling hard on her desire-swollen nipples.

She moved faster then, harder, and he moved with her, filling her again and again as she cried out her pleasure. Time seemed to stop as his entire world shrank completely down to this one woman who was touching him, loving him. Nothing else existed, nothing else mattered. He filled himself with her, all his senses working overtime as he watched his own ecstasy mirrored on her face, as he heard her cries and murmurs of pleasure, as her softness and warmth surrounded him completely.

He felt the shuddering thrill of her climax and he buried his face in the softness of her breasts as he, too, went up and over the edge. The rush of his release engulfed him, rocketing him to a dizzying height.

Mariah collapsed upon him as slowly, very slowly, the roar subsided, leaving him warm and relaxed and peacefully calm.

He became aware of Mariah's soft hair against his face. He became aware of the way her breath caught slightly as she sighed contentedly. He became aware of birds singing and the sound of water splashing enticingly down a steep hill.

A special place. Yes. This was a *very* special place.

Mariah turned her head and brushed her lips against his neck. She didn't say the words, but she didn't have to. He knew that she loved him.

This was what it was like to make love with someone who really cared. It was incredible—being loved so completely, on so many levels. It made the rather ordinary act of sex seem a miracle. It heightened all his senses and made his heart seem ten times as big. It took his breath away and filled his lungs with sheer joy and laughter. It made him want to smile—all the time.

Miller wondered if Mariah felt the wonder of this miracle. He wondered if she knew, if she felt it, too.

He didn't say the words, either. He didn't know how.

But he knew without a doubt that he loved her.

SHE LEFT THE PHOTO LAB CARRYING the box of negatives.

The nice man had seen no problem in letting her take them to her friend.

Once inside her car, she lifted the lid and looked inside. One by one, she held the strips of film up to the windshield, using the sunlight to illuminate them. She went through about twenty of the plastic-encased strips before she gave up.

She was going to have to burn the entire box.

She looked down into the box and saw there was a paper folder—the kind that drugstores use to enclose color prints. She pulled it out, almost on a whim. There were no photos inside, but there were several smaller strips of negatives.

She held one to the light and…

Quickly, she pulled out another and another.

These were other photographs of *her*. Somehow that bitch had taken more pictures of *her*!

Her rage was laced with fear. If there were negatives, then somewhere there were photographs.

She was going to have to go back.

She took a deep breath, calming herself. It didn't matter. She was smarter than they were. She could get the photos. She *would* get the photos. She would destroy the evidence and punish the bitch who had brought her this trouble.

Her calm soon turned to anticipation. She *was* smarter than they were. She could do all that, and more.

She put the lid back on the box and threw her car into gear. She had lots to do. *Lots* to do.

# CHAPTER TEN

MARIAH FOCUSED THE LENS of her camera on John. "Smile," she said.

He laughed as he glanced over at her. "You're taking a picture of me doing the dishes?"

She snapped several photos in rapid succession before looking up from the camera to smile at him. "No, I'm just taking pictures of you. The doing-the-dishes part isn't important. You know, I really wish I'd developed those pictures of you I took that day we first met."

He lifted an eyebrow as he drained the soapy water from the sink and dried his hands on a dish towel. "What? You mean you took pictures of me when I was lying with my face in the sand?"

She had to laugh. "No. I took pictures when I first saw you—when you were out on the beach with Princess. I wonder what I did with that roll of film. It's probably around here somewhere. But I wish I had those pictures to show you for comparison. It's amazing—you look so different now. You look so relaxed and...happy."

"That's because I got lucky this morning." John pulled her close and kissed her below the ear. "And I happen to know that the esteemed Dr. Gerrard Hollis recommends that particular activity we took part in as his number one means of relieving stress. So, yeah, I'm extremely relaxed."

"I'm not sure Dr. Hollis put it in quite those words," Mariah said, laughing in dismay. "Getting lucky."

He kissed her again, on the mouth this time, so sweetly she felt herself start to melt. "I got lucky all right," he said, searching her eyes. "I don't think I've ever felt this lucky in my entire life. I really hit the jackpot when I met you, Mariah."

Mariah's throat felt tight as she gazed back at him. What was he telling her? There was a softness, a gentleness in his eyes that, were she feeling foolhardy enough, she might interpret as love. But she didn't want to interpret it. She didn't want to hope or wish or even *think* about it.

The telephone rang, and she pulled away from him, grateful for the interruption.

It was the doctor's office, finally returning yesterday's call. The doctor seemed to think she could resume normal activities—provided she didn't push herself too hard.

Miller poured himself another cup of coffee as he watched Mariah talk on the phone. He wished he could take *her* picture. Dressed the way she was in only her silk robe, her hair still rumpled from the time they'd spent in bed, she looked incredible—as warm and welcoming and as satisfying as the breakfast they'd made together and shared out on the deck in the soft morning sunlight.

Normally, he resented anyone's intrusion into his morning routine. The morning was his private time. But as he gazed at Mariah, he knew he would enjoy having all of this on a regular basis—breakfast, watching her across the table, even doing the dishes. It was relaxed and easygoing. It felt right. Even the silences were comfortable.

He could easily imagine seeing Mariah's beautiful face first thing every morning, feeling her luscious body next to his every night. He could imagine coming home each evening and losing himself, *submerging* himself in her sweet warmth and love.

That was a dangerous way to be thinking. Mariah had done and said nothing to let him believe she was interested in anything more than a vacation romance. And before they could progress to anything beyond a casual love affair, they both had to come clean and confess as to why they were using false names.

Miller smiled wryly. It was only a matter of time before this investigation was declared defunct. But what was the best way to tell a lover that she didn't know his real name? When was the best time? Right after making love? Or maybe over a quiet dinner? *By the way, darling, you don't really know who I am....*

And he wasn't the only one working under an a.k.a. Mariah, too, had something of her own to share during show-and-tell. Marie Carver. Former CEO of Carver Software out in Phoenix, Arizona.

He'd checked the files. The company was doing fine. There'd been no reports of embezzlement—and no reasons for it either. Marie—Mariah—had inherited her father's share of the company when he had died and under her hand it had thrived. Even though she was no longer CEO, she still owned a large percentage of the business—which, if it was sold right here and now would easily put fifteen million dollars into her personal bank account. No, Mariah had no reason to turn to embezzlement. And according to the IRS, both her personal and business taxes had all been paid both accurately and on time.

So what was she doing, living under an alias, all these thousands of miles away from her home?

Miller had tried to find out during breakfast. Asking leading questions, giving her a clear opening to tell him the truth. But she'd sidestepped all his questions about her business, and somehow they'd ended up talking about Princess instead.

As she hung up the phone, he tried again.

"Mariah is such a pretty name," he told her, leaning back against the counter as he sipped his coffee. "What made your parents name you that?"

"Actually…"

Here it came. She was going to tell him the truth.

"Actually, my parents didn't name me Mariah," she said. "My grandmother did." She took his mug from his hands and set it down on the counter, then slid her arms around his waist.

Miller closed his eyes as she held him tightly, as his body leapt in response to her sweet softness.

"Mariah was *her* grandmother's name," she told him between dizzyingly delicious kisses. "My great-great-grandmother. She was born not far from here, in Georgia, before the Civil War. According to my grandmother, by the time Mariah was twelve, she was an active member of the Underground Railroad. That's partly why I came to Garden Isle. To see where she lived. I've always been fascinated by the stories Grandma told about her."

Miller was wearing only his jeans, and her silk-covered breasts felt incredibly smooth against his bare chest—but not as sinfully good as her skin would feel. Her belt was already loose and it opened easily as he parted the front of her robe and slipped his hands against the softness of her skin, pulling her against him.

She pulled his mouth down to hers and Miller lost himself in her kiss.

He felt her fingers on the button of his jeans and experienced a wave of euphoria. Was this great, or was this great? She wanted him again. Her own attraction to him was clearly as insatiable and intense as his was for her. Mutual overpowering lust.

*True, undying love.*

That thought came from out of nowhere, and Miller shook it away, unwilling to think about the way he'd felt as he'd held Mariah in his arms after making love.

But it was the way he still felt. It hadn't faded. It hadn't disappeared.

He kissed her harder, wanting only to feel the intense physical pleasure she gave him. It was overpowering, unlike anything he'd ever felt—desire of a caliber he'd never really thought existed. He'd heard people talk about the sensation of being hit by a truck, of being blinded to everything but need, but he'd always thought they were weak. They were weak, and he was strong, except here he was, unable to see anything but Mariah, unable even to catch his breath from the weight of the desire that bore down upon him like a runaway train.

He thought his need for this woman would be abated by making love to her, but that had only served to make him want her more. He'd had a taste of her heaven, and he was shamelessly addicted now.

He lifted her right onto the counter, and she willingly opened her legs to him as he kept on kissing her, his mouth trailing down her neck toward her luscious breasts, one hand working to free himself from his pants and...

Mariah pulled back. "John! We need to get a condom."

What the hell was he doing? He had been mere seconds away from thrusting deeply inside of her with absolutely no protection—without one single *thought* of protection. God help him, this woman drove all sane thoughts clear out of his head.

Mariah looked at the expression on John's face and started to laugh despite the adrenaline that passion had kicked into her system. He looked thoroughly, adorably stunned. "I don't want you to stop," she told him. "I just want you to get a condom." She slid down off the counter, pressing herself against him, loving the sensation of his arousal hard against her stomach. She kissed him quickly. "I'll get one. You wait here."

Mariah's heart was still pounding as she ran down the hall to her bedroom. Her bedside-table drawer was still open, the box of condoms on the top. She grabbed one and the phone rang.

Damn! The cordless phone was there in her bedroom, so she quickly picked it up, praying it wouldn't be one of the ladies from the Garden Isle Historical Society, wanting to talk on and on for fifteen or twenty minutes about the latest event at the library. "Hello?"

"I'm sorry to bother you again, Ms. Robinson, but is John still there?"

It was Daniel with the Asian-sounding last name— the dark-haired young man who was John's personal assistant.

"Um, yes, he is, actually." Mariah carried the phone

into the kitchen. "Just a moment, please." She covered the mouthpiece with her hand as she held out the phone to John. "It's for you. It's Daniel."

He fastened his pants before he took the phone—as if Daniel would somehow be able to tell that he was standing there nearly naked and mere moments from sexual fulfillment.

"Yeah," John said into the phone. "What's up?" He met Mariah's eyes briefly and smiled. Even with his jeans zipped, it was still very obvious—at least to the two of them—exactly what was up.

Mariah hadn't bothered fastening her robe, and John's smile faded and his eyes turned even a deeper shade of blue as he looked at her. Another woman might've found the intensity of his expression frightening. But Mariah loved it. She loved the way he seemed to burn for her. She stepped toward him, and he reached inside the thin silk to touch her.

"When?" he said into the phone. He glanced at the clock on the stove and swore softly. "That soon?" Another pause. "Yeah, all right. I'll be there."

He ended the connection with a push of a button, and Mariah took the phone from him, pressing the condom packet into his hand.

He swore again. "Mariah, I'm sorry, I have to go."

"Daniel can wait five minutes, can't he?" She unbuttoned his pants.

"Mariah—"

She pulled down his zipper. "*Three* minutes...?"

He groaned as she touched him, then crushed his mouth to hers. Before she could even blink, she found herself back up on the counter. She heard the tear of the wrapper, felt him pull back for just a second, and then she felt him fill her with a hard, fast thrust that took her breath away.

He groaned, too, still kissing her as he drove himself into her again and again, setting a wild, delirious, feverish pace. It was raw, almost savage sex, and Mariah dug her fingernails into his back, urging him on, wanting more, even more.

It was breathtakingly exhilarating. She had never been made love to like this before. She'd never had a man go so totally out of control over her before. It was more exciting than she'd ever dreamed. He was touching her everywhere, kissing her, caressing her in ways that filled her with fire, and she exploded almost instantly with pleasure, crying out his name.

He followed her lead, and she felt the power of his release as it rocketed through him, shaking him, pushing her even higher to a place of even more pleasure.

He held her tightly, his face buried in her neck as they both struggled to catch their breaths.

"I know you have to go now," Mariah said, when she finally could speak. "But is there any chance I can bribe you with the promise of dinner so that you'll come back later and do that again?"

He lifted his head and laughed. "The hell with dinner. I think we've discovered an entirely new use for the kitchen." His smile softened. "You know, I can go for days without a meal, but I don't think I can go for more than a few hours without making love to you."

John gently touched the side of her face, tracing her lips lightly with his thumb, as if he could see from her eyes how much she melted inside when he said things like that. And why shouldn't he see? She wasn't trying to hide anything from him. She'd told him she loved him. It wasn't a secret.

And for one heart-stopping moment, Mariah seemed almost sure that he was going to tell her that her feelings were mutual, that he loved her, too.

But he only said, "I'll be back by seven at the latest."

Still gazing into her eyes, John leaned forward and kissed her gently on the lips, then pulled her forward and helped her down from the counter. He kissed her again before disappearing for a moment into the bathroom as she straightened her robe and tied her belt. When he came back down the hall, he was pulling on his T-shirt.

"I've got to hurry now," John said, stopping to kiss her on the mouth—a quick brushing of the lips that turned into a much longer, lingering kiss. He groaned softly, forcing himself to pull away from her. "I'll see you later, okay?"

"Seven o'clock," Mariah said.

As he moved toward the sliding doors, past the dining-room table, he suddenly stopped short. "My God!"

"What?"

John picked up one of the pictures that were spread out on the table. It was a color photo she'd taken of Serena with that cheap, disposable camera. "Where did you get this?"

"I took it—I think it was a few weeks ago. Why?"

There was an intensity in his gaze that she'd never seen before. It made the blue of his eyes seem hard and flinty. He swore sharply, almost excitedly, adding, "This is good. This is *very* good. Do you have any other pictures of her?"

Mariah gazed at him, her heart sinking like lead into the pit of her stomach. Why should John care if she had photographs of Serena? Unless he was still... No, she refused to think that way.

"Yes," she said, moving toward the table and turning on several of the lights that were still positioned around that part of the room. "I managed to take four or five of them without her noticing. She's amazingly photogenic. Still, she doesn't like to have her picture taken. It's kind of strange."

"Yeah, I know," he said. He looked down at the seemingly haphazard piles of pictures as if he wanted to search through them but was afraid to mess up her organizational system. "Where are the others? Do you still have them?"

Unless he was still infatuated with Serena... This time she couldn't prevent the thought from coming through.

"They're here somewhere," Mariah said, quickly flipping through one of the piles, again cutting off that errant thought. He didn't want Serena. He wanted *her*. He'd told her that—she knew it was true. How could he have made love to her the way he just had if it wasn't true? "Probably close to where you found the first one." She unearthed three more pictures of Serena.

One photo caught the blond Englishwoman in nearly perfect profile. The three others were either three-quarter or full face.

"May I have these?" John asked.

Mariah laughed. "You're kidding."

He suddenly seemed to realize the inappropriateness of his request. Just a short time ago—mere *minutes* ago—he'd been making love to Mariah, yet now he wanted her to give him pictures of the woman he'd last dated. Dated—and at the very least, kissed. Mariah didn't want to think about the possibility that John had made love to Serena, but it was far too easy to imagine the two of them together.

John shook his head. "It's not what you think."

"It's not? Then please, tell me. What exactly *is* it? I'd like to know. Why do you want these pictures?" She was willing to give him the benefit of the doubt. Maybe he *did* have some genuine reason for wanting those pictures.

But John shook his head. "Look, I'm sorry. Never mind, all right?" He put the pictures back on top of the pile she'd found them in. "It's just…I was going to send one to a friend of mine up in New York. I think the two of them would really hit it off—she's just his type and…"

He was lying through his teeth. He was standing there and telling her some lame *lie* as if he actually thought she would accept it. But she didn't buy it, and he knew it.

He swore softly. "I can't tell you why I really need them, Mariah, but I promise you, my wanting those pictures doesn't have anything to do with you and me."

"I really don't want you to take them," Mariah said. "I'm sorry. Serena didn't know I took them, and…I don't want you to have them."

"That's all right." He nodded. "That's okay. I understand. Just…trust me, please?"

Mariah folded her arms. "You're going to be late," she said. "You better go."

But he hesitated. "I'm going to tell you everything really soon, all right?"

She tried to smile. "I'm not certain just what happened here, but sure. Whatever you want to tell me, whenever you want to tell it to me, would be nice."

"I will." John gazed at her steadily, real consternation in his eyes. "I'll tell you soon." But then he squinted out the door, up at the hazy blueness of the sky. "Damn, I don't have any sunblock with me," he said, and when he turned to look back at her, she could see a hint of that same dishonesty in his eyes. "I'm going to fry without it. Do you have anything number fifteen or higher that I could use?"

Mariah knew that if she left the room, he was going to pocket those pictures of Serena. He was going to *steal* them, even though she'd told him point-blank that she didn't want him to have them. Trust me, he'd said. Trust me.

She cleared her throat. "Yeah, it's in the bedroom—in my beach bag. I'll get it." She turned away. What could she do? Short of accusing him of theft or denying him the use of her sunblock? *Please let me be wrong.*

Miller watched Mariah walk down the hall and into her bedroom.

Quickly, he took two pictures of Serena—the profile and the best of the full-face shots—and slipped them into the back pocket of his jeans. He hated the fact he had to do it this way—to take them without Mariah's permission—but these photos would be invaluable in tracking down Serena Westford. With a photo of this quality on an APB sent to all law enforcement agencies, the FBI would actually have a chance of finding her again before she altered her appearance. It was a slim chance, but a chance just the same.

And it wasn't going to be long until this part of the

case was deemed over and done with, and he'd be able to tell Mariah everything. Surely if she knew the truth, she wouldn't deny him access to the photos.

She returned with the sunblock, and he quickly spread it across his nose and cheekbones.

He kissed her again, one last time, trying to tell her with his kiss the way she made him feel. Despite the wariness in her eyes, she kissed him warmly, sweetly.

"I'll see you later," he said. He slipped out the door and onto the porch where Princess was napping in the shade. "Come on," he said to the dog. "We've gotta run. We're already late."

He set off down the beach at an easy jog, Princess loping beside him. His legs felt weak, his body still buzzing from the pleasure he'd allowed himself to partake of only moments before.

On impulse, he turned to look back at the cottage. Mariah was standing on the deck, watching him. He waved, lifting an arm, and she waved back.

Picking up his speed, he smiled. Yes indeed, he was going to be late to this meeting with Pat Blake. When Daniel had called the second time, Blake's plane had already landed at the little airport on the mainland. His car would be pulling into the resort driveway in a matter of moments, and Miller would arrive a good five minutes after him—unshowered, unshaved and smelling distinctly like Mariah. Sweet, sexy Mariah. What a reason to be late….

Blake would nearly swallow his teeth at the sight of him—Miller couldn't remember ever attending a meeting such as this one in anything other than a dark suit and tie. But all would be forgiven the moment he produced these photographs.

Miller hoped Mariah would be as quick to forgive when he told her the truth. God, he wanted to tell her the truth soon. And maybe then she'd tell him why she was here on Garden Isle using a fake name.

*So Mariah was just a nickname. What did your parents call you?* That's what he should have asked. He should've pushed the conversation in that direction, but he'd been waylaid by her kisses. He'd been overcome by the promise of ecstasy. All rational thought had simply ceased to exist.

Damn, she drove him out of his mind.

He turned to look back once more at Mariah's house, but this time she was gone.

MARIAH WATCHED IN THE dim darkroom light as the photos she took just that morning slowly developed. She was feeling that familiar gnawing of worry and upset that she'd worked so hard to eradicate over the past few months.

Stress was making her shoulders tight and she rolled them, silently chanting her mantra: No worries. No problem.

But she was lying to herself. She *was* worried. There *was* a problem.

She was in love with a man who'd not only lied, but had stolen from her.

As she rinsed the chemicals from the paper, Jonathan Mills smiled directly up at her from the photo, his eyes warm and flashing with amusement. Mariah looked more closely at his eyes, trying to see if maybe his dishonesty had been captured through the camera's lens. She wanted to know if he'd been lying right from the start. But all she could see was warmth and life.

The pictures she'd taken in her kitchen were sharply in contrast to the shots she'd taken on the beach the day they'd met. Mariah had found that roll of film and developed it first. Those pictures now hung, drying. John's gaunt silhouette against the backdrop of a lightening sky. His profile—a face etched with pain. He looked cold and distant. But he didn't look deceptive.

She wasn't exactly sure what she was looking for— perhaps a shiftiness in the eyes. Or a glint of malice. In reality, it was probably the case that the most deceptive people gave away nothing at all. Her stomach started to hurt and she rolled her shoulders again. *No worries.*

Mariah carefully hung the more recent pictures of John next to the ones from the first roll of film. Someone glancing at them all would find it hard to believe this smiling man was the same person as in the others.

Mariah looked again into John's laughing eyes. This was the man who'd come to her for comfort as he'd finally allowed himself to grieve for his friend's death. This was the man who had made love to her so passionately. This was the man who had told her he wanted *her,* not Serena. She found it hard to believe that this was the same man who lied to her, who had actually *stolen* from her.

Mariah hadn't allowed herself to look through her piles of photos after he'd first left. And she'd hated herself for mistrusting him when she'd finally given in to the temptation. But she'd been right to mistrust him. Two pictures were missing. John had taken two of the photos of Serena even after Mariah had specifically said she didn't want him to have them.

The phone rang, and Mariah picked up the cordless extension she'd brought downstairs with her, half hoping it was John and half hoping it was not. "Hello?"

"Hey, girl, how's your back?" It was Laronda, the site coordinator from Foundations for Families.

"It doesn't hurt at all anymore," Mariah told her. "And I just got the all clear from the doctor this morning. I'm allowed to go back to work."

"God is truly watching over me," Laronda exclaimed melodramatically. "I'm in desperate need of roofers. Tropical storm Otto is heading on almost a direct path to the Washburtons' house. It wasn't supposed to rain— at least not hard—until the end of the week, and we gambled and took advantage of a local electrician who had some time off. We had the electrical work done before the roof was finished. But now the weather bureau is saying oops they made a big mistake. We're gonna get high winds *and* flooding rain. We need to get that baby sealed up tight before old Otto makes some bad voodoo by mixing water with those wires. Can you help? We're doing a blitz—round the clock from now until we're done. I'll take you for as long a shift as you can give me."

As usual, Mariah wasn't wearing a watch. "What time is it?"

"Nearly noon. Just say yes and I can have the van pick you up in fifteen minutes. Door-to-door service today."

"I'll be ready. But, Laronda—"

"Bless you, girl!"

"I have to be home by seven."

"We'll get you there."

Mariah took one last look at her pictures of John before she turned off the light and went up the basement stairs. She'd be back by seven, all right. And then she was going to get some answers.

## CHAPTER ELEVEN

MARIAH'S SLIDING GLASS door was open, the screen unlocked.

"Mariah?" Miller called.

No one answered. Nothing moved.

Miller stepped into the house and closed the screen door behind him.

Without Mariah to brighten the place up with her laughter and life, the room seemed almost shabby. Miller moved quietly to the dining-room table, intending to slip the two photographs he'd borrowed and had copied back into the pile. She'd never even know they were gone.

In theory, it worked, but in theory, Mariah hadn't checked up on him. In reality, she had. The other pictures of Serena had been separated out from the stack. She knew he'd taken two of them. He set the two in question down on the table with the others.

It didn't really matter. He'd had every intention of telling her the truth—and he could now. During his short meeting with Pat Blake, this portion of the case had been officially closed. Hanging around here and waiting for Serena to return had been deemed a waste of time and finances. Even at this moment, Daniel was back at the resort, packing up the equipment.

Miller had been helping him, determined to get the

work done and his report filed in time to meet Mariah for dinner at seven. But something Daniel had said during the meeting had started him thinking. Daniel had pointed out that in the past, Serena had always been so careful about having her picture taken. Was it possible that she knew about these pictures?

Miller knew it damn well was possible that she was on to him. She could have found the bugs in her house and correctly identified Miller as FBI. And if that was the case, she might've purposely left these pictures behind as part of some kind of weird game she was playing.

But what exactly was that game?

Had she left intending to alter her appearance so thoroughly that leaving photos behind didn't even matter? Was this possibly some kind of arrogant challenge?

Or had she truly slipped up? Had she found the microphones in her house and run scared? And after she calmed down enough, would she realize that because Mariah was a photographer it was more than likely she had pictures of Serena, taken either intentionally or unintentionally? And if that was the case, would Serena come back? And if she did come back, would Mariah then be in danger?

That thought had made Miller break out in a cold sweat, and he'd called Mariah, but she didn't pick up the phone. Thinking she might be on the beach enjoying the early-afternoon sunshine, Miller had left Daniel to deal with the equipment as he took the car and drove out to Mariah's cottage as quickly as he could.

"Mariah?" he said again, moving into the kitchen.

A jar of peanut butter was out and open on the

kitchen counter. She'd told him the first time they'd met that leaving food out in the kitchen was an invitation to disaster. Ants or enormous American cockroaches would come in almost immediately and they were nearly impossible to get rid of.

A plate with bread crumbs sat nearby—as if she'd made herself a sandwich there, then taken it with her as she'd left.

Left to go where? Her bike was leaning up against the side of the house. He'd seen it when he'd arrived. There was no sign of her in the yard or out on the beach.

Wherever she'd gone, she'd left in a hurry.

Miller made a complete circuit of the house. There were signs in the bathroom that Mariah had taken a quick shower—a wet towel had been tossed onto the floor along with the robe she'd been wearing this morning. A tube of toothpaste was open and left out on the sink. In her bedroom, the bed was unmade, the sheets still rumpled from their lovemaking.

Miller sat down on the edge of the bed, letting himself lie back among the sheets. He closed his eyes, breathing in the sweet scent of Mariah's perfume. Where had she gone in such a blessed hurry?

Even with his eyes closed, he could picture the house and all its telltale signs of a hasty exit. He was known for his ability to take the clues he'd been given and hypothesize the most likely scenario. Only this time, he didn't much care for the scenario he'd almost instantly come up with.

He had one Mariah Robinson living under an assumed name, telling him specifically that he could not have those pictures of Serena. He had Mariah go through the photos after he'd left, pulling out the shots of Serena and discovering that he had, in fact, taken two of those pictures with him. He had Mariah quickly take a shower, quickly make a sandwich and then leave the house in such a hurry that she didn't even lock the back door.

Going where? To meet Serena? To warn her that Miller had those pictures?

Miller could place Mariah—or Marie Carver, her real name—in Phoenix, Arizona, three years ago, during the time Serena had been there, too, preparing to off husband number five. The possibility that the two women had met at that time opened the door to all kinds of nasty questions, such as: Had Mariah/Marie come here to Garden Isle to act as some kind of accomplice or assistant? Was Mariah/Marie some kind of Black Widow killer-in-training?

Miller sat up. Dammit! He'd obviously been working for the FBI for too long. How could he possibly think such things about Mariah? Sweet, gentle Mariah…

He hadn't checked the basement because it was dark, but now he went down there anyway, hoping to find something that would tell him where Mariah had gone.

He'd never been inside her darkroom, and he turned on the light as he pushed open the door. It was a small room, with built-in counters lining the walls. It had a sink and shelves for chemicals and other supplies— even a small refrigerator for storing film. Different kinds of equipment were set up on the counters, including something big that looked like an enlarger.

Miller knew with just one glance that this room— combined with the beachfront property and the incredible view of the ocean—was the reason Mariah had rented this particular cottage. Dozens of places were more lavishly furnished or nicely decorated, but Mariah cared more about having a place with a darkroom.

There were photos hanging from some kind of clothesline assembly, curling slightly around the edges as they dried. Miller looked closer. The pictures were of him.

They were black-and-white photographs, but they still managed to capture the beauty of the sunrise. He and Princess were just silhouettes in many of them, but in several, Mariah had used her zoom lens, and he could clearly see his face, etched with relentless fatigue. The pictures echoed his pain.

But there, right in the middle of these pictures of his bleakly grim face, was a close-up. It was one of the pictures Mariah had taken just that morning. He was smiling at her, smiling into the camera.

Miller stared at the picture. It was him. He knew it was him. He remembered her taking the picture. He remembered smiling. But he'd never seen himself looking quite like that before. His eyes were reflecting the morning light coming in through the window and they seemed to sparkle with warmth and life. His smile was wide and sincere.

He looked nothing like a man who had been dubbed "The Robot."

And he wasn't, Miller realized. When he was with Mariah, he *wasn't* a robot. He was a real, live, flesh-and-blood man, capable of feeling—and releasing—deep emotions.

He closed his eyes, remembering the way she had held him as he'd given in and cried for Tony for the first time in two years. He remembered the strength of the emotion he'd felt as he'd held her in his arms after making love.

That man, that flesh-and-blood man would never have entertained such doubts about Mariah. It was only "The Robot" who could think that way—mistrusting everyone.

God, he wanted Mariah to come back. He wanted her to transform him once again into that real man. He despised himself for being this way, for having all these doubts about her.

With one last look back at Mariah's photographs, Miller turned off the darkroom light and went upstairs. As he locked the back door, he heard the crunch of tires in the gravel driveway and turned to look out the front window, hoping it was Mariah.

It wasn't.

It was *Serena's* car pulling into the driveway. It was Serena. My God, she'd come back. Miller's heart nearly stopped. Then it kicked back in, beating double time with a vengeance.

As he watched, she parked next to his car and got out. She didn't seem perturbed by the fact that his car was there—she knew he and Mariah were friends. And Miller knew from the time he'd spent with her that Serena had complete confidence in her sexual allure. Miller had no doubt that Serena didn't view Maria as any kind of a rival.

He moved to the front door, intending to step outside when Serena rang the bell. But she didn't ring, she just opened the screen and came in.

"Mariah's not here," he told her. "I stopped by to see how she was doing. The back door was unlocked, and—"

Serena kissed him. It was a kiss meant to curl his hair, to thoroughly numb him, to drop him—dizzy with passion and desire—to his knees.

Instead, Miller had to fight to hide his revulsion. She'd caught him off guard, that much was true. He kept close track of her hands, suddenly keenly aware that this woman might very well have killed at least seven times by forcing a knife blade into her husbands' hearts. It was true that he was not her husband, but it was possible she knew he was FBI. Although if she *did* know that, this was one hell of a dangerous game she was playing by returning to Garden Isle.

"Did you miss me?" she murmured.

"Absolutely," he lied.

As quickly as she'd started kissing him, she broke away, making a quick circuit around the room, stopping to look at the photos on the dining-room table. She picked up one of the pictures of herself.

"Oh, good," she said. "Mariah must've set these aside to give to me. I'd asked her about them last week. She's a remarkable photographer, isn't she? I mean, for an amateur."

"Yeah," he said. "She's pretty good."

"For an amateur," Serena repeated.

As Miller watched, she slipped all four of the pictures into her purse.

"So where did our little Mariah—or should I say *big* Mariah—go off to?" Serena mused. "Her tool belt's not by the door. I'll wager she's off trying to save the world, one family at a time."

Miller couldn't believe it. For all his highly touted skills as one of the FBI's top agents, he hadn't thought to check and see if Mariah's tool belt was missing. Sure enough. Her belt and her backpack were both gone.

"I've never been down this hall past the loo," Serena said, disappearing down the hallway that led to Mariah's bedroom. "What's down here? Her bedroom probably."

Miller followed her. "Serena, don't go back there."

"Why not?"

"Because you're invading Mariah's privacy."

"She left the door unlocked, didn't she?" Serena said almost gaily, sitting down on Mariah's unmade bed, surveying the small bedroom. "I don't know why she lives in a little dumpy place like this. She has plenty of money, you know."

Miller stood in the doorway. "We should leave."

He would've had to be a fool not to catch the meaning of the glint in her eyes. She was coming on to him. She was attempting to seduce him right there in Mariah's room, on Mariah's bed.

"I suppose we could go to your place." Serena leaned back on both elbows as she gazed up at him. "But I confess I like it here. Think of the excitement from knowing that Mariah could come home any moment and find us here together."

God, the thought made him sick, but he couldn't deny that this was what he'd wanted for so long. He'd wanted an opportunity to be in a position where it would seem natural for him to propose marriage to this woman.

But he hadn't wanted to do it like this.

Not here in this room where he'd discovered such pleasures with Mariah.

But he couldn't take Serena back to his room at the

resort where Daniel was packing up crates of electronic equipment. They'd brought the gear into the resort in inconspicuous suitcases, but there had been no need to leave with it that way, so most of it was clearly labeled with its destination, Quantico—FBI headquarters—in big black, official-looking letters.

"Why don't we take a walk on the beach?" Miller suggested.

"In these shoes?" Serena reached for his hand, tugging him down so that he was sitting next to her on the bed.

Mariah's bed.

It took everything Miller had in him not to stand up, not to pull away. Apprehending Serena was his job. Catching a killer was never fun. He didn't have to like it, he just had to do it.

He tried to convince himself that he wasn't betraying Mariah as he let Serena push him back onto the bed. He tried not to think about what Mariah would assume if she came home to find him here with Serena, entangled in an embrace in the very bed in which he'd made love to Mariah just mere hours earlier.

This wasn't real. He felt distant, removed both physically and emotionally from this woman who was kissing him so passionately. That distance worried him—surely she'd be able to tell that she left him feeling cold. Surely she'd realize that he wanted to kiss her about as much as he wanted to kiss Daniel. Less.

He'd made one hell of a mistake in assuming that Serena had gone for good. He'd messed things up royally. He'd made love to Mariah this morning, and this afternoon he was going to propose marriage to Serena.

Serena ground herself against him, and, suddenly

giddy, Miller knew the truth. He didn't want to do this. But what was he supposed to do? Was he supposed to tell both Daniel Tonaka and Patrick Blake that he was taking himself off the case? How could he do that after coming this far? The setup had worked after all—he had the suspect exactly where he wanted her.

Or maybe she had *him* right where she wanted him.

Daniel was sure to understand and forgive him. But Blake wouldn't. Not after getting to this point. Blake would send him in for that psych evaluation, assuming that Miller had finally snapped. The unit shrink was sure to find him crazy—crazy in love with Mariah.

Miller was just about to push Serena off him when she spoke.

"Please," she said, kissing his face and his neck as she sat straddling him, her head bent over him, her golden hair finding its way into his mouth. "Please, John. I know that you want me, darling, but please, can't we wait to do this until after we're married?"

Miller was astonished. He nearly laughed aloud. *She* was on top of him. She was the seductress, yet her words sounded as if she were an innocent being seduced. She was overpowering, yet she was presenting him with the illusion of being the powerful one. The approach must've worked well for her in the past. He'd never once—in any of their conversations—mentioned marriage, yet she spoke of it as if they'd been discussing it for weeks.

He spit her hair out of his mouth.

"Please, darling," Serena whispered. "We can fly to Las Vegas—be married by tonight."

It was too easy. He couldn't turn her down. He'd been after her for too long.

Still, he hesitated. Mariah would be devastated.

Yet to turn Serena down meant that when the photos of her next victim—and there was sure to be a next victim—crossed Miller's desk, he would know he could have prevented that death. And the next one, and the next one. He would know that he could have stopped her. And he wouldn't be able to bear that. He wouldn't be able to handle having failed. He *could* stop her, right now, right here.

"I'll charter a flight," Miller said to Serena.

He didn't want to do it, but he didn't have a choice.

# CHAPTER TWELVE

MARIAH COULD HEAR THE phone ringing and she took the stairs up to the deck two at a time.

Maybe it was John. Maybe he was finally calling to tell her why he'd left a message canceling last night's dinner plans.

His insomnia was contagious. She'd spent most of last night tossing and turning—sometimes feeling hurt, sometimes concerned, sometimes terrified that she'd been played for a fool.

She scooped up the phone, praying she'd reached it before the answering machine kicked on. "Hello?" she said breathlessly.

"Oh, good. You *are* there." It was Serena. "Can you come over and see my new place?"

Mariah cursed silently. "Now's not a really good time because I've—"

"I've rented that house right up the hill from you," Serena told her.

"The big one?"

"I suppose compared to *your* place, it might be considered big—"

"Serena, that house is a palace. You've wanted to live there since you first came to the island. How on earth did you manage to arrange to move in there?"

Serena lowered her voice. "Oh, I've only got it for a

short time. There was a week-and-a-half block in between renters. It's expensive, but considering that this is my honeymoon—"

"Your *what?*"

"I flew out to Vegas last night and got married," Serena said with a silvery laugh. "It was rather unexpected."

Married. Serena was married. Who did she know well enough to marry? Not Jonathan Mills? Dear God, had she gone and married John? Mariah felt a flash of disbelieving heat followed quickly by a blast of cold fear. "Who's the lucky man?" she managed to ask, somehow sounding casually nonchalant.

Serena just laughed again. "That's my surprise. I want you to come over and meet him."

Serena's new husband couldn't possibly be John. He wouldn't do that to her. Mariah refused to believe that he was capable of such a thing. He'd told her he wanted *her,* not Serena. He'd promised her he wouldn't sleep with Serena. Of course, she hadn't made him promise that he wouldn't *marry* Serena....

"Serena, just tell me who he is."

"If you ride your bike, it'll take you even less than three minutes to get up here," Serena said, laughter bubbling in her voice. "See you in a few."

Mariah stared at the telephone receiver, listening to the buzz of the disconnected line. With a curse, she hung up the phone.

She was going to have to go up there.

Not to please Serena, who clearly wanted to show off the house, but to put her own mind at ease.

She'd go up there, see for herself that the man Serena

had married wasn't John. She'd see for herself that he was probably some older man with the ability to write million-dollar checks without blinking.

This was good, Mariah told herself as she tied the laces of her sneakers and went out to where her bike was leaning against the side of her house. With Serena safely married, Mariah wouldn't have to worry about the blonde actively competing for John's time and attention.

Provided, of course, he came back from wherever he'd gone. And provided he came equipped with a good explanation as to why he'd stolen those photographs.

"WHAT ARE YOU LOOKING at?"

Miller turned to see Serena standing in the door to the elegantly high-ceilinged formal dining room. "Just…checking out the view from the windows."

She pointed through the treetops. "Look. There's the roof of Mariah's little cottage."

Miller nodded. He knew. That's what he'd been looking at.

He hadn't planned on living quite so close to Mariah. But Serena had rented this monstrously huge example of modern architecture on the morning before they were married and had insisted they return here for their "honeymoon."

He'd intended for them to stay in Nevada. He'd planned to call Mariah from a pay phone in one of the casinos to tell her that he was sorry, but he'd been pulled out of town on business—he wouldn't be back for a few weeks. He'd hoped Mariah would never have to find out about his charade of a marriage to Serena.

But…Serena hated Vegas.

And when he'd offered to take her on a honeymoon anywhere, *any*where in the world, she chose Garden Isle. She was adamant about returning there, and although Miller had put up a good fight, he'd eventually had to give in for fear she'd become suspicious.

That, of course, was assuming she wasn't suspicious of him in the first place.

"I love this room," Serena said, circling the banquet-sized table. "We ought to throw a dinner party."

"Sounds good to me."

She stepped closer to him and slipped her arms around his waist, embracing him from behind. "Or maybe we should just have our own *private* dinner party."

He tried to sound sincere. "That sounds even better." Miller gently pulled free from her arms. "Look, Serena, I called my doctor this morning," he told her. "He said it could be a few months before I'm…back to normal." He cleared his throat tactfully. "You know…"

He'd told her last night—their wedding night—that he was still suffering from the side effects of the chemotherapy he'd recently undergone. He'd informed her that one of those side effects was impotence. He'd told her it was a temporary condition, and he'd apologized for not telling her sooner.

She'd offered to see what she could do to arouse him, but he'd quickly made up some story about how he'd been advised not even to try since trying and failing could cycle into a more permanent psychological problem.

She hadn't been too upset.

They'd spent the night watching old movies on one of those classic-movie cable channels. Miller had stayed awake even when Serena had dozed off. He didn't much like the idea of waking up with a cold blade of steel in his chest. Or not waking up at all.

He'd slept some on the plane back east, knowing that Daniel was awake and watching out for him.

"I've decided what I want for a wedding gift," Serena told him.

"You have?" This time, he encircled her in his arms, brushing his lips against her forehead. Her perfume was too strong, too floral, too cloying. He forced himself to smile down at her.

"Yes," she said. "This house. It's on the market, you know."

This was good. This was very good. According to her pattern, she would ask him for a check or a transfer of funds into her private account. She would tell him that part of the gift would be the thrill of making the purchase herself from the money he had given her.

"I'll call the broker first thing tomorrow," Miller said.

She pulled back slightly. "You know what I would really love?"

"Something more than this house?"

She laughed. "No. But I'd like to negotiate this deal myself. I'd love to be able to write a check for a substantial deposit from my own account."

Miller kissed her again, as condescendingly as possible. "If that would make you happy, I'll simply transfer enough money into your checking account."

She kissed him again.

"Oh, my God!"

There was a clatter in the doorway, and Miller looked up from Serena's lips and found himself gazing directly into Mariah's horrified eyes.

Her bike helmet spun on the hardwood floor where she'd dropped it.

"Oh, hello," Serena said. "Funny, I didn't hear the bell."

"There was note on the door saying to come in," Mariah said, her eyes never leaving Miller's. Somehow she managed to sound completely calm.

"Isn't this the most exciting surprise ever?" Serena enthused, taking Miller's hand and pulling him toward Mariah. "Introducing Mr. and Mrs. Jonathan Mills. Can you believe it?"

"No." Mariah shook her head. "No, I can't, actually." She laughed, and as Miller watched, the sheer hurt in her eyes turned to scorn. "Or, God—maybe I can. Maybe the sad thing is that I *can* believe it. Excuse me, I have to go."

She scooped her helmet up off the floor and headed for the stairs.

Serena followed her. "Mariah, don't you want to see the house?"

"No," Mariah said, her voice echoing in the three-story entryway. "No, Serena, I don't want to see your house. I'm very happy for you. Just be aware of the fact that your husband doesn't think twice about breaking his promises, and you'll be fine."

"What is *that* supposed to mean?" Serena asked plaintively.

Miller opened the sliders that led to the small deck outside the dining room. There were stairs that led down and connected to the master bedroom's deck, and more stairs that went to the ground. He quickly went down them, intercepting Mariah just as she reached her bicycle.

"I don't have anything to say to you," she said tightly.

He held the handlebars of her bicycle to keep her from moving. "Yeah, well, I have something to say to you."

She threw her helmet onto the ground in anger. "Oh, yeah? Like what? What could you possibly have to say to me?"

"Mariah, I can't tell you what this is all about, but please, just trust me, okay? You *have* to trust me—"

She tried to jerk her bike away from him. "I don't have to do *any*thing—and the last thing I'm ever going to do again is *trust* you. You son of a bitch!"

Miller held tightly to her bike, talking fast and low. "Mariah, listen to me. Go away. Leave the island. Go to New York, or I don't know, back to Phoenix—it doesn't matter where you go. Just stay away from here for a week or two—"

She interrupted him with a terse phrase that instructed him to do the anatomically impossible as she wrenched her bike away from him. But she paused, looking back at him, heartbreaking hurt in her eyes. "To think I actually wasted my love on you," she whispered.

Miller watched her ride away, clenching his teeth to keep from calling out after her.

He turned back to the house, catching a flutter of movement out of the corner of his eye. Gazing up at the dining-room deck, he had to wonder. Had Serena been up there, watching them? And if so, what exactly had she seen?

THIS WAS GOING TO BE FUN. More fun than she'd imagined.

There was something between them. Something strong. From the level of her upset, it seemed pretty obvious that he'd done It to her. Silly cow. Didn't she know men were pigs?

She deserved to die—to melt along with all of those stupid pictures she shot, day after day.

And he... She was going to make him watch before she separated his ugly soul from his even uglier body.

Yes, this *was* going to be fun.


MARIAH STOOD IN THE BASEMENT, smashing dishes against the wall.

Maybe this would help. Each plate she threw was an outlet for her anger and hurt. Each plate she threw was accompanied by a bloodcurdling scream of rage.

Her voice was hoarse and her throwing arm was sore, but she kept at it, hoping, *praying* that eventually this raw wound where her heart used to be would begin to scab over.

She'd fallen off her bike on her way down the hill and scraped one elbow and both knees. But she hadn't cried. She *refused* to cry.

She cleaned up her scrapes in the bathroom, then took her suitcases down from the bedroom closet. She packed most of her clothes before she found herself here, breaking plates.

John had broken his promise.

Clearly, when he'd made it, that promise had meant nothing to him. *She* had meant nothing to him. He'd no doubt made love to her—no, not made love, had sex. It had been nothing more than sex, with the intention of never seeing her again. He'd probably already made his wedding plans with Serena.

Another piece of china hit the wall, shattering into a thousand pieces, just the way her heart had been broken.

And Mariah couldn't hold back her tears any longer. She crumpled onto the basement floor and cried.

"CAN YOU HEAR ME?" Miller said into the flower vase, making an adjustment to the miniature receiver he wore in his right ear.

"Roger," Daniel said from his position about a quarter mile to the south of the house. "Let's check those babies in the dining room once more before we move on into the bedroom."

Miller went into the elegant dining room where he'd planted a number of nearly invisible microphones underneath the huge table, along the sideboard, on several of the chairs and on the edges of one or two picture frames.

He stood in the center of the room. "Do you have me?"

"Loud and clear," came Daniel's reply. "Hang on a sec. Just let me fine tune this puppy... Got it."

The surveillance device in Daniel's car had been designed to look like nothing more than an intricate and expensive car stereo system. It was incredibly complicated to program—Miller was glad Daniel was the one doing it. He preferred the straightforward equipment that came inside the tinted glass of a surveillance van.

He wouldn't be able to wear his in-ear receiver tonight. Not as long as there was a possibility that Serena might find it.

"You know, I'm going to be fine here tonight. You could do this surveillance in comfort from the resort. She's not going to try anything until my bank transfers that money into her account," Miller told his partner.

"Yeah, I know," Daniel said. "I'd just feel better being close—at least for now. There's something in the air that's making my hair stand on end."

"Storm's coming," Miller said, moving to look out the window at the ocean.

A bank of dark clouds was gathering on the horizon. The late-afternoon sun was still shining, but the air was heavy with humidity and hard to breathe.

"Yeah, maybe that's it," Daniel said. "Whatever the case, I'll be out here, mainlining coffee and listening to every word you say. So don't say or do anything you don't want me to hear."

*That* wasn't going to be a problem. Miller found himself gazing down at the roof of Mariah's house. Was she in there right now, tearing all her pictures of him into tiny shreds? Was she in her bedroom, packing up her clothes and her CDs and her funny little speaker that made such realistic-sounding water noises? *Imagine yourself in a special place...*

"Any sign of Mrs. Mills?" Daniel asked.

Miller snapped himself back to the present, listening hard for any signs of movement in the house. When Serena had announced that she was taking a walk on the beach, he'd begged off. He claimed fatigue, but in fact wanted to use the opportunity to plant and test the surveillance system. He'd managed to get quite a number of the nearly invisible mikes placed while she was there in the house, but it was much easier doing it

SUZANNE BROCKMANN     227

this way. He looked at his watch. Serena had left fifteen minutes ago. It was entirely possible that she was on her way back.

"I, um, haven't exactly been keeping track," he admitted.

There was a long silence from Daniel's end of the line. "John, I need you here one hundred percent," he finally said. "If you can't do that—"

Miller cleared his throat. "Look, Daniel, *I* need you to run over to Mariah's and encourage her to leave the island. Can you do that for me?"

"I'm a step ahead of you," Daniel told him. "I tapped into the phone lines and I've been monitoring her outgoing calls. It occurred to me that she might be in a position to jeopardize your cover if she decided to share with Serena the fact that you and she spent the night together on the eve of your wedding." He paused. "I may be assuming too much here, but I know that you like this lady an awful lot. That and your lateness to the meeting with Blake clued me in to the fact that you and she—"

"What's your point?"

"The fact is, she *is* leaving. I heard her call for a taxi for this evening. For seven o'clock. She asked for a cab with plenty of trunk room. She told the dispatcher she had quite a bit of luggage."

"Thank God." Miller closed his eyes in relief. Mariah was leaving the island. He could stop worrying about her safety. He knew it was highly unlikely that Serena would hurt anyone other than her targeted victim. Still, he would breathe easier with Mariah off the island.

He would stop worrying about her, but he wouldn't stop thinking about her—and wondering if the truth would be enough to make up for the heartbreak.

## CHAPTER THIRTEEN

LIGHTNING FORKED ACROSS the sky, thunder boomed and the power flickered and went out.

Mariah swore like a sailor, bumping her shins on her suitcases as she felt her way into the kitchen where she knew there was a candle over near the toaster.

The matches were a little bit harder to locate, and with the candle held tightly in one hand, she felt along the counter with the other. She found the book of matches on the windowsill and lit the candle.

It had been burned down pretty far. Mariah estimated she had only about an hour or two of wax left at most. After that, it was going to be very, very dark in here.

But the kitchen clock was stopped at 5:37. With luck, her cab would arrive before the candle burned completely down.

She took the softly glowing light back downstairs into her darkroom. That was the last of the rooms she had left to pack. Her clothes were all ready to go, and she was going to leave what was left of her food behind for the cleaning lady.

She gazed around the darkroom at all of her photographic supplies—at the pictures of John, long since dried.

Tears filled her eyes, and she shook her head in disgust. She'd thought she'd already cried herself dry. She had, she tried to convince herself. These tears were just leftovers—kind of like an earthquake's aftershocks.

She'd cried, she'd gotten it out of her system and she was okay now. So she'd made a bad call. She'd guessed wrong, misjudged someone. Life was going to go on.

She could hear the rain pelting against the roof. Mariah thought about the Washburtons' house. She thought about the way she'd worked on that roof all yesterday afternoon, along with nearly two dozen other volunteers. They'd all worked in perfect cooperation, their common goal to get the job done and done well.

If she left Garden Isle, she wouldn't be able to see the completion of that house. She wouldn't go to the house-warming, wouldn't watch Frank and Loretta Washburton's eyes fill with joy and pride as they welcomed friends and Triple F workers into their home.

If she left, she would be leaving behind the friends she made, the work team she'd come to know so well. Laronda. There couldn't possibly be another site coordinator as cool as Laronda.

If she left Garden Isle, if she let herself be pushed out, chased away from her great-great-grandmother's childhood home, she'd never forgive herself.

Why should *she* be the one who was forced to leave? If Jonathan Mills was uncomfortable living two doors away from her, let *him* be the one to move.

Hell, she had the rent on this cottage paid through to the end of the month.

Thunder boomed, and she knew she was only kidding herself. What was she going to do? March up to John and Serena's house, interrupt their honeymoon and demand that they leave?

No, she couldn't do that, but she could just stay here, quietly keeping to herself-and feeling like crap every time John or Serena's car drove past, praying that she wouldn't run into them in the supermarket, dreading seeing them together on the beach, knowing that she still wanted him.

She still wanted him.

Jonathan Mills was a son of a bitch. The fact that he was confused, that he was tormented by painful nightmares, that he was stressed out from the strain of dealing with a potentially terminal illness—none of that gave him the right to make love to her one night and then marry Serena the next.

Yet she still ached for his touch.

She was a fool.

With a sigh, Mariah began packing up her darkroom equipment by candlelight, deciding what she had to take and what could be left behind.

Yes, she could refuse to leave the island. But as much as she hated the thought of slinking away, beaten down and defeated, she wasn't into self-torture.

She tossed the photos of Jonathan Mills into the trash can. Those could definitely be left behind.

"Wow, THIS IS FANCY." MILLER stepped into the candlelit dining room.

Serena had cooked a gourmet meal and set one end of the heavy wooden table with elegant china place settings, a myriad of wineglasses and what looked to be the entire silverware drawer. There were salad forks, shrimp cocktail forks, dinner forks, dessert forks.

Miller had to wonder—was she actually planning to

serve dessert tonight, or did she have something a little more macabre up her sleeve?

Actually, she wasn't wearing any sleeves. The dress she wore was black and sleeveless, timelessly chic, complete with an innocent-looking string of pearls around her neck.

"Fortunately, we have a gas stove," she told him as she opened a decanter of wine and poured them each a glass. "Or we'd be sending out to McDonald's for double cheeseburgers." She smiled at him. "And *that* wouldn't have done at all. I wanted this meal to be… special."

Special. The Black Widow's M.O.—*her* M.O.—was to serve her husband an elegant gourmet meal, drug him so that he couldn't fight back, then stab him in the heart shortly after the main course.

His nerves were strung much too tightly. Miller was as certain as he could possibly be that, just as he'd reassured Daniel that afternoon, Serena wasn't going to try to kill him tonight. It was too soon. She would wait until she had his money in hand—to do otherwise would be outside of her pattern, outside of her rules. And serial killers of this type rarely strayed from their set of rules.

"You should have told me we were going to have a formal meal," Miller said for Daniel's benefit. "I would have dressed for dinner."

Serena handed him one of the two wineglasses. "Let's have a toast, shall we?"

Right then and there, Miller knew he'd been dead wrong. She'd poured him a glass of red wine, but it smelled much too sweet and the liquid in the glass was much too thick. Opium. She was trying to drug him by putting opium in the wine. Right now. Tonight. Without having received a penny from him, she was preparing to kill him.

"I don't feel very much like red wine tonight," he said, setting the glass down on the dinner table.

Serena smiled at him. "Let's not be cute," she said. When she put her own glass down, he realized she was holding a gun. The rules were all changing, and changing fast.

"Is that a gun?" he said.

She laughed. "Yes, it's a gun," she told him. She raised her voice slightly. "Did you hear that, Daniel? Or, oh my. Maybe you're not listening. Maybe you're not *able* to listen. Maybe someone smarter than you *and* your partner waited until the call of nature pulled you out of that car you've been sitting in. Maybe someone much smarter sweetened that coffee you've been drinking to stay alert all night long—sweetened it with more than sugar. Maybe you're leaning against the steering wheel right now, drooling, about to slide into a narcotic coma. Eventually you'll just stop breathing, poor thing. What a shame to die so young…."

Miller took a step toward her and she lifted the gun, aiming directly for his head. "Sit down at the table," she ordered. "And keep your hands where I can see them."

He slowly sat down. Sitting down was good. It put his hands that much closer to the gun he had hidden in his boot.

"Hands on the table," she warned.

If she would only get close enough, if she would stop aiming directly at his head, he might have a chance to go for his gun. But she was carefully keeping her distance. Her aim seemed sure, her hands steady. Outside the windows, lightning flashed and thunder roared, but she seem oblivious, almost inhuman in her concentration.

But she may have finally met her match because there was no way in hell he was going to let Daniel die. No *way*.

"Drink the wine," she ordered him.

"No."

"Funny, I don't believe I phrased that as a yes or no question."

"I'm not drinking it."

She closed one eye as she aimed her gun and fired.

The slap of the bullet going into his arm nearly knocked Miller out of the chair. She *shot* him. He didn't let his disbelief get in his way as he went with the force of the bullet, pushing back his chair and landing on the floor, hoping to get a chance to grab that gun from his boot. But the chance never came as Serena moved around the table, aiming her gun at his head. He swore sharply as pain from his wounded arm rocketed through him.

"Get up." From somewhere, she'd procured a pair of regulation handcuffs. "Sit down. Put your hands behind you."

Miller sat back in another chair, aware of blood streaming down his left arm, aware of the teeth-clenching pain, aware of Serena's gun aimed, once again, directly at his head. He no longer had any doubts that she would use it. And once one of those bullets smashed into his brain, he'd be of absolutely no help to Daniel or anyone else.

Mariah. He closed his eyes briefly, praying that she was safe. She was due to be picked up at seven by a taxi that would take her off the island. He wasn't certain what time it was, but he knew it was close to seven. Please, God, let her be long gone....

He felt Serena cuff one of his wrists, felt her weave the metal through the heavy wooden back of the chair and then cuff his other wrist.

And then he felt her tug slightly at the hair growing at the nape of his neck. She was cutting a lock—probably as some kind of sick keepsake. A souvenir. She probably had an entire collection of hair, and once he found it, it was going to be the evidence he needed to tie her to *all* of the murders.

"I'm not going to let you keep that," he told her.

She just laughed. "Are you sure you don't want that wine?" she asked. "It works as a painkiller, you know." She sat on the table, her gun in her lap, but too far away for him even to consider going for her.

"I can't drink it by myself," he told her, willing her to get closer, to try to force-feed him that wine.

But she laughed again. "You don't really think I'm going to let you spit it in my face, do you?" she scolded him. "This is a designer dress. No, I think we'll do this another way."

She set the gun down on the table as she lifted one of the domed plate warmers. Instead of a roasted chicken, there was only a syringe lying there beside the parsley garnish.

"Morphine," she told him. "It'll make your arm feel all better in, oh, about five minutes." She moved behind him, and he felt the cold steel barrel of her gun pressed tightly against the base of his head. "If you as much as move," she warned, "I'll shoot you."

He felt her tug at his shirt, felt the sharp stab of the

needle into his back. Dammit, he hadn't had a very good look at that syringe. He had no idea how much she'd given him. He suspected it would be enough to paralyze, but not enough to kill. She would want the pleasure of skewering him with her sharp little knife.

"You'll have to forgive me for not disinfecting the area of injection," she told him. "But I think that stray germs are the least of your problems."

Miller watched her walk around to the other side of the table. Backlit by the stormy sky, she looked entirely in her element.

Five minutes, she said. In five minutes, he'd be stupid and drooling, just like all her other husbands had been. Or maybe he wouldn't be. Maybe he could hold on, fight the dizzying effects of the drug. Maybe he could make her believe he was weak and vulnerable. Maybe then she'd get close enough. Maybe she would let down her guard and he could overpower her....

"Oh, by the way, I have a little surprise for you," she said. "I want to tell you about it before the morphine starts working. It won't be as much fun to tell you if you don't really understand what's happening." She paused. "Are you listening?"

"I'm listening."

Serena smiled. "I put a bomb in Mariah's basement. All those pesky photographs that she had—I got her negatives out of storage and realized she'd been lying to me. She'd taken quite a number of pictures of me without my knowing it. I put the negatives next to some extremely flammable chemicals in her darkroom. This way, they all go up in flames—photos, negatives...and photographer, too."

Miller felt the cold fingers of death clutching at his heart. Mariah... "No."

"Don't worry, darling, the morphine I've given you will ease the sting." Serena looked at her watch. "The timer's set for six-thirty. That's in another six minutes. From where you're sitting, you'll have an excellent view of the fire. Of course, by then you probably won't care."

"Serena! God!" Miller's voice sounded harsh to his own ears. "Mariah doesn't know anything, I swear to you. Don't bring her into this."

"Too late."

"No, it's not. Call her. Call her and tell her to get out of the house. All you really want is to destroy those photos. You don't need to kill her!"

"My, my, my. You *do* care, don't you? You should have thought of that *before* you came after me. *Before* you listened in on me and stalked me like some kind of wild animal."

Her fingers tightened on the trigger of the gun and Miller nearly stopped breathing. Please, God, don't let her kill him now. Not yet. Not while there was still a chance that he could talk her into saving Mariah.

Her face was taut with anger. "Did you really think you could outsmart me? Did you really think I wouldn't notice that my house was *infested* with hidden microphones—just like the ones you hid here!"

"Mariah had nothing to do with that. Call her. Tell her to get out of there. Serena, she was your *friend*."

Something shifted in Serena's face. "Four minutes," she said. "And I can't call her. The phone lines went down when the power went off." She smiled. "Come on, John. I want to hear you scream."

Miller could feel a vein throbbing in his neck. It was

an odd sensation, countered by a feeling of floating, of drowsiness, of numbness. God help him, the drug was kicking in.

God, this was his worst nightmare happening all over again. Except this time, it wasn't Tony in a warehouse he wasn't going to be able to save. This time, it was Mariah, in a cottage where a killer had planted a bomb. This time he wouldn't hear her die. Instead, he'd see the flames that were devouring her. He'd see them over the tops of the trees.

Rage blinded him, and he used it to fight the unbalancing effect of the drug as he strained at his handcuffs, praying Serena would step just a little bit closer....

THAT WAS FUNNY. MARIAH couldn't remember putting that box down here, next to her supply of chemicals. The box had B&W Photo Lab's familiar logo on the side, and she pulled it off the shelf and opened it, holding the candle up to illuminate what was inside.

Negatives. The box was filled with dozens of plastic sleeves that held her negatives. That was weird. She'd been storing these over at the photo lab on the mainland. How on earth had they found their way back here? Who could have put the box on this lower shelf, where in the darkness she probably wouldn't have noticed it even with the power working and the overhead light turned on and...

She held the candle up again and looked deeper into the darkness of the bottom shelf. What the heck...?

She looked closer, then started backing away.

Whatever was in there, it looked a *hell* of a lot like a bomb. Not that she'd ever seen a bomb before—not up close and personal like this. But it looked like the bombs she'd seen in movies—some kind of sticks of explosive tied together, hooked into an alarm clock that was ticking quietly....

Mariah grabbed her candle and ran. She ran up the basement stairs, through the living room and out into the pouring rain. The candle went out the moment she burst through her front door, and she threw it down onto the lawn. She grabbed her bike from the side of the house and jumped on it, pedaling furiously down the driveway, taking a left to head toward town, toward the police station, toward somebody, *any*body who might have some sort of idea why there was a *bomb* in her basement.

The rain soaked her almost instantly, and the wind ripped at her hair and tore at her clothes. She had to squint hard, to squeeze her eyes nearly shut to see through the driving rain, but still she pedaled standing up, muscles straining.

Somebody wanted to kill her. Somebody wanted to *kill* her.

She hadn't gone more than a tenth of a mile before she saw car headlights up ahead. They weren't coming toward her, but rather, they were motionless, the light pointing crazily into the heavy underbrush that grew along the side of the road. As she drew closer, Mariah could see that the car had skidded off the road and slammed into a tree.

There was no way she was going to stop. Someone had planted a *bomb* in her basement. Someone wanted her dead, and she wasn't going to stop until she reached the safety of the police station downtown.

She would have gone past with a silent apology and a promise to herself to tell the police about the accident right away when she recognized the car. It was *Daniel's* car. And God, that was Daniel, still in the front seat, slumped over the steering wheel.

Cursing, she braked to a stop and dropped her bike along the side of the road. She cursed louder still at the sting of the branches that whipped against her legs in the wind. She moved as quickly as she could through the sodden underbrush, and bracing herself for the worst, she jerked open the driver's-side door of the car.

It looked as if the air bag had been inflated, and Daniel had somehow deflated it again. But he was resting his head against the steering wheel as if he had some kind of injury. Or as if he were drunk.

The radio was on—some kind of a talk show or a dramatized broadcast—a man and a woman were talking. And what looked to be close to half a dozen large thermoses of coffee littered the floor, along with an empty doughnut shop bag.

Mariah felt Daniel's neck for a pulse. It seemed uncommonly slow. But there was no sign of blood, no sign of any kind of injury. She touched the side of his face. "Daniel?" God, he *was* drunk. She smacked him lightly, then a little bit harder. "Daniel, wake up!"

He roused slightly. "Mariah!" he said. "Gotta warn you! A bomb!"

Mariah pulled back, aghast. "What did you say?"

"FBI," he mumbled. "Me an' John. Tracking a killer. Gonna blow up Mariah."

"Who's FBI?" Mariah was shocked. "*You're* FBI? You and…" John?

"Gotta save John, too." Daniel was fighting to stay awake, but it was clearly a losing battle.

"What's wrong with you?" Mariah shook him, feeling a flare of disbelief, of unreality. This couldn't be real, it couldn't be happening. "Are you drunk? What are you saying to me?"

"Somethin' in the coffee," Daniel breathed. "Gotta get help, gotta save John."

"Where is John?" Mariah asked, suddenly terribly, horribly afraid. Daniel's eyes were closed and she shook him again. *"Dammit, where's John?"*

But he didn't answer.

Something in the coffee. Someone had put something in his coffee—and a bomb in her basement.

Soaked to the skin and sobbing with frustration, Mariah used all her strength to push Daniel over into the passenger seat. She climbed in behind the steering wheel and tried to start the car. *Get help.* Unable to drive from the effects of whatever the hell had been put in his coffee, Daniel had crashed his car as he'd tried to go get help. Or maybe not to get help. Maybe to warn her. Maybe he was coming to warn her about the bomb.

Although how would he have known?

She turned the key in the ignition and the engine almost turned over. Almost. She tried again, but this time it only wheezed and died.

She tried again, but there was only silence. Silence, and those infernal radio talk show hosts talking and talking and talking and…

"Less than a minute now," the woman's voice was saying. "Thirty seconds and Mariah and her stupid photographs will be nothing more than a smudge of smoke in the sky."

"I'm going to kill you," the man's voice said. His speech was slightly slurred, slightly slow, slightly shaking with rage, but the voice was unmistakable. It was

John. "I'm going to break free from this chair, and I'm going to kill you."

And the woman's voice was Serena's.

Mariah couldn't breathe.

"Twenty seconds," Serena said. "Shall we count down together?"

"No!" John said. "No!" It was a howl of rage and pain nearly identical to the cry Mariah had heard the night he'd had a nightmare when he'd slept on her couch.

"Ten," Serena said. "Nine, eight, seven, six, five, four, three, two, one—"

The explosion rocked the car as flaming bits of shingles and wood rained down around them, extinguished almost instantly by the deluge. Mariah looked back up the road. Where her cottage had been was roaring flames—the fire too big and too hot to be put out by the rain.

"Oh, my God," she breathed.

Over the radio, she could hear John, his voice little more than a keening cry. "No," he said over and over again. "No!"

"Oh, please," Serena scoffed. "I know the morphine tends to make one overly emotional, but show a little backbone, won't you? I would've expected more from someone sent to catch *me*."

Mariah's heart was in her throat. John thought she was dead.

"I'm not dead," she said aloud, but, of course, he couldn't hear her.

"Mariah..." he whispered. "Oh, God, Mariah..."

"You really expect me to believe you cared that much about that great, huge *cow* of a woman?"

"You *bitch*," Mariah exclaimed. "I am *not* a cow!"

"You can stop the act," Serena continued. "I know what you're trying to do. You're trying to make me think that you're thoroughly anesthetized—totally helpless. You want me to come close enough so that you can try for me. What are you planning to do with your arms bound behind your back, John? Snap my neck with your legs?"

"Mariah..." he breathed. "No..."

John's arms were somehow tied. Serena had somehow managed to overpower him and tie him up. She'd given him morphine, too. That's what was making John's speech sound so slurred. Maybe Serena had put something similar in Daniel's coffee.

"I think I'll wait another few minutes or so before I get too close," Serena said. "I don't care to have my neck snapped today."

John took a deep, shuddering breath, then spoke softly, quietly. "Just do it, Serena," he said. "Just get out your stiletto and get it over with. Because I'm already dead. You killed me when you killed Mariah."

"No!" It was Mariah who cried out this time. "Oh, God, no!"

Whatever she was going to do, she had to do it fast. She tried to start the car again to no avail. She tried to rouse Daniel, but he was as unresponsive as the car's engine.

FBI, he'd said. He and John were FBI.

And FBI agents carried guns....

Mariah searched through Daniel's pockets and through his clothes. It wasn't until she pushed him over and patted around his waist that she found what she was looking for. A gun, in some kind of holster at the small of his back.

"I'm really sorry, but I think I need this," Mariah said to the unconscious man, as with shaking hands, she pulled his shirt free from his pants and drew out the gun. It was small and deadly looking, and warm to the touch from Daniel's body heat.

She pushed open the car door and stepped out into the driving rain, pushing the gun into the back pocket of her shorts, praying that it had some kind of safety attachment that would keep her from shooting herself in the butt by mistake.

She picked up her bike and pointed it back up the hill—away from town and the police. Her muscles strained as she started up the slight incline. She started to gather some real speed as she went past the still flaming ruins of her cottage.

The neighboring house that lay between hers and Serena's was silent and empty, and the last of her hopes for getting help sank. There was no one home there. There was no way anyone could be home and not be out on the porch, or at least at the windows, watching the inferno next door.

Still, Mariah kept pedaling up the hill. She didn't understand *half* of what was going on, but she knew one thing for damn sure. Serena wasn't going to kill John. Not if *she* had anything to say about it.

# CHAPTER FOURTEEN

"I NEVER QUIT," TONY SAID sternly. "I confess I did a stupid thing, I got myself into a situation that there was no getting out of, but I spit at Domino as his boys were squeezing the triggers of their guns to blow me away."

Miller's mouth was dry, his stomach queasy and his head felt as if it were floating a good twelve inches above his body. "Mariah's dead," he said. "She killed Mariah."

"No talking," Serena said sharply. "No more talking!"

Tony moved closer, lowering his voice. "You know, she's having some kind of ritualistic meal, getting into some kind of sicko trance while she's getting ready to skewer you, pal. And look at you. You've got your head on the table in a puddle of drool."

"I don't care," Miller told him.

It was amazing, actually. He had a bullet in his left arm, but it didn't hurt. He couldn't feel it. He couldn't feel anything. Nothing hurt. Nothing mattered. He honestly didn't care.

"I can't believe it," Tony said. "This bitch killed Mariah, and you're going to let her get away with it? You're going to just quit? I don't know what happened in the past two years, baby, but you're not the John Miller *I* used to know."

"I loved her," Miller said.

"Yeah, right, maybe." Tony didn't sound convinced.

"I told you to shut up!" Serena snapped.

"I did," Miller insisted. "I loved her more than anything."

"Not more than you love yourself," Tony pointed out. "If you did, you wouldn't quit. But you're scared because you know it's going to hurt you more than you can bear to wake up tomorrow morning and still be alive while Mariah's not. You *want* this bitch to shish-kebab you because Mariah's dead, because you couldn't save her, and because you can't deal with that."

"Damn right I can't deal with that! God, every day for the rest of my life?"

Serena clapped her hands together and the noise seemed to thunder around him. "I'm warning you!"

Miller lifted his head, working hard to focus his eyes. "Go to hell," he snarled.

"Attaboy," Tony murmured. "Get mad. Fight back."

Mariah was dead. Mariah was dead. Christ, Mariah was *dead*.

The pain of reality came stabbing through all of the layers of drug-induced numbness and apathy. Sweet, beautiful Mariah was gone forever, and Miller knew that Tony was right. As easy as it would be to quit, he couldn't do it. He couldn't just put his head down on the table and die.

Not without making Serena pay.

So instead, he put his head down on the table and waited for Serena to come closer.

With his eyes opened and focused, Tony was gone. He was on his own here, without even his dreams and hallucinations to back him up. He tried to formulate a plan, tried to make his brain turn back into a brain again, rather than the soggy basket of wet laundry it had become.

She would come close, and he would use every bit of strength he had left in his jellolike muscles, and he would…do something.

No, no! He had to come up with something specific. He had to figure out the details. He was always so good with details, good with alternate plans. He was good at making plans for every variable, every difference in every detail.

But for now, he'd have to skip the little details. For now, he'd focus on an overall plan. His mind was too foggy for anything but the big picture. It was hard enough to concentrate on how exactly to get from where he was sitting right now to being the one in control of the gun.

Gun.

There was something about a gun that he should remember….

He had a gun. He could…shoot her with the gun that was still inside his boot! Yeah. That was a great idea.

Except his hands were cuffed behind his back and he couldn't reach his gun.

Miller fought a wave of dizzying fatigue by calling to mind Mariah's beautiful face, her gorgeous smile. He focused on the dimples that appeared in her cheeks, the flash of laughter that danced in her eyes. That was gone, all gone, forever gone. Serena had stolen Mariah from him. Serena had taken all his hopes and his dreams when she'd so casually snuffed out Mariah's life.

He used the pain to bring himself back from the

edge, to push back the fog that threatened to over-power him.

Think. He had to *think*.

He had to figure out what he had to work with, his strengths as they were—not an easy task since he was finding it harder and harder to remember his name.

His legs.

His legs were free. They weren't tied.

He could kick the dining table over on top of her. Crush her. Or, like she herself had suggested, he could put her in a leghold and snap her neck.

He had the chair. He could throw himself forward, chair and all, and use the chair he was cuffed to as a weapon.

And the morphine. He could take that which weakened him the most and use it to his advantage. He could break his legs from the force of the blow he intended to deliver, and he wouldn't feel any pain.

Miller forced his eyes open. He could see Serena sitting way down at the other end of the table, eating her elegant dinner. She was halfway through the main course, and he knew that when the main course was through, she would take out her razor-sharp little knife.

And then she would come closer.

If he was lucky, he *would* break her neck. He'd take her out for good.

And if he was really lucky, she'd take him out with her and he wouldn't have to wake up tomorrow and know that Mariah was dead.

THE HOUSE WAS DARK and quiet.

Mariah stood in the pouring rain, straining to listen for something, *any*thing at all.

All she heard was the rain.

She'd rushed over here as fast as she could ride on her bike, but now that she was here, she wasn't quite sure what to do.

Ring the bell? Knock on the door as she pushed it open, calling, "Yoo-hoo, Serena, did you just try to blow me into a million little bits by planting a bomb in the basement of my house, and are you about to murder your husband and my lover—who, in fact, seems to be some kind of federal agent?"

Stealthily, she tested the doorknob. The door was unlocked. She turned the knob slowly and just as slowly pushed the door open.

It was as dark inside as it was out.

Darker.

Mariah silently closed the door behind her and stood for a moment, letting her ears adjust to the now muted sound of the rain on the roof, hoping her eyes would adjust to the eerie, smothering darkness, as well.

She became aware of a new sound—the sound of water dripping from her clothes and onto the Mexican-tiled floor. And as she took a step farther into the entryway, her sneakers squished. Moving as quietly as she could, she stepped out of them.

Her eyes *were* starting to adjust to the dark. She could see a dim light coming from somewhere upstairs. She looked around for a place to hide her sneakers, but gave up as she realized she might be able to hide them, but there was no way she could hide the puddle of water she'd brought inside with her. She might as well leave them by the door and pray she found Serena before Serena realized she had uninvited company.

Mariah heard a voice speaking sharply, echoing from

an upstairs room. It was Serena. She couldn't make out what the woman was saying, but she sure as heck didn't sound happy.

Mariah went up the stairs as quickly and quietly as she could, reaching into her back pocket and wriggling free Daniel's deadly little gun.

Dear God, she had no idea *what* she was going to do. She pictured herself leaping through the doorway, gun raised and held in both hands, like one of the cops on *NYPD Blue,* shouting for Serena to freeze.

And then what? What was she going to do if Serena had her own gun? Was she going to shoot Serena?

Now *there* was an unlikely scenario. Mariah had never fired a gun before, let alone fired one at a living, breathing human being.

As she drew closer to the top of the stairs, she saw that there was candlelight coming from the dining room—the room where all her dreams had come crashing down around her just this morning. It was the same room where she had found Serena and her new husband—Jonathan Mills.

She crept toward the door, careful to stay out of the light, pressing herself against the wall, gun raised. She held her breath and closed her eyes briefly, waiting for the trembling in her knees to stop, hoping that she would hear John's voice, praying that he was still alive.

The next move was hers. It was totally up to her. She could stand here for another two minutes, or she could get ready and—

"My gun is aimed at Jonathan's head." Serena's voice was crisp and clear, echoing in the silence. "I know you're out there, and if you don't step into the light with your hands held high, I'm going to kill him right now."

The next move wasn't Mariah's after all. Dear God, Serena must have heard her coming up the stairs.

"Do it now!" the older woman said sharply, "or I swear, I'll kill him."

Mariah stuffed the gun back into her back pocket and stepped into the light, hands held up over her head.

"You?" Serena laughed. Sure enough, she held a gun trained with steady confidence directly at John's head. "Well, well, look who's come to rescue you, John. It's Mariah, back from the dead."

"Run!" John shouted. "Mariah, run!"

Mariah couldn't move. It was as if she'd stepped into some scene from a horrific nightmare, and she couldn't move an inch.

John was sitting behind the long dining table, his hands behind his back. His left arm was soaked with blood. It looked as if it was all he could do to hold his head up. And Serena was standing across the room, perfectly dressed as usual in an elegant black sheath dress, with pearls and a gun as accessories.

It was unreal. Mariah didn't understand. What the hell was going on? Why was the FBI after Serena? What had she done? Why would she want to kill John and drug Daniel? Why would she put a bomb in Mariah's basement? It didn't make any sense.

But Serena held the gun calmly, confidently, as if she was accustomed to it. Clearly, she wouldn't hesitate to shoot—obviously she'd shot John once tonight already. She swung the gun toward Mariah.

"No!" Miller was drowning. The shock of seeing Mariah whole and alive had transformed rapidly from near euphoric joy to screaming fear. She was alive—but she wouldn't be for long if she didn't get the hell out of here.

"Well, isn't *this* different," Serena said. "You *are* a fool, aren't you? He married *me,* and yet here you are, rushing to his rescue, empty-handed. You know, he was only using you to get closer to me. Did you know that Jonathan Mills isn't even his real name? God, Mariah, I'm sure absolutely nothing he's told you is true."

Mariah took one step and then another and another toward Miller. "John, are you all right?" She was soaking wet, shivering slightly as she knelt next to him, as she touched his blood-soaked sleeve. He could smell her perfume, and reality shifted. For one incredible moment, he was back in her bed, making love to her and... He shook his head, trying to bring his focus back to here and now.

"Gun in my boot," he whispered, praying that she would understand, knowing that he had to act, and act fast. As much as Serena was loath to kill him with a gun, she'd have no problem using a bullet to kill Mariah.

"Of course, Mariah was playing her own game," Serena continued. "Mariah Robinson isn't her real name either. I wonder, John. Did you consider her a suspect because of that?"

Miller looked directly into Mariah's eyes. "Gun," he started to whisper again.

She cut him off. "I know. I'm really mad at you," she added, reaching behind him to touch his hand. Except wait—those weren't her fingers that touched him. It was something cold and...

It was amazing, but somehow she'd managed to get the gun out of his boot without his noticing. Without

Serena noticing. Miller's hands were numb, but he took the safety off, preparing the gun to fire.

Still, this gun wasn't going to do him a whole hell of a lot of good as long as he was holding it behind his back. He was a good shot—at least he was when he wasn't pumped full of narcotics—but trick shooting had never been his forte.

"Take it back," he told Mariah.

She shook her head. "I can't."

Serena's gun was still pointed loosely at Mariah, yet now she brought her hand up higher, taking better aim. "What are telling her?" she asked him sharply, then said to Mariah, "Move away from him."

"Take it," Miller said. *"Now!"*

Mariah didn't want that gun. She knew damn well there was no way she could aim it at Serena and pull the trigger.

But John dropped it into her hand as he used both of his legs and kicked the enormous table onto its side. A shot rang out as he tipped his chair over in front of her, and Mariah realized Serena was shooting at them. She lifted the gun, closed her eyes and squeezed the trigger.

The recoil knocked the gun out of her hands and she screamed.

Miller tried to shield Mariah as the shot she fired went wild. He could feel the dry wood of the old chair he was cuffed to splintering, and he pulled himself free of it.

His wounded arm should have hurt like hell as he contorted to slip his cuffed hands past his legs and around to the front of him, but he didn't feel even a twinge, thanks to the morphine Serena had given him. Weakness as strength. He was superhuman now. Nothing could hurt him, nothing could stop him—not even Serena's bullets.

He felt the force of one plow into his leg as he covered Mariah with his body, as he reached for the gun she had fired and dropped. He felt another bullet strike him as he took aim, and he saw Serena's eyes as she realized that only a direct hit to his head would take him down.

He fired.

And Serena fell instead, her gun falling from her hand.

In the sudden silence, he could hear the sound of sirens.

It was the sound of fire trucks, rushing to extinguish the blaze that once had been Mariah's cottage.

But they didn't stop down the street. They came all the way up the hill, all the way into the driveway. He heard the door burst open, heard the pounding sound of heavy footsteps on the stairs.

He leaned back, resting against the toppled-over table as Mariah tried to stop his bleeding.

Backup had arrived. Somehow Daniel had managed to call for backup, and they had arrived.

"I'm going to close my eyes now," he told Mariah.

"Don't," she said, tears in her own eyes. "Please, John, don't quit on me. Stay with me—"

He touched her cheek. It was wet with tears. "Don't cry. I never meant to make you cry. I'm so sorry," he murmured. "So sorry..." I love you, he wanted to say, but his lips didn't seem to be able to move.

"We need that stretcher up here stat!" he heard someone shout as the world went black.

# CHAPTER FIFTEEN

IT WAS THIRTY-SIX HOURS, seventeen minutes and nine seconds before John opened his eyes.

Mariah knew, because she'd been counting every second. The nurses had brought in a cot for her, and she'd slept fitfully, not convinced that she would be roused if John woke up.

But he hadn't.

He had an IV dripping steadily into his right arm. He was hooked up to machines that monitored his heart rate and his breathing. Doctors came and went, seemingly satisfied with his progress despite the fact that he slept on and on and on.

Daniel came to before John did, and he sat quietly for a while, next to Mariah. He told her about Serena, about all her other husbands, about the years John had spent tracking her down. He told her how, after Mariah had left him in the car, he'd roused himself and crawled out into the rain. He'd forced himself to keep awake, keep moving, and eventually, he'd flagged down a passing car. The driver had taken him to the Garden Isle police station, where a team of local cops had donned their bulletproof vests and driven like bats out of hell to John and Mariah's rescue.

Except by the time they'd arrived at Serena's place,

John and Mariah had pretty much managed to rescue themselves.

He told her that Serena was in custody, expected to recover from her gunshot wound. He added that her real name was Janice Reed and that they'd found her keepsake collection of hair, which tied her to nearly a dozen murders.

Daniel managed to answer only some of Mariah's questions. He said she'd have to wait for John to answer the others. Before John woke up, Daniel had been discharged from the hospital and he'd returned to the resort to finish packing their equipment.

And still Mariah sat next to John's bed.

Then, finally, he stirred and opened his eyes.

He just looked at her, and she just looked at him, fighting back the tears that immediately sprang to her eyes.

"You're not dead," he said when he finally spoke, and she realized that there were tears in his eyes, too. "I'm not really sure what I dreamed and what was real, but I'm glad as hell that you're not dead."

His mouth was dry, and she helped him by lifting the cup of water the nurses had left for him. She aimed the bendable straw so he could pull it into his mouth and take a long sip.

"My real name is Marie Carver," she told him without hesitation, "although my nickname has always been Mariah. I've spent the past few months on Garden Isle using the name Mariah Robinson because I read in a book that going on vacation and leaving your name behind was a good way to reduce stress."

He smiled very slightly as she put the cup back on

the table next to the bed. "It's also a good way to make the local law enforcement officials very suspicious."

"I never even thought of that." She paused. "You didn't really think I was...a killer?"

"We pretty much knew it was Serena right from the start."

"I can't believe you married someone you suspected of being a serial killer! Is that part of your job description as an FBI agent?"

He laughed, then winced, holding tightly to his side where one of Serena's bullets had cracked a rib. "No. No, that was above and beyond the call of duty."

Mariah was quiet for a moment. She almost didn't ask, but she had to know. "How could you...sleep with her, knowing that she'd killed all her other husbands?"

He took her hand, interlacing their fingers. "I didn't sleep with her—I didn't want to sleep with her. Besides, I promised you that I wouldn't, remember? I told her I was impotent—that my condition was a side effect of my chemotherapy."

Mariah gazed into his eyes. Chemotherapy. Cancer. "You never really had cancer," she realized aloud. "That was all just part of your cover."

He nodded. "That's right. I'm sorry—"

"Sorry?" She laughed, leaning forward to kiss him hard on the mouth. "Are you kidding? That's *such* good news! It makes all this hell we've just been through worth it. You're not going to die!"

Her reaction was pure Mariah. She was focusing on the good, not the bad. Miller felt his heart flip-flop in his chest. God, he loved her.

He caught her chin, pulling her mouth down to his for another kiss. This kiss was more lingering, and when she pulled away, her eyes looked so serious, so solemn.

"I don't even know your real name," she told him.

"It's John Miller."

"I don't know anything about you—who you are, where you're from—"

"Yes, you do," he told her. "You know more about me than anyone in the world. I told you more than I've ever told Daniel. More than Tony ever knew."

"Tony was real?" she asked.

"Yeah."

She looked down at their hands, their fingers still intertwined. "Serena said you were only using me to get close to her."

"If you really believe that, what are you doing here, sitting next to my bed?"

She looked up at him then. "I don't know," she confessed. "I honestly don't know. I just…I had to know you were all right before I…left."

Before she left. God, he didn't want her to leave. But if she *was* going to leave, he wanted her to know the truth.

Miller took a deep breath. "I did meet you to get close to Serena," he told her. "Yes, that's true. But I kept coming back—I couldn't stay away—because I fell in love with you."

Her eyes were so wide, so beautiful.

"I love you, Mariah," he told her quietly. "I have almost from the very first day we met. I made a lot of mistakes in this case—even though I tried my damnedest to keep away from you, I couldn't. And when Serena left the island, I was so sure she had gone for good. And then after we made love, and she came back…" He exhaled noisily. "I made some very wrong choices. I knew that marrying her would hurt you, but I couldn't stand the thought of letting her get away, and I nearly got you killed because of that."

He took a deep breath, afraid that what he was about to say was going to drive her away for good. "You see, that's who I am," he continued. "I'm a man who can't stand to fail. I have a record of arrests that's unrivaled in the bureau. I have a reputation for always catching the bad guys, for never letting them get away. I'm supposed to be some kind of superhero—the toughest and meanest in the field. I have a nickname—the other agents call me 'The Robot,' because nothing matters to me outside of my job. They think I have no heart and no soul, and maybe they're right, because the truth is I have no life outside of the work I do. I have no family and no friends—"

"Daniel is your friend."

Miller nodded. "Yeah. I don't get it, but yeah. He's my friend."

"I'm your friend, too."

Miller had to swallow. He had to take another deep breath before he could say, "That's all I can really ask. That you be my friend."

She was very quiet, just watching him.

"I had this crazy dream," he told her, "that morning we made love. I was thinking, this could be my life. I thought, maybe I could feel this good every single day. This woman could love me, and I could become this peaceful, relaxed, happy man. I could be so much more than I've ever been before—than I'd ever thought I'd be. And I could picture us, forty years from now, still making love, still holding hands, still laughing together. I really liked that picture."

Mariah's heart was in her throat as he looked away from her, as he was silent for several long moments. As she watched, he swallowed hard, and when he looked back up at her, his eyes were luminous with unshed tears.

"But I'm not that man. I'm 'The Robot.' And I don't blame you if you can't love me—if you don't want to love me. I'm hard, and I'm driven, and my job matters too damn much to me. I wouldn't wish myself on anyone—maybe especially not on you." He took another deep breath and forced a smile as he squeezed her hand. "So, go on. Get out of here. You've seen for yourself that I'm okay. You can leave."

Mariah couldn't move, couldn't speak.

"It's okay," he said. "I'm okay. I'm just…I'm glad I had the chance to love you. To, you know, know that I could actually feel this way and…"

One of his tears escaped, rolling down his cheek and splashing onto Mariah's hand. He swore, turning away and tightly closing his eyes. But that only served to make more of his tears fall.

"John," Mariah said quietly, gently touching his face. "Robots don't cry." She leaned forward and kissed him and when she pulled back, she whispered, "What would Jonathan Mills think if I told him that I made a mistake, too? What would he say if I told him that really, all this time, I've been in love with a man named John Miller?"

He could feel all his emotions cross his face. Disbelief. Amazement. Confusion. Jubilation. She loved him. She *loved* him!

He made a sound that was something like a laugh as he fought to keep his eyes from filling with tears again. And then he didn't fight anymore. Hell, with Mariah, he didn't need to fight it. He wanted her to know, wanted her to see the way she made him feel.

"He would wish you the best of luck," he told her, "and he would warn you that with me, you're probably going to need it."

Mariah touched his cheek, touched the tear he knew was shimmering there. "And what do *you* think about that?"

"I think that if you still have the urge to change your name, you should consider changing it to Miller."

He'd caught her off guard. "Are you asking me to *marry* you?"

"Yes," he said. "Yes, I am."

This time, the tears that fell were Mariah's. "Yes," she whispered, "I'd love to change my name." She leaned forward and kissed him.

It was the sweetest kiss Miller had ever known.

\* \* \* \* \*

# LETTERS TO KELLY

To my wonderful mother, Lee Brockmann,
who's been waiting a long time for this one.

# *CHAPTER ONE*

KELLY O'BRIEN LUGGED HER heavy canvas bag of books into the back door of the university newspaper office. The spring day was hot, and a trickle of sweat dripped uncomfortably down her back.

She heaved the book bag onto her desk with a crash, and pushed back the damp strands of long, dark hair that had escaped from her bun. With a sigh, she peeled off her jacket and undid the top buttons of her sleeveless blouse, shaking the neckline slightly to let fresh air circulate against her overheated body.

"Psst."

Kelly looked up to see Marcy Reynolds, the school newspaper's student photographer, hissing at her. Marcy's brown eyes were lit with excitement, her pixielike face alive with curiosity.

"There's some guy sitting in the front office, waiting for you," Marcy said, handing Kelly several pink phone message slips. "No. Correction—this is not just some guy. This is a Man, with a capital *M*. And quite possibly *the* most gorgeous man who has ever crossed the threshold of this humble establishment."

Kelly smiled. "Oh, come on—"

"I'm serious," the younger woman said. As she shook her head, her large hoop earrings bumped the sides of her face. "We're talking major heart-attack material. *Very* tall, blond, green eyes—he's a dead ringer for Mel Gibson's cuter, younger brother. The man is a walking blue jeans ad, Kelly. His legs are about a mile long, and those buns..."

Kelly laughed in disbelief. "He sounds too good to be true," she said.

"He looks like one of the heroes from those romance novels you're writing. He's been sitting there for forty-five minutes," Marcy complained, running her fingers through her short black hair, "totally blowing my concentration."

"Is he a student?"

"He's too old," Marcy said. "I mean, unless he took some time off from school, but not only a few years, like you. Like serious time, maybe ten years. I'd say he's maybe thirty. He's got those sexy little crinkly laugh lines around his eyes. Check him out—he's a total babe."

"Maybe he's a professor," Kelly said. "Did he say what he wants?"

"*You're* what he wants." Marcy smirked. "That's all he said. I told him I didn't know when you'd be back— that you could be gone for hours. But he just said he'd wait. He said something about waiting seven years, and that another few hours wouldn't kill him. Have you been keeping this man on the shelf for *seven years?*"

"Seven years ago I was only sixteen," Kelly said. She moved to the glass partition that separated the front office from the back. The blinds were down and shut, and she moved one aluminum slat a fraction of an inch and peeked out.

Her heart stopped.

T. Jackson Winchester the Second.

It couldn't be.

But it was.

He was the only person in the outer office and he sat by the door, one ankle resting on one knee, leaning casually back in his chair, as comfortable as if he were in his own living room. He wore a royal-blue polo shirt with both buttons open, revealing his sun-kissed neck and chest. His shirt was tucked into a pair of faded blue jeans that hugged his muscular thighs. On his feet he wore Docksiders but no socks. His ankles were strong and tan.

He was reading the latest copy of the school newspaper, and his eyes were down, hidden by long, dark lashes. Kelly didn't need to see his eyes to know they were a remarkable mix of colors, with a ring of yellow gold, like solar flares, that surrounded his pupils. The edges of his irises were brilliant green. And sandwiched between the green and the gold was the ocean. Like the ocean, his eyes changed. They could be stormy gray, or dark blue-black, or even a deep, mysterious shade of green. She could remember looking into his eyes, into a warm swirl of colored fire, his lips curving up into a smile as he bent to kiss her—

Kelly shook her head, pushing the thought away. She looked at him again, closely this time, searching for signs of age, signs of change.

He was wearing his golden hair longer than she'd ever seen him wear it before, hanging down several inches over his collar, thick and wavy and blond and soft. His face had a few more lines, but if anything, he was more handsome than ever.

He looked really good.

But he'd always looked good. He'd looked good when she'd first met him, and he'd been hung over at the time. She could still remember that morning as if it were yesterday, not eleven years ago....

Twelve-year-old Kelly had opened the door quietly, carefully, then slipped into the darkened guest bedroom. She had heard the clock ticking, and the sound of slow, steady breathing.

Her brother Kevin's mysterious college roommate was lying sprawled out on the bed, long legs escaping from beneath the covers that were twisted around him. One arm was flung above his head, the other lay across his bare chest.

His name was T. Jackson Winchester the Second. Kevin had called from school to tell her parents about the freshman dorm and about his roommate. Kelly had been particularly impressed by the length of his roommate's name. Kevin had told their father that T. Jackson was from Cape Cod, and he drove a Triumph Spitfire.

What did the T. stand for? Kelly had wondered. And what color was the Spitfire?

Red. She'd made a point of looking out onto the driveway first thing when she woke up. The Spitfire was shiny and red, with a black convertible top.

Kelly stepped closer to T. Jackson Winchester the Second, to get a better look at him in the dimness of the room, to see what a rich college roommate looked like.

He had an awful lot of muscles. Kevin was eighteen,

and he had lots of muscles, too, but Kelly had never given his muscles a second glance. He was her brother, sometimes a pain in the neck, sometimes a creep, but mostly fun.

This guy, however, was not her brother.

She swallowed hard, looking down at his messy blond hair and his handsome face. He was definitely a ten. A living ten. Kelly had seen some tens before on television or in the movies. But before this, she'd never met one face-to-face.

His face was perfectly shaped with a long, straight nose and a strong jawline. His eyebrows were two slightly curved light brown lines above the thick eyelashes that lay against the smooth, tanned skin of his cheeks. His lips were neither too thin nor too thick, and nicely shaped. Even in sleep, they tended to curve upward, as if a smile was his natural expression.

Kelly leaned even closer, wondering what color his eyes were, then wondering with a flash of giddiness what color his underpants were. She clapped her hand over her mouth to keep a laugh from escaping and backed away from the bed.

She'd come into this room with a purpose, and although checking out T. Jackson Winchester the Second was interesting, that wasn't why she'd crept in. She moved quietly to the closet. The door was closed, and she silently slid it open, carefully stopping it before it bumped the frame.

Oh, man, her mother had moved her rock-collecting gear up onto the top shelf.

Kelly was tall for her age, but she still couldn't reach

the backpack that sat on the top shelf in the closet. Not without climbing on a chair.

The only chair in the room was clear over on the other side, below the shaded window. Stealthily Kelly moved toward it. T. Jackson Winchester the Second had draped his jeans and shirt over the back of the chair last night before he climbed into bed.

Staggered into bed was more like it. Kelly wrinkled her nose as she smelled the odor of stale cigarette smoke and beer that seemed to cling to T. Jackson's clothes. He and Kevin had been to some kind of wild party last night. Some *illegal* wild party.

The drinking age in Massachusetts was twenty-one. She'd heard her father arguing with Kevin about that. Her brother insisted if he was old enough to register for the draft, then he was old enough to drink. Her father had countered by saying if he was old enough to drink, then he was also old enough to always pick a designated driver. Dad had added that if he ever caught Kevin drinking and driving, no matter *how* old he was, he'd be grounded for ten years.

From the looks of ol' T. Jackson Winchester the Second, Kevin had probably been last night's designated driver.

Kelly dropped the clothes onto the floor and wrestled the heavy chair toward the closet. But she didn't see the big high-top sneakers that were lying in the way, and she tripped, hitting the floor with a crash and a yelp as the chair fell on top of her.

Before she could move, the chair was pulled away. "Are you all right?" T. Jackson Winchester the Second said raspily, frowning down at her with concern.

Red.

He was wearing boxer shorts and they were red. As Kelly stared way, way up at him, she wondered whether it was a coincidence, or if he always matched his underwear to the color of the car he was driving.

"Did you hurt yourself, kid?" he asked, after clearing his throat noisily and swallowing hard as if his mouth was dry. He reached out a hand to help her to her feet.

His hand was big and warm, with long, strong fingers and carefully manicured nails. Kelly let go quickly, afraid to be caught clinging foolishly, grinning at him like an idiot.

"I'll live," she said. She was going to get some big bruise on her leg where the chair had hit her, but she wasn't about to tell T. Jackson Winchester the Second about it.

As she watched, he crossed to the bedside table and drained a glass of water that was sitting there.

"Ugh," she said, wrinkling her nose. "Isn't that warm?"

He glanced at her, putting the empty glass back down. "It's wet," he said. "That's all that matters." He ran his hands over his face and looked longingly at the bed. "What time is it?" he asked.

"About quarter to nine," she told him. "How tall *are* you exactly?"

He sat down on the bed, resting his forehead in his hands. "Exactly?" he asked, looking up at her through his fingers, a glint of amusement in his eyes. "Six foot four and one quarter inches."

"That's tall." Kelly nodded. "I'm Kelly O'Brien," she added.

T. Jackson Winchester the Second straightened up the best that he could and held out his hand. "Pleased to meet you, Kelly O'Brien," he said, somehow managing to smile. "I'm Jax, Kevin's roommate."

Kelly took his hand, shaking it firmly. "T. Jackson Winchester the Second," she said. "I know."

Green eyes. He had green eyes, rimmed with red. "Christmas in October," she said, and grinned.

Somehow he understood that she was talking about his eyes, and he smiled ruefully. "I look bad, huh?"

Kelly nodded. "You look like hell."

He laughed with a flash of straight, white teeth. Forget ten. He was clearly an eleven.

"Sorry I woke you up," she said. "I was trying to get my backpack down from the closet shelf."

"This isn't your room, is it?" he said, frowning slightly as he looked around at the impersonal guest room, at the blandly patterned bedspread, the flower print on the curtains, the beige carpeting.

"Nah," Kelly said. "I just use the closet because I'm overflowing my own. What does the T. stand for?"

He looked at her blankly. "The...what?"

"In your name," she said patiently. "You know. *T. Jackson...?* And you call yourself Jacks? Like the game? Or is it a plural, as if there's two of you?"

He laughed again, then winced as if his head hurt. "No, there's only one of me. It's spelled *J-A-X,*" he said. "It's a nickname."

"And the *T.?*"

"Tyrone," he said with a grimace.

"Ew."

"Yeah. That's why I keep it an initial."

"Tyrone," Kelly said slowly. "Ty. Well, it's not really *that* bad. But 'Jax' is pretty weird. Why don't you go for the entire initial thing? You know, call yourself T.J.?"

He stood slowly, steadying himself on one of the bedposts. "It's taken," he said. "My father is T.J."

"The First."

"You got it."

"Doesn't that actually make you *Junior?*" Kelly asked critically. "I mean, this 'the Second' stuff is kind of pompous, don't you think?"

Jax grinned, crossing toward the closet. "If you ask me, the whole Winchester existence is kind of pompous."

"I'll call you T.," she decided. "I like that better than Jax."

He turned toward her. "Look, if I get your backpack down for you, will you let me go back to sleep?"

She smiled. "Promise to take me for a ride later in your Spitfire and you've got a deal."

Jackson smiled back at her, his warm green eyes taking her in from the top of her boyishly short hair, to her faded turtleneck with the too-short sleeves and her skinny wrists sticking out, to her ragged jeans and right down to her worn-out cowboy boots. He stared at her for so long that Kelly wiped her nose, wondering if maybe it was running.

But his smile slowly faded, and he frowned down at himself, as if suddenly aware he was half-naked. "I probably shouldn't be standing here in my underwear, talking to you like this."

"I've seen Kevin in his underwear more times than I can count," Kelly scoffed. "It's no big deal."

"Yeah, but Kev's your brother," Jax said. "I'm not."

Looking at him, Kelly was glad that he wasn't. No one should have a brother who looked as good as T. Jackson Winchester the Second.

"Something tells me that your father wouldn't approve." Jax grinned. "And I don't want to be forced into any kind of a shotgun wedding, no matter how pretty you are."

Kelly felt herself blush. "Don't be a jerk," she warned him. "I know exactly what I look like." She was a skinny beanpole with a faintly feminine face. If she stretched her imagination, she could use the word *pretty* to describe her eyes. But only her eyes.

"Is this what you need?" Jax asked, pointing to a blue backpack in the closet.

She nodded.

He swung it down, but it was heavier than he thought, and he had to lunge to keep from dropping it. "God," he said, "what have you got in here? Rocks?"

Kelly smiled, taking the knapsack from him, her muscles straining as she slipped it over her shoulder. "Yeah. It's my rock collection."

Jax looked surprised, then he laughed. "You're into geology, huh?" he said. "Will you show me your collection later?"

"Yeah." Kelly nodded, smiling at him again. She turned to go, but looked back at him, her hand on the doorknob. "T. Jackson Winchester the Second," she said, "you're not a dweeb. I like you. My brother's lucky he got you for a roommate."

He'd laughed again as Kelly had gone out the door. "I like you, too, Kelly," she'd heard him say. "And *I'm* lucky that I got a roommate with a sister like you. See you later...."

Kelly now lowered the slat on the blinds, and looking down, realized that she had scrunched the phone message slips she'd been holding into a tight wad of paper.

"Do you know him?" Marcy's words finally penetrated.

"Yeah," Kelly said slowly.

"Who *is* he?"

Good question. Was he a childhood friend? A friend of the family? An almost-lover? Kelly went for the obvious. "He was my brother's college roommate," she said. She turned to Marcy suddenly. "Do me a favor and tell him that I just called and told you that I wasn't coming back in today."

Marcy was looking at her as if she had finally lost her mind. "And just which telephone line is it that you supposedly called on?" she said. "The one that rings silently?"

"Tell him—" Kelly was grabbing wildly now. "Tell him *you* called me."

Marcy folded her arms across her chest, the bangles and bracelets she wore on her wrists jangling. "I talked to the man for maybe five minutes when he first came in, but it was long enough for me to know he's no idiot," she said. "Now, if I go out there making excuses for you, girl, he's gonna realize that you took one look at him and ran away. And a man like that one—" she gestured toward the door to the outer office "—usually does only one thing when he's being run away from." She paused for emphasis. "He gives chase. So unless you want this guy following you all over town—and if you do, that's fine, because *I* sure wouldn't mind—you better take a nice deep breath, and go and talk to him."

Marcy was right. She was absolutely right.

Kelly walked to the door and, following her friend's advice, took a deep breath. She glanced back at Marcy for an extra dose of strength, then turned the doorknob.

## CHAPTER TWO

JAX STARED AT THE COLLEGE newspaper without reading it. He tried thinking about the book he was writing, tried to plan the next scene, but he couldn't even keep his mind on that. He was nervous. What if Kelly didn't show up?

What if she did?

Relax, he ordered himself. It's just Kelly.

Just Kelly.

It had been seven years since the night of her junior prom.

God, his life could have been so different if he hadn't been so stupid. But he made a mistake, and here he was, seven years later, no closer to getting what he wanted.

Seven long, wasted years...

Jax wished he could go back in time, do it all over again. Well, not *all*. He'd skip the trip to Central America, thank you very much. Yeah, he'd pass on *that* ten-day news-gathering expedition that had turned into a twenty-month nightmare—

He took a deep breath. He had dreamed about Central America last night for the first time in a long time. He'd dreamed he was back in the prison and—

But he didn't want to think about *that,* either. He was

better off just worrying about Kelly. Seven years was a long time. She must have changed. Lord knows he had.

But since yesterday, when Kevin had called and filled him in on the latest O'Brien family news, Jax felt twenty-two years old again. All of his optimism and hope flooded back, as if it had never faded and disappeared.

Kelly was back in Boston, Kevin had told him, finishing her college degree. She had gotten a divorce.

Even as Jax had talked to Kevin on the phone, even as he had made regretful noises over Kelly's failed marriage, he'd done a silent victory dance in his living room.

Kelly was single. She was single and she wasn't too young anymore. Jax smiled as he stared sightlessly down at the newspaper he was holding.

He could still see her, the way she had looked when he'd first met her. She'd been only twelve years old, no more than a child, but her dark blue eyes held the maturity and wisdom of a woman twice her age. With her dry wit, she was clearly intelligent, but it was her steady self-confidence that made him adore her—not to mention the promise of incredible beauty he could see in her face.

And as he found himself spending more and more time with the O'Briens, his feelings for Kelly grew as she did.

And though the O'Briens didn't have a fraction of the money that his parents had, in Jax's mind, the Winchesters were the losers.

Nolan and Lori O'Brien had been married twenty years when Jax had first met them, but they still loved each other, and maybe even more important, they still genuinely *liked* each other. And they truly loved their children. They couldn't give Kevin and Kelly expensive gifts, they couldn't even afford to send Kevin to Boston College without the help from his scholarship, but there was certainly no lack of love in that family.

And the O'Briens had opened their arms to Jax, encircling him with all the love and laughter and music that always seemed to shake the foundation of their little house.

Jax had even spent one entire summer living with them—along with Lori's recently divorced sister, Christa, and her three children. It had been a magnificent summer, the best he could remember. The house had been so crowded that he and Kevin had to sleep on bedrolls out on the screened-in porch. When it rained, they sought refuge on the floor in Kelly's room.

Kelly had been fourteen that summer, her long legs and arms beginning to change from skinny to willowy. She had grown her dark hair long, and she wore it in a single braid down her back.

She still called Jax "T." or sometimes even Tyrone. She was the only person in the universe he would let get away with that.

He hadn't gone out on a single date that entire summer, spending most of his evenings playing Risk or Monopoly with the ready crowd of O'Briens and relatives. But if anyone had accused him at that time of having anything other than a friendly, platonic love for Kelly, he would have furiously denied it. He was a twenty-year-old man, for crying out loud. Kelly was just a kid.

It wasn't until two years later, the night of Kelly's junior prom—

"T. Jackson Winchester the Second." Kelly's husky voice interrupted his thoughts, and he looked up from the newspaper into a pair of familiar blue eyes.

Kelly.

Jax forced himself to move slowly. He slowly folded the newspaper and put it on the table beside him. He slowly got to his feet and smiled down at her.

God, she had become even more beautiful than she'd been the last time he'd seen her, four years ago at Kevin's wedding.

Her eyes were a deep, dark shade of blue and exquisitely shaped. Her skin was smooth and fair, contrasting with her rich brown hair and her long, dark eyelashes. Her face was elegantly heart-shaped, with a small, strong chin and a perfect nose. She was gorgeous. She'd always been remarkably pretty as a girl, but as a woman, she was breathtaking.

"Kelly." It came out little more than a whisper.

"How are you?" she asked. "What are you doing here?"

Jax cleared his throat and ran his hand through his hair. "I'm in town on business," he said. It wasn't entirely a lie. True, the business could just as easily have been done over the telephone, but... "I thought I'd come and ask you to have dinner with me. I didn't realize you were back in Boston until I spoke to Kevin yesterday."

As Kelly looked up into his eyes, she was struck by how little T. Jackson had changed. He was still the same poised, confident, charismatic and utterly charming man he'd always been. There was no situation he would be uncomfortable in, nothing that could rattle him—no, that wasn't entirely true. She *had* seen him severely shaken up, even out of control. But only once. It had been the night of her junior prom.

"So how about it?" Jax smiled as he returned her steady gaze. "Will you have dinner with me?"

It was Plan "A." He would take her to dinner tonight, and again tomorrow night, and by Wednesday she'd remember how good they were together. She'd realize that their friendship had survived all those years they'd spent apart. And then he'd kiss her good-night, let her know he wanted them to be more than friends. By the end of the week, he'd ask her to marry him. It was fast, but it couldn't exactly be called a whirlwind courtship considering that he'd really started courting her back before he even realized it, back when she was only twelve years old.

It was a plan that would work. He knew it would work.

But he could see wariness in Kelly's eyes. "I don't think so," she said, shaking her head no.

She had turned him down. He hadn't figured *that* possibility when he was making his plan. This was one scenario he had never considered. Despite the heat of the day, Jax felt a sudden chill. Was he too late again? Was he destined to go through life with the woman he wanted always one step out of his reach?

"Are you seeing someone?" he asked.

Kelly looked away. "No."

Jax fought to hide his relief from showing on his face.

"It's just...not necessary for you to take me out to dinner," she said, pushing a wisp of hair from her face.

Jax laughed then. "Says who?"

She sighed and crossed her arms in front of her. "Look, I know Kevin called you because he's worried about me. I've been...a little down. Give me a break, I just got a divorce. I'm allowed to be depressed. I was brought up believing that marriage was permanent, but Brad and I didn't even manage to hold it together for three years."

As Jax watched, she looked down at the floor. Her unhappiness was clearly evident in her eyes, in the tightness of her mouth. Good grief, another variable he hadn't considered. "Do you still love him?" he asked softly.

She glanced up at Jax, and her eyes were filled with tears. "You know what the really stupid thing is, T.?"

He shook his head silently, wishing that he could take her in his arms. But he was held back by all those years of purposely not touching her. During the five years that he'd been in college, the five years that they'd been such good friends, he'd always been very careful not to touch her. Not casually, not at all. It was as if he subconsciously knew there could only be one kind of physical relationship between them, and that there would be nothing casual about it.

"I don't think I ever loved him," she said.

One of Kelly's tears ran down her cheek, and Jax couldn't stop from reaching out to brush it away. She took a step back, as if the contact had burned her.

"Don't."

"Sorry," he said quickly. "I'm sorry."

Kelly wiped her face with the back of her hand, blinking away the rest of her tears. T. was looking at her with such anxiety in his eyes, it almost made her laugh. T. Jackson anxious? She wouldn't have believed it possible. She managed a shaky smile.

"You think I'm a real basket case, right?" she asked.

"I think you could use a friend," he said quietly.

"Yeah," she said, hugging her crossed arms close to her body, as if she were cold, as if it weren't more than eighty degrees in the newspaper office. "I could. But not you, Tyrone. Not this time."

"Why not?"

But it was as if she hadn't heard him. "Just tell Kevin I'm okay. I'm going to be fine. But I'll be fine a lot sooner without you hanging around, doing my brother a favor."

Jax choked on the air he was breathing. "I'm *not* here to do Kevin a favor," he said.

"Yeah, well, it wouldn't be the first time," Kelly said, "would it?"

Jax laughed, but then stopped as the meaning of what she was saying washed over him like a cold bucket of water. "Oh, God," he said. "You believed what Kevin said that morning after the prom?"

"Of course I believed him," Kelly said. "You didn't deny it." She turned toward the door to the back office. "I've got to go. Thanks for dropping by."

"Kelly, wait—"

But she was gone.

Jax stood there for a long time even though he knew she'd gone out the back door, even though he knew that she wasn't coming back.

So much for Plan "A."

JAX SET HIS LAPTOP COMPUTER on the dining table in his hotel suite, attached the power cord and plugged it into the wall. He hit the On switch and the computer wheezed to life.

He pulled his spiral notebook and his collection of computer disks out of his briefcase and found the one labeled Jared.

This book was an historical, with most of the action taking place during the Civil War era. He'd written a number of Civil War books before, so the research he'd had to do for this one had been minimal. This book was going to be fast and easy, especially since the story was one he was extremely familiar with.

He put the disk into the computer's drive and called up the job. After less than a week of work, he was already up to page 163, and he'd just finished writing the explosive, pivotal fight scene between Jared, the hero, and Edmund, the heroine's brother.

He quickly skimmed the last few pages that he'd written, but it was all still fresh in his memory, so he went right to work, starting the next scene.

With bleakness in his eyes, Jared stared at the heavy wrought-iron gates that separated him from Sinclair Manor. The gates had been shut when night had fallen, just as they had been every night. In the morning the servants would come out, unlock them, and throw them open wide.

As Jared stood in the darkness, his gaze moving up to the brightly lit house on the hill, he knew without a doubt that, day or night, he was no longer welcome there. Those gates had been closed to him forever.

Jax stopped writing to take a sip from a can of soda. Now what? Now Jared had to get over that fence.

But Carrie was in there, and welcome or not, Jared meant to have her. With an effortless leap, he climbed up, up and over the sharp spikes that decked the top of the tall fence, letting himself drop lightly to the ground on the other side.

He'd made a promise to Carrie. It was a promise he intended to keep.

Keeping to the trees, moving quietly, the way he'd learned as a young boy in the wilds of Kentucky, he approached the manor house. He moved with purpose, his mouth set in a grim line of determination, making his dark good looks seem almost savage, making it seem as if more than just a quarter of the blood that ran through his veins was Indian.

His gaze quickly found Carrie's bedroom window—

"Whoa, wait a minute," Jax muttered as he stopped writing. "Where do you think *you're* going?"

In his mind he could see Jared turning to stare at him, arms crossed, eyebrow raised, impatience clearly written on the character's handsome face. "I'm going to see Carrie."

"Nuh-uh-uh," Jax chided gently. "According to my outline, you're supposed to meet her in the gazebo."

"Right," Jared said with exasperation. "Only, she doesn't show, her brother Edmund does, and he beats the crap out of me again, because I'm too noble to raise a hand against him on account of the fact that he used to be my best friend. In reality, I could whip him with one hand behind my back. I'm getting tired of this, and so will all your readers." He glanced up at Carrie's window again. "It's time for some sex."

Jax crossed his arms, leaning back with a sigh. His heroes were all alike. They all wanted immediate, instant gratification. They all loved the heroines desperately, and couldn't understand why Jax made them go through all sorts of contortions before being allowed to live happily ever after.

Of course, the *New York Times* bestseller list meant nothing to them.

"I love Carrie," Jared was arguing right now. "And she loves me. I know it—she told me in that last scene you wrote. Face it, Jax, there's no way on earth I'd get on a boat for Europe and leave her behind. It's entirely out of character."

"No, it's not," Jax said quietly. "Not if you thought it was the best thing for Carrie."

Jared sighed, shaking his head slowly. "Carrie? Or Kelly? This is fiction, Jax. Don't get it confused with the things that went wrong in *your* life."

"If things don't go wrong, there's no story," Jax pointed out. "You want to climb up into Carrie's room and make love to her, right?"

Jared nodded.

"And you plan to sneak her out of the house, and take her with you to Europe."

Jared nodded again, his eyes drawn once again to that dimly lit window on the second floor of the house.

"What are you going to do for money?" Jax asked. "Carrie is used to living a certain lifestyle. Have you thought about that?"

Jared shrugged. "I know she loves me more than money," he said with an easy smile. "As long as we're together, she'll be happy."

"You're too perfect," Jax said in disgust. "I've got to give you some insecurities, or some dark family secret."

"Oh, please, not the dark family secret thing," Jared groaned. "I'm already one-quarter Native American and dirt poor to boot. Isn't that scandalous enough?"

"Obviously not," Jax muttered. "I'd like this book to have more than 175 pages, if you don't mind."

"You want more pages?" Jared asked, his face brightening. "I've got a good idea. How about this—a hundred-page love scene? Just me and Carrie, and a hundred pages of bliss?"

Jax laughed out loud. "My, oh my, a little horny today, aren't we?"

Jared's eyes were glued to Carrie's window. "One hundred and sixty-three pages, and I've been trying to get my hands on Carrie since page one," he said. "Two different times you bring me right to the brink of ecstasy, only to snatch her away from me at the last minute. I'm dying here, Jax. Give me a break."

Jackson smiled suddenly. "All right," he said. "Go for it. Climb that trellis."

His hard gaze quickly found Carrie's bedroom window, and in a matter of moments, he was

scaling the side of the house, climbing the trellis, unmindful of the thorns from the roses that
scratched his hands.

Jared stopped climbing, and glared back at Jax. "You
could have chosen ivy, but you had to use roses with
thorns, didn't you? Man, you never give me a break."

"Roses are romantic," Jax said. "Besides, you're unmindful of them."

The window was open, and Jared quickly pushed
it wider and slipped inside. He knew as soon as
his feet touched her bedroom floor that something was wrong. With his heart pounding, Jared
stared at the carefully stripped bed, at the empty
vanity top, the barren bookshelf. Where were all
of Carrie's things, all of her clutter? He strode to
the wardrobe, swinging the doors open.

Empty.

All of her clothes were gone.

"Looking for something?" Edmund Sinclair's
taunting voice made Jared whirl around. Carrie's
brother was standing in the doorway, watching
him, a sneer on his aristocratic face. "Or someone?"

"Where is she?" Jared's voice was harsh.

"She's gone," Edmund said. "My father
thought it best if she went to visit some relatives for a while. Funny, I can't recall whether
she went to Vermont or Connecticut. Or maybe
it was Maine."

Jared spun to glare at Jax. "You son of a bitch," he
spat. Two large strides brought him toward Edmund,
and he hauled off and punched his former friend in the
face. Without another word, Jared disappeared out the
window.

Jax grinned and kept writing. Yeah, it was time for
Edmund to get knocked down. He'd keep that in.

JAX PARKED HIS SPORTS CAR on the street outside of Kelly's apartment. Looking up, he could see the lights on
in her windows. He got out of the car, grabbing the
handles of the bag that held the food he'd picked up at
the Chinese restaurant down the street.

If Kelly wouldn't come to dinner, dinner would come
to Kelly.

She lived on the second floor of a three-family house
on a quiet residential street in the Boston suburbs. Jax
climbed onto the front porch and pushed the middle of
three doorbells.

The evening was warm, and Jax sat back on the
porch railing, watching a couple kids ride their bicy-
cles around and around in a driveway across the street.
But then the porch light came on, the door creaked open
and Kelly was standing behind the screen, looking out
at him.

She was wearing cut-off jeans and a ratty T-shirt,
and her hair was loose around her shoulders, cascading
down her back in a long, dark sheet.

He smiled at her, and she returned the smile rather
ruefully, pushing open the screen door to come out onto
the porch. Her feet were bare, and Jax let his eyes travel
up the long length of her legs, feeling a still somewhat

odd surge of desire. But it shouldn't be odd, he told himself. She wasn't a child anymore. She was a beautiful woman.

He could still remember the first moment he'd realized his feelings for Kevin's little sister weren't brotherly any longer. It hadn't taken him much time to shake off the feelings of oddness *that* night.

She sat down on the top step, hugging her knees in to her chest and looking up at him. "Now, why am I not surprised to see you?"

"You were expecting me?" he said with a quirk of one eyebrow. "I'm honored that you dressed for the occasion."

"Tell me you don't wish you had shorts on," Kelly said.

"You win." He smiled, just looking at her. Her dark hair was so long. He wanted to touch it, run his fingers through its silkiness, but instead he gripped the railing. "How many years did it take you to grow your hair that long?"

She swept her hair off her neck, twisting it and pulling it in front of her and frowned down at the ends. "I'm going to get it cut. I haven't done more than trim it in almost four years. I'm thinking of going radically short for the summer."

"Radically?" he asked. "You mean, like Vin Diesel?"

Kelly laughed, and Jax was momentarily transported back in time seven years, to the night of her junior prom, to the night he'd danced with her in his arms, holding her for the very first time. It seemed as if they'd spent the entire evening laughing. *Almost* the entire evening...

"That's maybe a little *too* radical," she said. "But I am thinking of getting it buzzed in the back."

She pushed her hair up as if to demonstrate just how short she wanted it cut, and Jax's eyes were drawn to her slender neck. He liked her long hair the way it was, but she would look unbelievably sexy with it short. Her hair would curl slightly around her ears, frame her beautiful face and accentuate her long, graceful neck.

"I think it would look great."

"You do?" She looked up at him, surprise in her voice.

"Yeah."

She stood. "I've got to get back to work," she said, edging toward the door.

Jax was confused. They'd been having a normal conversation, everything was very comfortable and... He was coming on too strong, he realized suddenly. He'd been distracted, thinking about how much he wanted to kiss her neck, and he'd started mentally undressing her. She knew what he was thinking from the look on his face, and now she was running away again.

He looked down at the uneven floorboards of the porch. It was the only way he could hide the desire he knew was in his eyes. "I brought over Chinese food," he said.

She shook her head no. "Thanks, but I already ate," she said. "Good night, T."

"Kelly, don't shut me out."

His quiet words made her slowly turn around to face him. "Jackson, I can't handle seeing you right now. I need some time. I need my life to be simple for a while. And face it, our relationship has never been simple."

"We can make it simple." His voice sounded calm, matter-of-fact, betraying none of his desperation.

He took a step toward her, and Kelly took a step back, panic flaring in her stomach. If he touched her, she wasn't sure she could resist him. It was bad enough seeing him, talking to him. It was frightening the way her memories of the way she used to feel for him could consume her. It was almost as if they weren't memories at all.

But there was no way she could still be in love with him, not after seven years. No way.

"I have to get back to work," she said again. "I'm sorry."

She went into the house, closing the door tightly behind her. She leaned against it for a moment before climbing up the stairs to her apartment.

Dear Kelly,
Still no word from the American consulate.

The thought of serving ten years in this hell-hole scares me to death. It's unbelievable that this farce could have come this far. I've been framed. It's as clear as the daylight that I know is shining outside, despite the fact that it barely penetrates the thick walls of this stinking cell. I'm being punished for failing to cooperate with this country's current government, failing to reveal the location of the rebel forces, failing to reveal the names of the people who led me to my meeting with the rebel leader.

What's really ridiculous is that I don't approve of many of the rebels' methods in their fight for freedom. But if I betrayed them, it would mean the death of many people, most of them women and children.

So I sit here. Wherever the hell "here" is. Somewhere in Central America. I might as well be on the moon, a million miles away from the land of the free and the home of the brave, a million miles away from your sweet smile, writing letters to you in my mind, letters that have no hope of reaching you until I am free to deliver them myself.

With luck, that will be soon. Your eighteenth birthday is coming, and I intend to be there.

I love you.

Love, T.

KELLY SAT AT HER COMPUTER, staring at the empty screen.

Well, it wasn't quite empty. It said "Chapter Ten" about a quarter of the way down, and there were two carriage return symbols after that, along with a tab symbol. The cursor flashed five spaces in, ready to start the first paragraph.

But all she could think about was T. Jackson Winchester the Second, and the best and worst night she'd ever had in her life. It was the best because it had been an amazing Cinderella-like fantasy, with T. Jackson playing the part of Prince Charming. And it was the worst, because after it was over, after all the dust had settled, he had walked out of her life for good, and her world turned into a pumpkin.

Until now.

*Seven years later.*

KELLY CLOSED HER EYES, remembering that May night. Prom night. It had been a night like this one, hot and humid, more like summer than spring.

That afternoon, she'd modeled her prom dress for Kevin and T. Jackson. Kevin had just finished his first year of law school, and T. had finally graduated from college, having had a year off between his sophomore and junior years. T. was hanging out with the O'Briens, kicking back for a few weeks, taking a vacation before facing the realities of the working world....

"Tonight I'm going to wear my hair up," she'd said to them, twirling around the living room to show off the sweeping skirt of her long gown.

"Sweet Lord," Kevin said, staring at her. "When did *you* turn into a girl?"

She made a face at him. "Try opening your eyes sometimes, dweeb. I've been a girl for sixteen years."

She risked a glance at T. He was looking at her, a small, funny smile on his face. She smiled back at him, her heart doing a fast somersault. *He* knew that she was a girl.

"Sure could've fooled me." Kevin grinned. "I thought when you said you were going to get dressed up for the prom, you meant you'd wear your jeans without the holes in the knees and a new pair of cowboy boots."

"Ha ha," Kelly said.

"Just please don't tell me Mom bought that dress with the grocery money." Kevin made a face. "You look great, Kel, but I don't think a prom dress is worth having to eat hot dogs for the rest of the summer."

"This dress used to be Grandma's. It didn't cost a cent. Your stomach is safe."

The gown was outrageously retro, right out of the late 1930s, and it fit Kelly as if it had been made for her from some kind of shimmery, slippery cornflower-blue fabric that matched her eyes.

Kelly turned to find T. still watching her long after Kevin had gone into the kitchen to forage for a snack.

It hadn't been too much later when the telephone rang. Kevin answered it, and bellowed up the stairs for Kelly. She came clattering into the kitchen where T. and her brother were looking at the newspaper, trying to decide which movie to take Kevin's girlfriend, Beth, and one of her friends to that night.

"It's your boyfriend," Kevin said in a purposely obnoxious high voice, and Kelly snatched the phone away, glaring dangerously at him.

She covered the mouthpiece. "Frank's not my boyfriend. He's a *friend* who happens to be a *boy,* and we're going to the prom together. So don't be a jerk."

On the phone, Frank sounded terrible. He had some kind of stomach virus, he told her. There was no way on earth he was going to make it to the prom.

Kelly slowly hung up the phone.

"What did Frankie want?" Kevin asked. "Can't decide between the sky-blue or the chartreuse tux?"

She wheeled, turning on him angrily. "When are you going to grow up? You're in graduate school, you're supposed to be an adult now, so why don't you act like one? Frank's sick, so I'm not going to the prom, all

right? Does that satisfy your juvenile curiosity? Or is
there something else you want to know?"

"I'm sorry." Kevin was instantly contrite. "I didn't
mean to be—"

"I'll take you," T. said.

"What?" Kevin and Kelly turned to him at the same
time.

He was looking at Kelly, and he smiled his easy
smile when their eyes met. "I mean, I'd *like* to take
you."

Kevin stared at his friend in exasperation. "We're
double-dating tonight. What, are you just going to blow
off this friend of Beth's?"

"No." T. crossed his arms in front of him, and leaned
casually back in his chair. "I'll call her and tell her I
can't make it."

"Because you want to take my little sister to some
stupid high school dance?" Kevin laughed. "She's going
to love that—"

"It's *not* a stupid dance," Kelly protested.

"Kev, it's her *prom....*"

Kevin sighed, looking from Kelly to Jax and back
again. "Then I suppose *I* should take her."

"Gee, thanks," Kelly said. "A night out with Mr. Enthusiasm. I'd rather stay home."

But T. laughed, shaking his head. "No, Kev, you
don't get it, do you? *I* want to take her. I *want* to take
her. I would *love* to take her...."

Kelly swallowed. What was T. Jackson saying? She
heard the words, but the implications were too intense.

T. turned and looked at her, his green eyes lit with

an odd fire. "Kelly, will you let me take you to your prom?"

"Whoa, wait a minute," Kevin said before she could answer. He stared at his friend with growing realization, his voice tinged with disbelief. "Winchester, do you have, like, the *hots* for my little sister?"

But it was as if T. hadn't heard Kevin. He was just sitting there, his chair tipped back against the wall, smiling up at Kelly, waiting for her to answer him.

"Yeah." She'd smiled into his eyes as she'd nodded. "T., I'd really like that..."

Looking back now, Kelly knew that was the very moment she'd admitted to herself that she was in love with Tyrone Jackson Winchester the Second. And once she'd admitted it, she realized that she'd been in love with him for years. It wasn't puppy love. It wasn't a crush or an infatuation. It was solid, total, powerful love.

As she sat staring at her blank computer screen nearly seven years later, Kelly had to wonder.

What if T. had really been in love with her, too? What if they'd stayed together the way he'd promised, if he'd been the man she'd married when she was nineteen years old instead of Brad? Would her feelings have lasted?

JAX WOKE UP DRENCHED in sweat.

It was the nightmare again. The same old nightmare. He was back at that joke they'd called a trial.

He'd taken a flight from London a week earlier because the magazine he worked for had secured him a rare personal interview with the leader of the rebel

forces in the tiny Central American country. The interview had gone smoothly and he had returned to his
hotel room to type up his notes on his laptop computer.

Later that night he was roughly awakened by government soldiers and dragged to an official building where
he was questioned about the location of the rebel forces.
He'd been scared to death, but he refused to reveal even
what little he knew about where he had been and who
his contacts were.

Finally, after more than twenty-four hours of relentless questioning, he'd been released.

Back at the hotel, he'd considered calling the American consulate, telling them what had just happened,
but there was a flight to Miami leaving almost immediately, and he barely had time to get to the airport, let
alone make a phone call.

And he wanted to get out of there. Fast. He would
have taken the next flight to Hades if he'd had to.

It was then, on his way to the plane, that the government's military police stopped his taxi. A quick search
of his overnight bag led to the discovery of several large
sacks of cocaine tucked neatly next to his underwear.

It was such an obvious frame-up that Jackson had
laughed.

But as he sat in the ridiculous excuse for a court-
room the next day, listening to the announcement of the
guilty verdict and the resulting ten-year jail sentence,
he stopped laughing.

He'd managed to get in touch with the American
consulate, but they could do nothing for him. Drug
charges were out of their jurisdiction.

He was furious. It was so obvious. He was a reporter,

he had information the government wanted. It was such a blatant setup. The drugs had been planted in his bag. What about his rights? He was an American—

But Jax had no rights, the consulate finally told him. He wasn't a hostage. He wasn't a political prisoner. He'd been convicted of possession of drugs, and there was nothing anyone could do to help him.

So he went to jail. He did not pass go, and he sure as hell didn't collect two hundred dollars.

Be good, the warden told him, and maybe you'll get out in five or six years.

It had been hell.

Jax had been put, alone, in a dark, damp cell with only a tiny slit of a window. He was let out only for an occasional meal or a walk around the compound. He might've gone crazy, and maybe he even did a little bit, because he started imagining Kelly. He started seeing her there with him, keeping him company, giving him strength. He had no paper, no pencil, but he still wrote hundreds of letters to Kelly. He wrote letters in his mind, letters that would never be sent, words he vowed he'd one day put onto paper.

And somehow he'd survived for twenty horrific months.

For years after, he'd had terrible nightmares, but finally they'd stopped.

So why was he dreaming about it again?

# CHAPTER THREE

AFTER TIPPING THE ROOM-SERVICE waiter, Jax brought the breakfast tray to the table and set it down next to his computer. He poured himself a cup of steaming coffee and took a sip of the dark, pungent brew as he pulled his current story up on the computer screen.

Yesterday, when he'd finished writing, he'd left Jared in his horrible little room at the boardinghouse, fuming about the way Jax had spirited Carrie away from him.

Now. To get Jared on that boat for Europe.

Thinking hard, Jax took another sip of his coffee. He hadn't realized shipping Jared off to Europe was going to be this difficult. Jared was right—there was no way he would voluntarily leave Carrie, the way Jax had left Kelly all those years ago.

The two situations weren't exactly parallel, Jax reminded himself. Although Carrie and Kelly were both sixteen, back in Carrie's day, women frequently married at that age. And Jared wasn't Jax. Jared was a hero, while Jax was...only Jax.

He flipped through his notebook. In Jax's original outline, Jared had left Boston and gone to Europe, vowing to make his fortune and return a rich man, rich enough to wed the beautiful Carrie. But Jax had written that outline before he'd fleshed out the characters, before he knew just how bold and dauntless and damned self-confident Jared was going to be.

So now he was stuck with Carrie hidden away with some distant relatives, and Jared crossing his arms and refusing to leave until he found her.

How do you make a man do something he doesn't want to do?

Love.

No, it was because of love that Jared wanted to stick around.

Blackmail.

"Don't start with that dark family secret thing again," Jared said warningly.

"Cooperate, and I won't have to," muttered Jax.

That left money.

No, Jared had already said that he didn't need money to keep Carrie's heart.

What else?

Patriotism?

If Jared had the opportunity to make a fortune *and* at the same time help the Northern war effort...

England had provided weapons to the South during the Civil War. Despite the Northern blockades, English ships continued to smuggle guns to the Confederacy.

Enter Captain Reilly, the same old friend of Jared's father's who had appeared in chapters two and six, thought Jax with triumph. Reilly would offer Jared a chance to sail on his ship, to pirate the British vessels, seize their cargos and deliver the weaponry to the North—at a fair enough price to make a small fortune, of course.

Jax reached for his computer keyboard.

A sharp knock sounded on the door, rousing Jared from his sleep.

He sat up, his heart pounding as he stared into the darkness of his tiny room. Carrie, he thought. Carrie!

But even as he lit a candle, the knock sounded again, along with a familiar rusty voice. "Jared Dexter, you in there, boy? Open the damned door."

It was Captain Magnus Reilly, the owner of the ship called the *Graceful Lady Fair*.

Jax wrote quickly, bringing Captain Reilly into the room and letting the grizzled old man describe his plan to Jared.

"What do you say, Jared?" the captain asked. "Are you in? We've a chance to make a fortune."

Jared looked at Reilly in the flickering candlelight. Slowly he shook his head. "Sorry, old man," he said. "Not this time."

"No," Jax nearly shouted. "You're supposed to go with him, you fool. Don't you get it? It's your chance to serve your country *and* make some bucks. You'll come back rich, and then there's no way Carrie's family can refuse you."

Jared crossed his arms obstinately. "I'm not going anywhere until I find Carrie."

We'll see about that. Jax gritted his teeth as he deleted the last few sentences that he'd written.

Jared looked at Reilly in the flickering candle-light.

The boy's normally handsome, exuberant face looked pale and tired, thought the captain. And from the looks of things, he'd recently been in a fight.

"Magnus," Jared said slowly, "can you wait a few weeks? I can't leave the country right now."

What was wrong with him today? Jax pressed the palms of his hands against the headache that was starting to throb behind his eyes.

In his mind, Jared smiled nastily at Jax. "*I* know what's wrong with you," he said, then uttered the words writers hate most to hear. "You've got writer's block."

"I do not have writer's block," Jax said very calmly. "I simply have an obstinate, pigheaded, stubborn fool of a character who is refusing to cooperate."

Jared sat back on his bed, lacing his fingers together behind his head. "Don't worry, the writer's block is only temporary," he returned with equal calm. "Work this thing out with Kelly and you'll be able to write again in no time, whether I cooperate or not."

"Just tell Reilly you'll go with him." Jax ran his fingers tiredly through his hair. "Please?"

"Write me a love scene with Carrie and you've got a deal."

"Look, you're gonna have a happy ending," Jax promised. "I can guarantee that—"

"*That's* what's bothering you." Jared sat forward. "There's no guarantee that things are going to work out between you and Kelly. Bummer."

"Don't say 'bummer.' People in the nineteenth century didn't say 'bummer.'" Jax took a deep breath. "Will you *please* go with Reilly?"

"My offer holds," Jared told him. "Write me that love scene and your wish is my command."

This was ridiculous. Jax readjusted the keyboard and began typing, refusing to be held hostage by his own character.

Without warning, Reilly pulled a revolver from under his jacket, pressing the cold metal of the barrel to Jared's head.

"You're coming with me, boy," he growled. "And you're coming now!"

Jared burst out laughing. "Wow, Jax," he said, between gasps for breath. "That's *really* stupid. There's absolutely *no* one who's going to believe that."

"Oh, shut up," Jax muttered. Cursing under his breath, he saved the job, turned off the laptop computer and went searching for some aspirin.

Dear Kelly,

You appear in my cell again today, and again, even though I know you can't possibly be real, I am thankful for your presence.

You are twelve years old this time, and as you look around at the rough stone walls, at the damp dirt floor and at the wooden bench and dirty straw that I use for a bed, I can see anger in your dark blue eyes.

You look me over just as carefully, taking in my beard and my long, dirty hair.

You speak!

I can hear your husky voice clearly in the quiet of the cell. Last time you visited, you didn't talk. You only watched me.

"You smell," you tell me sternly, as if it were my fault, and I apologize.

"Sometimes," I say, "when it rains, the guards let us out with some scraps of soap and we can wash—"

You are looking at me oddly, and I realize I am speaking to you in Spanish. It's been so long since I've heard an American voice. I translate, and you nod.

"I guess it's been a while since it's rained," you say, sitting next to me on the straw.

"Soon it will do nothing but rain," I tell you, "and there will be five inches of brackish water on the floor of my cell."

You reach over and take my hand, holding it tightly with your slender fingers.

I notice the scabs on your knees and elbows, and you tell me about falling off your bike.

I sympathize. I am careful to hide my own healing wounds—three deep cuts from an irate guard's whip that I earned by helping a fellow prisoner to his feet when he stumbled on his way to the courtyard for another endless roll-call session.

But I can tell from looking into your eyes that

you know. You also know about the broken rib I received from an earlier beating.

"I didn't cry," I tell you. "They can beat me, spit on me, treat me like less than an animal, but I will not cry. I hold my head up when I walk. I look them in the eye. I am the Americano, and they both hate me and respect me for that."

You look at me as if I am your hero, and for a few short hours, I am.

"Hey," you say, looking more closely at the walls, "igneous rocks."

We spend some time identifying and arguing about the rocks that were used in building this prison.

I almost forget where I am as I chip at the wall to get you a sample for your rock collection.

You leave when the sun hits the correct angle. For forty-seven minutes it will stream into my little window. A narrow strip of sunlight will travel across the wall, and I will stand in it, letting it shine on my dirty face. It gives me hope to know that only a few thousand miles away, that same powerful sun is shining on you.

I love you.

Love, T.

JAX LEANED AGAINST THE CORRIDOR wall outside the university classroom, waiting for Kelly.

This was probably a mistake. No, not probably. Definitely. Following Kelly around this way was definitely a mistake. She would definitely be annoyed. But Jax knew only one way to achieve success in life, and it involved a large amount of tenacity and a great deal of perseverance, and all the stubbornness he could muster, which could actually be quite a bit when it came down to it.

He was going to marry Kelly O'Brien. That much was certain.

What wasn't so clear was how he was going to deal with the fact that the bride-to-be didn't even want to have a cup of coffee with him.

After rejecting his offer of Chinese food five days ago, she'd turned him down the next day for lunch. He'd tried brunch the following day, and breakfast the day after that, with similar luck. Yesterday he was reduced to asking her out for coffee, for God's sake, and she'd turned that down, too.

So what was he doing here, waiting for her to come out of class? What was he going to invite her to do now? Go out with him for a glass of water?

Maybe it was time to start over again with dinner.

Sooner or later, she was going to give in.

She had told him once that she loved him. And if she had loved him even only a tenth as much as he loved her, he would bet his entire seven-figure bank account that those feelings hadn't totally disappeared.

The classroom door opened, and students spilled out into the hall. Good grief, they looked so young. Some of them were twelve years younger than he was. Had he really been their age once?

Kelly didn't see him as she came through the door.

She was wearing a denim workshirt with the sleeves rolled up, a worn-out pair of jeans and cowboy boots. Her hair was back in a single braid. Except for the hint of makeup on her face and lips, she looked almost exactly as she had when she was fourteen.

Except almost ten years older, thank God. Her jeans hugged her body in a way that they never had when she was fourteen.

Jax followed her down the hall, not catching up with her until she stopped to swing open the big double doors that led into the building's main foyer.

Her eyes narrowed dangerously as she stared at him. "You're following me around," she said, not bothering to say hello.

"Yeah," he said, unperturbed.

She went into the foyer, moving out of the way of the steady stream of students who were going in and out of the doors. "Well, stop it," she said sternly. "You can tell Kevin that I'm really okay—"

"This has nothing to do with Kevin," Jax said, shaking his head. "I'm trying to get you to go out to dinner with me, Kel, and if you keep saying no, then you better get used to me following you around."

Kelly gazed at him. "Do you even *own* any socks?"

He looked down at his feet, lifting his pants slightly to get a better view of his bare ankles. "If I go back to my hotel and put on a pair of socks, will you have dinner with me?"

"I can't." She headed toward the doors that led out into the warm spring sunshine. "I have my last exam of the semester tomorrow."

"How about tomorrow night?" Jax followed her.

"How long are you going to be in town?" She stopped on the steps outside the building to fish in her backpack for her sunglasses.

As long as it takes. "At least a few more days." Jax put on his own sunglasses. "I've got some business to take care of on Friday, so..."

They began walking slowly down the sidewalk. The sun was hot on Jax's back, and he slipped off his jacket and rolled up his sleeves. "If you want, I could help you study tonight."

She slid him a sidelong glance. "For an advanced calculus exam?"

"Ouch." He winced. "Are you really taking calculus?"

"*Advanced* calculus."

"Yeah, right. Rub it in." He'd barely made it through trigonometry back in high school. And as an English major in college, he'd purposely stayed far, far away from the math building.

The sunlight glinted off his golden hair. With his dark sunglasses and his million-dollar smile, he looked like some kind of movie star. It was just Kelly's luck that T. Jackson had become better looking as he got older. Now, why couldn't he have thinning hair and a potbelly like some of Kevin's other old college friends?

"Why are you taking it?" he asked. "I mean, I've never known you to be a masochist."

She shot him a quick look, but he didn't realize the irony of his words. He was right, she wasn't a masochist, and that was one of the reasons she didn't want him hanging around.

"I'm taking it because I like science, and calculus is a prerequisite for some of the advanced science courses I want to take next year," she told him. Her cowboy boots made a clicking sound against the concrete sidewalk. "I'm sorry, T.," she added, "but I don't think you'll be any help as a study partner."

"It's been years since you've seen me," he protested. "How do you know I haven't suddenly become a math whiz?"

Kelly burst out laughing.

"How many more semesters do you have before you graduate?" he asked.

"Three," Kelly said. "I married Brad when I was a sophomore. Appropriate, huh?"

Marrying Brad had been incredibly sophomoric. She'd thought she knew what she was doing, what she wanted, but in reality, she had had absolutely no idea, not one clue. And apparently Brad hadn't known what he'd really wanted, either.

"We moved to California that summer," she told T. Jackson, "and there wasn't enough time for me to transfer to a school out there. So I got a job, and by the time the spring semester started, Brad had been laid off and we really needed the money."

"Are you going to take this summer off," he asked, "or do you have a job lined up?"

She shrugged. "Nothing definite. I've interviewed at a couple of places."

"Spend the summer on the Cape with me."

Kelly stopped walking. "What?"

"I live out on Cape Cod," T. Jackson said. He took off his sunglasses. She could see from his eyes that he was actually serious. "I've got a house on the beach, on the bay side, in Dennis. It's this huge modern monster—we've got lots of extra bedrooms, there's plenty of room." He stopped, laughed softly, shaking his head. "Look, I'd love to spend some time with you, and..."

"I won't even go out to dinner with you," Kelly told him. "What on earth makes you think I'd want to spend the entire summer with you on the Cape?"

He put his sunglasses back on. "I don't know," he said. "You always wanted to. You talked about it all the time, and I just thought..."

"I was *twelve,* T." She wasn't being completely truthful. She'd talked about it when she was older than twelve, too. Dreamed about it. A summer at the Winchester compound on the Cape.

Kelly stared up at him, seeing her face reflected in the lenses of his sunglasses. Truth was, spending the summer on the beach with T. Jackson would fulfill just about every single one of her childhood fantasies. And quite a few of her teenaged fantasies, too.

But as an adult, she knew her fantasies about T. were simply that. Fantasies. She knew what kind of man he was, because she'd been married to a man exactly like him. She no longer had any illusions about living happily ever after with T. Jackson, no matter how charming and handsome and sexy he was.

If she wanted happily ever after—and she did—she was going to have to find a different type of man. She'd gladly trade some of the spark, the sexual chemistry, for a man who would love only her. She wanted a man who gave as much as he took, a man who truly knew how to love, not just *be* loved. A man who kept his promises.

But there was something to be said for spending a few months with T. Jackson Winchester the Second. It would be one *hell* of a summer, that was for sure.

Unless this was just another of his favors to Kevin...

She could just imagine the conversation her brother must've had with T. "Cheer her up," Kevin must've told Jax. "Take her out, show her a good time. She used to have a crush on you, remember? Make her feel important. If anyone can do it, you can."

But it hadn't been a crush. What she had felt for T. Jackson had been so much more than a crush. And did she really want to wreck her romantic memories of her first love by going and having a tawdry affair with the man?

When the answer didn't come as an immediate no, Kelly shook her head in disgust. What was wrong with her?

"I'm going to be busy all summer," she said, starting down the sidewalk again. And she would be. When she finished writing her second novel, she'd start on a third. It was a never-ending process, but one that she loved. And right now her writing was a way to stay safe, insulated from the rest of the world. And from T. Jackson Winchester the Second in particular.

"Think about it," he said.

The annoying thing was, she would. In fact, she'd probably think about nothing else. She'd probably dream about spending the entire summer with T. He'd already appeared in her dreams last night, her imagination clothing him in a hell of a lot less than the bathing suit he'd wear as a standard uniform on the Cape. Her subconscious was giving her a very deliberate message—there was unfinished business between the two of them.

But it was a hormonal thing. It was pure sex, and

it had nothing to do with love. Even if she ended up giving in to T.'s persistent demands, even if she ended up sleeping with the man, she'd never let him back into her heart. Never.

"So are we on for dinner tomorrow night?" Jax asked as they stopped outside the school newspaper office door.

"Tomorrow night?" She shook her head. "I don't—"

"Friday night, then."

"No," she said definitely. "I'm going to a meeting in the late afternoon. I don't know how long it'll last."

"I've got something happening Friday afternoon, too," he said. "We can eat later—"

"No."

Jax looked at her, silent for a moment. Then he laughed. "I guess I'm going to have to keep following you around, then."

Kelly took off her sunglasses, sighing with exasperation. "Jackson—"

He kissed her.

It was little more than a light brushing of his lips against hers, but it was a kiss. And it was enough to make her system go haywire. She stared at him in shock.

"See you tomorrow, Kel." He smiled and walked away.

JARED WAS RIGHT. JAX realized it would be much more romantically tragic if Carrie were whisked away to the safety of distant relatives *after* she and Jared had a scene in which they planned to run away together. Jax just wasn't convinced it should be a love scene.

"She's only sixteen," he muttered. "She's too young."

"That's a load of crap, and you know it," Jared countered. "Just because *you* made the mistake of thinking that *Kelly* was too young—"

"She *was* too young."

"You ran because you knew you couldn't deny her anything," Jared said. "You knew if you stayed, you'd make love to her, because she wanted you to. You left because you were scared."

"I left because I loved her!" Jax argued.

"You didn't even have the decency to tell her you were going—"

"Because what Kevin threatened to do was—"

"So what are you saying?" Jared's dark eyes were intense. "Are you saying that you want *me* to make the same stupid mistake you did? I thought one of the reasons you were writing this story was to give yourself a chance to do it over, and do it *right* this time."

"Fine!" Jax threw up his hands. "I'll write that love scene. But I've got to warn you, friend. It's only going to be one night. And things are going to get much worse before you get your happy ending. I've got another 230 pages to fill."

JAX SAT IN HIS SPORTS CAR. From where he was parked, he could see light streaming from the front window of Kelly's apartment.

He'd left his hotel room this evening after writing a passionate scene between Jared and Carrie. Writing sensual scenes made him restless, in need of air. He'd intended to go to a movie, but somehow he'd wound up here.

He'd waited for Kelly this afternoon as she finished up her calculus exam. He'd asked her to go out to dinner again, and again she refused. This time he could barely keep up with her as she nearly ran to the newspaper office. She'd disappeared inside with only a quick good-bye, not giving him enough time to kiss her again.

God, he wanted to kiss her. He wanted to kiss her the way Jared had kissed Carrie in the scene he'd written only a few hours ago. Jax wanted to kiss Kelly the way he had on that night so many years ago—prom night....

At first Kevin had refused to let Jax take Kelly to the school dance. He'd followed Jax all the way down-town, to the tux rental place. A little bell had tinkled as they walked into the air-conditioned interior of the tiny shop.

"I need a tux," Jax told the skinny man behind the counter.

"No, he doesn't," Kevin countered, folding his big arms across his beefy chest. "*I* need a tux." He turned to Jax. "She's too young for you."

The shopkeeper removed a measuring tape from around his neck, and stood looking at them. "You both want tuxes?"

"No." Jax smiled. "Just me."

"No." The fierceness of Kevin's voice was a sharp contrast to Jax's cool control. "Not him. Me. I need it for tonight."

"I'm taking her," Jax said mildly to Kevin. He leaned against a glass-topped counter that held an assortment of bow ties and cummerbunds.

"She's a *kid*." Kevin's face was pink with anger. "You should be dating women, not little girls."

"Don't you trust me?" Jax asked, his voice level.

"No, not after the way I saw you looking at her this afternoon." Kevin ran his hands through his red hair in exasperation as he glared up at his friend. "Hell, Winchester, she's only sixteen!"

"I know how old she is."

"You better keep that in mind. She's jailbait, pal." Kevin took a threatening step forward, stabbing Jax's chest with his forefinger. But Jax didn't move a muscle, didn't even blink. "You mess with her," Kevin threatened, "and you'll end up in prison. And I'll personally escort you there."

The two young men locked gazes for several long moments. Then Jax smiled, shaking his head slightly. "You know I'd never do anything to hurt her, Kev."

"Mess with Kelly and I'll kill you," Kevin repeated, but the anger was gone from his voice.

"I'm crazy about her," Jax admitted. "I'll take good care of her, I promise."

"You *are* crazy." Kevin laughed with disbelief. "Beth has a gorgeous friend who's dying to get naked with you, but *you* want to go out with a girl who's barely out of diapers. I just don't get it."

Jax smiled. "You don't have to get it. Just relax. I want to go out with Kelly tonight, and you want to go out with Beth. We're both doing each other a favor, okay?"

"I still think you're nuts."

Jax looked at the shopkeeper, who was watching them with unabashed interest. "I need a tux for tonight," he said again.

But the shopkeeper shook his head. "What're you?

Six foot five? I'm sorry, no can do. I only had a few rental tuxes in your size, and they're out. Won't be back in 'til Sunday."

"Then I'll buy one," Jax said.

"You'll what?" Kevin's eyebrows disappeared under his thick red hair.

Jax smiled at his friend. "I'll buy one." He looked back at the shopkeeper. "And I'll pay extra if you get the alterations done by this afternoon."

By five o'clock, Jax had showered, shaved and finished putting on his brand-new tuxedo up in Kevin's room. He didn't remember being this excited about going to his own junior prom.

Kelly's door was still closed, so he headed downstairs to wait for her. Jax stopped in the kitchen first, pulling the flowers he'd bought her out of the refrigerator and carrying them into the living room.

Nolan O'Brien was lying on the couch, reading the newspaper as Jax came in, and he looked over the top of it, smiling. Kevin and Kelly's father was an older, heavier version of Kevin. He had the same red-orange hair, thinning a bit on top, though, the same beefy frame, the same cheerful disposition and millions and millions of the same freckles.

"So you're the sacrificial substitute date for the prom, eh?" the older man asked, not bothering to move from his relaxed position on the couch.

"It's no sacrifice, Nolan," Jax said easily, sitting down in the rocking chair that was across from the couch. He leaned forward to put the flowers on the coffee table.

"A corsage *and* a dozen roses," Nolan said, looking

at Jax appraisingly with a slow smile. "I was wondering when you were going to start noticing that Kelly's almost all grown up. Looks like it finally happened."

Jax smiled.

Nolan folded the newspaper. "I suppose I don't have to give you the normal 'date speech' that I give the rest of the boys that take Kelly out—you know, the 'no drinking and driving' speech, the 'get her home before midnight' speech..."

"I know your rules," Jax said, nodding. "Although you might want to cut loose with the curfew for tonight. Kelly told me there are after-prom parties scheduled one after the other until sun-up. And then, if it's warm enough, everyone's heading over to the beach."

Nolan nodded. "Okay," he said agreeably, swinging himself up into a sitting position. "Just don't forget, Kelly comes across as being much older than she really is. Keep in mind that she's only sixteen. There's a big difference between sixteen and twenty-two, Jax."

The older man's eyes were intense. Jax smiled, realizing that Nolan was giving him a polite version of the same message Kevin had delivered at the tuxedo shop: Don't mess with Kelly.

"I know," Jax said quietly.

"Good."

Ten minutes later, Kelly was sitting next to Jax in his little red Spitfire, and they were heading down the road toward town, toward the restaurant where he had made dinner reservations.

Jax glanced over at her, still struck by how beautiful, how elegant and poised she looked.

When she'd appeared in the living room, his heart had nearly stopped.

She was wearing that fabulous blue gown, and her hair was pinned up, swept back loosely, femininely, from her face. She was wearing makeup and her eyes looked more blue than they ever had before, with her long, dark lashes accentuated. Her normally pretty, fresh face looked exotically beautiful with her hair up, giving Jax a good look at the gorgeous woman she was destined to become in the next few years.

Kelly was a child-woman, a curious mixture of innocence and poise, elegance and enthusiasm. She was unconsciously sexy—well, maybe not entirely unconsciously. She wasn't wearing a bra beneath her slinky gown because the back of the dress was open. True, the top wasn't tight fitting, but the smooth material occasionally clung to her lithe body, and the effect was... extremely distracting.

He'd thought he'd have no trouble taking her out like this. He'd thought after four years of being close friends with Kelly that it wouldn't be hard to remember she was still only a kid.

So why was it that he could think of little else but how her lips would feel against his?

Jackson's pulse was running too fast, his heart pounding. Relax, he ordered himself, forcing himself to breathe slowly. Just relax. Stay cool.

"This feels...strange," Kelly said, glancing at T. from beneath her eyelashes. She laughed softly. "You look as tense as I feel."

"I'm not tense," Jax protested, reaching up with one

hand to loosen the tight muscles in the back of his neck.
"Are you tense?"

"Yeah," she admitted with her usual candor and a
brief, charming smile. "I just keep thinking...well...
maybe we should go Dutch tonight."

"Dutch?" he said, disbelief in his voice as he looked
over at her. "Nope. This is on me, Kel."

"It doesn't seem fair to make you pay for everything—" she turned slightly in the bucket seat to face
him "—just because I happen to be female. Especially
considering that I shanghaied you."

"Do I look like I'm suffering?" Jax asked, amused.

"You never look like you're suffering. That's why
it's so hard to tell whether or not you actually *are.*"

"I'll let you know if and when I start," he assured
her with a grin as he pulled up to a red light.

She looked up at him, and he returned her gaze.
Her face was so familiar. He knew her so well. Or did
he? He knew the child, not the woman. And sometime
during the past few months, she'd suddenly become
part woman. Her skin looked so smooth, so pale compared to the inky darkness of her hair. Yet her cheeks
were flushed with a soft glow of good health, her mouth
curved up into a small smile, her eyes bright, sparking
as they met his own. Jax could imagine himself drowning in the blue depths of her eyes. Imagine? Hell, he
*was* drowning.

A short beep from the car behind him told him that
the light had changed, and he forced his eyes back to
the road. After a moment, he glanced quickly at Kelly,
but she was looking down at the small clutch purse she

was holding in her lap, a faint tinge of embarrassment on her cheeks.

God, she knew everything he was feeling just from looking into his eyes. He'd learned a long time ago that he couldn't hide things from Kelly, so why should he expect to be able to hide this?

The main problem was that he wasn't exactly sure what "this" was.

Was he in love with her?

If he wasn't in love with her already, he was definitely teetering. No, not just teetering, he'd already lost his balance. There was nowhere for him to go but over the edge.

Kelly glanced at him again, smiling, and Jax felt a sudden lack of gravity deep in the pit of his stomach.

Free fall. He was in free fall, there was no doubt about it. He'd taken the plunge, and he was falling hard and fast.

Add into the equation all the feelings he was already carrying around for Kelly. It was one hell of an emotional attachment, and one he couldn't deny. Add to *that* this explosively intense physical attraction...

If she were eighteen years old, he would court her ruthlessly. He would use every trick in the book to get her to fall in love with him, too. He would take her out, buy her presents—hell, he'd even seduce her. He would tell her and show her in every way possible that he loved her. He would make love to her endlessly. And then he would get down on his knees and beg her to marry him.

God, he actually wanted to *marry* her, as in 'til death do us part, as in happily ever after. There was just one problem. She wasn't eighteen years old. She was sixteen. Jailbait, as Kevin had so indelicately put it.

For one wild moment Jax wondered if Nolan and Lori O'Brien would give their daughter permission to marry him now. But as quickly as the thought entered his mind, he pushed it away. It wouldn't happen. Kelly's parents would never agree to it. They would say that she wasn't old enough. And they would be right.

There was just no getting around it. Kelly was too young.

That left him only one option. He'd simply have to wait for her to get older.

"This *is* strange," Kelly said. "I think this is the first time I've ever seen you so quiet." She laughed softly. "Usually I can't shut you up."

"Sorry," Jax said. "I was thinking."

"About the job offer you got from that London magazine?"

He looked over to find her watching him, her face serious. "What do you think about that? Should I take it?"

She was quiet for so long, he thought maybe she wasn't going to answer. But when he glanced back at her, she was still watching him steadily.

"I can't answer that fairly," she finally said. "See, when I think about it, I can find all kinds of reasons why you *should* take that job. I mean, come on, T., you'd be living in *London.* That would be so great. You could spend your vacations in Europe." She looked away from him, out the window, at the spring wildflowers that were growing along the sides of the road. "It's true it's not a lot of money," she continued, "but you'd be paid to write. After a couple of years as a staff writer for the magazine, you'd have name recognition, so if you ever started working on that novel you keep talking about, you'd probably have an easier time selling it."

She was quiet, and he glanced at her again. "But..." he prompted her.

"I'd miss you," Kelly said simply. "That's why I can't answer your question fairly. I don't want you to live on the other side of the Atlantic Ocean."

Happiness exploded inside of Jackson. "Then I won't go. I'll find a job in Boston."

"Tyrone, don't tease."

"I'm serious."

"But—" she started, then stopped, her eyes widening as Jackson pulled his sports car into the parking lot of the Breckenridge Inn, the fanciest restaurant in the area. "Whoa, T., what's this?"

"This is where we're having dinner." Jax pulled into a parking space at the edge of the big lot.

"But this is too expensive—"

"You're worth every penny."

"I would've settled for Bertucci's," she said.

"Why settle?" Jax pulled up the parking brake and turned off the engine as he smiled at her.

Kelly's eyes danced with delight. "Why don't you have women falling all over you, T.?" she asked. "You're so smooth, you put James Bond to shame."

"It's the name." Jax sighed. "Winchester," he said in his best Sean Connery. "Tyrone Jackson Winchester the Second... No, see, my name's way too long. By the time I finish saying my name, all the gorgeous women have either fallen asleep or they've gone off with the guy with the shorter name."

Kelly laughed again and Jax glanced at the dashboard. The digital clock read 5:35. The prom didn't start until eight o'clock. There were two hours and twenty-five minutes before he could dance with Kelly, before he could hold her in his arms. He wasn't sure he would survive until then.

Of course, compared to the four hundred and fifty-nine days he had to wait until she turned eighteen, two hours and twenty-five minutes was a piece of cake.

She was looking at him, her lips moist and parted slightly. God, he wanted to kiss her. God, he wanted to...

"Shall we go inside?" he asked, opening his door. But Kelly put her hand on his arm. Even through his jacket and shirt, her soft touch made him freeze.

"Jackson—" she began to say, then stopped, pulling her hand back onto her lap.

"Uh-oh." Jax tried to be light, turning toward her. "You only call me that when you mean business. What'd I do?"

Kelly shook her head. "There's something I want to ask you, and I'm not really sure how to."

"You've never had a problem being direct before. Just ask."

She looked down at her hands for a moment, then shook her head again, laughing softly. "This is stupid, but..." She looked up at him. "Is this a real date?"

Kelly was looking directly into his eyes, and again Jax had the sensation of drowning. He was being pulled under again. Sooner or later, he was going to go down, and he wouldn't make it back up. "I think so," he said slowly. "What's the definition of a real date?"

She moistened her lips with the tip of her tongue, and Jackson's eyes were drawn to her mouth. He couldn't look away—he was hypnotized.

"A real date is when you go out with someone that you like enough to kiss good-night when it's over," Kelly said softly.

When, oh when, did the inside of his car get so tiny?

Jax pulled his eyes away from the delicately shaped lips that were only a few scant inches from his own mouth. "Yeah," he managed to say. "This is a real date."

"Could you—" Kelly said haltingly. "Could we—" She laughed self-consciously and started again. "T., this is going to sound really weird, but the thought of kissing you is making me really nervous and——"

"Then I won't kiss you," he said quickly.

"No, that's not what—" She shook her head, laughing again. "See, I was just thinking if you kissed me *now,* I could stop being nervous about it."

"Now," Jackson repeated. He held on tightly to the steering wheel, afraid that if he let go, he'd lose his balance. She wanted him to kiss her. Now.

"I mean, it would take some of the pressure off, don't you think?"

No. No, he did not think that it would take any kind of pressure off at all. Not for him, anyway. Still, when he looked into her eyes, he knew there was no way on earth he could turn her down.

He felt himself lean toward her, closer, closer. He reached out his hand to cup her face. Her skin was so soft underneath his fingers. He ran his thumb across her lips.

Jax could feel his heart pounding in his chest. He was going to be the first twenty-two-year-old to die of a love-induced heart attack. He smiled. There were certainly worse ways to go.

Kelly returned his smile, then closed her eyes, lifting her lips to him. He moved that final fraction of an inch, and then he was kissing her.

Her mouth felt warm and soft as he slowly, gently brushed his own lips across hers. It took every ounce of control he had to keep himself from deepening the kiss, to keep himself from touching her lips with his tongue, from entering her sweet mouth.

Breathing hard, he pulled back to look at her. Her breasts were rising and falling as if she, too, were having trouble pulling air into her lungs.

"T., don't stop," she whispered, and he groaned, knowing he shouldn't kiss her again, knowing he *should* stop right here and right now before this got out of hand.

"Please," she whispered, and everything he knew he should do went right out the window as he bent his head to kiss her again.

This time her arms went up around his neck. He felt her fingers in his hair as their lips met. He felt her mouth open underneath his, her tongue lightly touch his lips.

He swept his arms around her, pulling her against his chest as he gently met her tongue with his own. He wanted to pull her over the parking brake onto his lap, to reach under her light spring shawl to cup her breasts in the palms of his hands. He wanted to kiss her long and hard and deep, and he wanted to keep kissing her until she turned eighteen. And then he wanted to make love to her. He wanted to be her first lover, and her last.

"Kelly," he said between kisses, his voice raspy and thick. "Kelly—"

He had to do it. He had to kiss her just once the way he was dying to. Just one real kiss.

He swept his tongue into her mouth, fiercely, wildly, claiming her, possessing her. He could feel her fingers tighten in his hair as she pulled him even closer to her, as she met his kiss with a passion that equaled his own.

One kiss became two, then three, then more, and suddenly nothing else mattered or even existed. There was only Kelly. Kelly, who knew him better than anyone in the world. Kelly, with whom he shared all of his secrets. All of his secrets, including this one—he loved her, the way a man loves a woman.

But faintly he was aware that time was passing, and somehow, somewhere, he found strength to pull away from her sweet lips.

"Oh, T.," she breathed, "I've never been kissed like that before."

He closed his eyes, still holding her in his arms, her head against his shoulder as waves of emotion flooded him. It was an odd combination of relief and guilt and love, happiness and great sorrow, all mixed together, blended in a confusing blur.

He held her for what seemed like hours, until his pulse slowed. When it reached as close as he thought it would get to normal for that evening, he released her.

His hands shook as he tried to get the keys out of the

ignition, and he dropped them on the floor. He took a deep breath and combed his hair back with his fingers, then turned to look at Kelly.

She smiled as he met her eyes. "Well, I guess you're not gay."

Jax stared at her, momentarily floored. "What did you just say?" he asked in a burst of air, even though he knew he'd heard her correctly.

"A few days ago, Christa asked me if you were gay."

"You're kidding." Christa was Kelly's aunt who had lived with the O'Briens that same summer that Jax had.

"She's been wondering for a while why you don't have a girlfriend. I told her I didn't know what your sexual preference was," Kelly said with a nonchalant shrug.

"*Kel*ly!" Jax's voice reached up an octave in outrage before he saw the amusement sparkling in her eyes, before the smile she was trying to hide crept out.

"Relax, Jackson. I told her that you were straight... but I don't think she believed me. She's very big on proof, and frankly, I didn't have any."

This conversation was getting *way* out of hand. And the clock on the dashboard now read 6:03. Man, had he really sat here in his car for the past half hour making out with Kevin's little sister? Someone was surely saving a place for him in hell, because that was right where he was going to go after Kevin broke his neck.

And Kelly was looking at him as though she didn't want to get out of the car for at least another half an hour.

"Kelly, let's have dinner," he said desperately, his usual cool demeanor slipping. "Please?"

With a smile, she adjusted the rearview mirror and carefully reapplied her lipstick. Jax couldn't bear to watch, afraid he wouldn't be able to keep himself from kissing it off her lips, too.

He forced himself out of the car, picked his keys up off the floor, then went around to open Kelly's door. He offered her his hand to help her out, and she put her slim, cool fingers into his as she smiled up at him. He caught a quick, breathtaking glimpse of her shapely legs through the slit in her skirt and then she was out of the car. He closed the door behind her, reminding himself to keep breathing.

As they crossed the gravel driveway to the front entrance, Kelly slipped her hand into the crook of Jax's arm. He covered her hand with his, unable to keep himself from lightly stroking the tops of her fingers.

"T.," she said quietly as they approached the door to the restaurant. He looked down into her steady blue gaze. "It didn't really help, did it?"

She was talking about those practice good-night kisses. With a laugh, Jax shook his head. "No, Kel, it sure didn't."

"Well, at least I'm not nervous anymore," she said with a small smile.

Yeah, but Jax still was. In fact, now he was *twice* as nervous.

## CHAPTER FOUR

Dear Kelly,
Another day dawns and I am still here in this damned miserable cell.

One of the guards takes pity on me and slips me some American paperback books that were left behind in the hotel where his wife works as a maid.

There are three of them—all romances. One is a long historical, the other two are shorter and set in the present day. I read them eagerly, voraciously, in the dim light from my little window. I read them over and over again, taking great joy in the happy endings, the tender embraces of the lovers reunited at last.

You come after sunset, when it's too dark to read any longer, and I proudly show the books to you. They are my prize possessions, and I keep them carefully out of sight of the other guards.

Tonight you are sixteen, and you leaf through the books casually in the darkness, far more interested in the paper they are printed on than the words themselves.

"If you write really small," you tell me, "you can use this paper and write between the lines."

I stare at you stupidly.

You laugh. "T., you always said that you'd write a novel if you could only find the time," you say. You lift one eyebrow humorously. "Well, suddenly you've got plenty of time."

I am elated, but only briefly. "I have nothing to write with."

"Ask the guard who gave you these books. Ask him for a pencil or a pen."

"I will."

You smile, and I suddenly realize you are wearing your prom dress. You are so beautiful, my heart nearly stops beating.

You lean forward to kiss me, and I can feel your soft lips, smell your perfume. You take me with you, back in time, and for a while, I am out of my cell. I sit with you in my sports car, clean-shaven and smelling sweet, wearing my tuxedo, and we kiss.

You are still so young, and I'm even older now, and I still don't know better. I still can't stop myself.

I love you.

Love, T.

IT WAS WELL PAST 2:00 A.M. BY the time Kelly shut down her computer and turned off the lights in her apartment. She moved to the living-room window, remembering that she hadn't closed and locked it the way she did every night. As she pulled the window down, the sound of a car's engine starting out on the street caught her attention. As she watched, a sleek sports car pulled away from the curb, dimly lit by the streetlight on the corner. She looked closer, sure that she could see the glint of golden hair through the driver's-side window.

The first thing she felt was anger. What the *hell* was T. doing, spying on her until all hours of the night?

But it didn't take long for rational thought to intercede. He couldn't have been spying on her. The only way he could have seen into her windows was if he'd somehow gained access to the apartment across the street. And it was hardly likely that he had gone to such lengths. If he had wanted to know what she was doing, he would've no doubt simply knocked on her door.

So then, what *was* he doing? Sitting out in his car in front of her house for God only knows how many hours?

Why?

The only answer she could come up with was more than a bit alarming. It had to be the physical attraction, the same old irresistible pull that they had nearly given in to on her prom night, so many years ago. *She* still felt it tugging at her every time he was near. No doubt he did, too.

Kelly lay back in her bed and threw her arm across her eyes. She was exhausted, but sleep didn't come. Finally, too tired to fight, she closed her eyes and let her memories carry her back in time to that wonderful, terrible Saturday night of the prom.

She couldn't begin to remember what she ate for dinner at the Breckenridge Inn. She wasn't sure that she even knew at the time. Her attention had been so totally captured by T. Jackson Winchester the Second....

He'd reached across the table between courses, holding her hand lightly, playing with her fingers, making her think about the way he had kissed her in the car. He'd kept up a steady stream of conversation about books, movies, music, anything and everything, but there had been an odd fire in his eyes that had let her know he, too, had been thinking about kissing her again.

When the waiter brought their dinners, he also brought them each a complimentary glass of white wine. T. looked at Kelly, one eyebrow slightly raised, but he said nothing until the waiter left.

"People always think I'm older than I am," she said. "It was a drag back when I was eleven. I used to get into arguments with the ticket lady at the movie theater. I finally had to bring her my birth certificate to prove that I really was under thirteen." She smiled. "But now I'd say it's paying off." She toyed with the long stem of her wineglass. "I wish, at least, that I was eighteen."

T. was leaning back lazily in his chair, his handsome face lit by flickering candlelight. "I wish you were, too."

"I feel like I'm spending all of my time waiting." Kelly gazed into the stormy gray-green of his eyes. "I know exactly what I want to do, I know exactly what I want from life, but it's going to be another few years before I'm allowed to start living."

"Four hundred and fifty-nine days."

She looked at him in surprise.

He smiled. "I'm counting." He leaned forward suddenly. "What *do* you want from life?" His eyes were electric green now, and they seemed to shine in the dim light, intense, piercing.

You.

She almost said it aloud. Instead she said, "I want what I've always wanted, the same thing you want—to be a writer."

"So do it," T. told her. "Be a writer. Just because you're living at home, just because you're still in high school, doesn't mean you can't start sending your stories out to magazines. It doesn't mean you can't get published. If you really want something, if you've really figured out what you want, then go for it, work for it, do it. Don't hold back. No matter what else you do, just keep writing."

His face was so serious. A lock of hair had fallen across his forehead, but he didn't bother to push it back. Kelly gazed at his perfect features—perfect except for the tiny scar below his left eye, close to his temple, on his cheekbone. He'd been in a fight in high school, he'd once told her, being purposely vague.

That scar had always been a reminder to Kelly that there was more to T. Jackson than he'd let the world believe from his cool and collected outward appearance. There was a fire inside of him, ready to spark into flames if he was pressed hard enough.

She'd tasted that fire when he'd kissed her. But even when he kissed her so passionately, she'd felt his control, felt him holding back. She'd never seen him when he wasn't in control, and had only rarely seen him rattled. She smiled again, remembering his reaction when she'd mentioned that Christa doubted his masculinity. But still, even then, he'd really only been slightly fazed.

That scar, though, was proof that there was a side to T. that she'd hadn't yet seen. And although the scar interrupted the lines of his face, it added a mysteriousness and an unpredictability to him, and Kelly found that wonderfully, dangerously attractive.

As he gazed across the table at her, his eyes held the same fiery fierceness that Kelly had seen right before he had kissed her in the car—those amazing, industrial-strength kisses. As she watched, he forced his eyes away from her, down to his plate, and stared at the food in front of him as if he hadn't realized it was there.

*If you really want something,* he had said, *if you've really figured out what you want...*

She wanted T., there was no doubt about it. And she wanted him forever. It couldn't be much clearer to her, it couldn't be more obvious.

*Then go for it...don't hold back.*

"There's more," she said quietly, and he looked up at her. There was uncertainty in his eyes, and she realized he wasn't following. "There's more that I want," she explained.

As she watched, understanding replaced the confusion. As she gazed at him, she saw his sudden comprehension, along with a renewed flare of the fire that was burning inside of him.

*I want you.*

She didn't have to say the words. He knew.

He smiled at her, but it was tinged with sadness. "Oh, Kel," he whispered. "What am I going to do about this?"

She picked up her fork and toyed with the food on her plate for a moment before she answered. "You could start by asking me out on another date."

He reached across the table, lacing her fingers with his. "What are you doing tomorrow night?"

Kelly felt her heart flip-flop. He was taking her seriously. "I've got nothing planned."

"Will you go to a movie with me?" he asked. "We could get something to eat before or after, depending on what time the movie starts."

Kelly looked down at her barely touched dinner and laughed. "Maybe we should skip the meal. Neither of us seems to care much about food these days."

"Is that a yes?" His hand tightened slightly on hers.

"Yes."

"Will you go out with me Monday night, too?"

"Yes."

"Tuesday?"

Kelly laughed. "Yes."

"How about Wednesday?"

"I'm supposed to baby-sit for the Wilkinses. You know, they live down the street."

"I remember," Jax said. "Kevin and I filled in over there for you last year when you got that virus. Do you think they would mind if I came along?"

"No," Kelly told him.

"Good." Jax smiled. "Then that just leaves Thursday and Friday...and every other night for the next one year and ninety-four days. Will you go out with me those nights, too?"

As Kelly gazed into his warm green eyes, she was incredibly, deliriously happy. "Yes," she whispered.

He brought her hand up to his lips, gently kissing the tips of her fingers. "Good."

"Why only a year and ninety-four days?" she wondered aloud.

He lifted her hand to his mouth again, this time kissing her palm. Kelly inhaled sharply at the sensation, and heat raced through her body. She could see the same heat in T.'s eyes as the warm green turned hot. "Because in one year and ninety-four days, you'll be eighteen."

"What happens then?" She watched, mesmerized as he kissed the soft inside of her wrist, pressing her throbbing pulse with his lips.

"Lots of things," he replied, watching her through half-closed eyelids. His thumb now traced slow circles on the palm of her hand, and Kelly felt nearly overpowered by her feelings. She wanted to kiss him again. She wanted...

She knew about sex, even though she had no experience. She'd read plenty of books, seen movies, heard talk, but she'd never really quite understood what the big deal was all about. Until now.

"When you're eighteen, you'll start college," Jackson was saying lazily, still smiling at her. "You'll leave home. You'll marry me."

Kelly pulled her hand free. "Tyrone, don't tease about something like that."

"I'm not teasing."

She looked up at him. His smile was gone. Kelly felt a rush of dizziness, and she started to laugh. "I thought, according to convention, that a man is supposed to *ask* a woman to marry him, not simply *tell* her that she will."

"Oh, I'll ask," Jax had said. "The minute you turn eighteen, Kelly, I'm going to ask...."

But he hadn't. Even though he had disappeared a few days after the prom, even though he had broken all of the other promises he had made to her that night, Kelly had spent her entire eighteenth birthday waiting for him to show up, to call, to come for her.

But he never had.

Tears still stung her eyes as she remembered the bitter disappointment, the hurt. It was on that day she convinced herself that she had truly stopped loving T. Jackson Winchester the Second. It was on that day that she started moving ahead with her life. It was the day she finally agreed to go out with Brad Foster.

It was better it had happened this way. Better that she'd married Brad instead of T. Because although finding Brad with another woman had hurt her, it wasn't the end of the world. It was simply the end of their relationship.

But if it had been T. Jackson she had found in bed with someone else...that would have destroyed her. Her heart would never have recovered.

Now that Jared was cooperating, Jax's writing should have been going much more smoothly. But it wasn't.

Oh, he managed to write, but it was like pulling teeth, rather than the effortless, almost stream-of-consciousness outpouring of words he was used to.

He sent Jared off to sea for close to two long, dangerous years. But as his hero was triumphantly returning to Boston a wealthy man, the *Graceful Lady Fair* was taken for a British ship and attacked by the Union fleet. Instead of reclaiming Carrie, Jared was wounded and mistakenly sent to a prison camp for Confederate soldiers. It took him another year and a half, and about 100 pages, to recover from his injuries and successfully escape the prison.

But then, finally, *finally* Jared was in Boston.

With a spring in his step, Jared walked down the street that led to the Sinclairs' town house. He hadn't felt this good, this *whole,* in years. It wouldn't be long now before he held Carrie in his arms....

JAX STOPPED TYPING, his fingers poised on the keyboard.

Jared tapped his foot impatiently. "What's the matter? What are you waiting for?"

"You're not going to like this," Jax muttered.

Jared froze. "Don't tell me she's not here."

"She's here, all right." Jax started to write again.

And then Jared saw her, her dark hair gleaming in the summer sunshine as she stepped out of the carriage. Her shoulders were back, her head held high—she was exactly as he remembered her.

He wasn't close enough to see the smile that he knew must be on her beautiful face, and he began to run, shouting her name as he dodged the heavy traffic that cluttered the street.

Carrie's head turned, and Jared knew the exact instant that she saw him. Her eyes opened wide, her face went pale and her delicate lips moved as she soundlessly spoke his name.

As he skidded to a stop in front of her, it was all he could do to keep from pulling her into his arms and covering her mouth with his own.

"OH, COME ON," JARED FUMED. "After all this time, you're not going to let me kiss her?"

"Chill out," Jax muttered as he continued to write. "You're not alone."

But Jared was aware of the gentleman and two elderly ladies standing near her, so he reined in his desire and simply smiled at her.

She was more beautiful than ever. Dressed as she was, she looked every inch the proper lady, but Jared saw she still had a spark of fire in her deep blue eyes. It was that spark that had become a flame on the day they had met, the day he had found her riding her father's nearly uncontrollable stallion, dressed in her brother's clothes, in the field above the manor house. She had seemed as wild and untamable as the horse, and he had fallen in love with her instantly.

Jared could feel Carrie's eyes studying him, taking in the expensive cut of his clothes, the leanness of his body, the drawn, thin lines of his face.

"I thought you were dead," she whispered, her low voice husky with emotion.

"You know this man?" the gentleman standing beside her asked. He was several years older than Jared, with a round face and a pair of spectacles that magnified his brown eyes.

Carrie turned to look at him, as if she was startled that he was there. For the briefest of instants,
Jared saw what might have been fear in her eyes.

"Yes," she answered slowly, as if she was
choosing her words carefully. "Harlan, this is
Jared Dexter, an old friend of my family's." She
looked back at Jared, and he saw that her eyes
were nearly brimming over with unshed tears.
"Jared, I'd like you to meet Harlan Kent. My husband."

IT WAS EASY TO WRITE JARED'S reaction to the news that
Carrie had married another man. Jax knew firsthand
about the waves of disbelief, anger and pure heartbreaking sorrow that swept over Jared. He knew about the
misery and could describe the sensations in absolute
vivid detail.

With a few quick sentences, he brought Jared back
to the privacy of his fancy hotel room, where his hero
put his head down and cried.

Just the way Jax had done when he realized that
Kelly would not be his, that he had come home too late.

## CHAPTER FIVE

Dear Kelly,
August 24. Your eighteenth birthday.

I spend the day thinking about you. I remember how you invited me to spend your thirteenth birthday with you. We went downtown to the aquarium and looked in the top of the big fish tank. We stared at the skeletons of sharks hanging from the ceiling, sharks big enough to eat us both for breakfast and still go hungry.

For the first time in the three months I have been here, I cry.

Worse than the black eyes and the bruises and cuts and broken ribs, worse than the fear that today may be the day they drag me out of my cell and kill me, worse than the insults and the degradation, the filth and the stench, worse than all that, they have made me break my promise to you. That fills me with pain so great that I can't stop the tears.

I try to imagine your day, where you go, what you do.

Do you wonder where I am? Do you expect me at least to call?

Right now I'd sell my soul to the devil for a telephone.

I wonder if anyone even knows where I am.

The warden laughs and hits me when I ask, then tells me the government has told my London magazine that I died in a cholera epidemic.

But, Kelly, I am not dead.

You come to me tonight, eighteen years old and so lovely. Your eyes are so sad. We hold each other tightly, and I fall asleep with you in my arms.

But when I wake up, you are gone.

I love you.

Love, T.

FRIDAY MORNING DAWNED gray and rainy. Kelly worked on her novel straight through until the early afternoon, grabbing a peanut butter and jelly sandwich on her way to get dressed to go to the university lecture series.

Normally the dismal weather would have kept her inside, but today's guest speaker was none other than Jayne Tyler, one of the hottest names in women's fiction. Tyler had rocketed onto the *New York Times* bestseller list with her first novel three years ago, and since then she had written five books, each one better than the last. She created hot, spicy characters that seemed to leap off the pages, and stories full of intrigue and passion. She could have her reader laughing on one page and reaching for a tissue to dry her tears on the next. And Tyler really knew what romance was. She knew exactly the right amount of gentle tenderness to throw in to cut straight through to the reader's heart.

Today she was going to speak in front of a roomful of hopeful authors and fans, spilling her secrets. And Kelly was going to be there, paying close attention.

She dressed carefully in her favorite dress, a beige-and-tan-checked shirtdress with a flared, nearly floor-length skirt, and long sleeves that she rolled up casually to her elbows.

The rawness of the rainy day penetrated her apartment, and there was a decided draft up the full skirt. So Kelly pulled a pair of slim black leggings on underneath the skirt. Still feeling cold, she unbuttoned the dress down to her waist and slipped a tank-style undershirt on, then put her arms back into the sleeves. She adjusted the small shoulder pads and rebuttoned the dress. With her black cowboy boots on her feet, a wide leather belt around her waist, her hair back in a casual ponytail, and silver earrings with shiny black stones dangling from her ears, she was ready to go.

Amazingly, the trolley was running ahead of schedule, and as she disembarked, she put up her umbrella against the drizzle and glanced at her watch. She was nearly two hours early. She rolled her eyes. Just a tad overeager. Still, if she had timed it perfectly, the trolley would have broken down and she would have ended up being two hours late.

She eyed the row of shops across from the campus lecture hall as she pulled her denim jacket more tightly around her. Somewhere over there was a shop called Quick Cuts, and Marcy had recommended it soundly the last time Kelly had made noise about getting her hair cut.

She hesitated only a few seconds, then made her way across the street, dodging the puddles as she went.

JAX GLANCED AT THE CLOCK ON the dashboard of his sports car. They were running late because of this damned rain. Bostonians were notorious for their wild driving skills, and add a little rain to the equation—the end result was sheer chaos.

His sister, Stefanie, was sitting next to him, calmly filing her fingernails.

"There's no way I'm going to find a parking spot," he told her. "I'm going to have to drop you."

"Oh, no, you're not." She put her emery board into her purse and looked up at him. "I'm *not* going in there alone, Jax. We'll both be late together."

"Stef—"

"Relax, darling, they can't start this party without us." Stefanie pulled down the mirror that was part of her sun visor and checked her perfectly styled blond curls. "I'm the guest of honor, remember?"

"I'm not worried about that. I just want to be able to leave on time."

Stefanie's gray eyes were filled with speculation as she looked up from putting on another coat of lipstick. "It's a woman, isn't it?"

Jax kept his face expressionless. He didn't even glance in her direction.

"I *knew* it," she said triumphantly, reattaching the top to the lipstick and tossing it into her purse. "It is, isn't it? You're finally over that girl—what was her name? Kevin's sister. Kelly. The one you wrote that collection of letters to. The one who was so young."

Again Jackson didn't say a word. He just drove the car. They were close enough now to start looking for a parking space.

"You know, your entire affair with her was too dreadfully romantic." Stefanie wouldn't let up. "She was just a teenager, a child really, while you were a grown man. I know forbidden fruit has a rep for being sweeter and all that, but carrying a torch for her all these years borders on the absurd. Not that I don't appreciate the absurd, of course. And it *is* rather disgustingly romantic of you." She watched him carefully. "I was thinking it might be a good story idea for the next contemporary novel—"

Jax turned and glared at her. "No."

"Made you look." She grinned toothily, then laughed at his exasperation. "You're *not* over her, are you? Well, maybe this new woman can sufficiently distract you for a while anyway. Tell me all about her, darling. What's her name? Where'd you meet her— Look, that car's leaving!"

And so it was. Jax braked to a stop behind a small blue Honda that was pulling out of a miniature parking spot. As he wrestled his car into the space that was barely twelve inches bigger than the length of his car, a young woman standing at the crosswalk waiting for the light to change caught his eye. Something about the way she was standing looked familiar. He caught a glimpse of short, sleek, dark hair underneath her umbrella as she turned away.

As he pulled up the parking brake and cut the engine, Jax watched a transit bus speed past. It sent a sheet of muddy water into the air. The young woman jumped back, but not quickly enough, and her skirt was drenched.

"Oh, yuck." Stefanie was watching, too. "The poor thing."

Jackson checked his watch. "Stef, we've got to hurry."

But his sister's eyes had widened as she watched the movements of the young woman on the sidewalk. The woman had stepped back, away from the street, and had set down her backpack and umbrella under the awning of an ice cream parlor.

Jax followed Stefanie's gaze, and watched, too, as the woman calmly took off her denim jacket and placed it on the top of her backpack. She took off a wide brown belt, set that on top of her jacket, then began to unbutton her dress.

She pushed off the top of the muddy dress, revealing a black sleeveless tank top and long, slender arms. Feeling rather like a voyeur, Jax made himself look away. But there was something so familiar about her. He looked back to see her pushing the dress down around her thighs. She wore a pair of skintight black leggings on her long legs. She had very, *very* long legs.

"Do try to keep your tongue inside your mouth, Jax darling," Stefanie said dryly.

As Jackson watched, the woman stepped out of her dress, shaking it slightly to get her cowboy boots free—

Cowboy boots!

"She got her hair cut," Jax breathed, and Stefanie looked at him in surprise.

"You know her?"

But Jax was already out of the car.

KELLY FOLDED HER MUDDY dress small enough to fit into her backpack. She wished she could rinse it out, but the lecture was going to start in just a few minutes. She hoped the mud wouldn't stain before she had a chance to go home and wash it clean.

"God," she heard a voice say. "It *is* you."

Startled, she looked up from where she was crouching to see T. Jackson towering above her.

"I love it," he said simply as she slowly stood and faced him. "Your hair—it's great."

She was gorgeous. Dressed all in black, her leggings and tank top hugging every inch of her lithe body, and with her dark hair cut very short—shorter even than his—she looked like a chic New York City model. Her hair capped her head, cut so short in the front that she could barely be described as having bangs. Pointed sideburns of hair hung down in front of each ear, curving in to accentuate the prettiness of her face, framing her big blue eyes. Her hair was buzzed short around her ears and in the back, but the effect was remarkably feminine. Her neck looked long and graceful and very, very vulnerable.

She looked as if she were twelve again. His gaze dropped down to her body. Well, maybe not exactly...

Kelly pulled her jacket on, more as protection from his eyes than from the cold. "You're following me again." It wasn't even a question. "Do us both a favor, Jackson. Give up."

"You know I'm not going to do that," he said softly. "And actually, this time I'm not following you." He looked at his watch again. "I've got to go—"

"Aren't you going to introduce me?"

Kelly turned to see a tall woman standing next to Jax, her hand possessively on his arm. She was strikingly beautiful, tall and slim, with hair like spun gold that shimmered and curled around her face. Her perfect mouth was curved upward in a friendly smile, but her cool gray eyes were inquisitive, curious.

Surprise rushed through her. This had to be Jackson's wife. Funny how he hadn't mentioned he was married...

"Kelly, this is Stefanie Winchester," Jax said. "Stef, meet Kelly O'Brien."

Stefanie *Winchester.* Oh, Lord, she *was* his wife. The wave of jealousy that shot through Kelly shocked her. No, it couldn't be jealousy she was feeling. Maybe it was indigestion—something she ate. As she shook the cool, slim hand that Stefanie extended, Kelly missed the pointed look of surprise and interest that the blond woman sent Jax.

"My brother's told me so much about you," Stefanie said, her voice cool and cultured.

Brother?

Stefanie was T. Jackson's *sister,* not his wife. Of course. Stefanie. *Stef.* Jax had told her about his older sister, Stef.

Kelly looked up to find Jax's eyes on her. He was watching her steadily, and he smiled very slightly, as if he knew what she was thinking. But he glanced at his watch again and turned to his sister.

"We're late." He looked back at Kelly. "I'll see you later."

She shook her head and opened her mouth to protest,

but he stopped her by cupping her face with one hand and pressing his thumb lightly against her lips.

"I *will* see you later," he said, his voice soft and so dangerously positive. "You *are* going to have dinner with me and we *are* going to talk. Tonight."

Kelly couldn't move as she gazed into his eyes. He was looking at her with an intensity that was hypnotizing. As she watched, his gaze dropped to her mouth, and she knew with a flash of heat that he was going to kiss her.

But he didn't.

Instead he brushed his thumb lightly against her lips, letting his fingers linger before he turned to leave. He walked backward all the way to the curb, a smile spreading across his handsome face.

"You *do* look..." He shook his head, as if unable to find the words. "Wonderfully," he finally said, "amazingly, fabulously, unbelievably, deliciously—"

"You could probably stand to insert an adjective right about now," Stefanie said dryly.

"Sexy," he whispered, but his voice carried quite clearly to Kelly.

"I'll be over about eight," he said.

"No." Kelly finally found her voice, but it was too late. He'd already turned and was halfway across the street.

With a sigh of frustration, she picked up her backpack and her umbrella and went back to the curb, where the Don't Walk sign was flashing. She waited far from the puddles for the light to change.

"KELLY, HUH?" STEFANIE SAID, giving Jax a sidelong glance as they went into the university building. "So it's still little Kelly O'Brien that you've got it bad for, even after all these years. Although she's not so little anymore, is she?"

"No, she's not," Jax agreed.

"I thought she got married."

"She did. It didn't work out."

"Lucky you," Stefanie said. "So naturally you've got your catcher's mitt on, ready to grab her on the rebound."

"You're mixing your sports metaphors," Jackson countered, not commenting on the truth of what she'd just said.

"And *you're* going for the big, happy Hollywood ending," Stefanie decided. "You *are* a hopeless romantic, aren't you, darling?"

"Everything I've ever written has a happy ending," Jax told his sister. "It shouldn't be *too* hard to orchestrate a real one for my life."

"I hope so." In an unusual display of affection, Stefanie reached out and squeezed Jax's hand. "But you know, real people aren't as easy to manipulate as fictional characters."

Jackson's smile turned rueful. "You're telling me. And lately my fictional characters haven't been easy to manipulate, either."

Dear Kelly,
I have finished.

True, it's only a rough draft, but what more do you want for a first novel written in pencil between the printed lines of a paperback called *Passion's Destiny?*

It's a romance. Why? I needed to write a book with a happy ending, and since I've read nothing but these three romance novels in the past eleven months, I figured it was a good place to start.

And I promise in the next draft I'll change my heroine's first name from Kelly. She is you, though—beautiful and strong and proud.

I read my book over and over. Reading between the lines suddenly has a real meaning for me.

It has been nearly a year.

I pray that someday, somehow I will see you again. I live for that day.

I love you.

Love, T.

# CHAPTER SIX

KELLY WENT INTO THE crowded lecture hall, scanning the auditorium for an empty seat. As usual, there were chairs free in the front, so she went down the sloped aisle and sat down in the second row on the end.

It wasn't too long before the representative from the college lecture series came out onto the stage and, after testing the microphone, introduced bestselling author Jayne Tyler.

Kelly joined the enthusiastic applause, but then stopped suddenly, staring in disbelief at the woman who had walked out and now stood behind the podium.

It was Stefanie Winchester.

T. Jackson's sister was Jayne Tyler?

Why not? thought Kelly, laughing to herself at the irony. She knew Tyler was a pen name.

She spotted T. leaning lazily against the wall in the front of the lecture hall, his arms casually crossed. He was looking out over the audience, occasionally glancing up at the stage, at his sister.

But then his eyes met hers. He straightened up, staring at her, frowning slightly as if he couldn't figure out what Kelly was doing here.

She heard Stefanie introduce herself and her brother and agent, Jackson.

LETTERS TO KELLY

Brother and...

Agent?

Kelly looked back at T. Jackson. His gaze was fixed on her, and he smiled slightly.

JACKSON WONDERED WHAT Kelly was doing here, as she gave her full attention to his sister. He glanced at his watch. Stef's speech would take another forty minutes, then there'd be a question-and-answer period, during which he'd make an attempt to take control. Stef didn't like answering questions, and he couldn't blame her. People tended to ask the damnedest things.

He glanced up at his sister. She looked calm and collected, and her speech had been well rehearsed. She was doing fine. He stopped paying attention to Stef's words. He'd heard this speech too many times; hell, he'd written the damned thing.

He let his eyes drift back to Kelly. She hadn't put up a fight today when he'd told her he was taking her to dinner.

He wanted to hold her in his arms tonight. Quickly he ran down a mental list of posh Boston restaurants, trying to remember which places had a band and a dance floor. The last time he'd danced with Kelly, she had felt so good in his arms, and they'd both been so optimistic about the future....

The junior prom had been held in the high school gym. The lights had been down low, and the room had been decorated with crepe streamers and helium balloons. It had looked about as romantic as a badly decorated gymnasium could be, but Jax hadn't cared. Just holding Kelly in his arms had been nearly an overload of romance.

From the number of curious stares he and Kelly were getting, Jackson knew he was the object of much discussion among both the other students and the teachers. It was obvious that he was much older than Kelly.

He wanted to pull her close, closer than he was holding her, but he was afraid to. He was afraid of attracting even more attention. But most of all, he was afraid of what people would think. Not about him—he didn't care about himself. But he *did* care about Kelly, and he was afraid people would assume that since he was dating her, she must be sleeping with him.

She still had another year to go in this school, with these kids. It wouldn't be easy for her if she were labeled, tagged with that kind of reputation.

Jax looked down to see her smiling up at him. He smiled back, but concern instantly darkened her eyes.

"What's wrong?" she asked.

He laughed, shaking his head. "I can't hide anything from you, can I?"

Her fingers were twisted in the hair that went down over the back of his collar. She shifted her weight so that her body brushed against his. He could feel her long, firm thighs against his, the softness of her breasts against his chest. It felt like heaven, but he had to make her stop.

"Kel," he said, unsure how to explain. "Have you noticed the amount of attention we're getting?"

She glanced around the room, then smiled back at Jax. "I think it's because you're the most handsome man here."

"The key word is *man*." Jax took a deep breath. He had to just say it. "Kelly, I'm afraid if we dance too close, people are going to think we're...involved."

"We *are* involved." She watched him steadily. "Aren't we?"

He gazed into her lovely face for several long moments. She was so beautiful, so mature in so many ways, yet still such an innocent. "I meant... *intimately* involved."

A tinge of pink crept across her cheeks, but she didn't look away from him. "I don't care what other people think about me."

"But I do," he said softly. "I care very much. Once people give someone a label, it's almost impossible to change it. Trust me, I'm speaking from experience."

Kelly didn't say anything. She simply gazed up at him, waiting for him to go on.

"You know that I graduated from public high school out on Cape Cod," he told her. "Out in Dennis."

She nodded.

"I only went to that school for the end of my junior year and my senior year," he explained. "Before that, I went to prep school. Lots of different prep schools."

"I didn't know that."

Jax moved with her across the dance floor to the slow rock ballad. Every few minutes he had to remind himself to loosen his hold on her, because every few minutes he forgot his resolve and his arm tightened around her waist, drawing her closer to him. "Yeah." He had to clear his throat. "By the end of my junior year, I'd been kicked out of so many prep schools, there weren't any left that would accept me."

"Kicked out?" Kelly was surprised. "You?"

He released her to point to the tiny scar on his left cheekbone. "Remember that fight I was in?" He put his arm back around her. "Well, I won the fight, but I got booted out of school. And *that* didn't win me any points with the folks," he added with a grin.

"You never told me what you fought about."

"Freshman hazing. The seniors were merciless. I watched one kid after another get hurt by their supposedly harmless pranks, and when they went too far, I...um, went a little crazy."

"What did they do?"

Jackson grimaced. "They put something in the food and made the entire freshman class really sick. I was late to lunch that day, and when I walked into the mess hall and saw all the seniors standing around laughing at all the freshmen—and some of them were *violently* sick—I got upset. When I found out who had masterminded the scheme, I broke his nose." He shrugged. "Apparently making fifty kids blow groceries is good clean fun, whereas breaking a senior's nose is not."

The band segued directly into another slow, pulsating song. Jax could feel perspiration forming on his forehead as Kelly rested her head on his shoulder. He wanted to kiss her, he wanted to hold her tightly, feel the length of her slim, soft body against his. But she was only sixteen. It was good that they were here, with all these people watching. If there ever were a time he needed a chaperone, it was right now.

But even after tonight, he'd have to endure a year and a half of wanting something he couldn't have. He looked down into Kelly's eyes and he was overcome by a rush of emotions. He loved her, and he wanted to be near her all the time. Sex only played a very small part in the way he felt about her—

Who was he kidding? He would come damn close to selling his soul for a chance to make love to her. It wouldn't be easy to live through the next few years. In fact, if Kelly managed to remain a virgin until she was eighteen, they would both deserve sainthood.

"That was the first prep school," Kelly said, breaking into his thoughts. "Why were you kicked out of the others?"

"I kept getting kicked out because I went in with a bad reputation," Jax told her. "At the second school, I was in the wrong place at the wrong time. Someone set fire to the athletic supply shed, and because I came in pegged as a troublemaker, I ended up taking the blame. By the time I was a junior, I was at my fifth boarding school. I went in on probation, and managed to get asked to leave simply because I dropped my tray in the dining hall one morning."

"That's awful."

"It happens. Once you're labeled, it's all over." He shook his head. "I don't want that to happen to you, Kel."

"T., somehow I don't think my connection to you is going to hurt my reputation." Kelly laughed. "It just might help it, if you want to know the truth."

Jax looked down into her sparkling eyes, feeling his heart expanding in his chest. He loved her. Good God, he'd loved her for years, but he'd refused to admit it, even to himself, because she had been only a child. All that time, he'd wondered what was wrong with him,

why he never dated any of the women at school for
more than a week or two. He'd led himself to believe
that he was simply not cut out for long-term relation-
ships, that one woman simply didn't have the ability to
hold his attention for very long. He'd come to the conclusion that marriage and a family were simply not in
his future.

But the real truth was, he was more monogamous
than most men his age. Kelly owned his heart and soul,
had owned it for years. Jax knew without a shadow of
a doubt that he was going to love her until the day he
died.

She reached up and touched the side of his face,
catching a bead of perspiration that threatened to drip
down past his ear. "It's warm in here," she said, her low
voice husky.

"Yes," Jackson agreed, his eyes never leaving her
face. "It is."

In silent agreement, he led Kelly off the dance floor
and out of the gym. The air in the lobby was much
cooler, and they moved toward the refreshment table.

"Want a soda?" Jax asked and Kelly nodded.

"Thanks. I've got to go, um... What's the correct eu-
phemism?" She smiled. "Powder my nose? That's as
obsolete as dialing a phone, isn't it? I'll meet you out
here."

She pulled away from him, but Jax didn't let go of
her fingers until the last possible moment. He watched
her walk down the hallway. She was elegant and poised,
full of the self-confidence that made her so unique
among her peers. The heels she wore on her feet made

her hips sway slightly as she went, and he didn't look away until the girls'-room door closed behind her.

But then he turned and came face-to-face with an older man who had silently moved to stand at his side.

"Kelly looks lovely tonight," the man, obviously one of the teachers, said. He was smiling at Jax, but that smile didn't reach his eyes. "I didn't realize she was dating a college...boy."

It was obvious to Jax that this teacher didn't consider him a boy at all.

But he returned the smile, holding out his hand. "I'm Jackson Winchester," he said easily. "I've been a friend of Kelly's for some time now."

"Ted Henderson. What school are you going to?"

"I went to Boston College," Jax replied.

"Went?" Henderson's cold brown eyes probed for more information.

"I've graduated," Jax explained.

"You're *out* of college." Henderson made sure he got it straight. "Isn't Kelly a little bit young for you?"

"I don't see how that's any business of yours, Ted." Jax spoke pleasantly, but the older man's eyes darkened with disapproval anyway.

"I care about Kelly." Henderson crossed his arms in front of him, all pretense at pleasantness dropped. "I'm a friend of her father's—"

"Nolan approves of my relationship with his daughter." Jax didn't know if that was *exactly* the truth, but Nolan O'Brien wouldn't have let him take Kelly to the prom in the first place if he didn't want them to date, would he have?

"If that's the case," Henderson countered, "then I

truly doubt that he's seen the way you look at that girl." He shook his head. "You're a grown man, Winchester. She's only a child. You have no right to take the rest of her childhood away from her."

Jax kept his face carefully neutral, taking out his wallet as he turned past the teacher and headed toward the refreshment table. But Henderson followed.

"Kelly should be involved with boys her own age," he persisted. "She should be having lighthearted romances, she should be having fun. I'm sure she's flattered by the attention you give her—what young girl wouldn't be? I'm sure you don't need to be reminded about your good looks."

Jackson paid for two cans of soda, then turned back to Henderson. "Have you finished?"

"Just about." Henderson blocked Jax's way with his bulk, pinning the younger man against the refreshment table. "I just want to make sure you're aware of the laws in Massachusetts regarding statutory rape—"

"I don't need any lectures, Ted." Jax forced himself to speak slowly, without any trace of his anger evident in his voice. "Like you said, I'm a grown man. I'm well aware of any consequences my actions might bring. But I love Kelly, and I believe that she loves me. Now, if you'll excuse me?"

"I don't doubt that you love her, son," Henderson said, his voice surprisingly gentle. "But she's only sixteen. You don't really expect whatever she feels for you will last, do you?"

Jax saw Kelly come out of the bathroom and start down the hall toward him. "Yes," he said shortly to Henderson, nearly pushing past him. "I do. Excuse me."

He walked toward Kelly, watching her face break into a beautiful smile as she saw him. He watched her eyes dance with pleasure, watched her dress cling to her body as she moved. But Ted Henderson's quiet voice trailed after him. "High school should be a carefree, happy time. Your relationship with Kelly can only be a burden, Winchester. If you really love the girl, you won't do that to her."

Jax opened one of the cans of soda and handed it to Kelly when they met farther down the hallway. "They didn't have any cups," he apologized. "I wiped off the top for you."

"Thanks," she murmured, taking a sip of the soda.

He led her back into the dimness of the gym, where they found an empty table off to the side of the dance floor and sat down. He could feel Kelly watching him as he opened his own can of soda and took a long drink.

"You're not having much fun, are you?" she asked softly.

"I'm having a great time—"

"Someone in the girls' room told me that Mr. Henderson was giving you the third degree, telling you how wrong it was for us to be here together." She leaned toward him. "That doesn't sound like a great time to me. We can leave, T. I won't mind if you want to go—"

"Are you kidding? I want to dance with you some more."

Kelly covered his hand with hers, gently lacing their fingers together. "We could go somewhere else and... dance."

Jax felt a hot flare of desire shoot through him as he

met her steady gaze. She wasn't talking about dancing. She was talking about... He swallowed.

Sixteen, he reminded himself. She was only sixteen.

"I think we'd better stay here," he said quietly.

"Are you sure?"

Jax laughed desperately. "Kelly, come on. I need you to help me out, not make things harder than they already are." As soon as the words were out of his mouth, he realized just how full of sexual innuendo they were. To his relief, Kelly didn't seem to notice.

"While I was in the girls' room, I heard a little of the gossip that's going around about you and me," Kelly said. "And you were right. I *have* been relabeled."

"Oh, no." Jax frowned with concern. "Not already—"

But Kelly was smiling, her blue eyes shining with delight. "They're calling me...a studcatcher." She laughed. "You, of course, being the stud in question. It's a big step up for me from my last label."

"Which was...?"

"Math nerd." Kelly made a face. "Hardly flattering and particularly galling since I'm planning to major in language arts when I go to college. I like studcatcher much better." She grinned. "Wanna dance with me, stud?"

Jax feigned indignation as he followed her onto the dance floor and took her into his arms. "Is that all I am to you? Just a stud?"

Her smile softened and her eyes grew warm as she tipped her head back to look up at him. "Tyrone, I fell in love with you before I knew what a stud was."

*I fell in love with you....*

Her words echoed over and over in Jax's head. She loved him. She loved him!

"Oh, Kel," he breathed.

Both of her arms had been around his neck, and she'd pulled his head down to her waiting lips.

He'd kissed her. Right there in the middle of the dance floor. A slow, soft, lingering kiss...

The sound of three hundred pairs of hands clapping startled Jax out of his reverie. The crowd of people in the university auditorium was applauding. Stefanie's speech was over.

Momentarily off balance, he looked for Kelly. It had grown warm in the room, and she had taken off her denim jacket. God, in that outfit she looked good enough to eat.

As if she could feel his eyes on her, she glanced in his direction.

T. JACKSON WAS STARING AT her with that same hungry look in his eyes. He *wasn't* going to give up, Kelly realized with a flare of despair. He wasn't going to quit until they gave in to the desire that still burned between them, until they finally made love.

But maybe that was the answer. Kelly watched as he climbed the stairs to the stage and crossed to stand next to his sister. His blond hair glistened in the stage lights, and his teeth flashed as he smiled. He took over the podium from Stefanie, introducing the question-and-answer portion of the program. He spoke easily, confidently, his wonderful charisma set to full power as he fielded questions from the floor.

Making love to T. would probably be pretty damn good.

Kelly gazed at the wide expanse of his shoulders. His muscular arms were covered by the sleeves of his well-tailored tweed jacket, arms that led down to a pair of strong, long-fingered hands that now gripped the sides of the podium. What would it feel like to have those hands touch her body?

It was a rhetorical question, but Kelly's imagination took over, producing a vivid picture of T., naked in her bed, with fire in his eyes as he touched her, kissed her, made love to her— She shook her head, forcing herself to pay attention to the questions that were being asked.

"What's your writing schedule like?" a woman in the back of the lecture hall asked.

"Jayne usually gets up pretty early in the morning," T. answered, "and crawls straight from her bed to her personal computer, stopping on the way for a cup of coffee. She starts the day by reviewing and revising her previous day's work, then writes until a little before noon. She eats lunch in front of the computer, then about an hour later, takes about a two-hour break—runs on the beach, goes for a swim. After that, she writes until dinner, and usually again after dinner."

"It's pretty intense," Stefanie interjected. "But this way a book can be completed quickly. After it's all over, I take some time off, head for Club Med."

As people raised their hands, hoping to ask another question, Kelly lifted her own hand into the air.

Jax focused on her immediately. "Yeah, Kelly."

She cleared her throat, raising her voice so her question could be heard throughout the huge room. "What do you do when you've got a manuscript that doesn't work, but you can't figure out how to make it better?"

He stared at her, a curious look on his face. "Have you written a book?"

She nodded.

"You never told me that," he said, his voice sounding soft and intimate, even over the PA system.

"You never asked," she countered. She could feel the curious eyes of the audience studying her as she had what was essentially a private conversation in front of them all.

As if he realized this, Jax shifted his weight, looking out at the sea of faces. "Well, there are a couple of solutions," he said. "The first is to put that manuscript on a shelf and start something new. After you finish your next project, you can go back to the problem manuscript and look at it with a new perspective." His eyes found Kelly's face again. "The other solution is to find a critique partner. Work with another person, get another opinion. What may seem an insurmountable problem to you might be a quick fix for someone else." His eyes seemed to sparkle as he shot her his infectious grin. "Next question?"

Jax spent another twenty minutes answering questions, and then the program was over. He waited impatiently as the head of the lecture series shook his hand and long-windedly thanked him and Stefanie for being able to do the program for only a small honorarium.

He could see Kelly walking slowly toward the back doors of the lecture hall, talking to another young woman—Marcy something from the newspaper office. Marcy touched Kelly's hair and walked in a full circle around her. Kelly said something, and the two women broke up. Kelly's musical laugh cut through the ambient noise of the big room like a knife to his heart.

He turned to the lecture series head and skillfully interrupted her. "I'm so sorry," he apologized, "but we've really got to go. Jayne's got another appointment and—"

"Oh, yes, of course," the woman said. "So nice to have met you, and thanks again."

Grabbing Stefanie's arm with one hand and snatching up her coat and purse with his other, he dragged her down toward the main entrance of the hall.

Marcy was gone, but Kelly stood in the lobby, putting on her backpack. The light drizzle had turned into a heavy rain that fell like a sheet of water outside the open door. About to put her umbrella up, Kelly was ready to plunge into the downpour.

"Kel, wait!"

Kelly turned back to see T. striding toward her.

"Let me give you a ride home," he said. "You don't really want to stand in this, waiting for a trolley, do you?"

He wasn't really standing that close, but it seemed as if she could feel the heat from his body. Again, unbidden, the image of their naked bodies, intertwined as they made love, appeared in her head. Only, this time, the sound of rain on the roof and the duskiness of gray, late-afternoon light coming in through her bedroom windows completed the vision.

Oh, how she wanted him.

It was nothing but animal attraction. Lust. It was the remnants of years of fantasy. If only she could wipe those feelings from her memory, wash him out of her system.

Maybe she could....

Making love to T. Jackson couldn't possibly be as good as she imagined. But there was only one way to prove that, and that was to make love to him. By making love to him, she would satisfy both her curiosity and her desire, and prove that he was nothing special to her, not anymore.

He, too, would get what he wanted, and then maybe he would leave her alone.

"All right," she heard herself say, and saw the surprise in his eyes. He'd been expecting a fight.

"I'll pull the car around," he said, as if he were afraid that if he didn't act fast, she'd change her mind. "Wait here with Stef, okay?" With a quick smile, he was gone.

Kelly turned to find his sister watching her.

"I had no idea you were Jayne Tyler," Kelly said. "I've really enjoyed your books."

Stephanie shrugged almost nonchalantly. "Thanks."

"Is Jackson doing any writing these days?" Kelly asked. "That was always his dream."

"You *do* care about him." The older woman watched Kelly closely. "Don't you?"

It was Kelly's turn to shrug as she looked out the door at the street, watching for Jax's car. "Well, yeah. He was my best friend for years. I'll always care about him."

"Why did you marry that other man?"

Kelly looked up, surprised at the personal nature of the question, surprised that Stefanie even knew she'd been married.

Jax's car pulled up to the curb, saving Kelly from having to answer. "Come on, you can share my umbrella," she said instead, and the two women dashed out into the rain.

Stefanie got into the tiny back seat, so Kelly took the front, shaking her umbrella rather futilely as she closed it and pulled it into the car behind her.

The shoulders of T.'s jacket were soaked, and drops of water dripped from his wet hair onto his face. "I'm going to take Stefanie to the hotel," he said. "And if you don't mind, I'd like to change before we go out to dinner. We *are* going out to dinner, remember?"

"I'm not exactly dressed for anything fancy, T.," Kelly protested. "I don't want to—"

"I didn't mean fancy," he interrupted. "I meant *dry*. I stepped into a puddle, and my sock is wet." He grinned. "I *knew* there was a reason I don't wear socks."

Kelly had to smile. "And here, all this time, I thought you just didn't like to do the extra laundry."

He put the car into gear, signaling to move out into the steady stream of traffic. "If you want, we can get something to eat right at the hotel."

As T. Jackson headed toward downtown Boston on Commonwealth Avenue, Kelly settled back into the comfortable leather seat of his car. She looked out the window, through the drops of rain, and let her mind wander to the last time she'd been in a car with this man....

## CHAPTER SEVEN

IT WAS NEARLY 5:00 A.M., AND T. Jackson and Kelly were parked at the beach. After the lights and glare of three different after-prom parties, the intimate quiet of the predawn was wonderful.

They'd left the last party several hours early, and now they sat quietly talking and holding hands.

T. told her about his dream of becoming a writer. He wanted to write everything—novels, short stories, screenplays. He wanted to write comedies most of all, stories with happy endings.

He talked about growing up, about his family, his parents. They loved him, he'd told her, but they just didn't know how to show it. When T. had been kicked out of the last prep school that would accept him, his mother had been in Milan, and his father had been on a three-month cruise in the South Pacific. He'd talked to each of them on the telephone, and they both said the same thing—military school.

"So I told my mother that Dad was going to take care of everything, and I told my dad that my mother was making all of the arrangements, and I packed up my things and drove out to the summer house we had on the Cape." His voice was smooth and soft in the darkness. "I took a couple days off, did errands, restocked the house with food." He laughed softly. "Thank God for credit cards. Then I forged a letter from my parents and went over to the high school and registered. I had a copy of my school records, and I weeded out all the mention of disciplinary action. I left out anything that said I'd been expelled. I entered the school almost anonymously, and I kept a low profile and did okay."

"You lived by yourself?" She couldn't see his expression in the darkness, not until he smiled.

"Yeah. It was tough getting around those parent-teacher conferences, though."

"But your parents must've known—"

"Not until Christmas break during my senior year," he said. "By that time, I was almost eighteen, and they figured I had things under control."

"Weren't you lonely?" she asked softly.

T. was very quiet. "I didn't know what I was missing," he admitted. "Not until I met your family. Not until I met you."

Kelly could see that he was watching her, and she felt his hand touch the side of her face, felt his lips brush hers. She heard him make a low sound, a groan, as he pulled away.

"Kel, we should go home." His voice was raspy.

Her heart was pounding in her chest, making her feel as if she were about to explode. "Please, T., let's not go yet. Let's take a walk on the beach."

Even as she spoke, she slipped off her shoes and rolled down her stockings.

Outside the car, the night air was cold. In the east, the sky was starting to lighten. It wouldn't be long before the sun came up. Kelly turned to see T. standing almost uncertainly by the car. She took his hand and pulled, leading him out onto the soft sand.

"Wait a sec," he said, reaching down to pull off his own shoes and socks. He left them in a pile next to his car.

As they walked along the edge of the water, T. Jackson draped his jacket around her shoulders and held her close to him for added warmth. The water was icy as it occasionally splashed up onto their bare feet, but Kelly didn't care.

She was in heaven.

"I don't want tonight to end," she whispered.

T. stopped walking, turning her to face him, pulling her in even closer to him. "I don't want it to, either."

He kissed her then, and she could feel his restraint. He was holding so much back. She pressed herself against the hard muscles of his chest and, feeling shockingly bold, she opened her mouth underneath his and touched his lips with her tongue.

She heard him groan and felt his arms tighten around her as he parted his lips under her gentle pressure. His mouth tasted wonderful, so moist and warm and soft.

She could feel his control slipping as he returned her kisses. Each kiss was longer, deeper, more passionate than the last. His hands moved across her body, and his jacket fell off her shoulders onto the sand.

One of his legs pressed between hers as they both tried to get closer, even closer, to each other. She could feel his hands in her hair, pulling out the pins, letting it hang down around her shoulders.

He found the slit in the back of her dress, and the

sensation of his fingers on her bare skin made Kelly cry out.

He pulled back then, breathing hard. She could feel his heart pumping in his chest, echoing the crazy beat of her own heart.

"God, Kelly—"

She pulled his head down, pulled his lips to her and kissed him again. He resisted for all of half a second, then nearly crushed her mouth with his as his careful control slipped even further. Kelly felt an additional flash of pleasure, an even stronger flash of heat that seemed to spread throughout her entire body as she realized the power she had over him.

"Jackson, make love to me."

Her words made him freeze, until she began kissing his chin, his neck, instinctively pressing the soft place between her legs against the solid muscles of his thigh. That seemed to drive him crazy, and he kissed her, a savage kiss that made all of his other kisses seem tame in comparison. Together they lost their balance, falling backward onto the soft sand.

And still he kissed her.

She wrapped her arms around T.'s neck, feeling his weight on top of her. His hands swept her body, touching her in ways that left her breathless and wanting more. She felt his hand move up the long, smooth length of her thigh, pushing her skirt up, freeing her legs so that he could lie between them—

That was when Kevin showed up at the beach, looking for them.

That was when her wonderful night with Jackson turned into a nightmare.

LETTERS TO KELLY

Kevin was incensed, pulling Jax off her. "You promised me!" he shouted. "You gave me your word, you son of a bitch—"

The sky was light in the east, and the first rays of the sun shot up, over the edge of the horizon.

Kelly could see T.'s face in the pale light, and his eyes looked frantic, shocked, as he scrambled to his feet.

"Oh, God, what was I doing?" he gasped. "Kevin, man, I didn't mean to—"

Kevin charged him, but T. didn't make a move to defend himself. "No!" Kelly cried out as her brother's big fist slammed into T. Jackson's face.

T. reeled backward as Kevin hit him again and again.

"You bastard," Kevin kept saying. "You *bastard*—"

"Stop it!" Kelly sobbed, throwing herself onto Kevin's back, trying to hold his arms, trying to keep him from hitting T. again.

Jackson hit the ground, blood dripping from his nose and split lip. He pushed himself up onto his hands and knees until a well-aimed kick from Kevin sent him back down onto the sand.

Kelly threw herself down next to Jax. His face was bleeding, and he held his side as if one of his ribs had been cracked. "Oh, T., I'm sorry," she cried.

"Kelly, are you all right?" he asked, his green eyes trying to focus on her face. "I didn't hurt you, did I? I'm so sorry, what was I *do*ing?"

She shrieked, startled, as her brother roughly hauled her to her feet. "You stay away from him," he ordered her. "I oughta knock some sense into *you,* too."

He pulled his arm back, as if he was going to slap

her the way he had so many times when they were both children. Instinctively Kelly flinched, but then was nearly knocked over as T. suddenly lunged at Kevin.

Almost effortlessly, he took Kevin down. Before she could blink, her brother lay with his face in the sand, Jackson straddling him. T. had Kevin's arm tightly, savagely twisted behind his back, and he pushed it up until her brother cried out with pain.

"You *ever* hit her, it'll be the last thing you do," T. hissed. "Do you understand?"

"Yes," Kevin yelped. "Yes!"

Abruptly T. released Kevin, and they both sat in the sand, catching their breath.

Kevin looked up at Kelly. "Go wait in my car."

"No," she said, wiping the tears from her face. "No, Kevin, I'm going home with Jackson."

There was still a flash of anger in her brother's eyes as he looked up at her. "Jax isn't welcome in our house anymore." He turned to T. "I'll ship your things out to the Cape."

Slowly T. nodded.

Kelly couldn't believe it. He was going to give up, just like that?

"You were supposed to be doing me a favor," Kevin continued, accusingly.

Kelly froze.

"You were helping me out, taking Kelly to the prom, so I could go out with Beth," Kevin said, anger still tingeing his voice. "You *promised* me you wouldn't touch her, you dirtwad."

Jackson had only taken her out as a favor to her brother? Kelly felt sick. He had implied that he loved her, practically proposed marriage to her. But he'd never said the words. He never actually told her that he loved her. But she knew that he did. She *knew* it.

"T.," she started.

"Kelly, go get in my car," Kevin said again.

"Go on, Kel," T. said softly. "I'll call you later."

Numbly she'd walked back to the beach parking lot. Numbly she'd waited for ten, fifteen, twenty minutes until Kevin got into his car beside her and silently drove her home. Numbly she'd climbed the stairs up to her bedroom, peeled off her dress and fallen into bed. But she hadn't slept. She'd waited hours and hours for T. Jackson to call her.

But he never had.

He'd never called, he'd never shown up for their movie date or any of the other many dates they'd planned....

As Jackson pulled his sports car up to the valet at the hotel, Kelly still stared out the window. She'd only seen T. once between prom night and the afternoon last week when he'd shown up at the newspaper office—at Kevin's wedding, when she was nineteen.

Kelly looked up in surprise as T. opened the passenger-side door, offering her his hand to help her out. She took his warm fingers lightly, afraid to touch him, but more afraid that if she didn't touch him, he'd realize why.

All his promises had been empty. He had done nothing but let her down ever since prom night. So why in God's name was she still so damned attracted to him?

Because attraction had nothing to do with love. Love hinged on trust, not on broken promises. But hormones—now, that was an entirely different matter. Kelly's hormones didn't care that T. Jackson hadn't proved to be especially honor-bound. Her hormones only saw a tall, blond, handsome man with a killer smile and a body to die for.

"It was nice meeting you, Kelly," Stefanie interrupted her thoughts. "You should come out to the Cape and visit us sometime this summer."

"Gee, what a swell idea." Jax grinned as he helped Kelly into the hotel. "Why didn't *I* think of that?"

"Thanks, Stefanie." Kelly ignored Jackson. "It was nice meeting you, too. And I really *do* enjoy your books."

"Gotta fly," Stef said. "Emilio's waiting for me." She smiled at Jax. "See you when I see you, darling."

With a flash of blond hair and long legs, she disappeared, leaving Jax and Kelly standing in the posh hotel lobby.

"If you don't mind, I *would* like to change," Jax said.

He began walking toward the elevators, past the entrance to a lounge. To his surprise, Kelly went with him, rather than offering to wait for him in the bar.

"This is a nice place," she said, looking around at the elegantly decorated, airy lobby. The colors were muted shades of pink and rose, with a green-leaf print thrown in for good measure. It was all very soothing and quiet, with thick carpeting and overstuffed furniture to help absorb any excess noise. "I've never been in here."

Jax pushed the up button, and as they stood waiting for the elevator, he watched Kelly. Had she really relaxed enough around him to be comfortable waiting in his suite while he changed his clothes? But she didn't

seem relaxed. She seemed quiet, thoughtful almost to
the point of distraction.

"What are you thinking about?" he asked.

Her eyes focused on his face. "I was thinking that
it's a shame you don't write anymore."

Jax smiled. "Well, I do a little bit here and there."

"But it's not what you do for a living," she said.

The bell rang for the elevator, and Jax held the door
open so that she could step inside. As the door slid shut
behind him, he pushed the button that said Penthouse.
"I'm a Winchester," he said easily. "I open dividend
checks for a living, remember?"

"I thought you wanted to write screenplays." Her
tone was faintly accusing. "Or novels. Whatever happened to that?"

"Actually, I started a screenplay," he said.

"But you didn't finish it?"

"Other obligations got in the way. I haven't stopped
thinking about it, though. The same way I never
stopped thinking about you."

"Smooth line, T." Kelly glanced over at him. "But
somehow, I have trouble believing it."

"I guess you don't have to believe it," Jax said. "But
it *is* true."

He was leaning casually, nonchalantly against the
wall of the elevator, feet crossed in front of him, hands
in his pants pockets. His hair was mussed and still wet
from the rain. He smiled at her perusal, his eyes warm
and very green.

Was this elevator shrinking? Kelly looked up at the
numbers that were changing above the door. Eight more
floors 'til they reached the penthouse level. What was

that old saying, out of the elevator and into the penthouse? *Why* did she ever come up here with him?

"What do you want from me?" she asked, point-blank.

He answered with the same laid-bare honesty. "I want to marry you."

Stunned, Kelly heard a ding as the elevator reached the penthouse floor, and the doors glided open. She stared at T. in shock. He held the doors back with one hand and gestured with the other. "After you," he said calmly, as if he hadn't just told her that he wanted to... marry her.

He wanted to marry her.

The initial shock was starting to wear off, and as Kelly walked down the long hotel corridor, she began to laugh. He said he wanted to marry her. What a hoot.

Unperturbed, Jax used a plastic key card to unlock the door and opened it wide, stepping back to let her go in first.

His hotel suite was enormous. It had a spacious living room tastefully done in the same subdued colors that had decorated the lobby. But the best part of the room was the wall of glass that overlooked downtown Boston. The view was breathtaking.

As Kelly walked toward the windows, she saw a set of French doors that led into a huge bedroom. The bed itself was almost the size of her entire apartment. She pulled her eyes away, not wanting to be caught staring.

T. Jackson hung his wet sport jacket on the back of a chair, and as Kelly turned to look at him, she saw that his shirt was wet. He had been soaked by the rain clear through his jacket.

Slowly, she put her backpack down on the floor.

He smiled at her as he pulled off his tie and kicked off his shoes. "I'll be right back," he said, unbuttoning his shirt. "Help yourself to the bar."

There was a wet bar on the wall next to the TV, and Kelly tried to focus her attention on the various bottles of alcohol and soda, rather than the glimpse of hard, tan muscles she'd seen before T. had left the room.

She poured herself a tall glass of seltzer, added a few ice cubes and turned to look around.

There were a number of books scattered about the room. Two of them were Jayne Tyler's most recent releases. A third was a galley copy of what Kelly assumed was to be Jayne's next book, entitled *Love's Sweet Captive.* Seven titles that she recognized from the *New York Times* bestseller list, both fiction and nonfiction, sat on an end table. A week's worth of the *Boston Globe* lay in a pile on the floor. *Premiere* magazine and *Writer's Digest* were open and out on the coffee table, along with several news magazines.

"Grab me a cola from the fridge, will ya, Kel?" Jax called out from the bedroom.

She pulled a can of soda free from a six-pack that was in the refrigerator as Jackson appeared in the bedroom door. He was wearing a pair of faded jeans and a smile, turning a T-shirt rightside out.

Kelly tried not to stare. It wasn't as if she hadn't ever seen him without a shirt on before. But, Lord, he looked good. His body was well-toned and his skin was smooth and lightly tanned.

His muscles rippled as he pulled his shirt over his head and down across his broad chest.

"What do you really want from me?" Kelly heard herself ask. Her voice sounded faint and breathless.

His fingers brushed hers as he took the can of soda from her hand. "I told you," he said easily, his teeth flashing as he shot her a brief smile. "I want to marry you. I wanted to marry you seven years ago, Kelly, and I *still* want to marry you."

Kelly felt a prick of anger and she clung to it, unable to deal with the other emotions that were assailing her. "After all this time, *you're* finally ready—"

"No." He shook his head, his green eyes unyielding, pinning her in place. "*You're* finally ready."

"The hell I am," she said with an exasperated laugh. "I've just gotten out of one foolish marriage. Do you really think I'd be so eager to get into another right now?"

"Do you really think marriage to me would be foolish?" he countered.

"Absolutely."

T. took a step toward her, setting his can of soda on the coffee table. "Why?"

He moved another step forward. His eyes were green crystal, his face unsmiling and serious.

Kelly crossed her arms defensively, determined to stand her ground. "Oh, come on, T.," she said. "Why do you think?"

"I don't know," he said softly, shaking his head. "Seven years ago, you seemed to think marrying me was a good idea."

T. Jackson had that burning light in his eyes as he

took yet another step toward her. He was getting too close, close enough to be able to reach out and touch her.

Kelly stepped around him, bending down to pick up her backpack and jacket. "I took you seriously then because I was too young to know better." She put more space between them. "But I know better now."

She had to leave before the horrible memories of the hurt she had felt when he left brought the pain back. But he was standing between her and the door, blocking her way out of the suite.

"I know I disappointed you," Jackson said softly.

Kelly laughed. "Yeah, I'd say I was disappointed," she agreed. "For God's sake, T., you left the country without even saying goodbye to me!" She pushed past him toward the door. "I've got to go-—"

Jax caught her arm. "Please, Kel..." He suddenly wished desperately that real life could be as simple as fiction. He wished he could go back and rewrite some of the scenes in his life. But he'd made so many mistakes with Kelly, it was hard to know where to start. He wished at least he'd had a chance to make love to her, to show her how much he loved her. Suddenly he was glad that he had added that love scene between Jared and Carrie to his book. Their one night of love was what bound them together, and it would keep them bound together even as they faced the trials and tribulations he was going to send their way.

But he and Kelly had had no such night. He had never even said the words *I love you* to her.

She pulled her arm away and stared at him, anger and hurt in her eyes. "I loved you so much, T. But it was just a game to you-—"

"No!" He raked his hair back out of his face with his fingers. "That's not true—"

"The truth is, you were doing Kevin a favor by taking me to the prom," she said hotly. "But you went kind of overboard, took it a step too far." She reached for the doorknob, pulling the door open. "Well, not this time, Jackson."

But he pushed the door closed with the palm of one hand, and brought his other hand up against the door on the other side of her, effectively pinning her between his arms. "No," he said very definitely. "I won't let you run away. You've got to give me a chance to explain."

T. was standing so close, Kelly could feel heat radiating from his body. She could smell his sweet scent, a mixture of after-shave, shampoo and his own, individual familiar aroma.

"God, you even smell the same," she said, looking up into the swirling colors of his eyes. *I give up,* she suddenly wanted to say. *Take me to dinner. Take me anywhere. Take me.*

She knew all she had to do was ask. There was no mistaking the desire she could see in his eyes.

He leaned toward her, as somehow she knew he would, and he kissed her, also as she knew he would. What she didn't expect was the total meltdown she experienced as his lips touched hers.

Her bones became liquid, her muscles useless and her arms, the evil betrayers, wrapped themselves around T. Jackson's neck, pulling him even closer to her. She heard him groan as his tongue pushed past her lips, tasting her, possessing her.

Nothing had changed. Seven years had passed,

during which time Kelly had been married and divorced, yet all it took was one kiss from this man and all the old feelings came flooding back. As her fingers became tangled in his soft, blond hair, she tried to stop herself, but she couldn't.

He kissed her, harder, pulling her body in more tightly to him, his hands cupping the softness of her derriere, pressing her hips against him.

He lifted his head then, and Kelly stared into the turbulence of his eyes. "You know what I want," he said, his voice thick, raspy.

There was no mistaking the hardness of his arousal as it pressed against her stomach. Even though he hadn't asked a question, Kelly nodded, unable to speak.

"I wanted to make love to you the morning after the prom, too." He kissed her neck, her throat, running his hands lightly up her body, touching the sides of her breasts.

She closed her eyes, wanting him to touch her, wanting...

"I wanted you so badly," he whispered. "But you were only sixteen. And I—I didn't even care. I was so crazy in love with you, I couldn't see straight. If Kevin hadn't found us, if he hadn't stopped me, I would've done it. I would have made love to you right there on that beach. You were just a kid, and I didn't even have any protection, and I *still* would have done it, and, Kel, that scared the hell out of me." He shook his head, still amazed that he could have felt so out of control. "So I lost it, I totally lost it. Kevin was beating the crap out of me, and I didn't fight back because I knew I deserved it. And those things he said... I didn't deny it because I couldn't speak, I couldn't even *think*. But I didn't take you to that prom as a favor to your brother. After I saw you in that dress, I begged him to let me take you. I promised him I'd take care of you, and instead I nearly took your virginity—"

Kelly pressed her fingers to his lips. "You weren't the only one there that morning," she said steadily. "I was there, too. And I wanted you as much as you wanted me."

"Kel, you were a kid—"

"So what, T.? I knew what I wanted."

"How could you have known?" he asked. "You were only *sixteen*—"

"I'm not sixteen anymore," she said.

And then she kissed him.

It was a kiss of passion and need, filled with fire and heat and the promise that all they'd started seven years ago would not remain unfinished business. Not for long.

Kelly's backpack dropped to the floor as Jackson pushed her jacket off her shoulders. He heard her inhale sharply as his hands caressed her arms, and he was overcome by the need to touch more of her, all of her. He tugged at her shirt, yanking it free from the waist-band of her pants, and groaned as his fingers found the soft, warm skin of her back and her belly. He was lost, lost in the depth of her kisses, consumed by wanting her. Even after all those years, his control was still shot to hell when he held her in his arms. He was possessed, utterly, totally possessed by his burning need.

She moved away from him slightly to pull her shirt over her head. As if in a dream, Jax watched his hands unfasten the front clasp of her bra, releasing the soft fullness of her breasts. He wanted to take his time, to look at her, to touch her slowly, but he was on fire, and he couldn't hold back. He touched her almost roughly, driven nearly mad by the heavy weight of her breasts in his palms. Greedily he lowered his head and drew one taut nipple into his mouth, hungrily tugging, sucking until she cried out with pleasure.

Kelly pulled at his shirt then, and he quickly yanked it off. She reached out to touch him lightly, and the sensation was too exquisite, too intense. He crushed her to him, exalting in the feeling of her skin against his as he kissed her frantically. He was unable to think coherently, unable to think at all.

Jax felt her fingers at the waistband of his jeans, unfastening the button, tugging at the zipper.

"Kel," he groaned, knowing that if she touched him there, he'd never be able to turn back. "Kel, what are we doing?"

Her laughter was low and sexy. "Don't you know?"

He kissed her neck, her throat, letting his hands explore her body. Her hair felt like silk, her skin like satin. His fingers swept lower, and he realized with an electric jolt of pleasure that her leggings were gone. She'd somehow kicked off her cowboy boots and her pants, and now stood before him, naked.

She was beautiful—incredibly, perfectly beautiful.

He felt her tugging at his jeans, pushing them down.

"Oh, Jackson," he heard her whisper as she freed him from the confines of his shorts. And then she touched him. He nearly lost it right then and there, simply from the touch of her hand.

Seven years. For seven years he'd been waiting for this moment.

He touched the softness between her legs, feeling the heat and wetness that proclaimed her desire. Kelly opened herself to him, pressing against his exploring fingers. "Please, T.," she breathed, "I need you *now...*"

She had a condom. She must've had it in her backpack. She handed it to him and, as quickly as he could with shaking hands, he covered himself.

And then the waiting was over.

He lifted her up, and with one fierce thrust, he was inside of her. She cried out with pleasure as he plunged into her again and again.

Kelly's back was still to the door, her arms and legs wrapped tightly around T. as she moved with him. She'd never made love like this before. She'd never felt so desperately wanted, so fiercely desired. T.'s eyes were lit with a wild passion that both excited her and frightened her—frightened her because she suddenly doubted that making love to him once would be enough.

He pulled her down with him then, down onto the floor. He covered her body with his own, increasing the tempo of his movements. She met each thrust by lifting her hips, pushing him even more deeply into her. His hands and mouth were everywhere, adding to the sensations, driving her closer and closer to release.

And suddenly she was flying, hurtling through space as waves and waves of pleasure rocketed through her.

"Yes," she heard T. say through the storm that possessed her. "Come on, Kelly." And somehow, some way, she went even higher.

Jax had only imagined how good this would be, but

his imagination hadn't even come close to the reality. As the last tremors passed through her, she gazed up at him. "Oh, T., we should have done this seven years ago," she breathed, still moving with him.

She smiled up at him then, and it was the love he was so sure he saw in her eyes that pushed him over the edge.

He exploded. It was amazing, incredible, impossibly wonderful. He wanted to laugh and cry and...

And she held him tightly, her arms around him, until his breathing slowed. He rolled off her then, pulling her into his arms. He could feel Kelly watching him staring at the ceiling for several long moments before he glanced at her out of the corners of his eyes. He laughed, not without a certain amount of embarrassment.

"I have such amazing finesse," he said, more to himself than her. "I had seven years to plan the perfect way to make love to you for the first time, and what do I do? I don't even take you into the bedroom. I end up nailing you to the wall."

She laughed. "Is that what that's called? I liked it a lot."

Jackson moved his left arm out from underneath her so he could use it to support his head as he looked down into her eyes. "I'm glad," he murmured.

She reached up to push his hair back from his face.

Jax's smile was sheepish and utterly charming. "I really wasn't planning for this to happen, you know, for us to make love. I was totally unprepared. I'm glad you had a condom." He leaned down and kissed her, a long, lazy, unhurried kiss.

Kelly closed her eyes, feeling her heart begin to beat faster. Could she really want him again? Already?

When Jackson swung her up into his arms and carried her through the bedroom into the huge bathroom, she didn't protest. He set her down in the big shower stall and gently washed them both clean, and still she didn't protest. By the time he had wrapped her in the thick, white hotel towel, she was on fire again. And from the looks of things, he was, too.

He pulled her to his bed and sat down, holding her on his lap. He kissed her, another slow, leisurely kiss that made her tremble. As he held her close, she could feel his heart pounding and knew that he hadn't gotten her out of his system any more than she had removed him from hers.

Once had definitely not been enough.

"Kelly, why did you give in?" Jax murmured into her neck as his hands caressed the smooth, clean length of her body. "Don't get me wrong—I love it that you're here, but I'm just...kind of surprised."

She pulled back slightly to look at him. "I guess I figured that it's time to move on with my life," she said. "We've both had this attraction for each other for such a long time, and..." *Neither one of us would ever really have been free until we proved that sex between us wasn't the magnificent event we'd imagined,* she wanted to say, but couldn't. Because in reality, making love to T. Jackson had been far, far more magnificent than any fantasy she'd dreamed. Instead of being freed by finally making love to this man, she had simply made the chains that bound her to him that much tighter.

But Jax couldn't read her mind, and the words he heard filled him with happiness. She was ready to move on with her life, and it sure seemed as if she'd chosen to move in his direction. "Kelly, I want to make love to you again," he whispered. "If that's okay with you."

She told him just how okay it was with a kiss, and he pulled her back with him onto the bed.

Maybe this time, thought Kelly. Maybe making love to him this time would chase his memory back to where it belonged—securely in the past.

# CHAPTER EIGHT

KELLY AWOKE AS DAWN was beginning to edge its way past the hotel room curtains. T. lay in the big bed beside her, his arm possessively draped across her, holding her close, her back against his chest.

She felt the familiar jolt of sexual excitement that always shot through her when she was near this man. It flared into full-blown desire as she felt his most masculine part pressing into her leg.

T. Jackson even wanted her in his sleep.

Being desired so intensely gave her a powerfully strong feeling. It was similar to the way she'd felt as a kid when she'd climbed out onto the roof of the house. She felt daring, bold and adventurous. She felt an adrenaline high, a rush.

But that wasn't the kind of feeling she wanted from a relationship.

She wanted to feel safe and warm. She wanted to feel secure. She wanted to be cherished, not hungered for.

T. looked so peaceful, so serene, so content as he slept. With his hair disheveled, an unruly jumble of waves falling down across his forehead, with his long, dark lashes lying against his smooth, tanned cheeks, he was, truly, the most beautiful man she'd ever seen. He was funny, smart, bright and fun to be around. But he'd broken her heart once, and there was no reason to believe that he wouldn't do it again. No, she could not let herself love him again.

How could you love T. *again,* when you never stopped loving him? a little voice in her head asked.

But she *had* stopped loving him. She could remember the exact time, the exact hour it had happened.

That was when you *wanted* to stop loving him, the voice said. It doesn't mean you really stopped. People can't just turn their feelings off like a light switch. You still love him.

No, Kelly thought almost desperately. She *didn't* love T., and she could prove it.

Quietly she slipped out of bed and went into the living room. She dressed quickly and grabbed her backpack and jacket, and crept out of the room and out of the hotel.

Standing at the underground trolley stop, she waited for the train that would take her home.

See, she told herself, she didn't love him. If she loved him, she wouldn't have been able to walk away.

Okay, the little voice in her head said. So how come you're crying?

Dear Kelly,
Toilet paper.

They found my book and took it away and now they use the pages for toilet paper.

The warden laughs at the look on my face, at the tears I can't keep from my eyes, knowing he has at last found a way to hurt me.

You come to me then, for the first time appearing when others are around. They can't see you. They don't know it is your strength that keeps me from crumbling.

"Don't cry," you order me, your eyes fiery with determination. "Keep your head up. You've got that book practically memorized anyway. So what if they take the paper that it's written on? They can't take your memory. It's in your head, T., you can write it again."

You look so beautiful, trembling with your conviction. I smile at you, and I am rewarded by your bright grin.

The warden frowns and sends me back to my cell.

I love you.

Love, T.


JAX WOKE UP WITH A SMILE on his face that faded as soon as he rolled over and saw that he was alone in his bed.

"Kel?" he called out, going first into the bathroom and then out in the living room.

He saw right away that her things were gone. He looked around for a note, thinking maybe she had an appointment and she didn't want to wake him.

But there was no note.

Why would she leave like that, without saying good-bye? Why would she slip out of his room as if last night had been nothing more than a casual one-night stand?

Fear hit him, squeezing all of the air out of his lungs. No.

No, he wouldn't believe that. Things had gotten pretty intense last night. She must've gotten scared and felt the need for some time alone, to think about what was going on, about what was happening between them.

He crossed the room and picked up the telephone, quickly punching in her number.

She answered on the second ring. "Hello?"

Jackson took a deep breath, determined not to let his paranoia show. "Hey," he said, his voice light. "Good morning."

"Jackson," she said.

Not a very enthusiastic greeting. And was that trepidation he heard in her voice? Or were his insecurities making him imagine things?

"I missed you this morning." He still kept his voice easygoing. "I'm dying to see you again. What do you say I pick you up in about an hour and we have lunch?"

There was a brief moment of silence, during which time Jackson died over and over and over again. *Say yes,* he prayed. *Please say yes.*

"I'd planned to write all day," Kelly finally answered. "I'm not as far along as I'd hoped to be with this story and..."

It sounded like a lame excuse. But Jax understood what it meant to need time to write, so maybe it really wasn't. "How about I pick you up at six? You should be ready for a break by then. We can have dinner."

"I don't think so."

Her words echoed in the great, big, heavy silence that followed. Jax slowly sat down. His heart was in his throat as he finally said, "Kelly, what's going on? I don't—I don't understand."

"T., I already told you that I don't want to become

involved with you," she said softly. "I'm not ready to be in a relationship right now."

All that was left of last night's happiness crashed and burned. Jax's knuckles were white as he clutched the telephone. But still he managed to keep his voice calm. "I think you're too late, Kel. I don't know what you'd call last night, but I'd say at this point we've started something that's pretty involved."

"Last night we were finishing something, Jackson," Kelly said quietly. "Not starting it."

"Kelly, please don't say that." Desperation was starting to creep into his voice.

"I'm sorry. I've got to go—"

"Wait, please! Talk to me—"

But she'd already hung up.

KELLY SAT IN FRONT OF HER computer, trying to find the right words to finish her latest manuscript's final love scene. This was the hardest part of writing romances. At least it was for her. She kept her thesaurus handy, and had even made a list of words such as *tempestuous* and *untamed* but when she reread the scenes, there always seemed to be something missing.

The telephone rang again and she closed her eyes, trying not to listen as her answering machine intercepted yet another of T. Jackson's telephone calls.

"Kelly, I know you're home." His normally easygoing voice sounded tight, his words clipped. "So answer the damn phone. If you don't, I'm coming over."

She swore softly under her breath, then shut down the power to her computer.

The spring day had dawned warm and sunny after

yesterday's dismal rain. It was a perfect day to go running. And now seemed like an especially perfect time.

She changed quickly into a pair of running shorts
and her sneakers, pulling a T-shirt on over an athletic
bra. Automatically she reached up to pull her hair back
into a ponytail, then smiled as she realized that with
her new short hairstyle, that was no longer possible.
She tied her house key onto her shoelace, trying not to
think about T. Jackson.

She'd spent the entire day trying not to think about
him. She hadn't thought once about the way his green
eyes seemed to glow as he made love to her. She hadn't
thought about his rich laugh or the sexy catch that she
heard in his voice when he wanted her. And she certainly hadn't thought once about his hard, lean, muscular body, or about that golden tan that intriguingly
covered every inch of him.

No, she hadn't thought about him once. She'd
thought about him too many times to count.

But she was more than a walking hormone. And
there was more to life than good sex.

She wanted a man who would stick around for the
rest of his life, not just for a few years until he got tired
of her.

But what would it hurt, that pesky little voice popped
into her head and said, if you spent the summer with
T.? Spend one last summer with a man who drives you
wild, *then* start dating only safe, down-to-earth types.

No, she couldn't do that. The emotional risk was too
great.

What emotional risk? the voice argued. You say you

don't still love the guy. You say you're not going to fall in love with him again, no way—

Damn right. And the best way to not fall in love with T. was to avoid him. There was no doubt about that.

She closed her apartment door, checking to see that it was locked, then quickly went down the stairs. She pushed open the screen door at a run, went out on the porch, down the steps—

And skidded to a stop to keep from slamming into T.

How the hell did he get over here so quickly? Cell phone, she realized instantly. Of course. He must've called her on his cell phone. So much for making an easy escape. So much for avoiding him.

His face looked hard. There was definitely a determined set to his jaw, but his eyes held more than a glimmer of hurt as he stared at her.

"Going somewhere?" he asked.

Kelly sighed. "Yeah, I was going to go running."

"Running away, you mean," he said tightly.

"You're really angry at me." Her heart sank further. She had hoped he'd see that this was for the best.

He laughed, a quick burst of exasperated air. "Did you actually think I wouldn't be angry? Or hurt?" He shook his head. "God, Kelly, what are you trying to prove?"

"T., I didn't mean to hurt you." Her eyes filled with tears and she fought to blink them back. "I thought..."

"What?" T. pulled her chin up so that Kelly was forced to look him in the eye. "What did you think? That I wouldn't care? That I'd just walk away, disappear, stop bothering you? Say, 'thanks, it was a lot of fun?'"

"Yes," she said honestly, then backed away from the sudden flare of anger in his stormy eyes. "I thought that if we made—if we *had* sex, we'd both realize that the attraction between us wasn't real, that it was based on fantasy, on the past."

He turned away from her, screwing his eyes shut as if in sudden pain. "*That's* what you meant when you said you wanted to move ahead with your life. I thought you were talking about having a future with me, but damn it, you were exorcising me, weren't you?"

When she didn't answer, he turned back to face her. "Weren't you?"

Kelly stared into his accusing eyes, and felt a tear escape and roll down her cheek. "Yes," she whispered.

"Well, did it work?" T.'s voice was raspy. "Did you get me out of your system, Kel? 'Cause it sure as hell didn't work for me."

"I don't know," Kelly said, another tear joining the first.

Jax stared at her. Her eyes were so big in her pale face. She looked little more than a child. But she was no child. Not anymore. They'd both proved that last night.

"Did you really think that all I wanted was to make love to you?" He felt tears burning his own eyelids. "No, not make love, you called it sex. Is that really all it was to you, Kelly? Sex? Just a one-goddamned-night stand? God, I made *love* to you last night."

His voice shook with emotion, and he turned away, wiping the tears from his eyes. "Goddamn it, Kelly," he whispered. "*Goddamn* you."

"I'm sorry," she said.

"Are you?" He turned back to her. "Then have dinner with me. Spend time with me. Let this thing between us have a chance—"

"No." She realized how brusque she sounded, and tried to soften it. "T., I can't, I—"

"Come to the Cape with me." He took a step toward her, reached for her. "Please, Kelly. God, I'm begging you—"

She moved away. "No!"

He shook his head, defeated, and turned away, heading for his car. But he'd only gone a few steps before he came back. As Kelly watched, he took a business card out of his wallet and held it out to her.

"Take it," he ordered her, and Kelly reluctantly reached for it. "It's my phone number on Cape Cod. In case you need me for anything. In case..." His voice shook again, and he took a deep breath. "This is not over," he said, gazing directly into her eyes. "I'm under your skin—you just don't know it yet. But I'm under there and you're not going to be able to forget me. Especially now, after last night. If that really was just sex for you, Kelly, imagine how good making love to me could be."

Kelly stood staring, long after his car had disappeared.

## CHAPTER NINE

Dear Kelly,

For the first time in months I have hope.

A piece of paper has appeared, slipped by unknown hands through the crack under the heavy wooden door to my cell. It lies on the damp dirt floor, white and shining in the dim morning light.

I pick it up slowly, carefully.

It is a card. The paper is a thick linen blend and I run my fingers lightly over the texture of the fibers. It has the feel of a wedding invitation.

I turn it over. There's a picture on the front. A drawing.

A white dove flies up to the sky, escaping the bars of a prison cell. Inside the darkness of the cell, a single candle burns. It is wrapped in barbed wire.

My hands tremble as I open the card. There is writing inside—plain block letters. In English.

"Jackson Winchester, we know you are there," I read. "We are working and praying for your immediate and unconditional release."

There is no signature, but I know who it is from.

Amnesty International.

One month later I am free.

"OH, PLEASE, DON'T TELL ME *that's* your breakfast." Stefanie looked with pointed distaste at the cold slice of pizza Jax held in one hand as he opened the refrigerator with the other.

"All right, I won't tell you," he said, pulling out a bottle of beer and opening it.

"When was the last time you shaved?" She followed him up the stairs and into his office.

The spacious room had big windows that looked out over the bay, and an entire wall of bookshelves filled with books of all shapes and sizes, covering a vast plethora of subjects. Jax's computer was set up so that he could look out over the water with a simple turn of his head, but directly above the monitor was a huge corkboard to which he'd pinned information on his current characters and a brief list of the major plot points of his story.

There was a large oak table in the room, with several comfortable chairs placed around it. A couch ran along another wall. The floors were hardwood and the ceiling was high, angling up dramatically.

Jax stood in front of the windows, eating the cold pizza and staring at the sunlight on the water. There was a boat way out, almost beyond the edge of the horizon, and he could see only the tiny speck of its red sail against the brilliant blue sky.

He scratched the back of the hand that held the bottle of beer with the rough stubble on his chin. When *had* he last shaved? But who cared, really? "Why? Are guests coming today?"

"Just Emilio," Stefanie said.

Jax turned to look at her, smiling grimly after he

took a long swig of beer. "Thank God. For a minute I thought we were going to get a royal visit from the King or Queen of Winchester."

Stefanie laughed. "Someday you're going to have children of your own, and you better hope they treat *you* with a little more respect than you treat our parents."

His eyes clouded, and he looked back out the window. "I'm never going to have children."

"Ooh, ready to do some wallowing, are we? Poor baby—"

"Don't start," Jackson said sharply.

There was a long silence. The red sail had disappeared down behind the curve of the earth. What would it be like to be on that little boat right now? Out of sight of the land, nothing but the ocean and the sky...

"When was the last time you slept?"

Jax shrugged. "Probably shortly before the last time I shaved."

"Was that two days ago?" she asked. "Or three?"

He turned to look at her. His sister was a picture of health, dressed in her shiny Lycra workout clothes. Her sneakers were so new that Jax almost had to shield his eyes from the glare. Her hair was pulled back off her elegant face, and she wore a light coat of makeup. She was on her way to the fitness club.

"Who knows?" he answered. "I'm in the midst of a creative spurt. I'm not keeping track of pedestrian things like sleeping and eating."

"A creative spurt." She crossed her arms skeptically. "How many pages have you written?"

"Creativity and output aren't necessarily connected," he said, somewhat loftily.

"That many?"

He was silent, staring once again out the window.

"You still want me to screen your calls?"

"Yeah," he said. "I don't want to talk to anyone, except..."

"Kelly," she finished for him.

He didn't bother to say anything. Kelly wasn't going to call. He'd waited for two weeks, and he knew with a certainty that, as each day passed, it was less and less likely she would.

"Jax, maybe it's time to move on," Stefanie said quietly. "If you're going to give up, then do it. Give up. But don't sit here feeling sorry for yourself—"

"If I wanted therapy, I would've called my shrink." He saw a flash of hurt in her eyes, and he felt like a jerk. "I'm sorry."

Stef used the toe of her brilliant new sneaker to rub at an imaginary spot in the carpet. Dressed as she was, with her perfectly coiffed hair and her flawlessly applied makeup, it didn't seem possible that she was the one who'd refused to believe he was dead. She was the one who'd marched into that hellhole of a Central American country with the help of Amnesty International's London office and demanded to see either Jax's remains or the location where he was being held.

Stefanie, who had always seemed more concerned with getting her nails done and shopping at Saks, had almost single-handedly set up the letter-writing campaign that had secured his release.

He owed her his freedom, maybe even his life. Definitely his life.

"The publisher called again about that book you started," Stefanie said. "You know, the collection of letters? They're waiting for the final few chapters. Why don't you send it, Jax? I know you've finished it."

"I'm waiting to find out if that book's going to have a happy ending."

She shook her head. "How long do you intend to wait?"

"I don't want to talk about it."

"If you don't want to talk to me," Stef said, "maybe you *should* think about calling that psychologist...what was his name? Dr. Burnham."

Jax stood silently, just watching her.

"Call him," she urged. "Or call Kelly. Do *some*thing, darling. I'll see you later."

His sister turned and left the room, closing the door softly behind her.

With a sigh, Jax turned back to his computer.

His main characters had run into each other downtown on the Boston Common. They had exchanged pleasantries. It was all so polite and proper, yet they both couldn't help but think about the night they'd made love.

With breathtaking clarity, Jax had a sudden memory of Kelly lying naked on his hotel room bed, smiling up at him, her blue eyes half closed.

"God *damn* it..." Waves of anger and self-pity flooded him until he felt as if he might drown.

"Why the hell are *you* feeling sorry for yourself?" Jared's mocking voice cut through Jax's misery. "*I'm* the one who's in a real bitch of a situation. I'm starting to really wonder what you've got in mind here. Carrie's obviously mad as hell at me, and I don't have a clue why. I mean, for crying out loud, *she's* the one who married some other dude."

"Don't use words like *bitch* and *dude*," Jax reminded him tiredly. "You live in the 1860's, or have you forgotten?"

"Look at you." Jared ignored Jax's question. "You look like total crap—"

"*Crap.* Another fine word for a historical romance hero."

"—you haven't showered or shaved in days, and you're drinking beer at nine o'clock in the morning—"

"Morning, night, what's the difference anyway?" muttered Jax. "One's got the sun, the other doesn't. Big deal."

"So that's it then?" Jared asked, one eyebrow raised in surprise. "You're giving up on Kelly, just like that?"

Jax didn't answer right away. He just turned to stare out the window as he drank the last few drops of his beer. "I don't know what else to do," he finally said.

"Well, okay, but giving up is really stupid," Jared said. "You automatically lose when you give up. Think about all the heroes in your books. Think about Hank in *Night of the Raven.* He didn't give up when Anna told him she'd fill his hide with buckshot if he as much as set one foot on her ranch. And how about Daniel in *Too Late To Run?* Maggie swore on a stack of Bibles that she'd never fall in love with him, but he won her in the end. Think of all the books you've written—how many *have* you written anyway?"

"One too many, apparently," Jax said dryly.

"Kelly's not going to call," Jared told him.

"Thanks a lot. Rub it in, why don't you?"

"You've got to call her."

Jax looked down at the silent telephone that was sitting within arm's reach of his computer. If he called Kelly, she'd refuse to see him. He knew her well enough to know that. No, he was going to have to make her an offer that she couldn't refuse.

And in a sudden flash of inspiration, he knew just what to offer her. "No." He smiled. "*I'm* not going to call her."

THE TELEPHONE WAS RINGING as Kelly unlocked the door to her apartment. She was still breathing hard from her three-mile run. Her skin was slick with perspiration, and her clothes were soaked. But she unlocked the door quickly and bolted for the phone. Maybe it was T.

But you don't *want* him to call, she scolded herself as she picked up the kitchen phone. "Hello?" she said breathlessly.

"May I speak to Kelly O'Brien please?" an unfamiliar female voice asked.

Disappointment. She tried to ignore it as she opened the refrigerator door and pulled out a bottle of seltzer.

"Yeah, this is Kelly." The seltzer exploded slightly as she twisted off the cap, spraying her with cool water. She took a large swallow of the bubbling soda right from the bottle.

"Kelly, this is Stefanie Winchester. I don't know if you remember me. We met at that university lecture a few weeks ago?"

T. Jackson's sister. "Of course I remember you. How are you?" Kelly asked. *How is T.?* she wanted to ask. *And why hasn't he called me?*

*Because you told him not to,* she answered her own question.

"Fine, thanks," Stefanie said. "I'm actually calling to ask you for a favor. I'm doing some research for, um, a book, and I need some information on how small-press newspapers are made—everything from planning to layout to printing, and I thought I remembered that Jax had told me you work at the university newspaper...?"

"Yes, that's right."

"I'm going to be in town tomorrow," Stefanie said. "Would you mind joining me for lunch?"

Lunch. With Jayne Tyler. It smelled very fishy, kind of like *bait.* Now, why did that make her so happy? But if it *was* some kind of lure, she wanted to know about it.

"Lunch isn't necessary," Kelly said, testing her theory. "We can talk right now, on the phone."

"Well, uh..." Stefanie hesitated. "Now's not a really convenient time for me, and I, uh, really would like to get together with you, and, well... How about twelve-thirty at the Bookseller Café?"

"Stefanie, did Jackson put you up to this?" Kelly asked with her usual bluntness. She took another long drink of seltzer.

Stefanie laughed. "Yes," she admitted. "He did. He told me if you refused to come to lunch, I should offer to read your latest manuscript, you know, as a bribe."

Now Kelly laughed, pressing the cold bottle against

her forehead. She watched as droplets of sweat dripped onto the tiled floor. "He's shameless."

"May I be candid?"

"Of course."

"I don't know what happened between you two," Stefanie said, "but he's been an absolute mess ever since he came back from Boston."

Kelly felt a flash of pain as she remembered the hurt she'd last seen in T.'s eyes. She really hadn't meant to hurt him. She'd been carrying around guilt and remorse for two weeks now, wishing she'd somehow handled the entire affair differently.

She thought about T. Jackson all the time, because of the guilt. Every time she saw a tall, blond man, her heart leapt into overdrive, no doubt because she wanted another chance to apologize to T.

If she could turn back time, she would probably agree to go to Cape Cod with him for the summer. Not because she particularly wanted to go, she reassured herself, although as the mercury climbed higher and higher in the thermometer, it was difficult *not* to think about the cool, blue ocean and the fresh breezes sweeping across the beaches. Never mind how often she thought about a certain pair of eyes that changed color like the sea.

The truth was, she didn't want to feel responsible for that wounded look T. had had on his face the morning after they'd made love. She'd seen that same look in her own mirror the first few months after he'd left for London without telling her. The look was there again when he didn't show up for her eighteenth birthday.

"Will you come?" Stefanie asked.

"My manuscripts aren't perfect," Kelly said. "In fact, I'm having a real tough time finishing my second one. And I can't figure out what's wrong with the first one."

"Jayne Tyler to the rescue, darling," Stefanie said. "If anyone can help you, it is she. Can I expect to see you tomorrow?"

"Yes," Kelly said decidedly. "Will Jackson be there?"

"Do you want him there?"

Kelly was silent, finishing off the last of the seltzer. "Yeah," she finally said. "I guess I do." That way she'd get her chance to apologize again.

"I'm not sure what his schedule's like," Stefanie said breezily. "I've got to run. Bring whichever manuscript you want. See you tomorrow, Kelly."

Kelly hung up the phone and headed for the shower, feeling lighter than she had in weeks.

JAX SETTLED HIMSELF IN THE beach chair next to Stefanie as she opened one eye and glanced over at him. She took in his freshly shaved face and clean hair, and, most obviously, his smile.

"Well, well, if the smelly little frog hasn't turned back into the handsome prince," she murmured, closing her eyes and turning her face to a better angle to catch the sun.

"What do you think I should wear tomorrow?" Jax asked, pulling off his T-shirt and dropping the chair back into a full reclining position.

"Since when do you ask me for fashion advice, darling?" Stefanie opened both eyes to look at him this time.

"If I were writing this," Jax mused, "I'd have the

hero show up in an impeccably tailored suit, looking like a million bucks, never mind that the weatherman's predicting another hundred-degree day for tomorrow."

"Fictional characters are so nice," Stefanie said with a sigh, "because they never sweat unless you want them to."

The sun felt warm on Jax's face, and a wave of fatigue hit him. "If I fall asleep, wake me up in a couple of hours. I don't want to fry."

"A bathing suit," Stefanie said. "You should wear a bathing suit and one of those disgustingly sexy undershirt things that reveal more than they cover. As long as it's going to be hotter than hell, you might as well look good while you sweat. Have you ever noticed that when an athlete sweats, it's sexy? But a soggy businessman, now, that's an entirely different story."

Stefanie's watch alarm went off and she put on her hat, careful now to keep her face out of the sun. She only exposed her face to the sun for ten minutes each day. While crow's-feet looked good on men when they aged, women had to be careful.

She glanced back at her brother, but he was already fast asleep.

Dear Kelly,
I am writing this on a real piece of paper with a real pen as I sit on this 727 heading north to Miami.
I am free.
I am flying first-class, and the stewardess offers me champagne, but Stefanie, my sister, shakes her head no. She seems to think I've

picked up some nasty bugs during my stay in the tropical wilds of Central America. Her doctors have advised her to let me eat or drink nothing besides bottled water and fresh vegetables until they have checked me out.

There's a hospital bed and a bevy of doctors waiting for me at Mass. General Hospital. Stef tells me she's arranged for a private room, and I laugh. She doesn't get the joke, and I explain— I've spent the last twenty months in solitary. I don't want a private room.

I'll be in the hospital for three or four weeks undergoing medical tests. They'll also be fattening me up. I guess I'm a little malnourished right now.

The warden let me shower and gave me clean clothes before I was released. I have lost so much weight and my beard and hair are so long, I didn't recognize myself in the mirror.

I want to see you, but I don't want you to see me like this. So I'll wait until I'm out of the hospital to call you.

Tonight I will sleep on a bed with real sheets, but I will still dream about you.

I love you.

Love, T.

WHEN KELLY WALKED INTO THE café, Stefanie was already there, sitting on the outside porch, waiting for her. The older woman waved from the table where she was sitting.

She was alone. No T. Jackson.

Kelly was surprised. What was the point of using Jayne Tyler for bait if T. wasn't even going to bother to show up? Unless he had something else in mind...

The two women greeted each other as Kelly started to sit down across from Stefanie, placing her briefcase on the floor.

"Oh, sit over here." Stef patted the chair next to hers. "It's so nice to be able to look out on the street."

With a shrug and a smile, Kelly changed seats.

"Did you bring your manuscript?" Stefanie asked.

"Are you kidding?" Kelly was amused. "No one in their right mind would pass up an opportunity to get a critique from Jayne Tyler."

"Let me have it now, so I don't forget to get it from you."

Kelly pulled the heavy manila envelope out of her briefcase and handed it to Stefanie, who set it on the table next to her.

She sat still, returning Stefanie's gaze steadily as the older woman looked at her closely. She was pale, she knew, because she hadn't had much of a chance to get out in the sun. She still ran, but in the very early mornings, just as the sun was starting to rise. The rest of the day she spent inside, in the infernal heat of her apartment, slaving at her computer.

As Stefanie looked at her, Kelly fought the urge to put on her sunglasses, to cover up the dark smudges she knew were under her eyes, the shadows that betrayed the fact that she hadn't been sleeping well for quite some time.

But Stefanie didn't comment. She just smiled and

picked up her menu. "What do you say we order before we talk? I'm starving."

"But..." It came out involuntarily.

Stefanie looked at her, eyebrows delicately raised, waiting for her to continue.

What the hell, Kelly thought, and asked, "Isn't Jackson going to join us?" She only wanted a chance to apologize, to clear the air between them.

"He wasn't sure when he could get over here," Stefanie glanced down at her menu, "if at all. I hear the crab salad is wonderful."

Bemused, Kelly opened her menu. If T. Jackson was playing some kind of game with her, he just won a point. She was confused. If he was going to go to all this trouble to get her together with his sister, it seemed kind of silly for him not to show up.

After the waiter came up to their table and took their order, they began to talk. Stefanie was easygoing and self-confident, like her brother, and socially quite adept. She gracefully steered their conversation from one light topic to another. Although the two women came from entirely different backgrounds, they had a lot in common.

Before Kelly knew it, their lunches had arrived.

Stefanie somehow managed to eat and converse at the same time, and without ever talking with her mouth full.

"So I went into the fitness center—" the elegant blonde took a sip of her water "—expecting my personal trainer to be some kind of Nazi drill sergeant, or, even worse, a muscle-bound Amazon commando bitch, and Lord help me, but I must have done *some-*

thing worthwhile at *some* time in my life. I look up into *the* most soulful pair of brown eyes that I've ever seen in my life. And those eyes just happened to be attached to this incredible Roman god of a man. His name was Emilio Dicarrio, he told me in this wonderful Italian accent." She gestured at Kelly with her fork. "I'm telling you, it was love at first sight, for both of us." Another sip of water. "At first I thought, God, how tacky. Falling in love with your personal trainer—that's almost as gauche as having a thing for your shrink. Then I thought, he's a gold digger, just after my money. That's what Jax thought, too. But Emilio is one of the few people that I've ever met who's totally happy with his life. He's living in the United States, working in a job he likes. I tell you, the man's *content.* I offered him a chance to do some modeling for some of Jayne's book covers. He did a few photo shoots, but then turned down all the other offers because he thought the work was dull."

"He sounds perfect," Kelly said. "What's the catch?"

The blond woman's gray eyes were suddenly subdued. "He wants me to marry him."

"That's a problem?" Kelly asked.

"Emilio is only twenty-two years old. He's a baby. He's ten years younger than I am."

"So?"

"So when he's forty, I'll be fifty." She shuddered. "Darling, it's too terrible to consider."

"But that's eighteen years away," Kelly protested.

Stefanie shrugged, taking a sip of her iced tea. "So tell me." Her gray eyes were suddenly sharp and slightly accusing. "Why did you come to lunch today?

Was it purely mercenary, only to drop off your manuscript, or were you hoping to see my brother?"

Kelly returned her gaze steadily. "I wanted to apologize to Jackson. I'm afraid I treated him badly."

"You know, when he came back from Central America—" Stefanie stopped, looking at the puzzled expression on Kelly's face. "Don't tell me. He never told you what happened in Central America?"

"Was that before or after he went to London?"

"Oh, God." Stefanie sat back in her chair, staring sightlessly down at her plate. Why hadn't Jax told Kelly? He had a nearly completed 250-page manuscript of letters to her. Letters that he'd obviously never even told her about...

"Why? What happened in Central America?" Kelly asked curiously.

"No." Stefanie looked up at her again. "Jax will tell you if he wants you to know."

The waiter approached the table. "Ms. Winchester," he murmured. "Phone call."

Stefanie stood. "Excuse me. Maybe that's Jax."

Kelly put her chin in her hand and watched the traffic, both in the street and on the sidewalk. The café looked out on quirky Newbury Street in downtown Boston, so there was a wide variety of people passing by. Overheated men in business suits, delivery men without their shirts on, modern hippies in long, flowing skirts, teenagers with more earrings and nose rings than Kelly could count, tourists in Bermuda shorts and T-shirts with cameras around their perspiring necks....

From out of this teeming mass of humanity, Kelly suddenly saw him. T. Jackson Winchester the Second.

His golden hair reflected the sunshine. His eyes were covered by his sunglasses, but the rest of his face looked calm and relaxed. He was wearing...

Kelly swallowed. He was wearing a colorful bathing suit and a tank top that was nearly nonexistent. The only thing missing was his surfboard.

As he walked down the street, his muscles rippled. As Kelly watched, he turned in to the entrance of the café and opened the door. He hadn't spotted her yet, but it wouldn't be long.

She took a cooling sip of her water, and then there he was. Standing in front of her.

"Hey," he said with a quick smile. "Mind if I sit down?"

Silently she shook her head, trying not to stare at him.

Up close, she could see the light sheen of sweat on his muscles. His shirt was white, matching his teeth, contrasting with his tanned skin. A sudden vivid picture of T. Jackson wearing nothing at all popped into her mind.

She took another sip of water, wishing she could be hosed down. It was much too hot today.

T. sat down across from her, but he kept his sunglasses on. It was unnerving not to be able to see his eyes.

"How are you?" He leaned forward and casually rested his elbows on the table. "How's the writing coming?"

She had missed him.

She hadn't realized it until just now, but somehow she'd let herself get used to him hanging around, following her everywhere. And then when he was gone, something had been missing.

She'd missed his *friendship,* she told herself firmly. Because, face it, that was what their relationship had always been based on. Out of all those years of being close, they had only spent one day as lovers. Well, two, counting the night she'd spent in his hotel room.

Kelly leaned forward, too. "T., I'm really sorry about the way I treated you," she told him. "I don't want you to think that I slept with you as some kind of revenge thing or something like that, because I didn't. I honestly thought it would do us *both* good if we could be free from the past. I didn't mean to hurt you, and I'm sorry if I did."

His smile had faded, but she still couldn't see behind his sunglasses. "Kel, you're apologizing for the best night of my life," he said softly. "Don't do that."

He looked up suddenly, and Kelly turned to see Stefanie returning to their table.

"Well, well, look what the cat dragged in." Stef smiled, stopping to drop a kiss on the top of her brother's head. She turned to Kelly as she sat down. "Sorry about that. The publisher needs some revisions by yesterday. I'm afraid Jayne hasn't been on the ball lately."

"That's the second time you've done that," Kelly said. "You referred to Jayne in the third person, like she's somebody else."

"It's a funny thing about pseudonyms," Jax said easily. "They seem to take on a life of their own." He glanced at his watch. "If you're ready, Stef, I'll get the car and pull it around front." He stood, looking down at Kelly from behind his shades. "Nice seeing you."

He picked Kelly's manuscript up off the table, and left.

She turned to Stefanie, who was signaling the waiter for the check. "But we didn't talk about small-press newspapers."

Stefanie smiled. "Darling, we didn't need to in the first place."

"But..." Kelly laughed. "What just happened here? Did I miss something? Jackson set up this elaborate plan for me to have lunch with you simply to show up, say three sentences and leave? I don't get it."

Stefanie just smiled.

# CHAPTER TEN

OUTSIDE THE WINDOWS OF THE office, the beach was dark. Jax sat leaning back, his feet up on the conference table, as he read the last few pages of Kelly's manuscript.

It was good. It wasn't perfect, but it was pretty damn good. The heroine was a tough, feisty Katharine Hepburn type. In fact, the whole story read like a 1940s romantic comedy, with crackling, fast-paced dialogue.

In his opinion, the story had two major weaknesses. One was that the hero's motivation seemed unclear and some of his actions were contrived. The second weakness was in the love scenes.

Kelly wasn't comfortable writing those scenes, and it showed. Instead of being sensual explosions of emotion and feelings, they were sketchy and vague. And over much too soon.

Jax glanced at his watch. It was nearly midnight. Too late to call Kelly tonight.

With a sigh, he stood, stretching his muscles, heading toward the kitchen and the cold beer in the refrigerator.

Damn, but Kelly had looked good today. He was glad that he had been wearing his sunglasses, glad that she hadn't seen his eyes. If she had, she would've seen how badly he had missed her, and how much he wanted to be with her. She would have seen how badly he still wanted her.

He opened his beer with a swoosh and took a long sip.

It had nearly killed him to get up from that table after only sitting there with her for a few minutes. But his goal wasn't to have lunch with her. He was aiming for bigger things.

Such as forever.

He'd noticed her trying not to look at his body today. She hadn't been able to hide the flashes of desire that he'd seen in her eyes. Despite what she'd said about getting him out of her system, he knew that the magnetic pull of attraction he felt whenever he was near her was stronger than ever. And he knew she felt it, too.

She said he belonged only in her past, but she was wrong. He knew that he was her future. And she was his.

He would do whatever it took to prove that to her.

Well, almost anything.

He winced, remembering the way Stefanie had damn near chewed his head off in the car this afternoon. She didn't understand why he hadn't told Kelly about Central America.

When exactly was he supposed to have told her?

At Kevin's wedding maybe? Right after she'd dropped her own nuptial bomb?

He'd tried calling her when she was living in California, but Brad had answered the phone. Kelly's husband had told Jax in no uncertain terms that he didn't want him calling his wife. With a husband as jealous as Brad obviously was, there was no way Jax could resume his role in Kelly's life as friend of the family. He wasn't even sure he wanted to resume that role anyway. Instead, he'd stayed away from her for all those years.

So how could he have told her about Central America?

Maybe he was supposed to have told her in between her classes in Boston, as he chased her down the sidewalk. Yeah, he'd had *tons* of time then.

The night that they had made love, he had thought there would be plenty of opportunities to talk to her in the future, to tell her what had happened, what he had been through. But he'd been wrong.

And Jackson didn't want to tell her now. He didn't want her to pity him. He wanted her to love him.

KELLY COULDN'T SLEEP.

It was much too hot in her apartment, even with all of the windows open wide and the fans blowing directly at her.

Without the shades pulled down, light from the street lamp on the corner made bright patterns on the walls as it shone through the trees. She stared at them for a while, unwilling to shut her eyes.

Because when she shut her eyes, she saw T. Jackson.

T. Jackson. Looking better than a man had a right to.

T. Jackson. Giving in to his desire, unable even to walk the short distance to the hotel bedroom before he made love to her.

T. Jackson. Dancing with her all those years ago at her junior prom, smiling down into her eyes.

With sudden clarity, Kelly could see T., dressed

again in a tuxedo, standing in the church where Kevin had married Beth.

Kelly was one of the bridesmaids. She and Brad flew down to Beth's hometown of Atlanta to take part in the ceremony....

As the organist had begun to play the wedding march, she had followed the other bridesmaids down the aisle. The crowd in the church had all risen to their feet to watch. Kelly had smiled back into the sea of friendly, happy faces until suddenly she'd seen him.

T. Jackson Winchester the Second.

Kevin hadn't mentioned that T. was coming to the wedding.

But he was standing on the groom's side of the church, at the end of the pew closest to the center aisle. His blond hair was cut short, and his face looked pale and gaunt, as if he'd recently been very ill. But he was smiling at her, his eyes warm and so very green.

As she stared at him in shock, his lips moved as he silently spoke her name.

The ceremony passed in a blur, with Kelly standing up and sitting down with Beth's sisters, who were beside her at the front of the church.

Her mind was a whirlwind of thoughts. She'd never expected to see T. again. His estrangement with Kevin had seemed so permanent, so unmendable. The last time she asked Kevin about him, her brother had been vague, saying he thought Jax was still in London, but he wasn't sure.

Yet here he was. In Atlanta, of all places, for Kevin's wedding.

Kelly felt T.'s gaze on her throughout the entire ceremony. When she looked up to meet his eyes, he smiled at her. God, his smile could still take her breath away.

Her gaze flickered nervously toward Brad, who was sitting on the other side of the church. He hadn't wanted to come to this wedding. He hated flying, and he was already worrying about tomorrow morning's flight home. He was staring sightlessly down at the ground, the muscles in his jaw working.

As if he felt her eyes on him, Brad looked up at Kelly. But he didn't smile. He looked at her closely, the way he did a lot lately, as if he weren't sure exactly who she was. As if he couldn't figure out how he'd suddenly wound up married to her.

The events leading up to their marriage *had* happened fast. Kelly would be the first to admit it. She'd met Brad her senior year of high school, during an orientation session at Boston University. He was an upperclassman, and he had, as he later told her, fallen in love with her instantly.

He was tall, like T., and blond, like T., with the same zest for life evident in his winning smile. He was a senior when she was a college freshman, and almost before she knew it, he had taken her virginity and, she thought, her heart.

Carried along on the waves of romance, Kelly had married him in the fall of her sophomore year of college. Four months had passed since then, and now, looking into Brad's shuttered, expressionless blue eyes, she was starting to wonder just what they'd gotten themselves into.

The ceremony finally ended, and then the wedding party posed for pictures. When that was over, Kelly was whisked into a waiting limo with the other bridesmaids. As the big, white car pulled away from the church, she could see T. Jackson standing there, watching her. He lifted his hand in a wave.

It wasn't until the reception that T. caught up with her. Kelly and Brad were standing near the bar, talking to Beth's older sister as the band played an old, slow song. Couples were on the dance floor, swaying to the music.

Kelly spotted T. on the other side of the room, and knew that he was heading in her direction. She felt the urge to run or hide or—

"Kelly."

She looked up into the swirling colors of T. Jackson's eyes. He looked so thin as to be unhealthy, but his eyes were still the same marvelous mix of colors. Had it really been three years since she'd seen him last? Three long years since the night of her junior prom...

"You look beautiful," he said.

His lips curved into a small smile, and as he stepped even closer to her, he reached out and his warm fingers touched her arm, sliding gently down to her hand. As he pulled her toward him, his gaze dropped to her mouth.

He was going to kiss her, right there, right in front of *Brad*—

And he did.

T. Jackson gently brushed her lips with his.

"I need to talk to you." He smiled down at her. "Dance with me, will you—"

"I don't believe we've met," Brad's voice cut in.

T. looked up, surprised, and Kelly took the opportunity to step back, out of his embrace. Beth's older sister was watching with unabashed interest as the two tall, blond men sized each other up.

"No, you're right," T. said. "We haven't met. I'm sorry, Kelly tends to...distract me."

"Oh, really?" Brad crossed his arms in front of him.

T. looked slightly surprised at the hostility in Brad's voice, and he glanced at Kelly as if looking for an explanation.

That's when it hit her.

T. Jackson didn't know that she and Brad were married. Kevin hadn't bothered to tell him.

"Are you gonna introduce us?" Brad asked her, a touch impatiently.

"Brad, this is Jackson Winchester," she said. "He was my brother's college roommate."

She looked up at T., who had held out a friendly hand toward Brad. The two men shook.

"T., I'd like you to meet Brad Foster," Kelly said. "My husband." For some mysterious reason, her eyes had suddenly filled with tears.

T. stared at her, an expression of shock clearly written across his usually unflappable face.

"Oh, God," he breathed. "You're married?"

She tried to smile. "Yeah."

"How could you be married?" he asked, disbelief in his voice. "You're only nineteen."

He reached out, pulling her chin up so he could look into her eyes, as if he were hoping that something he saw there would prove her words wrong.

Brad stepped forward. "I'd appreciate it if you kept your hands off my wife."

T. Jackson let go of Kelly as if he'd been burned.

As she watched, tears formed in his eyes. He tried to blink them back. "I guess I missed your eighteenth birthday," he said softly.

Kelly nodded. "I guess you did."

"Oh, Kelly," he said.

She glanced back up into his eyes, and for one brief moment, he held her gaze, and she saw the white heat of his pain, the depth of his misery.

"Excuse me," T. whispered, and nearly ran from the room.

Brad stared after him. "People always have too much to drink at these things."

Kelly had spent the rest of the afternoon trying to convince herself that seeing T. hadn't really been that big a deal. Naturally she'd felt rattled; having him there had been a surprise. And as for the nearly overpowering urge to throw herself down on the floor and cry, well, that had had more to do with Brad's news that he'd found a job in California, than with anything else. Hadn't it...?

But as Kelly lay in the heat of the summer night nearly four years later, it all clicked into place.

She'd married Brad not because she loved him, but because he was so much like T. Jackson—or at least she thought he was—with his imposing height and blond hair. And even though she denied it, when she saw T. again at Kevin's wedding, deep down she realized the magnitude of her mistake.

Kelly stared at the ceiling, seeing T. as he had looked at lunchtime today, walking down the city street, dressed down for comfort in the afternoon heat. She could see the tanned planes and angles of his handsome face as he sat across from her at the café table. She could see the longing in her own eyes, mirrored in the reflective lenses of his sunglasses.

There was no denying that she missed him.

She missed him following her around campus all day and all night, popping up in the most unexpected places to give her a lift or ask her out. She missed hearing his voice and talking to him. She missed the way he listened to her as if every word she said was of the utmost importance.

She missed his friendship, that much was clear.

But she couldn't deny that she missed him in other ways, too. When she saw him at lunch, her body had responded with astonishing speed to his nearness, and she walked away feeling utterly frustrated.

God, she still wanted him.

Aha, triumphantly cried the side of her that always played devil's advocate. I've been right all along. You *do* still love him.

Don't get carried away, she chastised herself. Lust and love don't always go hand in hand.

Still, as she lay awake into the late hours of the night, she could see T.'s stormy green eyes and hear an echo of his voice saying, *This is not over. I'm under your skin.*

Around two-thirty, Kelly fell into a restless sleep, only to dream about T. Jackson Winchester.

"SO WHEN ARE YOU GOING to call her?" Jared asked.

Jax was sitting in front of his computer, arms folded across his chest. A glance at his watch told him it was still not even nine o'clock in the morning.

It was going to be another hot one. He could already see heat waves shimmering out on the sandy beach.

Jax had a similar heat cooking inside of him at the thought of calling Kelly and hearing her voice. And if everything went according to plan, he'd be seeing her in only a few hours.

He would be using her ambition as a means to get her out here, though, to put her within his grasp. It felt like cheating, but Jax reminded himself that he had to do whatever it would take to get her to spend time with him.

"All's fair in love and war," Jared supplied helpfully. "So why don't you call her?"

"Why don't you quit trying to distract me?" Jax said. "I'm not going to call Kelly until nine, and I should probably even wait until ten. Right now I *should* be finishing this damned book, and *you* should be helping."

"Hey, *I'm* not the one who left me hanging here on the Boston Common with Carrie for two solid days." Jared was disgruntled. "And on top of all that, she's still mad at me. Why am I here? What's the purpose of this scene? Maybe you just want to torture me. I suppose that could be it. God knows you *love* to torture me—"

"This is where you notice the bruises on Carrie's face," Jax said, starting to write.

Horrified, Jared looked closer.

Carrie had tried to cover it with powder, but he could see the fading bruise beneath her eye and across her delicate cheekbone. She ducked her head, turning away.

"I have to go—"

Jared caught her arm. "Who did this to you?"

"I fell." She couldn't meet his gaze as she pulled away.

He swore sharply, but it was the sudden tears filling his eyes that slowed her feet. "Why do you stay with him, Carrie?" he asked. "Lord—how could you *marry* him—"

But as she wheeled to face him, it was anger, not sorrow that made her voice shake. "How dare you," she said. "How *dare* you come back here, and how *dare* you look at me as if I were the one who betrayed *you?* God *damn* you to hell, Jared Dexter. *You're* the one who deserted *me!* You *promised* you would come for me—"

"Why didn't you wait?" It came out a whisper filled with his anguish and pain. "You should have waited for me."

He held her by her shoulders, and as he stared down into her deep blue eyes he could see...fear?

"Let go of me," she said. "You're making a scene. If someone tells Harlan they saw me here like this with you—"

Jared released her, feeling sick.


Jared looked up at Jax. "I don't like where this is going."

"You're definitely not gonna like where Carrie's going."

"Going? As in *away?* No, don't tell me—"

"She and Harlan are headed out west," Jax said. "Yippee-yi-oh-ki-ay. They're buying a ranch in California."

"California?" Jared threw up his hands in disgust. "Are you sure this book is going to have a happy ending?"

"I'm sure of nothing these days," Jax replied.

"Lord save me from depressed writers." Jared rolled his eyes.

"Relax," Jax said. "It won't be long now 'til Part Three. Part Three is three years later."

"Three *years!* What have I been doing for three *years?*"

"Getting richer. Your business ventures keep earning you more money. Everything you touch turns to gold."

"Everything except my love life." Jared sulked.

"You go west," Jax said, and Jared stopped sulking.

"Okay. Things are starting to look better. Where exactly did you say Harlan Kent's ranch was?"

"I didn't." Jax sat back in his chair. "But it's near Los Angeles."

"So what's going to happen?" Jared was still suspicious.

"First you go to L.A.," Jax told him, "where you find out that Harlan's dead."

The hard planes of Jared's handsome face softened into a smile. "Now you're talking. You had me worried there for a while."

Jax pulled himself back to his computer keyboard, but Jared shook his head.

"It's after nine," he pointed out. "You should call Kelly."

"Just let me get this started," Jax said distractedly.

"You're stalling."

Jared was right. He *was* stalling. No more stalling.

With a click of his mouse, Jax cleared the computer screen.

Taking a deep breath, he turned and looked at the telephone, then glanced at his watch to be sure it really was past nine.

He picked up the phone and dialed Kelly's home number. It rang once. Twice. Three times. Four.

"Hello?" She was breathless, as if she'd run for the phone.

"Hey, Kel," Jackson said. "It's me. Jax. How are you?"

"Soaking wet, actually," she said in her familiar, husky voice. "I was just turning off the shower when I heard the phone. Can you hold on a sec while I dry off and grab my robe?"

A sudden vivid image of Kelly, standing with only a towel around her, took Jax's breath away. He almost couldn't answer. "Yeah, sure," he managed to say.

He heard the sound of the phone being put down and then silence for about thirty seconds. Then she was back.

"Sorry about that," she said.

"No problem." He wiped the sweat off his upper lip with the back of his hand.

"It's funny. I was just thinking about you."

In the shower? He shook his head. It wasn't going to do him any good to start thinking along those lines.

"What's up?" she asked.

Funny you should ask... He cleared his throat. "I read your manuscript. It's good."

There was silence.

"*You* read it." Another pause. "I thought Stefanie was going to."

Mentally Jax froze. God, of *course.* Kelly thought that *Stef* was Jayne Tyler. She had no reason to think anything else. He realized that she was waiting for him to say something, that his silence was stretching longer and longer.

"Yeah," he finally said, hoping his next words would take her attention off the vagueness of his comment. "Look, your story could use some revisions. And that's why I'm calling. I thought you might be interested in letting Jayne Tyler help you with the rewrites."

It was his ace in the hole, his secret weapon, his only shot, and he prayed desperately that it would work.

"You're kidding."

"No."

More silence. He could almost hear the wheels turning in her head.

"Our offices are here at the house in Dennis," he said, mostly to fill the empty space. "I figure you could have the revisions done by the end of the summer."

"Dennis, huh?" She made a sound that might've been a laugh. "It's a hefty commute, considering I don't have a car."

"Um," Jax said. "There's plenty of room for you to stay over."

She laughed. "Now, how did I know you were going to say that?"

"Oh, come on, Kel." Jax closed his eyes and prayed. "Summer on the Cape...?"

"T., will you be honest with me?"

"I'll try."

"Is my writing really any good, or is this just a ploy to get me out to Cape Cod?"

"Yes, and yes," he admitted.

Kelly laughed. "Right," she said. "Okay, answer this one. What does Jayne get from doing this? I mean, I understand *your* motivation, but what's in it for her?"

"Whoa," Jax backpedaled. "Wait a minute. Kelly, this isn't some kind of sexual bribe. I don't want you to think that you owe me anything. I just want you to have a chance to get to know me again. That's all." He took a deep breath. "I'm not trying to buy your love. Or anything else. I'm just trying to get you out here. Once you're here, I'm hoping...you'll fall in love with me again."

"Well." Kelly was slightly breathless. "As long as we're being honest with each other, I have to tell you that I have no intention of falling in love with you *ever* again, Tyrone."

She'd already made that way more than clear. "I know. Will you come anyway?"

"What kind of computer do you have?"

"A PC," he said. "Why?"

"I knew it," she said. "More proof that we're not compatible. I've got a Mac. I better plan on bringing it."

Jax stood, twirled around in a silent dance of victory and then untangled himself from the phone cord. Yes. *Yes.*

"Can you pick me up?" she asked. "Or is that a stupid question?"

"Stupid question," he agreed. "Really stupid. I'll be there before noon. Don't forget to pack your bathing suit."

"Of course," Kelly said dryly. "I always wear my bathing suit when I write."

"Oh, come on. It's summer. This is Cape Cod. You can't *not* bring your bathing suit."

"I won't be packed by noon," Kelly warned him.

"I'll help you pack."

"I must be crazy."

"I promise you, Kelly," Jax said, "you won't regret this."

"I already regret this." But then she laughed. "I *am* crazy. See you later, T."

Jackson hung up the phone and let out a whoop that could be heard clear across the bay.

## CHAPTER ELEVEN

"RULE NUMBER ONE," KELLY SAID, sitting in Jax's little sports car as they sped down Route 3 toward Cape Cod. "No touching."

"I can live with that." Jax smiled as he glanced at her. "With exceptions, of course—"

"No exceptions," she said sternly.

"Well, what if I have to pull you out of a burning building?" Jax asked. "Or push you out of the way of a speeding car? Or—"

"I don't intend to spend much time in burning buildings or near speeding cars this summer. Rule number two."

"All rules have exceptions," Jax told her stubbornly. "And you know it."

"Rule number two," Kelly repeated, crossing her arms. She could be just as stubborn. "No looking at me like you want to eat me for dinner."

Jax exhaled a loud burst of air as he laughed. "Like *what?*"

"You know what I mean."

"No, I *don't*—" He was *laughing* at her.

"Yes, you do." She smacked his arm.

"Uh-uh-uh. That was a direct violation of rule number one. No touching."

"You *know* the look I mean," Kelly insisted, choosing to ignore him. "It's like you're taking off my clothes with your eyes."

"Rule number two," Jax repeated. "No taking off your clothes with my eyes. It's gonna make it hard to undress you, considering rule number one. How about taking off your clothes with telekinesis? Is that permitted?"

Kelly couldn't hide her laughter, which was only serving to make him act sillier than ever. "T., you're not taking me seriously."

"On the contrary. I'm taking you extremely seriously." The road was flat and straight and empty, and he took his eyes off it for a long moment to study her. Despite the car's air-conditioning, she was sticky and hot and—

"*That's* the look," she accused him. "You were giving me that look—"

Startled, Jackson pulled his eyes back to the road. "I was *not*—"

"Yes, you were."

"Well, if I was, I didn't know it. How can I stop doing something I don't do intentionally?"

"Wear your sunglasses."

"Day and *night?*" he said. "Inside the *house?*"

She shrugged. "Whatever works. Rule number three."

"There's more?"

"No sweet talk, no marriage proposals, no constant reminders that you want us to be more than friends, no sexual innuendos."

Jax sighed. "I'm not sure I'll be able to stand the pressure."

"Rule number four—"

"Kelly, you're not giving me an awful lot to work with here."

"No trying to distract me with your body."

"Excuse me? No trying to *what?*"

"No walking around half-naked," she elaborated. "You know."

"Kel, we're going to be living at a beach house," Jax said. "*Every*one walks around half-naked. Including you. I hope."

"Rule number five—No flirting." She looked over at him. "That's going to be a hard one for you. I don't think you're capable of communicating with a woman without flirting."

Jax was silent for a long time. Finally he looked over at her and lifted an eyebrow. "Every single way I could think of responding to that statement could be interpreted as flirting. You're right. I'm completely doomed."

He pulled off the highway and down to the end of the exit ramp. There were no cars behind him, so he put the car in park and turned toward Kelly.

"T. Jackson Winchester the Second's Only Rule." He had a dangerous glint in his eye and Kelly tried to back away, but there was nowhere to go. "Once a day," he told her, "every single day, I intend to break each and every one of your rules. Rules number one and two..." He touched the side of her face, pulling her chin up so that her gaze met his. He looked into her eyes, letting his desire for her simmer. "Rule number three," he whispered. "Kelly, I want to make love to you for days without stopping. Please, will you stop this nonsense and just marry me?"

"No," she breathed, caught in the turbulent green of his eyes. Oh, God, this was a mistake.

He leaned closer and kissed her, but instead of a passionate attack, his mouth was soft, sweet. "The kiss was a variation on rule four," he explained, then he smiled. "These rules are going to kill me. But frankly, I can't think of a better way to go."

She could kiss him. She could lean forward right now and kiss him, and, like the man said, stop this nonsense.

Instead, Kelly closed her eyes until she felt the car moving forward. She couldn't give in. She *wouldn't* give in.

Not unless she wanted him to break her heart all over again.

THE WINCHESTER HOUSE was enormous, and it sat on a craggy hill overlooking the beach. It was modern, with lots of odd angles and high ceilings. No single corner came together absolutely square.

The large living room was a few steps down from the entryway, and it had huge sliding glass doors that led out onto a wide wooden deck. The furniture looked surprisingly comfortable, and the room was decorated all in white and various shades of blue and green—the colors of the beach. There was a fireplace and an expensive sound system and a wall full of books. It was not the cold, imposing room that Kelly had expected from T.'s descriptions of the Winchester estates.

"Nice," she said.

T. laughed at the tone of her voice. "Why so surprised?"

She turned to face him, and caught a glimpse of her own rueful smile in the reflective lenses of his sunglasses. He was making a point to wear them inside the house. "Isn't this your parents' house?"

"Not anymore." He shifted the weight of her suitcase to his left hand. "I bought it from them a few years ago."

"But this *is* the house you lived in when you were in high school," Kelly said.

He smiled, setting the suitcase down. "This is it. Come on, I'll give you the grand tour."

She followed him back up the stairs and then up several more steps into the kitchen. It was huge and gleaming, with two different refrigerators, what seemed like miles of counter space and a center island that contained a second sink. All of the cabinets were made of a light knotted pine, and on the floor was cream-colored ceramic tile. Shining pots hung from a grid on one wall, and fruits and vegetables sat in baskets that dangled from the center beam.

"I keep a grocery list on the refrigerator," Jax told her. "If you want anything special, just add it to the list. I'll pick it up next time I'm at the store."

"I didn't know you could cook."

"I'm a whiz at grilled-cheese sandwiches," he said. "My other specialty is cornflakes. I pour a mean pitcher of milk."

Kelly followed him several steps down the hall. "This is the dining room." He didn't bother to go inside the large room that held a banquet-size table and about sixteen chairs. "But I don't use it. I eat out on the deck." He smiled. "Or in a restaurant. Usually in a restaurant."

He led her up a full set of stairs to the second floor. A long hallway stretched both right and left. He turned left. "This is my wing. It's over the garage." He pointed at several doors. "Guest bedroom, guest bedroom, bathroom. This is my office."

After peeking into the two very tastefully decorated guest rooms, Kelly followed T. Jackson into his office. It was a big room that, like the living room, overlooked the beach.

"I can move a desk in here for your computer," Jax said. "Or you can set it up in your room, whichever you prefer. Some people don't like writing when someone else is in the room, so..."

Kelly turned to him and smiled. "T., at school I work in the newsroom. If you don't mind, I'll put my computer in here. Unless you think having Stefanie and me working in here will disturb you?"

"Um..."

"What's in here?" Kelly curiously pushed open the door that connected his office to another room.

"My bedroom." He came to stand behind her, finally taking off his sunglasses.

His room was dark, with the shades still pulled down and the big bed unmade. Clothes were draped over chairs and in piles on the floor. His closet door was open, revealing a row of neatly hung shirts and jackets. The room was cool and dim and smelled good, like Jackson.

It wasn't hard to picture T. asleep in that bed, his hair tousled, his muscles relaxed.

His arms around her.

Kelly took a step back and bumped into him. Her entire back pressed against his entire front, and he put his arms around her to steady her. But he moved away almost immediately, giving her space.

"Sorry," she said.

His mouth twisted into a quick smile that didn't quite reach his eyes. "Hey, it's your rule. If it were up to me..."

Kelly followed his gaze back to his rumpled bed.

It wasn't hard to figure out what he was thinking. It would have been even easier to give in, to throw her arms around his neck and pull him toward that bed.

Kelly was suddenly very grateful that she had set up those rules, because she knew that if T. so much as touched her right now, her willpower would dissolve.

But he barely even glanced at her before putting his sunglasses back on. "I'll get the rest of your stuff in from the car. Why don't you pick which guest room you want to use? There's one more at the end of this hall, and three down on Stef's wing."

He disappeared, leaving Kelly still standing in the doorway to his bedroom. She looked back at his bed one more time, then quickly went into the hall. Moving down to the other side of the hall, Stefanie's wing, he had called it, she picked the room that was farthest away from T.'s.

It was decorated all in green. Green wallpaper, green bedspread, green curtains. There was a dresser and a rocking chair and a huge walk-in closet that was empty.

The room also had its own bathroom. Maybe all the bedrooms did, Kelly thought suddenly, wondering at the value of a house this size, with all those bathrooms, *on* the beach.

As T. Jackson carried her suitcase in, he didn't comment on the geography of her room choice. He set her luggage on the floor and nodded toward the bed. "Did you know that's a water bed?"

Kelly looked at it in surprise. "No, I didn't." She sat down on the bed, and felt waves rolling back and forth inside the water-filled mattress. It was fun, kind of like an amusement park ride. She lay back on the bed, letting herself float.

She bounced higher as T. jumped onto the bed next to her. "My parents got it in the seventies," he said with a grin. "Needless to say, this is the room I slept in when I was in high school."

Kelly sat up, staring at him. "Forget this room. I can't stay in here. It's probably haunted with the ghosts of high school girlfriends past. I'd never get any sleep."

T. laughed, propping his head up on his hand, his arm bent at the elbow. "I never brought anyone home, because I didn't want to risk people finding out that I lived alone," he said. "Well, no, that's not entirely true. Mary Jo Matthews came over once. Uninvited, though. We went steady for about a month during my senior year. She dumped me for the captain of the football team."

"Ouch."

"I got over it."

Stretched out next to him on the gently rolling bed, she could remember him as an eighteen-year-old. No doubt all the girls in the school had sighed over him, some of them doing more than sighing.

"I'll bet you did," she said.

"If we had gone to high school together, I would've been scared to death of you."

"Why?" she asked.

"You were a math nerd, remember?" He grinned. "I really stank at math."

"I could've tutored you." God, why did she say that?

"I would've invited you over anytime."

"I think I'd rather have a room with a regular bed," Kelly said.

The water shifted as Jax stood, and the force of the internal waves knocked Kelly over. She laughed helplessly, trying to regain her balance.

Jax held out his hand to help her up, and she reached for it automatically. But he let go of her almost immediately, and she bounced back down onto the rolling surface of the water bed.

"Rule number one," he reminded her.

No touching.

Trying not to swear too loudly, Kelly scrambled for the edge of the bed and got herself back onto the steadiness of the floor.

T. had already carried her suitcase out of the room, and she went into the hall and watched him walk back down toward his wing.

"What's wrong with this room?" Kelly asked, stopping in front of the next-closest guest room.

He glanced back at her. "That one doesn't have its own bathroom."

"And this room?" She pointed to the door directly across the hall.

"No bay view."

"Figures," she muttered, following him into a guest bedroom that was on the bay side of the house, one door down from his office, two doors down from his bedroom.

It was larger than the green room, with bigger windows and a bigger bathroom. The carpeting was a dusty rose, and the curtains and bedspread were white. Besides the double bed, the room held a dresser and a wicker chair.

T. Jackson put her suitcase down on the bed. "I'll bring your computer up to the office while you unpack."

Kelly followed him out into the hall again. "Hey," she said, and he turned around to look at her. At least she thought he was looking at her. It was hard to tell since he'd put his sunglasses back on.

"I don't want to unpack," she told him. "At least two years have passed since I've been within twenty miles of a beach. I'm going to go for a swim."

"Mind if I come along?"

*Yes. No.* Oh, brother, she didn't know what she wanted.

No, she knew *exactly* what she wanted. And what she wanted and what was good for her were two very different things.

What had she been thinking when she agreed to come and spend more than two months here with T.? Had she really thought she'd be able to come to Cape Cod and *not* wind up in bed with him? She couldn't be in the same room with him without wanting him. Heck, she couldn't be on the same continent, the same *planet* with him without wanting him.

But she had no intention of giving in to her desire. No, thank you. There was just no way she was going to risk letting him back into her heart. And if she let him get close to her in any way, he was bound to be able to break through her protection. And then she'd wind up hurt.

If T. cooperated and followed the rules she'd set down, that would be only half the battle. The other half was her own feelings, her own wants. Please, God, don't let me start sleepwalking, because my subconscious will surely lead me directly to T.'s bed.

Maybe it would be easier when Stefanie was here. After all, it was Stefanie she'd be working with day after day, not T.

Meanwhile, he was standing at the top of the stairs, watching her, waiting for her to answer his question.

"I'll meet you out on the deck," she finally said, and was rewarded by a quiet smile.

It was the quiet smiles that were the most dangerous.

She went into her room and tightly closed the door.

KELLY STOOD OUT ON THE restaurant patio, leaning on the rail, watching the sunset and drinking a beer. Despite all the sunblock she'd put on today, she'd gotten a slight sunburn, just enough to give her skin a tingling, sensitive feeling. In order to avoid the discomfort that a bra would cause, she had put on a sundress with a halter top.

At first she had hesitated, not wanting to give T. the wrong idea. In fact, for precisely that reason, she had intended to wear either jeans or shorts and T-shirts during her entire stay, but she had a particularly bright red stripe of sunburn at the edge of her bathing suit on her back, and the thought of pulling jeans or even shorts on over that was just too dreadful.

On the other hand, if she'd intended to only wear androgynous, casual clothes while she was here on the Cape, then why had she even packed this sundress in the first place? Or the three other skirts and dresses she'd brought?

"Am I allowed to tell you how beautiful you look?"

She turned to see T. standing next to her.

"Or is that against the rules?" He leaned next to her against the railing, taking a sip from his own glass of beer.

"I think you already managed to tell me." She stared out at the water. "And, yes, it's against the rules. But thank you, anyway."

"Oh, now, wait. If I'm going to break a rule, I'm going to do it right." He looked at her, letting his eyes caress her face. "You're incredibly lovely," he told her. "Your beauty rivals the sunset and—"

Kelly laughed. "Oh, ack."

"Ack?" he repeated, eyebrows elevated. "I'm waxing poetic, and all you can say is ack?"

"Rule six—No waxing poetic. Especially not on an empty stomach. Speaking of empty stomachs, are we going to eat sometime this century by any chance?"

"It shouldn't take more than another ten minutes." Jax sighed melodramatically. "I remember a time when food didn't matter to you, when my kisses were sufficient nourishment."

"Yeah, well, I'm on a diet, remember?" Kelly countered.

"Just let me know when you're ready for a little bingeing," Jax said.

"Tyrone," she said, all kidding pushed aside. "You promised. I'm not going to stick around if I have to fight you off for the rest of the summer."

"So stop fighting," Jackson's eyes were equally grave. "Surrender, Kel. I guarantee you won't regret it."

The breeze ruffled his blond hair and he carelessly pushed it out of his face as he watched her.

*Surrender.* She could imagine how good it would feel right now to lean back against his chest and watch the sunset with his arms wrapped around her. She could imagine the way his breath would feel against her neck as he leaned close to whisper soft, seductive words to her—

"Winchester. Table for two," a voice announced.

Saved.

Not that she had any intention of actually surrendering, Kelly told herself as she followed the hostess through the restaurant to the small, lantern-lit table at the railing of a covered open deck. She slid into her seat, watching as T. Jackson somehow managed to squeeze his long legs into the small space opposite her.

"Please, will you ask the waitress to bring us a couple of bowls of clam chowder right away?" T. asked the hostess as she handed them their menus. He smiled across the table at Kelly. "My friend here is starving. I don't want her to start eating the tablecloth."

Kelly could see the bold interest in the woman's eyes as she smiled down at T. Well, sure, why not? T. had to be the best-looking man in the place. Kelly was getting quite a number of envious glances from other women. But if he noticed, he was hiding it well. To look at him, anyone would think he was oblivious to everyone in the restaurant besides Kelly.

Another woman might've been flattered, or made to feel special by his undivided attention. But not her, no way. In fact, she'd prefer it if he found someone else to look at that way.

He was being careful to keep that hot, hungry, gobble-her-up look from his eyes, but this soft, faintly amused adoration was unbearable in its own way.

The soup came out almost right away, and T. soon gave some of his attention to eating. As they ate, and throughout the rest of dinner, he kept the conversation light and almost pointedly not flirtatious.

Kelly felt herself relax.

JAX FELT HIMSELF START TO SWEAT. He wasn't sure how long he could keep up the big-brother act.

Somehow he'd managed to spend three and a half hours on the beach with Kelly without breaking any of her damned rules. Despite the fact that her bathing suit was a chlorine-faded one-piece, she *did* look good enough to eat. And watching her rub sunblock onto her long, slender legs...

God, he was in trouble here.

Jax couldn't wait until tomorrow, until he could break her rules again. What was that expression? Go big or stay home. Maybe tomorrow he'd break those rules in a big way. Like by crawling into bed with her in the morning.

Inwardly he laughed, imagining the expression on her face.

On the other hand, he didn't want to push so far that she'd go running back to Boston.

How was he going to live through the rest of tonight? How could he continue to sit here and pretend that Kelly didn't own his heart?

Worst of all, how was he going to tell her the truth about Jayne Tyler? He had to tell her. Tonight.

As the busboys cleared the table, as the waitress brought out mugs of coffee, Jax was silent, staring out at the darkness that had fallen over the water. How was Kelly going to react to his news?

She was probably going to be angry, upset maybe, annoyed at the very least. She might think that he had purposely tricked her, purposely lied to her.

Jax considered waiting until they got home to tell her, but figured maybe if he told her in public, here at the restaurant, she might not yell at him quite as loudly.

She met his eyes as she took a sip of her coffee.

"You're so quiet," she said. "What are you thinking about?"

This was it. The perfect opportunity. "I have a secret I've got to tell you."

Kelly stopped drinking and slowly put her mug down. He could tell that she was thinking carefully, trying to decide what her response should be. He didn't give her time to say anything.

"I haven't told anyone," he said. "Ever. Not in the three years since—well, it's been four, really."

Kelly watched him as the light from the lantern on the table flickered across his face and reflected the shiny gold of his hair. What kind of secret could it possibly be? She was curious and a little worried. He looked so serious, so solemn.

"Well, Stefanie knows," T. said, then smiled. "She'd have to know. I mean, of course she knows."

Kelly hadn't said a word. She just sat there, watching him, the soft light playing across her beautiful face. Her eyes were dark and almost colorless in the dimness, and her hair curled slightly in the damp ocean air.

"I'm not sure I really want to know what this secret is," she said finally. "But I'm dying of curiosity. What'd ya do, T.? Kill somebody? Rob a bank? Run for office? Have an illegitimate child? What?"

T. Jackson laughed. He was fooling with the container that held little packs of sugar for coffee, and the salt and pepper shakers that were in the center of the table. His large, strong fingers toyed with them nervously.

Nervously. If T. was so nervous that it showed, if he was *that* nervous about telling her whatever this secret was, then it must be serious. Kelly swallowed. Was it his health? Was he sick? She remembered how terrible he'd looked at Kevin's wedding. That was just about four years ago, wasn't it?

Even though she knew she shouldn't touch him, Kelly reached across the table and took T.'s hand, lacing her fingers with his. He looked up at her, his eyes momentarily opened wide in surprise. For that one instant, he was stripped of all his pretense of ease and his self-assuredness. His face looked younger, more vulnerable.

This was the same T. Jackson she'd had a glimpse of the night she'd gone to his hotel room with him. She'd seen that same look in his eyes the second time he'd made love to her that night. She hadn't thought they'd be able to surpass their first explosive joining, but T. had made love to her again so slowly, so unhurriedly, so sensually, the memory could still leave her feeling weak. And as she had gazed up into his eyes, as he had touched her, caressed her, filled her, it had been as if he let her see into his soul.

Now he looked down at her hand intertwined with his and smiled.

"Tell me," she said, squeezing his hand gently.

Jax looked into the depths of Kelly's eyes, carefully hiding the surge of triumph that he felt. She cared about him enough to take his hand. She cared about him enough to worry that this secret was something serious. She cared—

Great. Inwardly he shook his head with disgust as the triumphant feeling vanished as quickly as it came. She had cared enough to break one of her rules—no touching—and that was a step forward, that was real progress in his fight to win her back, but as soon as he told her the truth, she was going to take about twenty-five giant steps back. Toward Boston, no doubt.

"Kel." He wondered if there was some easier way to tell her this. "I'm really..."

She was waiting.

Crap. "No, it's nothing."

"T.!" She let go of his hand, her eyes lit with exasperation.

Now that she wasn't touching him, it was easier. He didn't have to be afraid she would release his hand when he told her, because she already had.

"You're really *what?*" she asked, her steady gaze giving him no quarter.

"Whom." He smiled weakly. "It's not a what, it's a whom."

She blinked. Then laughed. Then pinned him to the seat with a look of disbelief. "Don't tell me. Don't you dare say this is some kind of secret identity or alter ego thing."

"Yes," T. said, and Kelly knew that he wasn't kidding by the amount of guilt she could see in his eyes. "That's it exactly."

Kelly pushed her coffee away, reaching instead for the half-full glass of white wine that she hadn't finished with her dinner. She took a calming sip and slowly put the long-stemmed glass back down. For several long moments she studied the light from the lantern as it shone through the wine, before she looked back at T.

"Are you trying to tell me that you're, like... *Bat*man?" she said, one eyebrow raised.

Jax laughed. "Close." He braced himself. "I'm Jayne Tyler."

She stared at him in shock. Gee, maybe a superhero would've gone over better, Jax thought.

"You're... *what?*"

"Whom," he said gently. "Jayne. Tyler. She may have my sister's face on the book covers, but the words are all mine."

He looked down at his mug of coffee, resisting the urge to shut his eyes tightly against the accusations he was so sure were going to follow.

But Kelly didn't make any accusations. She laughed.

Jax looked up at her.

"You're not kidding, are you?" She was smiling at him.
Wordlessly he shook his head no.

"I can't believe it." She laughed again. "I mean, I *do*
believe it, and *wow!* I'm so proud of you, T. You're a
writer, a *real* writer, an author. My God, Jayne Tyler is
so good. I mean, *you're* so good! Where did you learn
to write like that?"

She was still smiling at him, her eyes sparkling with
enthusiasm. She wasn't angry. She was...*proud* of him?
Jax fought the urge to lean across the table and kiss her.

"You're not mad at me?" he asked.

Kelly shook her head. "No," she said. "Well, maybe
a little disappointed that you didn't trust me enough to
tell me before this."

"I haven't seen an awful lot of you since I started
writing," Jax pointed out. "This is the first time we've
really had a chance to talk."

"Uh-oh." Sudden realization dawned. "This means
I'm going to be working with *you* all summer, huh?"

*Surrender.* The word came immediately to mind as
Kelly looked into the stormy gray-green of T.'s eyes.
She'd only spent half a day with him, and already she
was considering giving in. She could picture them
working together during the day, taking breaks out in
the sun on the beach, sharing a quiet, candlelit dinner
like this every night and then going home to share T.'s
bed. She could picture him kissing her. On the beach,
in his office, in the car on the way home from dinner...
With very little effort, she could picture them making
love.

Kelly swallowed. There was a time not so very long

ago when a summer like that would've been a dream
come true. She had loved T. so much back then. She
would have given herself to him for the summer, believing that the summer would last forever. But if there
was one thing the past had taught her, it was that nothing lasted forever.

"Is the thought of working with me so terrible?" T.
asked softly.

"No," she said, meeting his eyes. It wasn't. And
that's what alarmed her. God help her. If she was with
him all the time, she might actually start to believe him
when he said that he loved her, that he wanted to marry
her. And if she started to believe him, God knows she'd
only end up hurt.

KELLY SAID GOOD-NIGHT TO T. out in the hall, leaving him
standing there as she went into her room and carefully
locked the door behind her.

*Surrender.*

Instead, she kicked off her shoes, went into her
bathroom and brushed her teeth. She pulled down the
shades and stepped out of her dress, gently rubbing
lotion onto her sunburned skin. The big T-shirt she slept
in was still in her suitcase, so she rummaged for it, then
put it on, wincing as it hit her shoulders.

When they got home from dinner, T. had found a
note from Stefanie on the kitchen table. She had left on
a cruise to Alaska with Emilio. She wouldn't be back
until the first week of August.

Kelly and T. Jackson were alone in this big house. It
smelled like a setup, but Jackson swore he knew nothing about Stef's plans.

Right.

As she went to pull the white spread off the big bed, she saw an envelope resting on one of the pillows. Curious, she picked it up. The flap wasn't sealed, and she pulled out a single sheet of heavy bond paper and unfolded it.

It was a letter. From T. From his computer's laser printer.

Dear Kelly,

If it were up to me, I'd be in there with you right now. Instead I'm sitting in my office, staring out the window at the night, burning for your touch.

I want you.

I want to feel your lips on mine, your body against me. I want to entangle myself with you, bury myself, lose myself in you.

It is such heaven and such hell having you close enough to touch—

But we're playing by your rules.

So I'm not going to speak the words that are always on the tip of my tongue and constantly tell you how much I love you. I'm not going to show you how much by holding you in my arms and making love to you, the way I want to.

But I am going to write down the words I long to say, hoping that you'll read them, giving me at least a fighting chance to win back your heart.

He had signed it with his bold handwriting. *"I love you. Love, T."*

Kelly carefully folded the letter and put it back into the envelope. She turned off the light but lay awake for a long time before finally falling asleep.

## CHAPTER TWELVE

WHEN KELLY GOT BACK from her morning run on the beach, T. Jackson wasn't in the house. On her way into the kitchen, she glanced out the window and saw that his sports car was gone from the driveway.

There was an envelope with her name on it on the kitchen table and, drinking directly from a half full bottle of seltzer that she'd pulled from the refrigerator, she opened it.

Another of T.'s letters. Love letters, she guessed she could call them. Since she'd arrived over a week ago, he'd left at least a dozen of them around for her to read. She hadn't even acknowledged them, and *he* certainly didn't bring up the subject.

It was as if he were two very different people. One was the good old friend who was helping her rewrite her novel, helping her straighten out the problems with her hero's motivation. The other was this ardent lover who had no shame when it came to writing his desires and passions, all of which involved her.

In this latest note, he described in extremely specific detail just how he wanted to kiss her when he returned home from the errands he was on.

Kelly felt her pulse increase as she read his words. It was scary to know that he was going to kiss her sometime today or tonight. Part of her was really looking forward to that kiss, and knowing *that* scared her even more.

As T. had promised that very first day, he broke all of her rules once a day, and only once a day. He would kiss her, tell her he loved her, ask her to marry him. She was never sure just when during the day that romantic attack was going to come. Several times it had happened first thing in the morning, but other days he had waited until afternoon or even after dinner. As a result, she was kept on edge almost all the time. And even after he kissed her, she found herself anticipating the next day's onslaught.

She also looked forward to his letters. And as much as she realized he was using them to break down her resolve not to get involved with him, she couldn't stop herself from reading them, sometimes over and over again.

Kelly took this latest letter back onto the deck with her and sat down on the steps as she finished the seltzer. Wow, it was going to be another megahot day. She wasn't even going to bother to shower. At least not before she put on her bathing suit and went into the bay for a swim.

She leaned her head back against the banister, feeling the hot sun on her face. She needed to put more sunblock on, or her fair skin was going to burn again. She'd probably already sweated off the stuff she'd applied earlier this morning.

"Hey."

Kelly jumped, opening her eyes and turning to see

T. Jackson standing by the sliding glass doors into the living room.

"Morning," he said. He already had on his neon-green bathing suit with an Amnesty International T-shirt on top. Don't Discount The Power Of The Written Word his shirt proclaimed in large block print. Write A Letter, Save A Life. Kelly glanced down at the letter she still held in her hands. The power of the written word, indeed.

"I picked up some groceries." T. looked at her over the top of his sunglasses. "Wanna help me unload the car?"

Kelly hauled herself to her feet. "Sure."

He stepped back to let her go through the door first, and she glanced up nervously as she passed within inches of him. But his face was relaxed, he was smiling. She couldn't see his eyes through the dark lenses of his sunglasses.

"How far did you run?" he asked.

"About three miles." She took a detour to put the empty seltzer bottle and the letter down on the kitchen counter. God, she wished he would just kiss her and get it over with. "I've got to start getting up earlier," she added. "It's getting too hot, even first thing in the morning. As soon as we're done here, I'm going for a swim."

Jackson pushed open the screen door and went out onto the driveway, where his car was parked.

The trunk was open wide and filled with cloth grocery bags. T. was environmentally correct. Somehow the realization didn't surprise her.

"I got you a present," he said.

"Fudge ripple ice cream?" Kelly lifted two of the bags out of the car and lugged them back toward the kitchen.

"I thought you outgrew that when you were fifteen." Jax carried two bags in each hand.

"Yeah, well, I've regressed." She tried to ignore the way the muscles in his arms and shoulders flexed as he almost effortlessly lifted the weight of all four bags up onto the kitchen table.

With an easy underhanded throw, he tossed her a small bag that bore the label of a local fashion boutique. "I bought you a new bathing suit."

Kelly looked from the bag she had caught to Jackson and back to the bag. "If it fits in this little bag, something tells me I'm not going to be eating much fudge ripple ice cream in the near future."

When she looked up again, T. was standing directly in front of her, and she knew from the look in his eyes that he was going to kiss her.

"Oh, T., yuck, I'm all sweaty." She tried to sidle away from him along the edge of the kitchen counter.

But he put his hands against the countertop, one on either side of her, penning her in. "I want to marry you, remember? For richer or poorer, for better or for worse... I don't think there's an exception for sweaty." With one finger, he caught a bead of perspiration that was dripping down past her ear. "Actually, it's kind of a turn-on."

Leaning forward, he smiled into her eyes and then he kissed her.

The bag with the bathing suit dropped to the floor as Kelly was surrounded by T. Jackson. His fingers left trails of fire where he touched her, his mouth met hers with a blaze of heat.

"Marry me, Kelly." His breath was hot as he whispered into her ear.

But she pulled free of his arms, and this time he let her get away. "No. I'm sorry." It was the same answer she'd given him every day since she'd arrived.

And just like every day, it didn't faze him. Cheerfully he bent down and picked up the bag she'd dropped and handed it to her. With a smile, he went back to the car for another load of shopping bags.

How could he do it? Every day she wondered how he could kiss her like that one minute, then act as if everything were completely platonic the next. Kelly always felt as if she needed a few hours to recover.

She waited for her pulse to return to near normal, then slowly opened the bag. A bikini. Black and very tiny, although allegedly it *was* her size. She held it up, looking at it skeptically.

T. came back into the kitchen carrying the last of the groceries. "I figured you needed a new bathing suit," he said as he started to unload the groceries. He looked at her and smiled. "That one-piece you have is on the verge of becoming transparent when it's wet. Do you know they actually make bathing suits these days designed to do that?"

Kelly stuffed the bikini back into the bag. "You don't *really* expect me to believe you, do you?"

"Scout's honor. They were totally see-through. I saw 'em in a catalog. It was this amazing catalog with—"

"I meant about my bathing suit," she interrupted. "It's not *that* old."

He looked up from loading liter bottles of seltzer into the refrigerator. "Hey, *I'm* not going to complain if you want to wear a see-through bathing suit, Kel. I just thought you might want to be warned. If you don't believe me, try it on and step into the shower. You'll see."

JAX FOUND KELLY IN THE office, hard at work. The windows were open wide and all the fans in the room were on and it was still hot.

"I thought you were going for a swim," he said.

She didn't look up from her computer. "I changed my mind and took a shower instead."

He grinned. "You tried on your old bathing suit, and you found out that I was right."

"All right. Fine." Kelly turned around and sighed. "Go ahead and say it."

"Say what?"

"I told you so."

But he didn't say anything. He just looked at her. Kelly quickly turned around. Damn. She knew she shouldn't wear this halter top, but even the thought of putting on a T-shirt on a day this hot was too unbearable.

"I'm almost done with these revisions," she announced, making her voice as businesslike as possible. "Actually, I *am* done, I'm just inputting the changes. It shouldn't take more than an hour or two."

"Good," Jax said. "I haven't worked on my novel all week. That'll give me some time to touch base with my characters. After lunch we can work on fixing up your love scenes."

Kelly cringed. "Do we have to?"

"Well, no. We don't *have* to. But you'll never sell your book if we don't."

"I guess when you put it that way..."

Jax sat at his computer, waiting the few seconds it took his word processing program to boot up. He popped in his Jared disk and quickly read through the last chapter that he'd written.

Jared was out in California, in Los Angeles. He'd bought himself a horse, a big black stallion, and he was riding out toward the ranch Carrie and her husband, Harlan, had bought nearly three years ago. He'd just found out that Harlan had died some months ago from a fever.

Jax started to write.

As Jared rode the trail, it was clear the entire area was having one hell of a drought. Dust rose up from the ground, covering his dark suit, making him cough. He tied his handkerchief around his mouth and nose, and pushed the wide brim of his hat down a little lower.

"Yo, so that's Kelly, huh?" Jared said. "Lord, will you look at those *legs!* Oh, baby!"

"Shut up," Jax muttered.

"I didn't say anything," Kelly said.

Jared laughed, his dark eyes sparkling with amusement. "This is great. Finally I can get the last word in. If you talk to me, Kelly's gonna think you're bonkers. And she'll be right. Man, she's beautiful. No wonder you've been so distracted. She's *hot*. I bet you're dying to kiss those shoulders—"

Jax scowled and started writing again.

He saw the dust kicked up by the running horses before he heard the familiar sound of their hooves on the hard-packed ground. Taking his rifle from the back of his saddle, he stuck the heels of his boots into his stallion's sides. The beast reared up on his hind legs, then launched like a Chinese rocket.

Jared saw sunlight reflecting off the barrels of at least four guns as he glanced over his shoulder. Four horses, four riders, four guns. Damned if he knew what they wanted. Damned if he was going to find out.

They fired their first shot at him when he was within eyesight of the gate of the Double K ranch. Carrie's ranch. The bullet zinged just over his head.

Jared took the turn into the Double K at a dangerous speed, the big horse scrambling for a foothold in the loose dirt.

"There better be a good reason for this," Jared shouted. "If this is just some kind of stupid punishment, I'm going to be very, very annoyed."

"There's a good reason for everything I do," Jax muttered.

"Did you say something?" Kelly asked.

Jax looked up, meeting her inquisitive gaze. "Just arguing with my main character."

"Ah." She turned back to her own computer.

"I can't *believe* you actually told her," Jared said.

"She took that rather well," Jax murmured.

Kelly laughed. "T., do you do this all the time?"

"Do what?"

"Talk to yourself?"

"Hah! See, now she thinks you're nuts," Jared said.

"Do you think I'm nuts?" Jax asked Kelly.

"Are you really having a conversation with your main character?" she countered.

"I'm afraid so," he admitted. "Right now he's on the back of a galloping horse, with four men chasing and shooting at him. He's not very happy with me."

"I don't blame him. If you put me in that situation, I'd argue with you, too." Kelly laughed. "Why don't you stop arguing and just write the end of the scene, get him out of there?"

"Did you hear that?" Jax said to Jared. "Stop arguing."

The stallion was still running like a demon out of hell as he approached the ranch house and the barn. With his rifle in his hand, Jared tried to rein in the big horse, even as he turned to double-check that the four gunmen hadn't followed him this far.

A shot rang out, and Jared felt a tug of pain in his right arm. The rifle clattered onto the dry ground. Damn, he was bleeding and his arm hurt like the devil. He turned, trying to figure out where that gun had been fired from when a clear voice said, "Keep your hands up where I can see them."

Jared nudged his horse, who obligingly turned to face the owner of both the voice and the gun. With his left hand, he swept his hat off his head.

"Hello, Carrie," he said.

Jax saved the job, cleared the screen, stood and stretched.

"I'm going to get a cup of coffee," he said. "You want something?"

"Are you talking to me or your imaginary friend?" Kelly asked.

"Very funny," Jax said.

"How'd you end that scene?" she asked.

"It was an obvious solution. I had the heroine shoot the hero."

Kelly laughed. "Did it shut him up?"

"Not a chance."

KELLY SAT OUT ON THE DECK, eating a salad for lunch. She heard the screen on the sliding door open and close, heard Jackson's bare feet as he approached. The heavy wooden deck chair groaned slightly under his weight as he sat down, and there was a soft hiss of escaping carbonation as he opened a can of soda.

She glanced at him, and he smiled at her from behind his sunglasses. He'd taken off his T-shirt, and as she tried not to watch, he rubbed sunscreen onto his broad shoulders.

"You know, we can work out here this afternoon," he said. "You're not really ready to start rewriting. We have to talk about the scene first, and we can just as easily do that out here as inside."

Kelly closed her eyes. She was going to sit here and talk about rewriting the love scenes in her book with this man who clearly wanted to have a physical relationship with her. Add into the confusion the fact that she and T. *had* made love not so many weeks ago, and it had been the best sex she'd ever had in her life. To top it all off, her hormones wanted more, particularly when T. sat around half-naked the way he was, like some bronzed, blond sun god.

Kelly sighed. "All right. Start by telling me what I did wrong."

"For one thing," Jax said, "the scene's too short. It's over too soon. Essentially you've been building up to this scene, you've been building up to your characters making love since page one. Your readers are going to feel disappointed if you don't give 'em their money's worth."

Kelly put her salad bowl down on the deck and picked up T.'s soda can. Caffeine-free cola. Good, she didn't think she could stand a jolt of caffeine right now. "Can I have a sip?"

He nodded, still watching her.

She took a long drink of the sweet liquid. It wasn't as cool as she'd expected. The hot sun had already warmed the aluminum can.

"So, okay." She felt a trickle of perspiration drip between her breasts as she handed the soda can back to T. "How many more pages am I going to have to write?"

"It's not a matter of pages," T. said. "I've read great

love scenes that were only one page long. I've also read
at least one that was twenty-two pages—"

Kelly stared at him. "Twenty-*two*? Pages? Of sex?"
She laughed. "I don't think my thesaurus has that many
synonyms for the word *passionately.*"

"Relax. I'm not telling you to write twenty-two
pages. Five or six should be fine—"

"Five or *six*? I ran out of things to describe after two
paragraphs." The sun was beating down on her. She
could feel herself starting to burn. "Can I use some of
your lotion?"

T. sat up, his muscles rippling. "Feelings, Kel."

She looked at him. "What?"

He dragged his chair closer to hers, sitting on the
edge of it, his elbows resting on his knees. "It's not
enough simply to describe who's on top, and who's kissing whom and where."

Kelly felt her cheeks getting warm.

"You should use the actual physical descriptions of
the sex to reveal more about your characters," T. Jackson continued. "Do they take it slowly, take their time,
or do they tear each other's clothes off? How they do
it, particularly the first time, can say a lot about them."

Kelly looked up at T., remembering how they had
made love that first time in his hotel room. Oh, boy,
that had been explosive.

He looked at her for a moment over the top of his
sunglasses, and she could tell from his eyes that he
was thinking about that night, too. What did that night
reveal about her own character? Kelly wondered. What
did it say about the intensity of her feelings for him, that

she was willing to make love to him so wildly, abandoning all conventions, ignoring all proprieties?

Not feelings, she corrected herself quickly. What she had with T. had nothing to do with feelings. It was all attraction. All good old-fashioned lust.

Are you sure? that voice in her head asked.

"But that physical description shouldn't be your main focus," T. said as he handed her the bottle of suntan lotion. He took off his sunglasses and gently set them down on the deck next to his can of soda.

Kelly put some lotion into her hand and carefully applied it to her face as he stood.

"You've got to get inside your characters' heads," he said as he walked behind her deck chair.

She turned, surprised, to look back at him as he pushed the big wooden chairback up slightly, releasing the frame from the bar that held it in place.

He smiled at her as he lowered her chair into a more reclined position. "You've got to tell the reader exactly what the characters are feeling."

He leaned over the back of the chair and gently took the bottle of suntan lotion from Kelly's hand. He squeezed some out onto his palm. "And I'm not just talking about physical sensations," he added, looking down at her with a small smile, "although they're good, too."

She pulled her gaze away from him and sat up with her arms tightly hugging her knees. She felt him sit down on the edge of her chair, slightly behind her, and she looked back at him, startled.

He began rubbing the suntan lotion onto the top of her shoulders and her bare back, and she inhaled sharply. The lotion was cool against her hot skin, but it was the touch of his hands that sent chills down her spine.

"It's how your character feels about the person who's touching her that's important," T. continued softly. She could feel his warm breath against her ear as he rubbed a generous amount of lotion down her arm. "Think about it. Your character could get touched exactly the same way by a friend and then by a lover. It could be a handshake, or an embrace, or maybe...maybe some-one—a friend, or a lover—is putting suntan lotion on her back."

T. stopped to squeeze more lotion out onto his hand. Kelly turned toward him. "T.—"

"Relax," he said. "And pay attention. Maybe you'll learn something."

He reached behind her and began rubbing the lotion onto her other shoulder. Right, thought Kelly. If she was going to learn anything from this, it was that she liked T. Jackson's touch way too much. And she already knew that.

"So what's the difference?" T. said as if he hadn't been interrupted, as cool and collected as if he were giving a lecture from behind a podium instead of work-ing the lotion down her other arm. "It's in the way your character feels for the person she's being touched by. It's her emotion that can make a simple, innocent caress—" he ran his fingers lightly back up her arm "—outrageously erotic."

Kelly closed her eyes, feeling her insides turn to jelly. No, she did *not* love this man, she told herself. It was just the sun, the heat, making her light-headed.

"The same theory applies in a love scene when the hero, the man your character loves, undresses her." With one deft pull, T. untied the top knot of her halter.

"T.!" Kelly caught the fabric before it fell forward, modestly holding it up against her breasts.

"I didn't want to get any lotion on your top," he explained as she felt his hands on the back of her neck. Wow, that felt good. She closed her eyes again, swallowing her words of protest.

"Your character would have a very different reaction if a stranger walked up and started undressing her," T. continued. "But there's no embarrassment with a lover, only—" his voice lowered slightly "—anticipation." His hand slipped around to her neck, her throat, as he rubbed lotion into her hot skin. He spread the cool, sweet-smelling cream down, lower, covering her collarbone and the tops of her breasts.

Jackson could feel Kelly's heartbeat underneath his hand. He could feel the rapid rise and fall of her chest. Even beneath the loose folds of the fabric that covered her full breasts, he could see the hard buds of her nipples. He was dying to touch all of her, to kiss her, suckle her. This was torture. He smiled wryly. But it was the best kind of torture he'd ever experienced.

He stood, and her eyes opened as he gently pressed her shoulders back against the lounge chair. Nudging her hips over slightly, he now sat facing her. She watched, wide-eyed, as he spread suntan lotion onto her stomach, onto the wide strip of soft skin that was between her halter and the waistband of her shorts.

Kelly stared up into T. Jackson's eyes. How could he be so cool and calm when she was about to have a heart attack? She'd been long reduced to a puddle of desire, and he was sitting there smiling at her as if they were discussing the weather.

She saw it then. One lone bead of perspiration traveling down the side of T.'s face, next to his ear. He *was* rattled. He was just very, very good at hiding it.

But it was as if somehow he knew he'd given himself away. His eyes flooded with heat as he slid the tips of his fingers down below the loose waistband of her shorts. Kelly stopped breathing as his gaze locked with hers. He leaned forward, as if he was going to kiss her, closer, closer, until his mouth was just a whisper away from her lips.

"Foreplay," he whispered, his breath warm and sweet against her face. "When you write a good love scene, you've got to have plenty of foreplay. It's all part of the anticipation."

He straightened up without kissing her, but his eyes held hers as he said, "And if you do it right, most of the love scene can take place while your characters still have their clothes on."

He turned slightly then and squeezed a long, white line of suntan lotion first on one of her legs and then the other, from the tops of her thighs all the way down to her instep. Starting at her feet, he used both hands to rub the lotion into her skin.

His hands moved up her leg at a leisurely, deliberate pace. It was shockingly sensuous, and unbelievably delicious. Kelly opened her mouth but couldn't find the words to stop him. Truth was, she didn't *want* to stop him.

"If you do it right—" T.'s voice was low now, like a

caress "—one look, or a simple touch between lovers, can be as intimate as making love. But you've got to reveal what your characters are feeling."

His eyes were smoky gray-green as he looked at her, and now there was no hiding the sheen of perspiration on his forehead and upper lip. Kelly could see his pulse beating hard in his neck. His face held undisguised hunger as his fingers lingered on the soft skin on the inside of her thigh. The lotion had been long since rubbed in, but still he didn't pull his hands away.

"Imagine," he said, his voice husky, "if you loved me."

This was it. He was going to kiss her. And then they were going to make love, and she wasn't going to protest. She wasn't going to say one word. She couldn't. Not even if her life had depended on it.

But he didn't kiss her.

Instead, he reached for her hand, and taking it, he brushed her palm lightly with his thumb, drawing circles on the sensitive skin, round and round. "Imagine how you would feel," he whispered. "Imagine the *emotions* you'd feel just from a simple touch."

Kelly stared up at Jax. Emotions. Imagine the emotions. She must have one heck of an imagination, because those imaginary emotions were damn near bowling her over.

He put the bottle of suntan lotion into her hand. "That's what it's really about. Love and emotion. Try rewriting your scene, focusing on what your characters are feeling in their hearts. You'll write a lot more than two paragraphs. I can guarantee it."

He stood, put his sunglasses on and walked calmly down the steps, heading for the cool water of the bay.

Kelly watched him until he was out of sight.

*Imagine if you loved me.*

She didn't have to imagine. She just had to remember.

And that wasn't very hard to do at all.

## CHAPTER THIRTEEN

THE MORNING DAWNED hazy and humid.

After spending the evening writing and rewriting the first love scene in her book, Kelly had had a restless sleep. The setting sun had lowered the record high temperatures by only a few degrees, and the night had been almost impossibly hot.

Never mind the fact that she couldn't stop thinking about the way T. Jackson's hands had felt as he had spread suntan lotion on her legs.

She'd skip her run this morning, take a nice, cool swim instead.

It was a good plan, until she got onto the beach and found T. already sitting there.

"Good morning," he greeted her.

"What are you doing up so early?" she asked suspiciously.

T. shrugged. "Too hot to sleep." He was wearing the same neon-green bathing suit he'd had on yesterday. His hair was wet, and water beaded on his muscular body. He'd already been in for a swim.

It was a new day, Kelly realized, looking down at him. It was a new day, and sometime today he was going to kiss her. Her stomach knotted in anticipation.

As Jax watched, Kelly put her towel down on the

sand chair next to his and kicked off her sandals. With one big yank, she pulled her T-shirt over her head.

She was wearing the black bikini. God, she looked fabulous. He grinned his appreciation, but she ignored him.

Jax followed her down to the edge of the ocean, watching as she walked directly into the water until it covered all but her shoulders. He crash-dived in, surfacing near her. Shaking his wet hair out of his face, he moved closer.

"Couldn't you at least have picked out a bathing suit that had more *suit* to it?" she asked, backing away.

"But you look so good in black," T. said as innocently as possible as he moved toward her.

"Where's the black?" Kelly asked. She kept backing away, heading for the beach, exposing more and more of the bathing suit in question to the open air. "When I looked in the mirror, all I could see was skin."

"You look good naked, too. The combination is...very nice."

The water was only up to her waist now, and his eyes swept over her body. Here it comes. Kelly braced herself. He was surely going to kiss her now. But T. just smiled and dove back out into the deeper water.

She had been so positive he was going to kiss her, *so* sure. She had actually started feeling relieved that today's waiting was over. But then he went and didn't do it, damn him. He was driving her crazy, and she couldn't stand the uncertainty another minute longer. "Tyrone Jackson, get your butt back here."

"Uh-oh," he said as he swam back toward her. "What'd I do now?"

"Kiss me. Will you just kiss me, damn it, and get it over with?"

He stood up then, and water fell off his body in a sheet. Two big steps brought him right to her side, close enough to put his arms around her, close enough for her to see that the swirl of color in his eyes matched the sunlit ocean almost exactly. She swallowed and looked away, unable to hold the intensity of his gaze.

"Do you want me to?" he asked softly.

"No!" T. started to turn away. If he didn't kiss her now, she'd spend the entire day on edge— "Yes, okay? *Yes!*"

He looked at her and it wasn't the sizzling look of desire she had expected. Instead, he smiled rather wistfully. But he still didn't kiss her.

"Please, T.," she whispered.

He touched her then, one hand lightly brushing her hair back from her face, his eyes soft. "Aw, Kel," he breathed. "I didn't want to use up today's kiss right now, but you know I can't refuse you anything."

He leaned forward and his lips brushed against hers, gently at first, then with increasing pressure.

Kelly felt his arms go around her, his hands on her bare back, pressing her against him. It was as if the sensation of their two wet, nearly naked bodies was too much for Jackson, because he didn't end the kiss when she expected him to. He just kept kissing her, harder, deeper now. Of course, maybe it had something to do with the fact that her arms were up around his neck, and that she was kissing him as hungrily as he was kissing her.

She wanted him. She couldn't deny it any longer. She

was ready to surrender, ready to stop pretending that she didn't lie awake all night, wishing that she were in T.'s bed.

"Kelly, I love you so much," T. said, kissing her face. "I need you."

She could feel his heart pounding, hear the raggedness of each breath as his mouth found hers again.

He pulled her out with him, deeper, and under the private cover of the water, he touched her, cupping the softness of her breasts, caressing, stroking. Kissing her hard, harder, he pressed against her. There was no mistaking what he wanted.

And, quite clearly, Kelly knew that making love with T. Jackson was what she wanted, too.

But suddenly he tore himself away, backing off about five feet. He just stood there, breathing hard and looking at her. His eyes seemed luminous, and Kelly realized it was unshed tears that made them shine.

Before she could say a word, he turned and dove into the water. He surfaced far down the beach and kept swimming, hard, away from her.

"T., come back," Kelly whispered, but there was no way on earth he could have heard.


BY DINNERTIME KELLY convinced herself that her moment of surrender when T. had kissed her in the water had been merely that. A moment.

She had been temporarily insane, momentarily crazed. Hadn't she?

Of course, the fact that T. Jackson hadn't returned from the beach until she was in the shower helped her regain her misplaced sanity. By the time she was done, he had vanished, taking his car with him. He hadn't left a note saying where he'd gone and when he'd be back.

It was definitely much easier to convince herself that she didn't want him when he wasn't around.

She worked all day, pretending she wasn't wondering where he was as she rewrote that damned love scene.

It wasn't until six o'clock, when the sun was sinking in the sky, that Jackson appeared.

"How's it going?" He set cartons of Chinese food on the big conference table, along with several plates he'd brought from the kitchen.

He was still wearing his green bathing suit, though it had long since dried. His hair was a mess, but it only made him look even more charming than usual.

As Kelly met his eyes, she knew immediately that everything she'd been trying to tell herself about T. Jackson all afternoon had been a load of hogwash. If he as much as said a word, she'd throw herself into his arms.

"You getting that scene rewritten?" He opened a carton of steaming brown rice.

"I'm trying." Kelly had to clear her throat before the words came out.

"Want me to read what you've got?"

"I don't think so."

"You've got to let me read it sooner or later." T. flashed her a low-watt smile.

She stood and stretched, then sat down across from him at the table. "Later. Much later." She reached to open the third carton. It was unidentifiable, but it smelled great. Wow, she hadn't realized how hungry she was. She'd worked straight through lunch.

T. handed her a pair of paper-wrapped chopsticks, and they ate in silence.

Finally he cleared his throat. "Kel, I want to apologize for this morning."

She glanced at him, and his eyes were a very serious shade of green. But he couldn't hold her gaze, and he looked away.

"I went too far," he said quietly. "I'm sorry and I—"

"T.—"

"Please, let me finish, okay?"

He looked up at her, and she nodded slowly.

"I don't seem to have very much control when it comes to you. I'm afraid—" He cleared his throat again. "I'm afraid I'm not going to hear you or understand you when you tell me to stop, and I can't deal with the thought that I might—" He shook his head and took a deep breath. "Anyway, you don't have to worry, I'm not going to kiss you again."

It was then that Kelly knew with absolute certainty that she wanted him to kiss her again. Wanted? Hell, she *needed* him to kiss her.

She stood. "Let me get this straight. You're not going to kiss me again, because you don't want to make love to me."

Jax shook his head, laughing with frustration. "That's the problem. I *do* want to make love to you." He watched as she walked around the table and sat down in the chair next to his. "Desperately." He pushed his half-eaten dinner away from him. "You've read my letters, Kelly. You know how I feel. I love you. I'm just afraid—"

"That when I say no, you won't be able to stop,"

Kelly finished for him. "The message won't get through."

"Yeah." Jax rubbed his forehead as if he had a headache. He stood suddenly. "I need a beer. You want a beer?"

She stood, too. "T., wait."

Even with the windows open wide and the salty ocean breeze blowing into the room, Jax could smell Kelly's sweet scent. She was standing much too close. He tried to take a step backward, but bumped into the table. She moved even closer.

"Watch my mouth," Kelly said. "And listen really carefully."

"Kel—"

"Come on, T.," she said. "Watch and listen."

Jax couldn't find any answers in her eyes, so he dropped his gaze to her soft lips.

"Are you listening?" she asked, and he nodded.

Her lips curved upward into an enchanting smile, and then she said, quite clearly, "No."

Jax closed his eyes. Torture. She was torturing him.

"You have any trouble understanding that?"

Eyes still closed, he shook his head. "Of course not. But these are hardly the same conditions that—"

"Okay, then, kiss me," Kelly ordered him.

He opened his eyes. "What?"

She smiled at him again. "Put your arms around me and kiss me," she repeated. "Gee, I didn't think I'd have to ask you *twice*."

"Kel—"

"Come on, Tyrone. *Kiss* me. I can't prove my point until you do."

"And which point is it that you're trying to prove?"

Kelly laughed. "Kiss me and you'll find out."

Forget torture. She was trying to kill him. "I'm not sure this is such a good idea." He looked down at her mouth, and it was his undoing. She was moistening her lips with the tip of her tongue, and, God, he *had* to kiss her.

She was standing close, but not close enough, and as his mouth went down to meet hers, he pulled her in toward him. Just as his lips brushed hers, she reached up and, pressing the palms of her hands against his chest, she pushed herself back, away from him.

He let go of her instantly.

Kelly laughed. "You seemed to understand that, too."

Jax closed his eyes and pressed the heel of his hand against the bridge of his nose. This was going to be one *hell* of a headache when it finally arrived. If he lived that long. When he opened his eyes, Kelly was still standing directly in front of him, smiling up at him.

"Understand what?" he asked wearily.

She reached out and pushed against his chest with the palm of her hand again. "That," she said. "You know what it means when I do that, right?"

"Yeah. It means stop, don't, no."

"Well, there you have it. Two perfectly understandable ways to say no—one verbal, one not."

She looked so pleased with herself. "I hate to break it to you," he said, "but if you've just made your point, you lost me somewhere."

"Well, actually, no," she told him. "I haven't made my point yet. In order for me to do that, you have to kiss me again."

Jax sat down tiredly on top of the table. "Kel—"

They were nearly the same height now, and Kelly stepped in between his legs and draped her arms around his neck. "I suppose *I* could always kiss *you*." Leaning forward slightly, she did.

Her lips were soft, and tasted so sweet. She pulled back slightly, looking into his eyes and smiling before she kissed him again.

Jax opened his mouth under the gentle pressure from her tongue. She was kissing him. Kelly was kissing *him*. He couldn't decide whether to laugh or cry, so he did neither. Instead, he put his arms around her, crushing her to him, devouring the sweetness of her mouth with his own.

Kelly laughed, arching her head back as he rained kisses down her neck. "The reason you didn't hear me say no this morning was because I didn't say it. And if you listen very closely, you still won't hear me say no."

Jax couldn't breathe. "And how about if I pick you up and carry you into my bedroom?" he asked. "Will you still not say no?"

"Maybe you should give it a try," Kelly answered huskily.

He swung her up into his arms.

T.'s bedroom was lit only by the evening sunset. Red and orange light streamed in through the windows, making the white walls seem warm and pink. He set her gently on his bed, and Kelly reached for him, pulling him down next to her. She kissed him and slid her hands up, underneath his T-shirt, glad she'd finally given in.

"Kelly, wait," he said. He was breathing hard, and

she knew by the accelerated beat of his heart that he didn't really want to stop. But he caught her hands. "You know how much I want to make love to you." His face was serious as his eyes searched hers.

She nodded. "I want it, too."

"Do you?" A muscle flickered in his jaw as he clenched and unclenched his teeth. "Do you really want to make love? Or is this just going to be sex?"

Kelly tried to smile. "Can't we figure that out later?"

T. was trying to smile, too, but she could see the hurt in his eyes. "An evasive answer. You still won't admit that you love me, will you?"

"Jackson—" Kelly looked down at the floor "—I'm just not ready—"

"For this," he finished with her. "I know."

He was still holding her hands, and he laced her fingers with his, squeezing them gently. "This might come as a shock to you, and God knows it's one hell of a shock to *me,* but I'm not going to settle for sex. I'm not going to settle, period. When you decide to admit to yourself that you love me, then I'll make love to you. But not until then." He drew her hands to his mouth and kissed them before he released her.

Kelly *was* shocked. She was shocked that he would actually turn her down, but mostly shocked at how disappointed she felt. "Well." Her voice sounded breathless and odd. "Who would've guessed that you'd end up being the one to say no?"

But T. shook his head vehemently. "I'm saying yes," he said. "To the question that really matters, Kel, I'm the one saying yes."

## CHAPTER FOURTEEN

Three o'clock in the morning, and Jax still sat in front of the computer, staring sightlessly at the screen. God, would this night never end?

He couldn't sleep. He'd tried that already, and all he did was lie in bed and think about the fact that Kelly wasn't there with him.

She should've been, and worst of all, she *could've* been. He'd lost his mind. That had to be the answer. No red-blooded, *hot*-blooded American man in his right mind would've turned down a woman like Kelly the way he had. He had suddenly been possessed by the spirit of these damned romantic heroes he obviously spent too much time writing about.

"So go and tell her you were wrong," a familiar voice cut through his thoughts. Jared was sitting on a bed in one of the guest rooms of the sprawling ranch house. He looked dashing, as usual, his thick, glossy hair disheveled and his shirt off. His arm was still bleeding. The bullet had gone clear through, and Carrie was bandaging both sides of the wound. "Tell Kelly," Jared said, "that you were temporarily insane and that you'll gladly settle for a pure, uncomplicated sexual relationship— Ouch!"

He looked up at Carrie in surprise as she was none

too gentle with his arm. "He *loves* her," Carrie said to
Jared. "Has it occurred to you that he might actually
want more than just a sexual relationship? And I don't
care what you say, *no* relationship is *ever* uncomplicated."

"Look, guys," Jax broke in. "We're coming up on the
ending to this story here. Could we maybe be a little
nicer to each—"

"*I'm* being incredibly nice," Jared declared. "Man,
she *shot* me, and I'm still offering to stick around and
help her defend her ranch and her water rights against
those outlaws—"

"I don't want or need your help," Carrie said tightly.
"As soon as I'm done wrapping you up, I will thank you
very much to take your oversize horse and your oversize ego off my land."

"Hang on!" Jax said. "Let me get some of this on
disk." He started to write.

"You need help," Jared said bluntly. "Who're you
gonna get it from? That old man you got working in your stables? Or maybe that little boy I saw
running across the yard a minute ago?"

"Well, at least I know they won't desert me."

"Whoa now," Jared said, catching her arm
before she could turn away. "I never deserted you.
I *told* you I would come back for you. You didn't
wait for me!"

"I couldn't wait."

"You didn't want to wait," he accused her.

Carrie laughed, but there was no humor on her

pretty face. "No, Jared, I *couldn't*. I was carrying your child."

Shock. Complete numbing shock. A...*child?*

"We have a child?" Jared breathed.

"A son."

Outside the window, across the yard, the little boy was helping the old man brush down Jared's stallion. Slowly Jared pulled himself to his feet, crossing to the window, staring out at...his son?

Jared turned to her. "Carrie, God, I didn't know."

It had been purely by accident that he had deserted Carrie more than eight years ago. If he had known she needed him so desperately, he would've walked through hell to get to her.

Now she was in trouble again, and he was damned if he was going to desert her a second time.

KELLY COULDN'T SLEEP. SHE SAT on her bed, looking at the pile of letters T. Jackson had written to her in the few weeks she'd been here.

He loved her.

There was proof of that in these letters. As if she'd really need any other proof after tonight... T. never would've refused a chance to go to bed with her if he didn't love her.

She felt tears welling up in her eyes. She couldn't let herself love him back. It would hurt too much when he stopped loving her. And he *would* stop loving her. Or maybe he just wouldn't love her enough to stick around. He'd loved her seven years ago, but not enough to fight for her, not even enough to come back for her when she turned eighteen the way he'd promised.

No, she couldn't risk letting herself love him.

The best thing for both of them was for Kelly to pack her things and go back to Boston.

She wiped her eyes on the sleeve of her T-shirt and took her suitcase out of the closet. It didn't take her long to pack her clothes, but the sun was starting to peek over the edge of the horizon by the time she was done.

One more walk on the beach. She'd take one more walk before she woke up Jackson to ask him to drive her to the bus station.

The dawn air was damp, but the sun was already hot enough to start burning off the mist and ocean fog. The beach was deserted and quiet, with only the sounds of the water and the seagulls breaking the calm.

In just a few hours, she'd be back in Boston, back in the noisy city, away from the beach. Away from T.

She'd be alone again, working in the solitude of her apartment, unable to turn around and ask a stupid grammar question or share a joke, a comment, a smile.

Fact was, she was going to miss T. Jackson.

Kelly's bare toes dug into the wet sand as she walked, and she tried to brush away the tears that had gathered again in her eyes. She was going to miss more than T.'s keen sense of humor and his help editing her manuscript. She was going to miss the way his eyes crinkled up at the corners when he laughed. She was going to miss the fact that he could get dressed up to the nines for dinner in a hand-tailored suit and *still* not wear any socks. She was going to miss his teasing, his jokes, the way he smiled at her when he said "Good morning."

And she was going to miss his kisses.

Her tears were falling faster now, and Kelly just sat down in the sand at the edge of the water and cried.

Who was she trying to kid? She was in love with T. Jackson Winchester the Second. There was no doubt about it.

A ROMANTIC HERO WOULD stick to his guns and not give in.

But Jax wasn't any kind of romantic hero, and the fact remained that as much as he wanted Kelly to admit that she was in love with him, there was no guarantee that she was going to.

The fact also remained that after a long, sleepless night, Jax realized as much as it would hurt him in the long run, he was willing to take whatever Kelly was willing to give. And if that meant having a no-strings, no-commitment relationship based on a sexual attraction...well, at least there would be some pleasure with his pain.

When it came to Kelly, he was weak. He would be the first to admit that.

He stood outside Kelly's bedroom door. There was no sound from inside. Of course there wasn't. It wasn't even 6:00 a.m.

Jax knocked softly on the door, but there was no answer. He tried the knob, and it turned. The door was unlocked, so he pushed it open.

The room was empty; the bed hadn't even been slept

in. And Kelly's suitcase was packed and standing in the middle of the floor.

She was going to leave.

Pain hit him hard and square in the middle of his chest, and he struggled to breathe. Kelly was going to leave.

He heard a sound, and turned to see her standing in the doorway. She looked so beautiful. Her hair was tousled from the wind and curling from the humidity. Her T-shirt was damp from the ocean's spray and it clung to her soft curves. Her cheeks were flushed, her eyes bright with tears—

Jax swallowed the last of his pride. "Kel, please don't go." His voice cracked slightly. He tried to smile. "You win. I'll play by your rules. We'll do this your way."

Kelly watched him rake his fingers through his thick blond hair. He wasn't trying to hide his desperation from her, and she could see it in his eyes, hear it in his voice.

"T.—" she started.

"You don't have to love me." He took a step forward. "I know that you care about me, and that's good enough for now."

He was making a sacrifice. He was willing to toss aside the things he wanted in order to keep her near him.

"No, T.—"

"Kelly, please." Another step, and he took her hands in his. His eyes were fiercely determined. "If you leave, I'm just going to follow you. I can't live without you. I don't want to live without you. I *refuse* to live without you—"

He kissed her, a hard, demanding, hungry kiss that sent fire racing through her blood. With his arms around her as he held her tightly to him, she could feel his heart beating as he whispered, "Please, don't go. I was wrong—"

"No, you were right." Kelly reached up to touch the side of his face and realized her hand was shaking. God, what she felt for this man scared her to death. She didn't want to say the words aloud. But she had to, if only to relieve the look of desperation in his eyes. "You've been right all along—"

"Right now there is no wrong or right," Jax said, shaking his head. "All I know is that I'd do damn near anything to make you stay."

She was in his arms, and he was looking down into the bottomless depths of her eyes. His memories of those eyes had been his savior, his connection to sanity, blurring the line between reality and fantasy during a time when reality would have broken him.

Now her eyes were filled with tears, tears that escaped to run down the exquisite softness of her cheeks.

"You don't have to," Kelly told him quietly, "because, God help me, I love you, T."

Did she just say that she loved him? He stared at her. Had her words been fantasy or reality?

"What did you say?" he whispered.

"I love you. God knows I don't want to, but I do."

Reality.

With a sudden blinding flash, Jax could see his future stretching out in front of him, and for the first time in ages, it was lit by sunshine and laughter. She loved him. Kelly had finally admitted that she loved him.

He kissed her, tasting the salt of her tears, the sweetness of her lips. He could see the love in her eyes. It wasn't new—he'd seen it there before—but she wasn't trying to hide or ignore it now.

"T., make love to me," Kelly said.

"Come to my room," he breathed, and she nodded.

Holding her hand, Jax led her down the hall to his bedroom, drawing her inside and locking the door behind her. He closed the door that led to his office, then turned to look at her.

Kelly stood in the center of the room, watching T. He looked exhausted, and she knew that, like her, he hadn't slept at all last night. But he smiled at her, a smile that erased the fatigue from his face and lit his eyes with happiness.

She realized she couldn't let herself think about the future. She couldn't think about the pain and heartache that would surely come from loving him. There would be plenty of time to suffer when he was gone. But right now he was here, and here and now were what mattered. Here and now his heart was hers.

Kelly smiled at him. "Can we take this from where we left it last night?" She crossed to the bed and sat on the edge. "I think I was over here."

T. walked across the room almost impossibly slowly, holding her gaze every step of the way. The fire from his eyes burned into her body, infusing her with a heat that seemed to rise from deep within her. As he sat down next to her on the bed, he picked up her hands, lacing their fingers together.

He kissed her, and Kelly could feel his restraint. He

was holding back, as if he were afraid to overwhelm her, as if he were afraid he'd lose control.

"It's not many people who get a second chance to make love for the first time," he said with a crooked smile.

"I'm going to have to disappoint you," Kelly admitted. "That night in your hotel room? That wasn't just sex. We *were* making love. I loved you then—I was just too stupid to admit it."

"I'm not disappointed." He kissed her again, still so carefully.

Kelly reached up, lightly tracing the small scar on his cheekbone as she looked into his eyes. Like the high school boy who had scarred him in that fight, she knew firsthand about the passion that burned inside of T. Jackson.

She loved T. because he was sweet and kind and funny and smart. But the fact that he could manage so successfully to hide his passion behind a cool and collected facade of control made her love him even more. Especially since she knew that she had the power to take that control of his and tear it to shreds.

Which was exactly what she intended to do right now.

She knelt next to him on the bed and kissed him fiercely, pulling him closer to her, running her hands up underneath his T-shirt, against his smooth, muscular back. She could feel his control slipping as his arms tightened around her, as he returned her kisses. Drawing her leg across him, she straddled his lap, and he groaned.

Together they pulled his T-shirt off, then hers, tossing them onto the floor. Her bra soon followed.

Picking Kelly up, Jax turned, pushing her back onto the bed, covering her body with his. "I love you, Kel," he breathed, touching, caressing the smooth softness of her neck, her shoulders, her breasts.

As he kissed her again, his fingers fumbled with the button on her cutoff jeans. Nearly growling with frustration, he pulled away from her. Laughing, she unfastened the button, then, holding his gaze, slowly drew the zipper down.

As she slipped out of her shorts and her panties, Jax could barely breathe. He was frozen in place, spellbound, hypnotized. "Are you real?" he whispered. "Are you really here with me, or am I dreaming?"

For a long time after he'd returned from Central America, he had been struck by feelings of unreality, expecting at any moment he would awaken still locked in his prison cell. He felt that way now.

Kelly sat up, putting her arms around his neck as she kissed him. "If you think you're dreaming, maybe you better hurry up, get your clothes off and make love to me before you wake up."

Jax laughed, then gasped as her hands found the hardness of his arousal pressing against his shorts. She deftly undid the button and his shorts quickly followed the rest of their clothes onto the floor.

He quickly covered himself with a condom, then slipped between her legs. His hands and mouth were everywhere then, touching her, kissing her, drinking in the softness of her skin, the wet heat of her desire.

"Tell me again that you love me," he whispered, looking down into her eyes.

He was poised over her, the muscles in his arms and shoulders flexed as he kept his weight lifted off her. His golden hair was a jumble of unruly waves, messed from her fingers.

She smiled up at him, and he kissed her again, as if he couldn't bear to be separated from her lips for too long.

"I love you," she said. "I always have."

He filled her then, both her heart and her body, and for the first time in her life, she felt truly whole. She had loved him forever, a love so pure and true, it had triumphed over the passage of time and all of her pain and heartache. She knew in that instant she would love him until the end of time, long after he'd moved on.

She held him close, moving with him, pushing him farther, more deeply inside of her, hoping if she held him tightly enough, he would never go away.

"I love you," she cried, the waves of her pleasure exploding through her.

She felt T.'s body tighten with his own stormy release, heard him call her name, his voice hoarse with passion.

*Don't ever leave me,* she thought.

It wasn't until T. answered her that she realized she had spoken the words aloud. "I won't, Kel," he said, kissing her sweetly. "I promise I won't."

But it was a promise he'd already broken once before.

# CHAPTER FIFTEEN

"DO YOU WANT TO GO FOR a swim or make love?" T. asked, nuzzling Kelly's neck.

The morning sun was streaming through the windows of his bedroom, and Kelly stretched. "What day is it?"

He smiled at her lazily. "I can only give you a rough estimate—I can tell you the month and the year. Well, wait a minute, maybe I can't even do that. Is it July or August? It could be August."

Kelly laughed. "Impossible. August was at least a week away. I mean, all you need is love and all that, but I just can't believe someone as spoiled as you—"

"Spoiled?" T. feigned insult.

"—could go for a whole week without food," Kelly finished teasingly.

But suddenly he wasn't laughing anymore. His eyes were strangely haunted and his smile disappeared. "You'd be surprised at how long I could go without food," he said quietly. But just as quickly as that odd mood had fallen over him, it was gone. He smiled with a quick flash of his white teeth and pulled her on top of him, kissing her hard on the mouth.

"I have a deadline coming up," he told her, "and I'm having a bitch of a time finishing this book. Argh!

I don't want to think about it. I don't even want to work on it anymore." He kissed her again, then looked thoughtful. "Of course, if it *is* August, then I'm already late with the manuscript, and there're probably twenty-five very irate messages from my editor on my answering machine."

"And if it's August, Stefanie and Emilio are back from their cruise," Kelly pointed out.

"Oh, damn, there goes our privacy." T. closed his eyes with pleasure as she ran her fingers through his hair. "No more running naked through the house."

"Have you been running naked through the house?" Kelly teased. "Without me?"

"Well, no." He caught her hands and kissed the tips of her fingers. "But you know how it is. As soon as you can't do something, you immediately want to do it."

"If I tell you that you absolutely *can't* work on your manuscript, will that make you want to finish writing it?"

"No. But I just got a sudden wild craving to play miniature golf."

Kelly laughed.

"And then I want to call your parents and tell them that we're getting married."

She froze. T. was smiling up at her. He hadn't shaved in days and his hair was wild, but with his eyes lit with love, he was so utterly handsome he took her breath away. But she wasn't going to marry him. She couldn't. "T., we're not getting married."

He was unperturbed. "Yes, we are."

"No, we're *not*. Besides, that's not the sort of thing

you're supposed to just *tell* someone. You're supposed to *ask*— Didn't we have this conversation once before?"

He turned suddenly, flipping Kelly onto her back, pinning her to the bed with his body. "Marry me," he said, all teasing gone from his voice and eyes. "Kelly, please, will you marry me?"

As she looked up at him, her eyes filled with tears. "How many years do you want to marry me for, T.?" she asked. "Two? Maybe three?" She pushed him away from her and sat up on the edge of the bed. "I can't go through that again."

"I'm not Brad," Jax said quietly. "I want you for forever."

She turned to face him. "That's what Brad said, too. But he changed his mind."

"Maybe he realized that you didn't love him. Maybe he figured out that you were still in love with me."

Kelly just watched him quietly, and Jax wished he could get inside her head, read her mind and know what she was thinking.

"I love you," he said. "And you love me. We should have been together right from the very start—"

"If you believe that, then why did you go to London?"

It was a direct question, deserving of a point-blank answer. Jax looked straight into Kelly's eyes and fired both barrels.

"Because Kevin gave me a choice between going to London or being brought up on charges of attempted rape."

Kelly was shocked. Attempted *rape?* "That's ridiculous—"

"You were underage." His eyes were intense as he tried to make her understand. "If Kevin had made any noise, there would've been an investigation at the very least. It would've been horrible, Kel, not just for me, but for you. You would've been examined by doctors, questioned by the police and all kinds of social workers and psychologists. And God, if any word at all had slipped out to the papers, it would've been a total media circus. Your reputation would have been shredded." He was silent, looking out the windows at the deep, clear blue of the sky. "I didn't give a damn about myself, but I couldn't do that to you, so I went to London."

"Kevin was bluffing!"

"I sure as hell didn't think so."

"Why didn't you at least talk to me about it?"

"It was part of the deal," Jax said. "I couldn't try to see you. I couldn't call. I couldn't even write to you."

"I thought you didn't love me," she said softly.

He shook his head. "It was because I loved you that I left. And if I had to do it over again, I'm not sure I wouldn't do exactly the same thing."

Kelly was older now, but he could still see that sweet sixteen-year-old girl when he looked into her eyes. He had let her down all those years ago.

"You broke my heart." It wasn't an accusation. It was a fact. And somehow that made it even worse.

"That part I'd do differently," Jax told her.

JAX SAT AT HIS COMPUTER, looking out his office windows. If he craned his neck, he could see down to the deck where Kelly was sitting, reading the unfinished draft of his manuscript. She was wearing the black bathing suit he'd bought her. Black bathing suit, black sunglasses, all that lightly tanned, smooth skin...

"Aren't you supposed to be writing?" Jared's familiar voice broke into his thoughts. "Look, Kelly's a real babe, but can't you take your eyes off her for even a few minutes?"

Jax dragged his eyes back to the computer screen. He had left Jared out in the barn, brushing down his stallion. A light rain was falling outside of the open barn door.

"Kelly's finally mine." Jax laughed. "I am *so* lucky—"

"Yeah, well, she hasn't agreed to marry you, so don't send the tux out to the dry cleaners yet." Jared wiped the sweat from his brow with the sleeve of his cotton shirt. "You may have the 'happily' part down, but the 'ever after' needs some work."

"You're just jealous—" Jax crossed his arms and leaned back in his chair "—because Carrie still won't have anything to do with you."

"Yeah, well, she doesn't trust me," Jared admitted. "But hey, you know what they say about art imitating life."

Jax frowned, leaning forward. "Are you intimating that Kelly doesn't trust me?"

"That's exactly what I'm 'intimating.'" Jared grinned. "Man, where do you come up with these words?"

"I'm a writer," Jax said absently.

"Coulda fooled me," Jared said dryly. "I've been hanging out, waiting for you to write me out of this barn for days."

Jax was deep in thought. Kelly didn't trust him? Yeah, it made sense. "Is it men in general that she doesn't trust?" he wondered out loud. "Or is it me?"

"Mostly you," Jared guessed. "You hurt her badly once already. She's waiting for you to do it again."

"So what am I supposed to do?" Jax asked, adding, "God, I must be desperate if I'm reduced to asking *you* for advice."

Jared leaned against the doorframe, crossing his arms in front of him. Thinking hard, he looked down at the toes of his dusty boots as he scuffed them in the dirt. When he looked back at Jax, there was a twinkle in his dark eyes.

"Maybe you should let life imitate art for a change," he said with a smile. "How do you plan to get Carrie to agree to marry *me?* Just do the same thing with Kelly."

Jax ran his fingers through his hair and laughed, a short, humorless burst of air. "It's hardly the same situation—"

"It's *exactly* the same—"

"If you must know, you're going to take a bullet that was meant for Carrie," Jax told his character. "When you nearly die, she's going to realize how much you mean to her."

"You're going to have me get shot *again?*" Jared straightened up. "That's one gunshot wound for every... what? Every hundred and ten pages? Thank the Lord this book's only four hundred and fifty pages long. I'm beginning to feel like I'm walking around with a sign around my neck saying 'Shoot me, I'm a romantic hero.'"

"Stop complaining," Jax said, tipping his chair back

on two legs. "It's going to get you what you want, *and* you're going to save Carrie's life."

"Just watch your aim, okay?" Jared began to pace. His big horse snorted and glanced back over his shoulder at him. "Well, obviously you can't use that same solution for your problem."

"Obviously."

"Ahem."

Jax lost his balance and his chair went over backward with a crash. "Hi." He smiled weakly up at Kelly from the floor.

In the barn, Jared was laughing.

"You really do talk to yourself, don't you?" She put the notebook that held his manuscript down on the table.

She'd put a big, filmy gauze blouse on over her bathing suit. The tails came down to her knees, but she'd left the front unbuttoned. The flashes of smooth, tanned skin that Jax could see beneath the white gauze made his mouth go dry.

She held out her hand to help him up, but instead of getting to his feet, he pulled her down onto the floor with him.

"I wasn't talking to myself," he said, kissing her. "I was talking to Jared."

"Jared." She nodded. "You outdid yourself with him. He's a real hunk, and I mean to-die-for in a major way. I think he's your best hero yet."

"Oh, yeah!" Jared strutted across the barn. "She likes me. Watch out, Winchester, you're history."

"Yeah, well, you're fictional," Jax countered. Kelly was looking at him, one eyebrow raised, and he kissed her quickly. "Sorry. Just...you know..." He cleared his throat. "So you liked Jared, huh? And how about Kelly— *Carrie,*" he corrected himself, then rolled his eyes.

Kelly laughed. "Ah, the truth comes out with the old Freudian slip. I *thought* she looked suspiciously like me. Well, a glorified, perfect me, anyway. And Jared's obviously you, only not blond and a little bit more stupid."

"Hey!" Jared was insulted.

"More stupid!" Jax repeated happily. "That's a great way to describe him. I like it. More stupid. I can picture the blurb on the back cover now. 'Jared Dexter, stronger and braver than most, more stupid than some—'"

"Oh, shut up." Jared turned his back pointedly, picking up the brush and starting in on his horse's coat again.

Laughing, Jax kissed Kelly. "He's pouting now."

"If you told me you planned to shoot me, I'd pout, too," Kelly said, pulling herself to her feet.

"How long were you listening to me—"

"Talk to yourself?" Kelly finished for him with a grin. "Long enough to know that you're planning to get Carrie and Jared together with the old hero-almost-dies ploy. It's been used before, but that's okay."

She was standing with her back to the windows, and the sunlight streamed in behind her, making her cover-up seem to disappear. "There's just one thing I need to ask you."

Jax held up one hand. "Wait. Let me get rid of some distractions." He cleared the computer screen, then walking toward her, he took her gently by the arm and switched their positions, so that he had his back to the window. From where he stood now, the sunlight streaming in made her shirt opaque again. "Okay, now I'm listening."

"Why hasn't Jared told Carrie where he was all those years?" Kelly asked. "I mean, my God, he went through hell, and Carrie doesn't have a clue. As far as she's concerned, he *did* desert her. Why doesn't he say something?"

Jax frowned down at the floor. This was it. He had to tell her. As much as he didn't want to, he knew he had to. It was definitely time.

Kelly leaned back against the table, waiting for his reply. As she watched, T. moistened his lips and cleared his throat. When he finally looked up at her, he had the strangest expression on his face.

"What's he gonna say?" he asked her quietly. "How's he going to bring it up? It's not easy for him to talk about, you know, what he went through. And it's sure as hell not a topic of conversation to have over dinner. He can't just say, 'Oh, by the way, I spent twenty godforsaken months of my life in a rat-infested prison in Central America.'"

Kelly frowned. What? Wait a minute, Jared hadn't been anywhere near Central America and...

"How *do* you tell someone something like that?" T.'s voice sounded oddly tight. "Do you just walk up and say, 'Sorry I missed your eighteenth birthday, but I was a political prisoner in a country where the phrase "human rights" isn't in the dictionary?' How do you tell someone you love that you were locked in a four-by-eight room, given barely enough food and water to stay alive for nearly two years?"

"Oh my God," she breathed. He wasn't talking about Jared. He was talking about...*himself!*

With a sudden flash of memory, she saw T. as he was at Kevin's wedding, thin to the point of gauntness, as if he'd been ill or...nearly starved to death. She heard an echo of Stefanie's shocked voice, from the day they'd had lunch together. *He never told you what happened in Central America?*

Kelly felt sick.

"What's he going to say to her?" T. said again. He turned away and looked out the window at the sunlight dancing across the water.

Heart pounding, Kelly crossed toward him. As she put her arms around his waist, he looked down at her and forced a smile. "It's just not easy to talk about."

"What if she asks?" she said softly. "Will he tell her then?"

"Yeah."

"T., tell me about...Central America?"

He closed his eyes and drew a deep breath, then slowly let it out before turning and looking out at the water again.

"I went there for an interview with an opposition leader," T. said. He was trying to sound normal, as if they were talking about last night's Red Sox game instead of his...incarceration. Oh, God. Kelly could see tears in his eyes, but he staunchly ignored them, managing to look only slightly less cool and collected than he usually did. "After I talked to him, the government thought I might have information on the whereabouts of the rebel forces. They failed to, um, persuade me to part with any of my information—of which I had very little—and on my way to the airport, I was arrested. Someone had planted a small fortune in cocaine in my overnight bag. I was sentenced to ten years in prison. I was really a political prisoner, but the American consulate couldn't do anything to help me, because of the drug charges."

Tears escaped from his eyes, and he brushed them brusquely away. "I'm sorry," he said quickly.

Kelly punched him, and he looked at her in surprise.

"Don't you *dare* apologize," she said hotly. "My God, I can't even imagine how terrible it must have been. Jackson, how can you stand there like that and give me the impersonal Journalism 101 synopsis?"

"I'm sorry—"

"*Stop* apologizing!" she shouted. "You should be furious, angry, *outraged* that this happened to you. God, T., did they hurt you? Did you cry? Were you alone? What did you do? Did they make you work? Tell me what it smelled like. Tell me how you found the strength to survive! Tell me how you *felt!*"

Kelly paced back and forth, nearly shaking her fist in the air. She whirled to face him. "*Show* me how you felt, damn it. Get pissed! Throw something! Break some furniture—"

"I love you," Jax said. "And you love me. That's all I need to feel now, Kelly." He pulled her into his arms. "I can show you that, and I will—every day for the rest of our lives, if you'll let me."

She was crying, hot, angry tears, and Jax gently caught one with his finger. "Besides—" he smiled slightly and kissed her "—I don't break furniture. I write."

He pulled away from her and crossed to his big bookshelf. Reaching up, he took a heavy blue three-ring binder down from among all the other notebooks and handed it to her. "This will tell you how I felt."

Kelly looked down at the manuscript as she wiped the tears from her face. "A story?"

"Nonfiction," T. told her. "Although, when I publish it, I should probably give cowriting credit to my psychologist. I'd meant to get this all down on paper when I first came back, but it was my shrink who finally forced me to sit down and write it."

He kissed her again. "I'll be on the beach," he said, but she'd already sat down at the table, opening up the thick manuscript to the first page. She didn't even hear him as he slipped out the door.

It was called *Letters to Kelly,* she realized with shock. Leafing quickly through, she saw that the entire manuscript was a series of letters—all addressed to her. Heart pounding, she began to read.

After the first few pages, she was in tears again.

Dear Kelly,
I regain consciousness in my cell, and I am surprised—surprised that I am still alive. I'm lucky. I saw the bodies of less fortunate men being dumped into the back of a pickup truck the last time I was in the courtyard.
    But then I move, and my entire body screams with pain. And I wonder. Maybe *they* were the lucky ones....

Dear Kelly,
Four days since I've last been fed. You come and keep me company, and we talk about Thanksgiving dinner. You take my hand and pull me back

with you, back in time, and I'm at your house. Your dining room table has been extended, and your parents and your grandmother, your aunt Christa and your cousins, Kevin, you and I all sit, bowing our heads as your father says grace.

I stare at the feast on the table, realizing that the leftovers from this meal could keep me alive for months....

OUTSIDE THE OFFICE WINDOW, the sun moved across the sky, but Kelly was aware of nothing but the words on the paper. T.'s words. Letters he'd written her, from hell.

T. JACKSON WAS SITTING on the beach, arms wrapped loosely around his knees, watching the sunset. The wind ruffled his golden blond hair, and the sunlight flashed as it hit the reflective lenses of his sunglasses. He had a bottle of beer in his hand—he was a living advertisement for the good life.

He looked at Kelly as she sat down next to him. She knew what she looked like—her eyes were puffy and the tip of her nose was red. He put his arms around her and kissed the top of her head. "You all right?" he asked quietly.

"Shouldn't I be asking *you* that question?" Kelly reached up and took off his sunglasses so that she could see his eyes. They were beautiful, greenish-blue in the late-afternoon light, and so warm and loving.

"I'm extremely all right." He touched her hair and kissed her mouth. "In fact, I keep wondering if maybe I haven't actually died and gone to heaven. We're finally together, and you love me, too—"

Kelly started to cry, pressing her face into the warmth of his neck, holding him as tightly as she could.

"Hey," he said. "Hey, come on—"

"I'm sorry." Sobs shook her body. "Oh, T., I'm so sorry. You came back from that...that...*place*, and I wasn't there for you."

"Kel—"

"All this time I thought you had deserted me, but *I* was the one who deserted you. All that time you were in that horrible prison and I didn't even try to find you—"

"It's okay, Kel." His voice was gentle, soothing. "You didn't know."

"T., I wasn't there for you."

"You're here for me now."

Kelly looked up at him, tears running down her face. "Yes, I am," she said, and she kissed him.

"You know, I meant it when I said that I won't ever leave you," he told her.

He had never stopped loving her. He would never stop loving her. Kelly believed that now. "I know."

T. smiled at her then, and wiping her eyes on the sleeve of her shirt, she managed to smile back at him. It was shaky, but it was definitely a smile.

"So," she said. "You want to go play a few rounds of miniature golf?" She laughed weakly at the surprised look on his face. "Or do you want to skip the golf and just call my parents and tell them that we're getting married?"

T. stared at her, his eyes opened wide, for several long seconds. Then he started to laugh. He kissed Kelly hard on the mouth, then jumped up and started dancing down the beach, whooping and shouting.

Kelly stared at him in shock, her mouth open. T. was acting so utterly uncool. She started to laugh. She loved it.

He froze suddenly, looking back at her.

"Are we really getting married?" he asked, as if he were making a quick reality check.

Kelly nodded. "I take it you still want to?"

He grabbed her hands and pulled her to her feet. "Oh, yeah." He kissed her, a deep, fiery kiss that left her dizzy. He swung her effortlessly up into his arms. His long legs covered the ground quickly as he carried her back toward the house. "This is definitely the best day of my life," he said, taking the stairs to the deck two at a time.

Jax opened the screen door into the living room and carried Kelly inside. He set her gently down, but her arms stayed around his neck and she kissed him. He groaned, opening his mouth under the pressure from her lips, sliding his hands underneath her big gauze shirt. Her skin was so soft and warm. He kissed her harder, deeper, shifting his hips so that she could feel his desire against her. She slid one smooth leg up, twisting it around his own leg, and breathing hard, he reached for the string that would untie the top of her bathing suit—

"Well, well, you two have certainly been busy since I've been gone," Stefanie's well-polished voice cut through.

Startled, Kelly sprang away from Jax, blushing and clutching her overshirt together.

"Stef," Jax said. "On your way in or out? Hopefully out."

She was in the entryway, a small suitcase in her hand. She laughed, amusement in her gray eyes. "Gee, what a welcome home. But no, lucky you, I'm going away for another month or so. Emilio's waiting in the car. We're flying to Italy to meet his parents." She rolled her eyes. "I've totally lost my mind. I've agreed to marry the man."

"Congratulations," Kelly said.

"Maybe we can make it a double wedding." Jax pulled Kelly in close to him, kissing the side of her face.

Stefanie's eyes softened. "Oh, darling, I'm so happy for you."

She looked at Kelly. "Thank God you finally came to your senses. I was ready to wring your little neck."

Kelly laughed. "I'm glad you didn't have to."

"Our flight leaves Boston in just a few hours." Stef's hand was on the doorknob. "I've got to run, but I *am* very glad." She waved to them. "See you when I see you, darlings."

The door closed with a bang behind her, leaving T. Jackson and Kelly staring at each other in the sudden stillness.

T. smiled, a slow, sexy smile that made Kelly's heart race. "Where were we before we were so rudely interrupted?" he asked.

She smiled. "I think we were about to run naked through the house."

"No, we've got a whole extra month to do that," he murmured, kissing the delicate skin under Kelly's ear. "We don't need to do that right now."

She closed her eyes, humming her approval of the placement of his lips and hands. "Maybe you wanted to go upstairs and finish writing your novel?"

"No, no, not the novel," he said. "But there was definitely something I wanted to do upstairs."

He took her hand and led her up to the second-floor landing.

"Maybe you wanted to write me another love letter."

At the top of the stairs he stopped and kissed her again and she melted against him.

"Haven't you read enough for today?" He lifted her up and carried her the last few steps into his bedroom.

"There's no such thing as too many love letters," Kelly pointed out.

He placed her gently on his bed, softly kissing her lips.

"Dear Kelly," he said, gazing into the depths of her eyes. "Let's skip the miniature golf, and call your parents much, *much* later—"

"Tomorrow," Kelly suggested, pulling his lips toward hers.

*Tomorrow.* Jax liked the sound of the word. Tomorrow, and the next day, and the next tomorrow after that, sliding way out into the infinite future, he'd have Kelly by his side. It was the only future he'd ever wanted, and it was finally his.

"Tomorrow sounds perfect," he breathed. "I love you. Love, T."

\* \* \* \* \*